A Solitary MAN

SHIRA ANTHONY
And
AISLING MANCY

Published by

DREAMSPINNER PRESS

5032 Capital Circle SW, Suite 2, PMB# 279, Tallahassee, FL 32305-7886 USA
www.dreamspinnerpress.com

A Solitary Man
© 2015 Shira Anthony and Aisling Mancy.

Cover Art
© 2015 Reese Dante.
http://www.reesedante.com
Cover content is for illustrative purposes only and any person depicted on the cover is a model.

ISBN: 978-1-62380-719-1
Digital ISBN: 978-1-62380-727-6
Library of Congress Control Number: 2015945180
First Edition November 2015

Today, in the United States, more than 900,000 sworn law enforcement officers put their lives on the line for the safety and protection of others. That protection comes at a price, and each year there are approximately 60,000 assaults on law enforcement officers, resulting in nearly 16,000 injuries. Sadly, over the past decade, an average of 146 officers per year have been killed in the line of duty. Throughout US history, more than 20,000 law enforcement officers have made the ultimate sacrifice. This story is dedicated to honoring all of America's law enforcement heroes—those who have died in the line of duty and those who continue to serve and protect.

ACKNOWLEDGMENTS

Thank you to Elizabeth North, Lynn West, and all the wonderful people at Dreamspinner Press who made this book possible. Thank you to our fantastic editors and beta readers for invaluable opinions and not holding back. To Reese Dante, thank you for the beautiful cover. Thank you all for your support in bringing this book to life.

Authors' Note

The drug trafficking, child abuse, and child sex trafficking described in this work of fiction are based on real events.

The task of the solitary man is to be even more solitary.
—*Emile M. Cioran*

PROLOGUE

DIEGO TAPPED the barrel of his Heckler & Koch G3 rifle against the doorjamb of the small mud hut situated high in the Bolivian Andes. "¿Qué estás haciendo?" he demanded.

Xavier ignored him as he ladled the repulsive cassava gruel they called food from a bucket into a tin bowl. The bitter smell of wild roots was nauseating; the only redeeming quality to the soup, if there was one, was that it had boiled long enough to be rid of its natural deadly cyanide.

"Hey! I'm talking to you, Green Eyes!"

Xavier continued to ignore Diego but moved aside to reveal that he was ladling the gruel into a bowl.

"Too much!" Diego slapped the ladle and gruel splattered the dirt floor. The drops pooled and glistened in the flickering candlelight.

Xavier looked at him, careful to keep his expression neutral. "They're weak and too thin."

Diego grunted. "Easier to control the little *maricónes*."

Xavier fought not to show his hatred of Diego and disgust for the pejorative. "You will lose money on them."

Angry now, Diego shoved the nose of his rifle into Xavier's side. "You and your *boca linda*. You work here more than a month and you think you know something. If I tell you it's too much, it's too much!"

Xavier set the ladle in the bucket and awaited dismissal, his eyes riveted to the floor.

Diego burst into cruel laughter, the stench of his rancid breath almost too overwhelming to bear. "Eh, maybe you're right. We want them to look good for delivery tomorrow. You take the bowl and you come back for more and maybe I approve it."

Xavier kept his gaze downward as he nodded and turned to leave with a mumbled "Sí, mi jefe."

"You learn fast. I like that."

THUNDER RAGED overhead and lightning struck on the distant mountaintops as Xavier crossed the filthy, muddy camp. The Altiplano storms were famous for their brutality, often washing away entire villages.

Careful to note the positions of the *cocaleros* in his peripheral vision, he made his way to the squat hut where they kept the two boys. He went down on a knee and lifted the wooden bar on the door. He opened the door slowly, knowing even the dimmest glow from the firelight would be hard on their eyes after six weeks in pitch-dark captivity. The two boys huddled in a corner, their wrists and ankles bound, and the terror Xavier saw in their blue eyes made his gut clench. He carefully slid the bowl over the dirt toward the boys.

They glanced at it and huddled closer together as if trying to become one.

Xavier slid a small cloth pouch from his pocket and set it next to the bowl.

The boys glanced at it and then back to him.

One of the boys leaned forward, grabbed the pouch, and opened it quickly. He withdrew a small piece of paper and read it. His eyes went wide and he shook his head fervently.

Xavier nodded once before backing out of the hut on all fours. He closed and barred the door, stood, and resumed his paces as guard of the hut.

TWENTY MINUTES later Xavier returned to the food hut with the empty tin bowl. Diego blocked his entrance with an extended rifle barrel. Xavier waited, unsure of Diego's next move. "Not too much," Diego ordered.

Xavier nodded. "Sí, mi jefe." He entered the hut and ladled but one cup of gruel into the bowl. He stopped in the doorway for Diego's approval on the way out.

Diego sneered at him, pinched his cheek, and patted it. "You learn very fast. This is good. No more food tonight."

"Sí, mi jefe," Xavier offered softly as he headed back to the hut.

THUNDER CRACKED the sky, and Xavier nonchalantly looked up and then beyond the hut. There it was: the telltale signal lamp for extraction.

As before, he dropped to one knee, set the tin bowl on the ground, and unbarred the door. He opened it, carefully slid the tin bowl to the boys, and then held his hand up, five fingers splayed.

One of the boys whispered, "Five minutes?"

Xavier gave him the barest of nods.

The other boy shook his head again.

Xavier's gut twisted again. If he didn't get them out tonight, it would be too late. They'd be shipped off to the buyer tomorrow and gone for good. "Has to be now," he whispered ever so softly.

Tears filled the terrified boy's eyes, and a faithless drop spilled over. "They'll shoot us."

Xavier shook his head slowly. "I'll keep you safe."

"Eh! You better not be touching the merchandise!" Diego yelled as he shoved Xavier hard in the side with a boot.

Xavier gritted his teeth and fought to ignore the pain. He raised his hand again, four fingers splayed.

The braver boy nodded.

Xavier quickly poured the gruel out at the edge of the hut and backed out with the tin bowl in hand. "Just getting the bowl, *mi jefe*."

"Gimme that!" Diego grabbed the bowl. "Get back to your post, *puto*, or you go back to the fields!"

"Sí, mi jefe." Xavier shouldered his rifle and began his routine patrol around the hut as Diego walked away.

Lightning struck in a nearby field and deafening thunder rolled across the sky above them. He continued his patrol and prayed heaven would wait a little longer before unleashing her fury. Each time he passed the back of the hut, he withdrew a sheaf of straw. On his fourth pass, the far-off signal blinked thrice, letting him know it was time.

Within seconds, a grenade exploded on the other side of the camp. Lightning cracked with a riot of color directly above them right before a barrel of coca paste exploded, the sound nearly drowned by thunder. Chaos descended and guards scattered in every direction as the sky opened up to lay waste to the land. Wild gunfire began, and Xavier drew a knife from the leather sheath on his aguayo belt, bent quickly, and snapped the skimpy wooden frame on the back of the hut. He reached in and grabbed the first boy, who came willingly. He quickly cut the bindings on the boy's wrists and ankles. The second boy refused to come, and Xavier dragged him out by the arm. He cut his bindings and pushed both boys into the copse of coffee trees behind the hut. "Run!"

Xavier half ran and half dragged the boys along as they cleared the trees and raced down the muddy, crooked rows of coca plants. Lightning momentarily obscured the blinking Morse code of the signal lamp, but, after nearly two months working this field, Xavier knew exactly where to go. Gunfire sounded behind them, and Xavier's hopes of a covert escape were dashed as a bullet whizzed past his ear. "Faster!" he shouted in the pouring rain.

As they crested a rise and descended to the edge of the field, a DEA helicopter rose out of the trees and hovered, skids just off the ground. Xavier looked for the second chopper, and when it didn't show, he swallowed back panic as a sickening dread threatened to overwhelm him. Automatic gunfire sounded and the helicopter's M60s swiveled and fired in response, but without the firepower of the second chopper, they had no chance of getting out alive. Amid the shower of bullets, one of the boys slipped and fell in the mud, and the other boy ran back to help him. Xavier ran back and grabbed them both by the shirt, lifted them, and half ran, half dragged them again. "Get to the helicopter!" He shoved them in front of him, and they ran for the chopper.

As the boys neared the skids, tracer fire lit the blackened sky and bullets strafed the mud at their feet. Xavier didn't dare look back. He ran at the boys, taking them both to the ground, but not before bullets arced, nearly tearing them in half. Warm red rain showered him, made brilliant by the riot of lightning overhead. He reached for them, still believing he could save them, right before his world turned to black.

CHAPTER ONE

Two weeks later....

FOUR BLUE eyes looked out at him from the dark, angry and accusatory. "You promised you'd keep us safe!" the boys shouted in unison as their eyes filled with blood.

Xavier Constantine woke with a shout. Terror held him in its vicious grip as vivid images tore jagged wounds in his mind. His heart pounded, his breathing labored, and sweat coated him like icy syrup. His hands shook and the nightmare clawed at his nerves as he tried to gather his fractured mind and pull himself together.

A nurse quickly entered the dimly lit hospital room as the cardiac monitor droned on. She checked his vital signs and noted them in the chart. "Another nightmare?" she asked gently.

He said nothing. He'd been stuck at Saint John's Hospital in Santa Monica, California, for two weeks, and he'd been ready to leave since day one.

"Do you want something to help you sleep?"

He shook his head.

"Let me know if you do." The soft squeak of her shoes faded as she left the room.

He slowly sat up and swung his feet over the side of the bed. His side ached where the artillery shell had pierced it. He ran a tired hand through his long hair and wondered yet again how the cartridge hadn't taken a vital organ with it.

The boys hadn't been so lucky.

Pain banded his heart, and he put the heel of a hand to his chest and pressed, as if the futile effort could somehow ease the ache... and the guilt that accompanied it. He wondered if either would ever leave him. He didn't know, but he was sure their blue eyes would haunt him forever. Still shaking, he slowly rose from the bed and found his legs stiff. He desperately needed a workout. He stretched and worked each leg before heading to the bathroom to take a piss. He couldn't take the sloth that came with hospitalization. If they didn't discharge him tomorrow, he'd leave on his own.

THE NEXT morning Xavier dressed to leave the hospital, the loss of the two boys already casting a morbid pall over his day. The doc had been in to see him and they'd argued, but he eventually won out and was discharged and cleared to work pending a satisfactory session with the company shrink. He pulled on his favorite raggedy-ass MIT hoodie. With its stretched-out cuffs, stains, and holes, it reigned supreme in his dress code. Maybe he'd stalk The Coop when he got home and splurge on a backup. He'd worked so long undercover for the FBI he wasn't sure he still owned a suit.

William Benson entered the room with an entourage as Xavier laced and tied his Vince Adam Revolvers. He wondered what in hell he'd done to deserve a visit from the executive assistant director of the Criminal Investigations Division. Behind Benson was Daniel Ward, Xavier's boss at CARD, the Child Abduction Rapid Deployment program; Reggie Cook from the Evidence Response Team; Theo Mendez from the Innocence Lost National Initiative; and a woman he didn't know, but who wore a T-shirt bearing the DOJ's Project Safe Childhood logo. It looked as if a violent crimes against children convention had let out and his room was the doughnut lobby.

The belated entrance of Dick Blueblood told him why Benson was here. Dick wasn't only Xavier's least favorite yahoo from the Drug Enforcement Agency, he *was* a dick. After the loss of the two boys, Xavier had come to hate the arrogant, stubborn pig who'd fucked up their operation.

Xavier gritted his teeth and stood, vowing to keep his temper in check. He shook Benson's hand, then Ward's, and ignored everyone else.

"You've been cleared by Internal Investigations," Benson said without preamble and handed the Smith & Warren wallet containing Xavier's identification badge to him.

Xavier narrowed his eyes at the man as he accepted the wallet. He hadn't realized they'd opened an investigation, let alone investigated him during the two weeks he'd been hospitalized. He looked at Ward, who shook his head dismissively and raised his hands to shoulder height in mock surrender. "Standard protocol."

Xavier looked at the others in the room. "Who told the parents?"

"I did," Ward answered solemnly.

"What about the other boy? Who was he?"

Reggie chewed his lower lip before he spoke. "No identification yet."

Xavier frowned. "He looked to be about twelve. Someone had to have reported him missing."

The Project Safe woman extended a hand. "Tucker. Lacy Tucker. We're working on it with NCMEC, the National Center for Missing and Exploited Children."

So that's her connection, Xavier thought idly as he shook her hand and turned to Theo. "The buyer?"

Theo shook his head. "Yacht's in international waters, so we can't touch it, but we know it. The *Camarón*. We've been watching it for a few months."

Xavier almost snickered. *Camarón* meant shrimp in Spanish. What a dumbass name for a rich bastard's football-field-sized boat. "Who owns it?"

"We're looking into the foreign registry. She flies Norwegian."

That didn't make sense, but Xavier let it go in favor of pissing in Blueblood's cornflakes. "What are you doing here?"

"Need you to sign off on our report," he said with a cocky grin.

"Go fuck yourself."

"Constantine, it was a joint effort," Benson said smoothly.

Xavier fumed and told himself again not to lose it. "There was nothing joint about it."

"Xavier—" Dick began.

"You blew it! *You* fucking blew it!" Xavier fought not to grab the man and beat the shit out of him. "We agreed to two choppers! You sent one! You and your goddamned cost cutting! You killed those kids to save a lousy fifty grand! You put a price on their heads!"

"Screw you, Constantine! I wasn't the one who couldn't get my ass to the chopper fast enough!" Dick yelled back.

That was it. Xavier punched him.

"Xav!" Reggie and Theo shouted in unison. They grabbed him before he could land another and he fought them as they wrestled him away from Dick.

Dick pulled a handkerchief from his pocket and wiped his bloody nose. "You're off the team!"

"I was never on your team, asshole! You were on mine!"

CHAPTER TWO

XAV PROPPED himself on hands and arms and leaned back to watch the sun set from the end of the Santa Monica pier. He was restless with indecision and kicked his legs aimlessly as they hung off the wooden planks. He always came to the shore when he was unsettled. The taste of the salty sea air on the back of his tongue, the caw of gulls overhead, and the ceaseless rhythm of the waves—all were natural, steadying forces for him. A nearby angler turned his old transistor radio up and Coldplay's "Lost" filled the air. The angler offered him a beer in a brown paper bag. He smiled, nodded his thanks, but begged off with a wave of a hand. A kid on a skateboard narrowly missed his fingers as he sped to the railing and crashed into it. The board flipped and went over the side, and the kid tried to catch it. Xav shot to his feet and grabbed the kid's T-shirt to keep him from following the board over the end of the pier.

"Whoa!" the kid shouted, part in fear, part in relief.

"Whoa is right. No flyers off the pier."

The kid straightened his shirt and peered over the railing. "Shit, that was a Plan B with Shecks, man."

"Looks like you need a plan C."

The kid looked up at him, clearly confused. "No way, man. Plan B is the best."

The boy's eyes were sparkling blue diamonds in the bright sunlight, and they hit Xav like a sucker punch. He fought to smile. "Guess you'll have to retrieve it the old-fashioned way."

"How?"

"Go swimming."

The kid groaned. "Yeah, shit. I better or my dad'll kill me. Thanks for the save, man." The kid trotted off.

Xav resumed his place at the end of the pier and looked out over the water. He'd worked for the FBI since he'd graduated from U Penn with a master's in criminology, after an undergrad stint at MIT in mathematics. He began as an analyst and worked his way into field operations. He'd served his three years' penance in surveillance and had his choice of teams after a successful antiterrorism raid. He'd chosen CID's Violent Crimes Section, and when they'd formed the Violent Crimes Against Children division in 2000, he'd joined CARD and gone undercover to stop commercial sexual exploitation of kids. He shook his head to himself. He'd never lost a kid. Not one. Damn good stats. He knew that. Now he'd lost two in what should have been a simple extraction.

A seagull screeched overhead, and he looked skyward. The day was warm and clear, the sun bright, the heavens infinite. The lone gull coasted on air currents and flawed the celestial sky. Nothing was perfect. He knew that too, but it was time for a change.

HIS FIRST day back at the office sucked. Someone had been using his office and left it a mess, someone else had stolen his leather armchair, and nobody had made coffee. He walked down the hall to Ward's office.

"Welcome back." Ward stood and shook his hand. "The company shrink cleared you. How are you feeling?"

Xav nodded and plopped into the leather armchair that was his. "Can I have my chair back?"

Ward looked up and smiled. "No. I like it."

Xav rolled his eyes. "Did they ID the other kid?"

"They did better than that. Go see Reggie, and then go see Theo."

Xav stood. "Who's in charge of java?"

Ward smiled up at him again. "You are."

Xav headed for the door. "When I'm caffeine fueled, I'm taking my chair back."

"You can try. Get your hair cut!"

"No. I like it."

XAV WALKED to the elevator and pushed the down button. How Reggie worked in a basement lab with no windows was beyond him. He'd suffocate. He rubbed his side and thought of the boys' blue eyes again. No matter what he did, he couldn't get their eyes out of his mind.

The door opened and he stepped into the sterile lab environment. Reggie was easy to spot. Other than himself, Reggie was the only feeb Xav knew of with long hair. Blond dreads, no less. He also had a couple of badass ultraviolet tattoos you couldn't see in daylight but could see coming a mile away in a club.

"Be still my heart. He's back." Reggie greeted him with a cuff to his shoulder and a slap on the back. "How's it going?"

"It's going. Ward said you had news for me."

"I got better than that. Come on over here and check this out."

Xav followed him to a computer station, and Reggie kicked a stool over to him.

"Take a seat. One of the kids had this on him." He hit a few keys and the screen filled with a three-dimensional image.

Xav squinted and studied the image closely. "A Bible?"

"Of sorts." He hit the Print key and a single page spit from the printer beneath the computer. He handed it to Xav. "You ask me, looks like the kid got away with *el jefe's* black book."

Xav studied the page. It was an enhanced image of a ledger of some sort listing transaction after transaction in bolivianos in thousands. As far as Xav knew, the boys hadn't been in proximity to steal anything. Then again, he hadn't been there when the boys arrived. His stomach roiled at the thought of what they'd done to the boys before he got to the camp.

"I sent it to Crypto. They said they'd have it back in a few days."

"Did you ID the other kid?"

"No, but I got you this. And before you bitch about the quality, it was soaked with blood and I had to recreate it, so shut up in advance." He hit a few more keys and a ticket stub appeared on the screen. "Greyhound. LA to Dare's Landing, North Carolina, on April 2."

"Print."

Reggie looked at him as he hit the Print key and handed him the printed image. "You know, you need to get that thing fixed."

Xav studied the picture. "What thing?"

"Your personality. I mean, it's like you're missing everything but your amygdalae."

Xav glanced at him. "My what?"

Reggie shook his head. "I can't believe I work with you. The things in your brain that control sexual orientation."

"I have more than one?"

Reggie blew a long breath. "You're an asshole."

"How long will it take you to print that Bible out?"

"For you? A month."

"I'll be back after lunch."

XAV MADE his way to the Innocence Lost office on the fourth floor to
see Theo. Theo was on the phone when he arrived, and he waved Xav
to a chair. He searched through the piles of paperwork that made up his
desk as he yelled into the phone. "What do you mean how soon do I want
it? Yesterday!" He held a paper up and squinted at it, and then held it out
to Xav.

Xav took it and a seat. The document clearly wasn't made in
the USA.

Theo slammed the phone down.

"What is this?" Xav asked.

"The Norwegian registration for the buyer's yacht, the *Camarón*."

"Who owns it?"

"I don't give Norsk. Take it to Crypto."

AFTER VISITING the Cryptography Division, Xav checked the kitchen
and, to his fortune, found that someone had made coffee. He searched
in the cabinets and located his mug buried in the back. At least someone
hadn't taken that. Then again, the stuffed shirts in his office wouldn't be
caught dead with a cup emblazoned with *If you had my job, you'd drink
too*. Which was why he'd purchased it.

He headed to his office and was surprised to find it clean and his
leather armchair back in its rightful corner. The document strategically
placed in the center of his desk for his signature made him see red. He
dropped it in the wastebasket without as much as a cursory review.
Fuck Dick. Arrogant, selfish, cheap pig. Xav suddenly chuckled to
himself. Would that be pig dick or dick pig? *Whatever*. He turned to
the computer screen on his credenza, logged in, and checked e-mail.
He'd been gone for less than two months. How in hell could he have
twenty-three hundred e-mails? He selected all and clicked Delete. His
intercom buzzed. He hit the speaker button and answered with a crisp
"Constantine."

"Did you forget that our sophisticated information system tells us
when you don't read e-mails?" Ward asked.

"Nope."

"Fine. Did you sign Dick's report?"

Xav looked at the document in the wastebasket. "In a manner of speaking."

"Don't fuck around. Sign it." Ward hung up.

Xav signed off the computer and retrieved the report from the wastebasket. It was definitely time for a change.

XAV DROPPED by The Farms on the way home and bought shrimp, fresh pasta, and a bottle of still Voss. Next, he dropped by the Wine Garden and ordered truffle fries to go and a bottle of ZD Chard. His mouth watered just thinking about them.

One of the hazards of riding a hog was no storage. He stuffed his groceries into the saddlebags and hoped the fries wouldn't be mashed in the few minutes it took to get to his high-rise condominium overlooking the beach.

HE LOOKED through the images of the ledger Crypto had given him as his shrimp scampi simmered and he sipped chardonnay. He'd tried ZD at last year's Out in the Vineyard weekend in Sonoma—the last time he'd had a vacation—and liked it. It had also taken the gold in the San Francisco Chronicle wine competition. Deservedly so.

The ledger listed transactions by numbers, but otherwise the information meant nothing to him or to Crypto. He picked up the translated boat registration. The registered owner was a dead end until Theo finished digging through layer upon layer of corporate ownership. Next, he looked at the picture of the Greyhound ticket stub. Everyone with stars in their eyes made their way to LA only to have their dreams crushed beneath the heel of reality. But *to* North Carolina? And a kid of maybe ten or twelve? *No way.*

He stood and checked the shrimp. The sauce was perfect. He drained the garlic pasta, dressed a plate with it, and graced it with the shrimp scampi. It smelled delicious. He poured another glass of wine and took the meal, along with his tablet, to the table on the balcony.

He researched Greyhound's schedules from LA to Dare's Landing, North Carolina. They ran daily. The kid could have jumped on it any day of the week. The trip was pricey and he filed that information away in his mental archives as he jotted the bus numbers beneath the picture of the ticket stub. Next, he read pig Dick's report. It never ceased to amaze him how intra-agency operations could generate reports with just enough truth to avoid an indictment. He was tired of that too.

For shits and giggles, he jumped onto the government jobs website and created a login and password. Within seconds, Information Systems would notify his boss. He didn't care.

After setting the search parameters, he expected few openings to fill the screen. Rather, he ended up scrolling through job after job. He passed one in North Carolina and scrolled back to it. It was a position on the Carver County Sheriff's Crimes Against Children Task Force in Dare's Landing. He dug into the listing. It was the answer to his current dilemma.

He reached for pig Dick's report and wrote on it in big red letters, *FAILED OPERATION: INADEQUATE DEA REPRESENTATION DURING EXTRACTION*. And signed it.

HE WENT into the office at dawn, set pig Dick's report on Ward's desk along with his resignation and ID. He turned to leave and found Ward standing in the doorway.

"It's because I told you to cut your hair, isn't it?"

Xav smirked. "It's time."

Ward ambled into the office. "Theo'd be more than grateful if you joined his department."

Xav shook his head. "I need a change of scenery."

Ward took a seat behind his desk, locked his hands behind his head, and leaned back in his chair. "I have it on good authority they can't even spell gay in North Carolina."

In spite of his dour mood, Xav laughed. "You'll make the call?"

"You're lucky I speak North Carolinian and know the head honcho in those parts."

Xav approached the desk and held a hand out for a shake.

After a long beat, Ward stood and grasped it with both hands.

"Thanks, Ward."

"We'll keep your desk warm."

Xav smiled but knew he'd never be back.

XAV PULLED up to the curb in front of the two-story house in Woodland Hills and parked his bike. He looked at the clean, all-American neighborhood and the average house with its perfect lawn as he removed his helmet. He winced as he thought about the epidemic of child sex trafficking in the US. No one would guess that the heinous crimes against children had invaded even safe middle-class neighborhoods such as this.

With a heavy heart, he approached and knocked on the front door. The boy who opened the door had the same blue eyes as the boy he'd gone after. Eyes that would forever haunt him. The pretty woman who approached behind him looked haggard. She shooed the boy away. "Go watch your sister." She turned back to Xav. "Agent Constantine?" she asked with strained politeness.

"Good afternoon, Mrs. Helm."

"Your agents have already been here."

Xav nodded. "I came to offer my condolences."

Her face crumpled, tears threatened, and her voice was breathy. "Don't come back here." She closed the door in his face.

HE RODE hard and fast down the 101 freeway with Linkin Park's "Burning in the Skies" filling his helmet. He turned south onto the 405 through the Sepulveda Pass toward Sunset Boulevard. He exited amidst Getty Center construction and sped east on winding curves past UCLA, the west gate of Bel-Air, and the mansions of Beverly Hills into West Hollywood. He had one more stop to make before he left town.

THE ARTIST dabbed at Xav's chest and then held an ultraviolet light over the tattoo. Xav held the mirror up and four beautiful blue eyes looked out at him from his heart. Satisfied, Xav paid the guy in cash.

"Once it heals, you won't see it in incandescent light or daylight," the artist said.

"Thanks, man."

"Come back anytime."

CHAPTER THREE

"...AND OF course my office will ensure the citizens of Dare's Landing are made aware of the extraordinary efforts of law enforcement to stem the tide of illegal drugs into our county."

Assistant District Attorney C. Evan Fairchild rubbed the bridge of his nose and sipped his fourth coffee of the day. Lukewarm, but he needed the caffeine or he'd start yawning—a surefire way to piss off his boss. Not that the man's self-serving speeches deserved better, but after three years working under James Faison—Jimmy, as he liked to be called—Evan had managed an uneasy peace with the man. Though an elected DA, Faison couldn't toss Evan out on his ass, but he could make life miserable for him. It was always better to make nice and pretend Faison had something intelligent to say.

They'd been holed up with representatives of the sheriff's office and city hall in the largest conference room at the new justice center building for hours. Faison droned on. Nothing new in anything he said. No surprise to Evan—most were *his* words, not Faison's—but his boss liked to add fill just to hear himself speak. Evan had spent the last three days compiling all the stats and details so his boss would sound as though he knew what he was talking about. Still, he wouldn't complain about the long hours and lack of credit. He'd given up private practice five years before, after winning a few big cases, and he had no intention of returning to billable-hour hell.

The only new detail Evan had heard in all of Faison's political posturing were rumors that drug mules were using alternatives to the I-95 corridor to transport product. I-95 highway had been so heavily trafficked that law enforcement had dubbed it "Cocaine Lane," but now the busts were down.

"...efforts have reduced the amount of product on the streets." Faison laid the Carolina accent on thick as he finished speaking. He always did at the end of a rally-the-troops speech.

Evan had objected to categorizing the stats as a reduction. "Overall use is up substantially countywide," he'd pointed out when Faison had asked him to rework the figures to exclude all but the area within the city limits. More drugs meant more gang violence. More ODs. More kids in lockup and foster care. And Evan gave a shit about all that, even if Faison only gave a shit about his reelection bid. Faison had brushed him off, as he usually did. Evan was fairly certain it had to do with the fact that he had backed Faison's opponent in the last election. Or maybe Faison's gaydar was better than he gave him credit for. Or both.

"Walk with me," Faison said after he'd wrapped up the requisite after-meeting ass-kissing with the sheriff and the mayor. Evan didn't really have a choice, since they'd ridden to the meeting together.

"How do you think it went?" Faison asked.

Loaded question. Safe answer. "Great. The mayor looked happy."

"Donny Smith's always happy someone else is doing the work." Faison waved at one of the deputies as they headed out into the sticky heat of the day.

"I still think it's a mistake to limit the data," Evan said. "By giving the task force the broader picture, they'd be able to help move resources—"

"We can handle it just fine on our own." Faison shot Evan a *we've been through this before why are you bringing it up again* glare that Evan met without blinking. "Ain't no reason to invite the SBI or, God forbid, the DEA, in for a piece of this county."

Of course not, because then everyone would know you don't have a handle on it.

"Have you heard anything from the other DAs?" Evan asked casually as he opened the passenger-side door of his black '71 Jaguar E-type convertible for Faison. The car was cliché, but Evan didn't give a fuck. He liked it. Sometimes he wondered whether Faison always asked him to drive because he loved the car just as much.

Faison waved a dismissive hand. "Wesley James over in Nash County says there's a decrease in the number of busts on 95. They've been cleaning things up without outside help. You lookin' for a role model for handlin' things internally? That there's one. They're keepin' it local and getting it done."

Evan got into the car and buckled his seatbelt. "But we're seeing more of the stuff in the schools too. That's not something I'm hearing from other counties." Faison had clearly forgotten who'd spent the better part of a week sculpting the stats. Evan hadn't wanted to downplay the link to the schools, but Faison had insisted they "accentuate the positive" and omit it, which only made Evan feel worse about the spin. *Maybe if you focused on something other than the next election, we'd be able to get some of that shit off the streets.*

Faison pulled out his phone and tapped the screen a few times. "Sylvia? Anything more from the governor's office about getting me a spot on the Child Fatality Task Force?"

Evan strangled a sigh, gripped the steering wheel, and focused on the road. The air shimmered above the asphalt. It wouldn't rain tonight, judging by the nearly clear sky. He turned the AC up a notch and tried to ignore Faison. Jimmy didn't give a shit about kids. He wanted more visibility. And cozying up to the folks in Raleigh was at the top of his agenda.

If the couriers aren't using I-95, how the hell are they getting the stuff into the state? Evan made a mental note to talk to one of the deputies and see what he'd heard. Evan trusted one in particular who'd kept him in the loop. Despite what Faison believed, Sheriff Ralph Winston was a decent man, and he hired good cops.

Faison always withheld information, and Evan sometimes wondered if that was because Faison worried someday Evan might run to unseat him. He'd laughed the thought off, but one of the other ADAs had said the same thing. It didn't matter—Evan would work around Faison to get his job done. He always did.

"I'll be lead counsel on your next drug case," Faison said after he finished the call. "Show the assholes I can get down in the dirt with them and get the job done."

"Sir, we have the cases under control." Faison hadn't tried a case since he'd been elected. Of course he could, but—

"I think it's high time we show them who's in charge. What better way than to nail their asses in court?" Faison didn't add what Evan already knew: Faison wouldn't be doing any of the work to prepare for trial.

"Of course." Evan gritted his teeth and turned onto Carver Street. This would be all about the show, and it would be up to Evan to make it look good for Faison. Evan had made his peace with that when he'd taken the job five years before. He hadn't come to work for the DA for the limelight. He just wanted the drugs, dealers, and all the trash that came with them out of Dare's Landing. He'd give Faison his most experienced witnesses, make him look good, and limit the potential damage.

Faison leaned back in his seat, and Evan had no doubt he envisioned himself in Raleigh, shaking the governor's hand. "We need to get this in front of the people. Drum up a little interest."

Interest, as in press coverage. Free advertising, Evan thought.

"Talk to Walter Talley," Faison continued, on a roll now. "Get his thoughts on how to play this."

Talley was Faison's Yale Law School buddy and a former prosecutor the legislature had hired to appeal a ruling overturning the state's ban on same-sex marriage. Talley had offered up the first fifty grand of his work on the case pro bono, and Evan guessed Talley had seen the freebie for what it was: a potential cash cow and a prelude to a campaign for state senate.

"I don't think that's necessary," Evan said as he tightened his grip on the wheel. "I've got plenty of experience working with county law enforcement to—"

"Walter's more experienced."

Only at kissing your political ass. "I don't see that we need—"

"Call him." Faison was back to texting before Evan could answer.

Dismissed yet again, Evan pulled into the parking lot without another word. He knew his place. He didn't have to like it. He'd put up with Faison's shit if it meant getting the drugs out of the schools and off the streets.

BY THE time Evan made it to his house downtown, it was nearly seven. He grabbed his briefcase out of the trunk, gazed up at the Victorian, and smiled. The fading summer sunlight hid her imperfections and brought out the personality that had drawn him to the place. Back then, she'd been more of a promise than a house, with her cracking paint and termite-infested wood. But he'd imagined her as she might be returned to her former glory, her high turret neatly covered with slate tiles, her tall windows inviting the sun inside, her front porch a haven where he might sit and read on a warm Sunday morning.

For five years, he'd spent nearly every weekend restoring what the Historical Register called the Mather-Wilkinson House. The designation had spared her from being destroyed by area developers, but she was also the bane of Evan's existence. For the first year he'd owned her, he'd hit every local auction and antique store trying to find hardware to match the brass handles on the cabinets. He'd even driven as far as Georgetown, South Carolina, to find three matching cut-glass doorknobs. He soon realized that was the easy work—replacing the termite-damaged wood on the exterior and stairs was enough of a workout that he didn't need his weekend weight lifting. Another month of good weather and he'd be able to start remodeling the guest bathroom he'd been neglecting for the exterior work. Not that Evan ever entertained guests, but he enjoyed the interior work.

He walked up the steps and unlocked the front door. The third step always creaked, but after numerous attempts to fix the riser failed, Evan finally let it go. He considered it a victory of sorts that he didn't require perfection in all things. Maybe it was why he loved the place—he could forgive her failings, large or small, where he couldn't even forgive the small ones in himself.

After setting his briefcase on the dining room table, he pulled off his suit jacket and hung it on the back of a chair, then loosened his tie. He picked up the mail from behind the slot next to the front door, glanced through it: bills, junk mail, and another plea for donations to the Columbia University Law School alumni fund. He set the stack down in a neat pile. He'd deal with it later.

Once in the kitchen, he turned the iPhone on and Matt Corby's "Resolution" filled the air. The universal docking station did its job well, charging the iPhone while it served as a damn good music system. He snagged a Guinness and the remains of last night's takeout from the fridge. He put the leftovers in the microwave, hit the one-minute cook button, and then opened the beer. Beatty's pulled pork was nearly as good the next day, especially with a few splashes of Texas Pete Pepper Sauce.

He washed the barbecue down with the beer as he watched the birds in the backyard fight a squirrel for a perch on the neighbor's feeder. A moment later, he heard a flutter of wings and a few frightened chirps. He smiled as he got to his feet and opened the back door. Two deep green eyes gazed up at him through the screen door.

"Back again?" he asked with a chuckle. He knew he shouldn't keep feeding the stray, but he couldn't bring himself to take the starving animal to the pound. *Not starving anymore.* Not that he'd ever admit to buying cat food and feeding it. He set a dish of food on the step and refilled the bowl of water. The cat glanced up at him in thanks and set to eating.

He took a long, slow breath and tried to forget the day of bullshit. He'd spent the better part of an hour on the phone, trying to convince Walter—"call me Wally"—Talley he didn't need to make the three-hour drive to Dare's Landing to figure out the best way for Faison to "get in on the drug issue." Of course, Wally wouldn't hesitate to bill for his travel time.

Evan knew this for what it was: political exploitation, pure and simple. Talk and more talk. All the talk did nothing. Not a damn thing. In the meantime, John Carson, one of the few deputies Evan spoke to on occasion, had told Evan about another cocaine bust—this one at a local middle school. *Middle schools, for crissake.* And Jimmy had the gall to pitch that drug use was down.

The sound of his beer bottle falling over and hitting the table brought Evan back to himself. He ran a hand through his hair and tried to release the tension that coiled like a snake in his gut, ready to strike. Thinking about Faison's bullshit always pissed him off.

Dr. Sampson's words echoed through his brain. *"Imagine your anger is a train running on the tracks, slowing down as it comes to the station. You don't have to buy a ticket and board the train. You can just watch it pull away."*

When they'd forced him into therapy while he was in juvenile detention, he'd tried his best to ignore her. But Evelene Sampson refused to be ignored, and by the time the state cut the funding for the program that paid for his therapy, Evan was sorry to see her go. Nearly fifteen years later, she still called him from time to time to see how he was doing. He knew she was a good part of the reason he'd gotten his shit together. She'd recommended him for the scholarship at UNC-Chapel Hill, and she'd encouraged him to apply to law school.

"If you hate the system, then get off your lazy ass and change it," she'd told him when he'd hesitated to take the LSAT. He'd laughed and told her she was a crazy old lady to think that a kid who'd spent two years in detention could become a lawyer. But he'd listened.

He popped up out of his chair, cleaned the spilled beer off the table, and made his way upstairs to change. He needed to do something. Drive. Blow off some steam. Get Faison's stink off him. He'd get it out of his system and spend the rest of the weekend tiling the guest bath.

CHAPTER FOUR

XAV PARKED his bike at the marina in Dare's Landing and looked out at the Neuse River and the shrimp trawlers that made their way through estuarial waters. It was hot, humid, downright muggy. The scent of the Atlantic was different from that of the Pacific, and he breathed it in. Where the Pacific had a smooth, salty smell that rested on the back of your tongue, the intracoastal waters of the Atlantic were brackish and sent the acrid stench of fish to flight on the air. He turned and looked behind him and asked himself, yet again, how he'd ended up in a redneck town, on a force with a tacit DADT policy, and on a coast where the sun didn't set in the right place. No sunset over the water was sure as hell going to take some getting used to.

He'd checked out the City of Dare's Landing, population thirty thousand, the seat of North Carolina's Carver County and his new home. The town was picturesque from the outside looking in. A plethora of historical buildings and monuments attested to an interesting history, and the quaint contemporary shops and restaurants gave it a homey feel. But he knew better. All belied a seedy underbelly. He rubbed a hand over his chest where the fresh tattoo was still healing, and thought of the blue eyes that never left him. They reminded him of his purpose.

He'd met Sheriff Winston and found him to be a decent guy. He got the impression Winston was a little sloppy around the edges, but most straight men were.

Speaking of men, he needed to get laid.

EVAN SAT in the parking lot of the bar, fingers clenched around the steering wheel. Faison had pushed him to his limits. It pissed him off beyond reason how the man blew off the important stuff and focused only on what would help move his political career forward. Evan had never liked politicians. Even the DA before Faison, who now had a seat in the state senate, hadn't been anything to write home about, but at least he hadn't made Evan want to scream in frustration. With Faison, Evan felt he was spinning his wheels, where before he'd at least made progress toward cracking down on drug suppliers. Too many people—kids in particular—were falling victim to the drugs they should have taken off the street. Evan hated that, and he'd come to hate Faison for doing so little about it. Worse still, Faison had done nothing at all to make a dent in the problem but wasted no time distorting facts in order to spin things for his next campaign. *Hypocrisy at its finest.*

Breathe. Normally Evan let Faison's bullshit roll off his back. But when Faison blew off the things that were important to Evan, the frustration he'd felt as a child and the accompanying rage came roaring back. Faison didn't give a crap about illegal drugs, but those drugs had nearly destroyed Evan's life.

He inhaled for four counts, held his breath for four, and exhaled for four counts. His heart slowed and tension began to leave his body—one of many useful things Evelene had taught him when he was a kid.

The other thing that worked for him when he felt as though he might spontaneously erupt into flames?

Evan smiled and eyed the sign over the entrance to the bar. It read The Velvet Lounge. Wilmington was just far enough from Dare's Landing that he didn't have to worry about being seen. He kept his head down and his sex life firmly in the closet. Faison and his political backers probably couldn't fire him for being queer, but he didn't need the bullshit that came with being out. He'd had enough bullshit to last him several lifetimes already. The inside of his closet was perfectly comfortable, regardless of who they married at city hall these days.

The bouncer nodded to Evan as he walked inside. The sound of Easton Corbin's "Baby Be My Love Song" hit him at the same time the icy-cold air conditioning blasted him, and the sweat-soaked curls at the back of his neck gave rise to goose bumps. Nothing like August in North Carolina. Hot, muggy. Vacation Bible school over. Pulled pork and a gallon of sweet tea. If things slowed down at the office, he'd take next weekend and sail his boat to Cape Lookout, have fresh fish for dinner, and sleep under the stars.

The thought of work had him clenching his jaw again. He forced himself to breathe deeply and took a seat at the corner of the bar. Trading his expensive suit for a button-down and jeans had done little to erase his frustration. He needed something stronger.

"Patrón Silver and a Bud." He drank the shot as soon as the bartender set it down, ordered another, and took a pull of beer. He welcomed the tendrils of alcohol that eased his tight shoulder muscles.

Satisfied the evening was getting better, he glanced around the bar. The place wasn't a dive, but it wasn't what Evan would have called upscale either. The paneling was dark and weathered; the polished wood floor reflected the track lighting. A dozen tables, all of them occupied on a Friday evening. Country music played in the background, something Evan didn't recognize but that reminded him of the songs his mother had played when he was young. Over on the tiny platform that served as a stage, someone had begun to set up for the live band that would play later in the evening. It was too early for live music, but not too early for what Evan had come looking for.

He nodded to a few familiar faces—Evan didn't do repeats—then checked out the new ones. A ginger with a bit of a paunch at the end of the bar. A twink giggling and sipping an umbrella-laden drink at one of the nearby tables. A man with a dark ponytail seated at the middle of the bar sucking on an imported beer, the corded muscles of his arms straining against the fabric of his dark blue T-shirt. Lean, thirtyish, with the honeyed skin of someone who spent a great deal of time outdoors. Surfer, here to improve his broceanography at Wrightsville Beach, Evan concluded. Since the *Nat Geo* article, he'd seen a lot more of them. Even better? The guy was looking back at him.

Bingo.

Evan raised his beer and nodded. The guy nodded back and Evan walked over. "Hey."

"Hey." The smile that lit the man's face made his green eyes sparkle. Evan couldn't quite place the accent. Definitely not Southern.

The man flagged down the bartender, who had just set Evan's second shot in front of him. "Two of what he's drinking, on me."

"Thanks." Evan set his empty on the bar and leaned languidly on the edge.

"Xav."

"Chance," Evan said.

Xav chuckled. "You're serious?"

Evan nodded. He only used the name at bars, but it *was* his first name. "My mother had a twisted sense of humor." And a serious coke addiction, but he wasn't going to share *that*.

Xav raised a quizzical eyebrow. Evan didn't care if Xav wanted to know more. He downed the second shot and shed his Evan persona the way he'd shed his suit. For tonight, he was Chance. Evan and all his crap could wait until the morning.

"You from around here?" Chance asked as he sat next to Xav.

"No." Xav didn't elaborate.

Chance could work with that. Didn't matter given his no-repeat policy.

"You?"

"Grew up in Bertie," Chance said truthfully. "Near the Virginia border."

The bartender set their drinks in front of them. "Never heard of it." Xav's words didn't seem to judge, just state a fact.

"Half the people in the state haven't." Chance picked up one of the beer bottles and handed it to Xav, the brush of his fingertips against Xav's calculated. Xav's short intake of breath pleased him, Xav's fingers lingering just slightly too long against Chance's. Years ago, Chance might have looked away. But he'd come to enjoy the self-confidence and power he felt when he didn't back down, much as he'd come to enjoy locking horns with defense counsel in court.

Xav didn't look away either.

Nice. His past few hookups here had been low-key—translate: jejune. This one held more promise.

"I'm staying at Wrightsville Beach," Xav said.

Chance repressed a laugh. *Yep. Surfer.*

"I've got a few beers and a day-old pizza." The edges of Xav's very kissable mouth quirked upward and his thigh brushed Chance's.

Someone at one of the tables laughed, and the sound of a guitar being tuned mingled with the clanking of beer bottles. Chance hoped they'd be out of there before the music started. He wasn't in the mood.

Chance went to pull his wallet from his pocket, but Xav stood and leaned over him and handed the bartender a few bills before Chance could extricate it. *Nicely done.* Chance caught a whiff of cologne, subtle and citrusy. From his close vantage point, Chance watched the rhythmic pulse of a vein beneath Xav's chin.

Chance stood straighter, his hard cock straining against the heavy fabric of his jeans. "Thanks."

Xav didn't cede any territory as Chance stood, his shoulder pressing against Xav's chest. Chance hadn't realized the man stood nearly half a head taller. Chance clenched his jaw and felt his shoulders and neck tense as he fought the urge to shove Xav out of his personal space. He didn't like it when people got too close to him. The only exception was when he was getting laid. He took a slow breath, met Xav's eyes, then moved away and downed his second beer. "I'll follow you," he said.

CHAPTER FIVE

CHANCE COULDN'T recall who'd made the first move, but they barely made it out the door of the bar when they tangled and he pushed Xav against the bar's brick façade.

Holy fuck. Chance moaned and gripped the front of Xav's shirt. Xav ground his knee into Chance's groin. Xav licked and nipped at Chance's neck, the hint of five-o'clock shadow brushing Chance's cheek. Chance liked the roughness and the way tendrils from Xav's hair slipped from his ponytail and tickled his skin.

Xav found the waist of Chance's jeans and slipped his hand inside to cup his ass. He squeezed just enough that it stung. Chance pinned him harder against the wall, but Xav didn't release the pressure on Chance's ass.

"Thought we were going to do this at your place," Chance hissed and let go of Xav's shirt. He'd have been happy to fuck the guy here, but Wilmington wasn't so far away from home that he'd take a chance on getting busted for indecency.

Xav grunted and headed across the parking lot, bypassing a silver Ford Fusion for a black Harley with California plates. Chance barely registered putting the key in the ignition of his car as Xav pulled on a black helmet.

"NICE WHEELS," Chance said as they climbed the stairs to the second floor of a motel a half an hour later. Xav shrugged but said nothing, instead opening the door onto a shabby-looking hallway with faded pink-and-green floral carpeting.

Man of few words.

The crappy '80s time capsule of a beach motel was quickly forgotten as Xav closed the door to the room and got to work on the buttons of Chance's shirt. His skin exposed, Chance leaned against the door as Xav tongued one nipple and tugged on the other.

"Oh, fuck!" Pain and pleasure shot through Chance. He wriggled his arms out of his shirt and allowed it to fall to the floor. By now, Xav was using his teeth on that already sensitive bud. Xav might not say much, but his mouth was a fucking revelation.

Chance closed his eyes and let himself free-fall into that feeling of need, wanting the oh-so-fucking-good contact that zinged from Xav's tongue straight to his dick. He came back to himself when Xav worked open his belt buckle and unbuttoned his jeans. Xav snaked a smooth hand between Chance's boxer briefs and skin to cup his ass, then worked Chance's hard cock through the fabric.

Too much, too soon. Chance needed to take back control. Move it along at *his* pace.

He pushed Xav back, then pinned him against the closed door before Xav could pull his boxers and jeans off. Xav clearly didn't mind. He hissed his pleasure as Chance held him there with a knee pressed against his erection as he rid Xav of his shirt. It only took a moment before he had Xav entirely naked, his cock jutting out, tip glistening.

Satisfied he had Xav where he wanted him, Chance traced his fingers down Xav's chest and sides, reveling in the feel of smooth skin over hard muscle. When he reached Xav's waist, his right hand met the raised skin of a recent scar. He ignored it and continued his downward exploration until he clasped Xav's cock.

He went to his knees and glanced up to meet Xav's eyes before pushing back the foreskin and wrapping lips and tongue around his delicious cock. Chance teased at first, waited until he felt the first tremor rip through Xav's body before swallowing more down. With each erotic response, he allowed Xav in farther, stopping only when the tip touched the back of his throat.

"Fucking hell," Xav groaned as Chance wrapped his fingers around the base and fucked his cock with his mouth.

With his other hand, Chance squeezed Xav's ass, listening to his pants and moans until he had his answer: Xav liked it a little rough too. Chance licked around the crown, nipping at the edge, and worked his tongue over the top, pausing only long enough to lave the slit. Xav's powerful thighs shook against his arms.

"Bed," Chance said as he came up for air. He wanted to see all of Xav, and the musty shag carpet wasn't what he'd come here for. Xav grunted as Chance got to his feet, and they stumbled over the cast-off clothes on their way to the bed.

He wriggled out of his jeans and underwear, then tossed them aside and turned back to Xav. The ponytail caught his eye. He'd always cut his hair short. It kept him under the radar. But he liked long hair. He reached out and pulled off the elastic, freeing Xav's hair and causing it to tumble over his shoulders. He caught a whiff of something citrusy as he carded his fingers through the silk of it and laved Xav's neck.

A moment later Xav pushed him onto the bed and landed beside him. The mattress creaked beneath their combined weight and sagged at the center, causing them to roll toward each other.

Perfect. Maybe there were benefits to flea-trap motels and overly used mattresses after all.

Chance realized Xav must have tapped the ancient clock radio by the bed, because the thrumming bass of the Rolling Stones' "You Can't Always Get What You Want" drowned out the squeak of the mattress. Rock 'n' roll was always better than country for fucking.

They rolled, legs entwined, mouths pressed together, tongues tangling, each struggling for control. Xav pulled Chance to him by the ass and ground their cocks together, using his weight to increase the friction.

"Want to fuck you into the sheets," Chance gasped as he rolled Xav onto his back, lacing his fingers with Xav's, pressing his arms over his head. He expected an argument, but Xav merely grunted and inclined his head to the bedside table, where a bottle of lube and condoms lay scattered. Chance grinned but didn't immediately move to snag the stuff. Instead, he leaned down and sucked a particularly hard nipple, then gripped it between his teeth until Xav swore and canted his hips up to press his cock harder against his.

"Thought you were going to fuck me." Xav didn't seem all that disappointed as Chance slipped a hand between them to cup his balls.

Chance ignored this. He didn't usually enjoy drawing out this part of the dance, but he liked the slight tremor in Xav's voice. He released Xav's nipple and repressed a grin as the bud began to color and Xav groaned, "Oh fuck."

The room felt hot, the antiquated air-conditioning unit wheezing to keep up with the temperature outside and the activity inside. Sweat dripped down Chance's back as he worked his fingers farther back and skirted Xav's hole. When Xav moved to meet his probing finger, Chance backed off, circling the entrance, denying Xav what he was now moaning for.

Xav dug his fingers into Chance's back until it stung. Reaching the limits of his own patience, Chance retreated and snagged the lube. He poured it onto his hands and warmed it, then met Xav's glazed eyes as he pushed Xav's thighs apart and slid a finger behind Xav's balls. This time he pushed inside without hesitation.

"Better." Xav was clearly struggling to keep his eyes open as Chance worked his entrance with a second and a third finger. He wasn't particularly gentle, but each time Chance fucked him with his fingers, Xav tensed around them and groaned.

No more waiting. Chance sheathed his cock and slid inside Xav's tight heat. Xav lifted his legs and rested them on Chance's shoulders, opening to him, rising with each thrust. Like this, the muscles of Xav's abdomen tensed and released with the movement. Xav was slick with sweat, which made his skin appear to shimmer in the low light. Chance grunted and ghosted his fingers over Xav's belly, needing to explore the tantalizing heat of it and reveling in the hard muscle beneath the smooth skin. Not a surfer's body at all. Where Chance was lean from miles upon miles of pounding the pavement, Xav looked as though he spent hours honing his body into a powerfully built instrument. Xav's neck muscles strained, bringing the sharp edge of his square jaw into stark relief.

Xav grabbed him by the upper arms and squeezed, the intense green of his eyes forcing Chance to look away and catch his breath. Chance thrust harder as the slapping sound and the squeaking of the bed intensified. Xav met each movement, grunting, muscles tensing as he lifted his ass farther, hips pistoning. Overhead, the ceiling fan wobbled and spun, and the window unit blasted cold air into the room, but sweat dripped between Chance's shoulder blades and ran down his back. Beads of moisture appeared on Xav's brow, and a few strands of hair stuck to his temple.

"Fuck!" Chance shouted, at the limit of his endurance, knowing he would come soon and fighting it with every fiber of his being. He watched Xav's expression as he changed the angle of his thrusts, satisfied that he'd nailed the right spot when Xav's lips part in a throaty growl.

Xav sucked in air and panted before releasing one of Chance's arms and wrapping his hand around his own cock. He followed the rhythm of Chance's movements and stroked himself, his eyes never leaving Chance's. Chance couldn't look away. Couldn't retreat one iota. Couldn't hide, not without letting go of the fucking amazing hardness of

Xav's body and the heat from inside. He ignored the whispers at the back of his mind that warned him of the danger of getting too close, of letting Xav in even a little bit. It all felt too good. Too hot. Too right.

Xav tensed around Chance's cock as if challenging him to keep it together. Chance thrust harder, meeting the demand with his own, fighting back, telling himself he was in control and knowing it for the lie it was. As he spiraled beyond himself, he came with a shout at the same time Xav spurted on his belly. No winner here. At best a draw, but if all draws felt this fucking good, Chance could learn to embrace not winning.

WITH XAV asleep and Beck's "Blue Moon" emanating softly from the cheap clock radio on the nightstand, Chance slipped out of the hotel room as the first hint of pink warmed the dark sky. He and Xav had fucked again only an hour before, but old demons nipped at his heels and he felt an urgent need to distance himself again. He silenced the part of him that wondered what it might be like to wake up next to someone he cared about. *No.* He'd sleep alone in his own bed. He liked it better that way.

CHAPTER SIX

AT EIGHT forty-five Monday morning, Xav parked his bike in one of the two spaces at the sheriff's office that were reserved for the Crimes Against Children Task Force. He couldn't remember the last time he'd worn a suit, and the heat and humidity of the North Carolina summer made him feel like he'd just walked through a sauna. But the Andrew Christians clinging to his ass were a pleasant reminder of the Friday night before. He smiled to himself as he removed his helmet, reached in the saddlebag for his suit jacket, and hoped it hadn't been destroyed in the short ride to his new office. He shook it out and it looked surprisingly good. He unzipped and slipped off his leather jacket and stowed it, and pulled on the suit jacket. He'd braided his hair neatly that morning, and now he slid the braid into the collar of his jacket. Satisfied, he locked his helmet to the handlebar and headed to the building.

A deputy escorted a young couple from the building as Xav approached. The man demanded that someone find his boy, the woman was in tears and nearly hysterical, and the deputy appeared to be doing his best to assure the couple the sheriff's department was doing everything within its power to locate the missing boy. Xav glanced back at the distraught couple, the scene somehow ominous. Hot, muggy air suddenly gusted around him, carrying with it the scent of a coming storm. A sense of foreboding took root in Xav, burrowing deeper with each step as he ascended the wide portico to the sheriff's station.

He entered the office to find it bustling with activity. Strategically placed state-of-the-art surveillance equipment unobtrusively decorated the ceiling, and slim computer monitors graced the desks. It was a typical bullpen setup with offices surrounding the floor area, but nicer. The rich green carpeting, oxblood leather swivel chairs, and white wainscoting and chair railing all gave it the flair of Southern elegance. And the half-height walls between the desks, though useless, gave the impression that someone cared about privacy. It was nothing like the austere glass office he'd had in LA, and he liked it. Though the chandelier and baroque mirror in the waiting area could go the way of the dodo.

A woman in her late twenties with hair the color and shape of a neon tangerine—and pink-frosted lipstick to clash—looked up at him from the reception desk. "Can I help you?"

"I'm here to see Sheriff Winston."

"Is Sheriff expecting you?"

The accent was going to take some getting used to. He smiled. He couldn't help it. "He is. The name's Constantine."

"Oh, yeah. You're the fella from the FBI here to take Charlie's place. Have yourself a seat and I'll tell him you're here."

Xav stifled a chuckle as he read her nametag. "Thank you, Twyla Fay."

She eyed him suspiciously before picking up the phone and pressing a button. "Mr. Constantine is here to see you." She hung up. "I said have yourself a seat."

"Thank you, ma'am."

"You aren't from around here, are ya?"

Now he did chuckle. "No, ma'am, I am not."

Sheriff Winston strode to Xav and greeted him with a warm handshake, and led him back to his large office in the corner of the building. Xav entered and Sheriff Winston closed the door behind him. "Have a seat."

Xav obliged and waited as Sheriff Winston filled the oxblood judge's chair behind his massive oak desk. "I've known Danny Ward nigh on thirty years and trust him like a brother. He says you're the best at what you do, and from what I've seen of your records, I tend to agree with him."

"Thank you."

"I know why you left, and I'm sorry about that, but it can't be a problem for you here."

"It won't be."

"I don't doubt that or I wouldn't have hired you. But let me be frank. You and I know that our chances of finding kids gone missing for more than forty-eight hours are slim to none, much less finding them alive. This is going to be a gruesome task."

Xav nodded his agreement. "Thoughts? Suspicions?"

"None I can speak aloud and certainly none I should tell you for fear of tainting your investigations."

"Enlighten me?"

Sheriff Winston gave him a long considering look. "While I'm willing to admit that a few of my deputies need additional training, none are lazy and all are sharp as tacks. It makes no sense that we haven't found one missing kid. Not one. Second, drugs are showing up in our schools at four times last year's rate. Why isn't the DEA sniffing around? Third, the SBI hasn't jumped all over this. I find that queer as a three-dollar bill. They—" Sheriff Winston stopped his recitation abruptly, his cheeks lightly flushed. "No offense intended."

Xav smiled. "None taken. Please continue."

"They have the same access to data from NCMEC we do and should be all over this like a wet rag. Not to mention half the town is ablather and the press is breaking down my door. Yet the SBI hasn't so much as sent me an e-mail."

"In sum, your gut feeling is there is a connection between the drugs and missing youth. Further, that there may be an internal problem."

Sheriff Winston's expression was dour. "And I don't have a stitch of evidence to back up my thinkin'."

Xav met his even gaze. "We never had this conversation."

"Good man. Don't hesitate to ask for what you need to get this job done." Sheriff Winston stood and Xav followed.

They shook hands. "Thanks, Sheriff."

"Let me introduce you to everyone before they think we've gone and planned the next town barbecue without 'em." Sheriff Winston sized him up. "You're liable to catch hell over that hair."

Xav smiled again. "Nothing I can't handle."

Sheriff Winston huffed a laugh and opened the door. He went to the center of the bullpen and called for everyone's attention, and the room quieted. "This here is Xavier Constantine. He hails from the FBI's Child Abduction Rapid Deployment division in California, and we're fortunate to have him here to replace Charlie Cooper as the new head of our Crimes Against Children Task Force. He's here to help us find all the kids who've gone missing. What do you like to be called, son?"

Xav forced himself to keep a straight face. The accent was killing him. "Xav."

"You'll be working with John, over here, and Twyla Fay will make sure you know who's who and will get you set up with a desk and whatnot until your office is ready. Coffee and Krispy Kremes are in the kitchen."

A deputy stood and came around the side of his desk to shake hands with him—the same deputy who'd been on the front steps trying to calm the distraught couple. "The name's John Carson."

Xav shook John's hand and fleetingly wondered if he was old enough to drink.

Winston hiked his pants by the belt. "Once you get settled and have a chance to review the files, come see me."

"Thank you, Sheriff."

Winston clapped him on the back and the staff resumed activity.

"Coffee? Or are you one o' them water types?" John asked.

"Coffee would be great."

John led him into the kitchen, opened a cabinet, and gestured to the coffee mugs. "These here are for guests. I reckon you'll bring your own. Just put it on this side with the others. Cream's right there on the counter with the sugar. Spoons in the drawer. Twyla Fay's real good about keepin' us full with doughnuts." He gestured to the table.

Xav reached for a mug. It wasn't entirely clean, and he went to the sink and washed it. After drying it with a paper towel, he reached for the coffee pot. The aroma was more of a stench.

"Oh, here. Let me make a new one. That's been on for God knows how long."

Xav watched John as he rinsed the carafe, not bothering to wipe out the residue, and made a fresh pot of coffee. It suddenly dawned on him that John was nervous. "Thank you."

"Well, yeah. It's the least I can do."

"Don't be nervous."

John blushed and half snorted. "Guess it shows. Sorry. I never met anyone from the FBI before."

"I'm a deputy sheriff now. Just like you."

John looked at him curiously. "Yeah, why is that? If ya don't mind my asking."

Xav's humor dissipated on the air. "Needed a change of scenery."

"Ah-huh. Lots of stress? I hear they got some bad cases out that way. Serial killers and such."

Xav's humor returned and he nodded. "Whole towns full of them."

John's eyes went wide. "Man, no wonder you wanted to leave. All we got here is the occasional robbery or arson, usually drug related. Well, except we got all these boys gone missing."

Xav frowned. He thought it was interesting to note that only boys had disappeared. "All boys?"

"Yeah."

"How many?"

"As of this morning, eighteen just since spring. Mr. and Mrs. Thompson woke up at four this morning to find Ray Jr. gone from his bed. No sign of foul play, but the window was wide open. Techs are still out there lookin' around. Couple of our guys are still searchin' the woods."

The number of children who went missing was always much higher than reported. A sense of unease filled Xav, and he worked to keep his face devoid of expression. "That's quite a few missing boys," he said as he poured a cup of what smelled to be decent coffee and made a mental note to find the closest Starbucks.

John became excited. "The whole town's up in arms. Everybody suspicious of everybody else. Everybody judgin' everybody else's kids. And it's the craziest thing. It's a wonder it isn't on the national news. These boys just up and went missing. From homes, schools, the movie theater. Even from the grocery store and old man Spencer's butcher shop. And it's always the same. No foul play, just gone. You want cream and sugar with that?"

Child sex trafficking is rarely, if ever, reported on the national news, Xav thought bitterly. "No, thank you. How old is Ray?"

"Midthirties. He and Emi been sweethearts forever and married right out of high school. I was just walkin' 'em out when you came up the front steps."

"I'm sorry. I meant Ray Jr. How old is Ray Jr.?"

"Oh. He'll be eleven Saturday after next." His expression saddened. "Emi set up a surprise party for him and everything on regatta weekend. She's mighty broke up."

"I'm sure. Shall we get to work?"

John brightened. "Right this way, boss."

Xav caught him looking at his braid, a mixture of curiosity and envy plain on his face. Xav stifled a smile. He found a small satisfaction in straight men envying his hair. Yet there was an art to admiration. Gay men appreciated. Straight men ogled. *Downright plebeian.* The fauxmosexuals who admired his hair just left him wondering if Mother Nature had taken up drinking. "Xav. Just Xav."

"Never heard of a Z name except for Zeb," John said as he led Xav to a desk that sat behind a half-height partition. "This is your desk. Mine's right here on the other side of the wall. As I understand it, you'll be getting an office, but Twyla Fay hasn't had a chance to clean it out yet. It's still all full of props from last year's Shrimp Festival."

Twyla Fay hurried over. "I made sure your desk is stocked with everything you need. This note tells ya how to log into the computer. Your first name's your temporary password. Be sure to change it when ya log on. Those boxes on the floor are your files. Let me know if ya need anything else."

"Thank you, Twyla Fay."

"You California people have the strangest accent." The phone rang and she hurried away.

"Don't mind Twyla Fay. She's always been one to say what's on her mind, but she's nice about it. Mostly." John gazed with unvarnished longing at the empty space left when she walked away.

Xav repressed a chuckle. "Are you familiar with all the cases?"

John noticed that Xav sensed his interest in Twyla Fay, and a hint of pink stained his cheeks. "Yes, sir. Spent the last two days reviewing every one of them so the information'd be fresh in my mind."

"Why don't we sit at your desk and go through the files and you can tell me what you know?"

"Fine by me, boss."

"Xav. Just Xav."

CHAPTER SEVEN

A COUPLE of hours later, Xav flexed his back and arms and sat back in his chair. He and John had gone through only a third of the files. The number of boys missing within five months was astounding, particularly for a county with a population of just over a hundred thousand. The boys had nothing in common. Different towns, different neighborhoods, different schools. Good behavior, bad. It didn't make a difference. Not even the same Boy Scout troops. All disappeared without a trace. And it all began in March. "What happens in this town in March?"

John gave him a quizzical look. "Nothin'. Well, I mean, there're lots of art exhibits, a concert or two, but nothin' else unless you want standup paddleboard lessons or an electric bicycle tour."

Xav couldn't help it. Laughter bubbled up from inside him. "Come again? Standup what?"

"Paddleboarding. It's fun."

"I'll take your word for it."

John's eyes drifted to Twyla Fay's desk. "Oh boy," John said softly. "Here comes trouble."

Xav glanced at him and followed his gaze. Two men entered the station. Xav didn't think twice about the older gentleman who pointed at Sheriff Winston's office and walked past Twyla Fay without breaking stride, but the man following in his wake made Xav do a double take. *Chance*. Xav fought to keep his expression neutral and stifled the stab of heat to his groin as he briefly met Chance's eyes. Xav thought he detected squelched surprise, but Chance didn't blink an eye as he followed the older man into Sheriff Winston's office.

Chance's ass was haute in a suit. "Who are they?" Xav asked nonchalantly.

"That's Walter Talley. Slick bastard who does all the DA's dirty work. Watch out for him. Smooth enough to charm the skin off a snake, and windy as a sack full of farts. Man behind him is Mister C. Evan Fairchild, the assistant district attorney who prosecutes drug crimes. We talk from time to time about cases, but generally he don't allow much. Guys here like to say his nose is so high in the air, he'd drown in a rainstorm."

Xav smiled. "Beg your pardon?"

"You know, he acts like he's real satisfied with himself. Like he's better than everyone else."

"Why is that?"

John shrugged. "Always been that way. No one really knows anything about him except he came from up in Bertie County and went to some big-name law school up North."

"Full of himself?"

John shrugged but didn't say more.

AFTER SEEING Chance, Xav had trouble concentrating on the files and John's information. Images of Chance's lean body, rebellious auburn hair, and dusty blue eyes flashed through his mind and only served to rekindle his lust. Chance was just plain hot. Their night together had been more than a little memorable, and Xav had been disappointed when Chance had left at dawn without a word. Not that he expected his hookups to stick around and cook breakfast for him, but for the first time in a long time, Xav had wanted to wake up next to someone. He also thought he'd sensed something in Chance. Some… something. Something he couldn't identify but that made him consider that Chance could be more than a fuck. He shook his head, clearing it of useless thoughts, and returned to reviewing files.

An hour later Talley and *Evan* left the office. Evan met Xav's eyes deliberately this time and gave Xav a look. *The* look. The "I don't know you, never heard of you" look. And it pissed Xav off. Evan wasn't out. So what? Xav sure as hell wasn't going to out him, and Evan didn't need to be a prick about it. "Let's get through the rest of these files," he said to John.

EVAN HAPPILY deposited Talley at Faison's office. He'd had more than enough of the asshole telling him how to do his job and blathering on about the governor this and the speaker of the house that. Seeing Xav hadn't done much to improve his shithole of a day. *A fucking sheriff's deputy?* No matter the man's assets—and they were substantial—eight years of Evan's no-fraternization policy had just landed in the crapper.

When Sheriff Winston asked him to share his drug case information with Xav, he almost lost his temper. It would be a cold day in hell before Faison let him do that, and he wasn't going to risk his job to help a newbie. *He was a good fuck. That's all!*

He was losing his mind. Sure, Xav was probably a great guy. *Even worse.* Judging by the braid that snaked down his way-too-sexy back, Xav probably wouldn't hesitate to be out if given the opportunity. Evan ran a hand through his hair, causing a rogue lock to tumble onto his forehead. He smoothed it back with a hand. He hadn't expected to see Xav again, much less find him working for the damn sheriff's department.

On the way out, he'd swung by Twyla Fay's desk while Talley finished kissing up to Sheriff Winston.

"New guy?" he asked.

"Xavier Constantine. California. Ex-FBI. Here to take over where Charlie left off," she said as she eyed him carefully. "Why do you care?"

"Don't."

"Liar." She said it in long syllables, so it sounded almost as if she'd said "lawyer."

"Yep." He leaned a hand on her desk and smiled. "Tell me something I don't know."

Twyla Fay was the second person in Dare's Landing who'd guessed he was gay—the first being a twit clerk at the coroner's office—and he'd never confirmed it for her, but it was nice that she didn't seem to care one way or another and never pushed him. He trusted her not to gossip about it, although he wasn't sure why. Dr. Sampson would probably say he didn't feel threatened by her, but he was pretty sure it was because she never tried to bullshit him.

She'd become a bit protective of him, and he guessed it was because she had some misguided notion that he needed her protection because he was gay. But he thought it was sweet, and she was one of the few genuine people he interacted with at work. She'd discovered he'd graduated from Carolina, so most of their conversations centered on NCAA basketball. Other than Carol, his administrative assistant, Twyla Fay had been the only one who'd checked on him when he'd been laid up with the flu. He also appreciated how she kept him in the loop on sheriff business when most of the force made it a point to keep their distance from him.

She nibbled her lower lip and raised an overly plucked eyebrow. "Constantine comes highly recommended," she said as she studied a

Carolina blue fingernail. "Few of the guys who applied for the job are pissed. Thinking he shouldn't have leapfrogged his way to the top of the task force. But I saw the recs with his application. Guy's some sort of maverick." She grinned, then added, "I think we're going to get on just fine."

"Fairchild?" Talley said from behind him.

Evan nodded his thanks to her and turned to Talley. "Sir?"

"I'm supposed to meet with Jimmy in ten. Time to go."

Evan fought the urge to tell the asshole he wasn't a chauffeur. Instead, he smiled blandly and headed toward the waiting area.

Evan forced himself to look Xav in the eye again, a reminder to himself that, as long as Xav was on this turf, nothing but a fuck had happened between them. This proved to be a mistake, since revisiting those bright green eyes made his traitorous cock twitch its approval. It took all his self-control and imagining Talley in his underwear, belly plunging over the waistband, to fight his body's reaction. The conjured image had the desired effect, and Evan hoped he wasn't entirely transparent. At this rate, Twyla Fay wouldn't be the only one to figure things out, and that was one pile of shit he didn't want to be buried under.

He needn't have worried. Xav looked away, clearly bored. Fine. *Fuck him, anyhow.* Evan didn't care as long as Xavier Constantine kept his mouth shut.

"…get in touch with Raleigh," Talley was saying as Evan focused once again on the task at hand.

SBI. Just what they needed. And Faison had already told the DEA in no uncertain terms that he didn't want them sniffing around his garbage. Too many fingers in the pot meant even less would be accomplished as things became more polarized, more unwieldy to manage, and Evan's workload doubled with more low-level busts, more low-level dealers to put away, none of whom would give up anyone valuable. Same old shit. No one ever looked for the suppliers. No one ever looked to cut the head off the snake.

CHAPTER EIGHT

XAV STOPPED by Whole Foods Market on Front Street on the way home. The thought of shopping at a place called Harris Teeter was just... *no*. It smacked of a cheap horror dramedy. DollyCam tilts up and down as Hannibal Lecter teeters on totter with playmate. Cue music sting. Steadicam pans in artificial blood spray as Hannibal Lecter eats playmate. Cue audience boo. Close up: Hannibal Lecter sits alone on teeter-totter. *Silence of the Seesaws. Just... no.*

He wasn't sure he liked the new condominium yet. It was a fully furnished corner unit in a historic building, with a nice view of the river. The building had a dry cleaner, a quaint restaurant that served a mean veggie omelet for breakfast, and a Starbucks. The Starbucks had sealed the deal for him. He'd been even more ecstatic when he found a Starbucks around the corner from his office. It lent hope to survival in this man-versus-shrimp town. All said, he missed the sound of waves crashing against the shore and hated that the sun set in the wrong place. Not to mention the mosquitoes were big enough to suck the fender off a Hummer—proboscis size no doubt the subject of many a Friday-night brag at the local salt-marsh cantina. He needed to remember to buy industrial-strength bug repellent.

Xav stood in the checkout line and read the back of a can of bug repellent emblazoned with *Guaranteed to eradicate mature tiger mosquitoes*. Xav immediately had visions of striped mosquitoes the size of prehistoric felines coming at him, jaws agape, saber-proboscis bared. *Bad visual*. He dropped the can back into his handbasket of purchases as harsh whispers from the women behind him infiltrated his hearing.

"...that Tommy was a troublemaker, Betty. Always actin' up in school and he knew his mama'd beat him for it, so he ran away. Pure and simple."

The second woman nodded with certainty. "It's a fact he'd been runnin' with the ruffians down at the docks. Why, his family even stopped comin' to church a few months ago. Ain't that somethin'?"

"Mmm-hmmm. That boy had it comin' to him and he just up and left."

Xav shook his head as he moved forward and set his basket on the conveyor for the cashier. It pissed him off when people spoke of missing kids in past tense, as if it were a foregone conclusion they were gone for good. Even more, he hated when people inferred kids deserved the horrors adults rained down on them. If only these gossips accepted the truth. There was an epidemic of missing children in the US, and it all stemmed from abuse and neglect. Very few parents were responsible anymore. Most were breeders who didn't give a shit about the end product.

The young cashier's expression showed that she'd noticed his irritation with the biddies behind him, and she gave him a sympathetic smile. He paid for his items, thanked her, and left the store.

As a tenderloin marinated in extra-virgin olive oil, lime juice, garlic, onion, and sage, he spread files out on his antique dining room table. He poured a glass of the Childress merlot that had been airing and sipped it as he sifted through the files. The local vintage was decent, but nothing compared to a California wine. He turned the volume up on his cell phone as Spotify played Peter Gabriel's "In Your Eyes." Deciding to pick up where he and John left off, Xav opened a file marked Department of Social Services: Child Protection Services Unit—the only case where the missing kids had been in the custody of the state. He opened it and read.

Quinn and Winter Haverty, eleven-year-old twin boys removed from their home after the father was caught attempting to sell one for a fix. On a street corner, no less. The father was sentenced to a mere thirty days in county jail. The boys' conditions were what you'd expect from the home of violent, drug-addicted parents. Bruises, history of ER visits, stitches and broken bones, underweight, unvaccinated, no social interaction at school, but by all accounts smart and courteous. They'd had a horrid home life, and DSS took custody of them during an onslaught of violence and placed them in Bright Horizons Group Home six months ago. The boys had disappeared from Bright Horizons on a Saturday during a routine visit to the park next door. What was to say the kids hadn't run away? He noted that DSS had filed the appropriate reports with the sheriff's office and the SBI, but the SBI had taken no action other than the cursory interview of the social worker. Xav reached for a double-sized sticky note and wrote *John, 1. Why no SBI follow-up? 2. What do you know about Bright Horizons?*

His mind drifted to C. *Evan* Fairchild, and he immediately began to get hard. He smirked and wondered how many people knew what the C stood for. *If* it really did stand for Chance.

Get out of my head, Chance. He closed the DSS file, redoubled his efforts to focus, and opened the next file. Twelve-year-old Jeremy Wrigley disappeared from a Greyhound station. An insistent thought niggled at the back of his mind like a rabid tapeworm and…. *Click.* Xav dug into the file. The boy had arrived from Los Angeles after visiting relatives out west. *Click.* On April 2. *Click.* He'd been waiting for his father to pick him up when he disappeared. According to the statement taken from the father, he'd been running late, called the station, and asked the ticket clerk to keep an eye on him. According to the statement taken from the clerk, Jeremy had arrived with another boy about the same age. *Click.* On bus 1072.

Xav reached for the folded, now worn and tattered paper that occupied the granite counter with his keys, wallet, and weapon—the paper that had become his touchstone. He read down the list of potential buses that applied to the ticket stub. Bus 1072 was one of them. *Click.* His nervous system ratcheted like a machine gun as he searched the file and found a picture of the boy. He held it in trembling fingers as he studied the blue eyes that never left him. He swallowed hard and propped the picture against the cracked-pepper carafe on the table. The Helm boy from LA had ridden to Dare's Landing with the Wrigley boy? Why? For now, it would remain an unanswered question. He rubbed the tattoo on his chest and continued to stare at the picture as he reached for his cell phone and hit the icon to call Daniel Ward.

"I knew you'd come crawling back," Ward answered, humor clear in his voice.

"I found our other boy from Bolivia."

"No shit? *Now* I know your motive for going to North Carolina. Next time I can't put two and two together, at least let me buy a clue. Why isn't he in NCMEC's system?"

"File says he is. I'll send the encrypted file, prints, and DNA report to you tomorrow for verification."

"Your desk is still warm."

Xav terminated the call and looked at his watch. *Fuck it.* He dialed John's cell phone.

"Hello, Xav. Everything okay?"

"Everything's fine. I have a question that can't wait until morning."

"Shoot."

"Who, in our office, enters data into NCMEC's system?"

"Oh, well, that used to be Twyla Fay, but Charlie took over doing it about six months ago. Said she wasn't being thorough enough with details."

The irritation Xav heard in John's voice only fueled the burgeoning dread in the pit of his stomach.

John continued. "I know it hurt her feelings 'cause she's real thorough about that kinda stuff and she's taken the matter of our missin' kids to heart."

"Why don't we give that responsibility back to her?"

"I guarantee she'd be pleased as punch if you did that!"

"In fact, why don't we have her audit our data in NCMEC's system?"

"Sure thing! You got anything in particular you want her to look for?"

Xav weighed his options carefully and decided to tell John the truth. "I might have a disposition on one of our missing boys from a case I worked in LA. We couldn't identify him because he wasn't in NCMEC's system."

"Well, hot diggity dog! Which boy and where's he now?"

Xav mentally kicked himself in the ass for not thinking before he opened mouth and inserted foot. "He's dead, John. I'm sorry."

"Ah, hell! Who is it?"

"Jeremy Wrigley."

"Shit! That's the worst news ever. The Wrigleys are gonna be all tore up."

"It'll take a day or so to get confirmation from LA. Let's not say anything until we know for certain."

"Yeah, shit. That's just horrible news. How in hell did he end up bein' one of your cases in LA?"

Xav wanted to shoot himself. The last thing he wanted to do was tell John about Bolivia. "Don't know," he lied. "I want to know why he isn't in NCMEC's system."

"I'm sure he is, Xav. Charlie used to stay after hours to work on that stuff."

Man, Xav hated it when cops went bad. "Let's ask Twyla Fay to find out why we couldn't find a match to his data."

"Shit, yeah. She'll be mighty pleased you trust her to do that. But hell, Xav. It's just awful that we're asking her to audit because one of our boys is dead. Ah, hell, that's not what I meant. Because law enforcement couldn't ID him. His remains, I mean."

"I know what you mean. See you in the morning."

"What time are you comin' in?"

"I'll be there by ten. Why?"

"'Cause me'n Twyla Fay will be there at seven. If you trust me, I'll go ahead and give her the news and get her started."

"Go for it. You're my partner, remember?"

"Yeah, I do. Just want to make sure I'm handling things right."

"Go ahead, but don't say anything to anyone else until we know where the glitch is." John was silent and Xav thought he'd lost the call. "You still there?"

"Yeah, sorry. I was just thinking that Sheriff Winston's going to be madder than a wet hen if something's wrong with our data."

"All the more reason to wait for me to get there."

"Yeah, okay. See you in the morning."

Xav terminated the call and stared at Jeremy's picture for a long moment. He'd been the more afraid of the two boys, the one who didn't want to run. Xav closed his eyes as the horror of the failed rescue fought for territory in his mind. He opened them again and placed Jeremy's picture back in the file, determined to think of another set of blue eyes. Blue eyes that would comfort him as he cooked dinner.

CHAPTER NINE

"MR. FAIRCHILD?" Carol said over the phone. "I've got Fred Lewis on line two."

"Thanks." Evan pressed the button on his phone to connect. "Freddy? What did you find out?"

Fred laughed. "For this, I'm going to exact a price."

"You mean the keg I sprang for at graduation doesn't get me a freebie?" Evan shot back.

"We've been out of law school for how many years now? Eight?"

"Nine this year," Evan corrected.

"Credit's no good anymore," Fred answered. "I'm thinking dinner at Ivy at the Shore next time you're in LA. On you, of course. Including a bottle of Veuve Clicquot."

"For that," Evan said with a chuckle, "this had better be good."

"It's good. And it was hell to get."

"Okay, okay. Dinner on me. Assuming you and Margie put me up for the night," Evan replied. "I'm looking forward to seeing your McMansion."

"Deal. Took a little digging. Seems your mystery man did some undercover work for the FBI."

"And?"

"My buddy in the US Attorney's office wouldn't give details, but word is Constantine got fed up with the bullshit after a case went bad somewhere down in South America."

"Drugs?" Evan asked.

"No. He dealt with human trafficking. Specifically, child sex trafficking. My friend says the guy's good. He tried a few cases where Constantine was the government's key witness. Knows his stuff. Works his ass off and gets into his work. I got the impression sometimes he gets a little too close."

Now that *was* interesting. "Why?"

"Seems the guy's rabid about protecting kids."

"Any idea why?"

"Nothing anyone would tell me," Fred replied.

Evan leaned back in his chair. At least Xav wasn't a slacker, but it didn't make Evan feel any better about the prospect of bumping into him at work. "Anything else?"

"Constantine grew up in LA, went to school in Boston."

"Boston?" Even more interesting. So much for his initial assessment of Xav as a broceanographer.

"Yeah, you'll love this."

Evan could almost hear Freddy's grin over the phone.

"He did undergrad at MIT. Mathematics major. Master's in criminology from U Penn with an emphasis in cryptology. The FBI was probably falling all over itself to recruit him."

No shit. This just got better and better. "What the hell's a guy with that kind of background doing in North Carolina?"

"I could ask you the same question," Fred shot back. "Of course, if you decide you want your own McMansion...."

"You couldn't pay me enough to come to work for you," Evan joked. Fred was serious—they'd had this discussion a half-dozen times before.

"Try me." Fred paused for a moment and then asked, "This personal?"

Evan had no intention of telling Fred he'd slept with Xav. "Not personal."

"'Cause word has it he's gay," Fred said. "Out but not advertising." When Evan didn't take the bait, Fred added, "But you already knew that, didn't you?"

Evan shook his head and sighed theatrically. "Don't even go there, Freddy. You know I don't mix business and pleasure. I just want to know what I'm dealing with. That's all."

"You can't bullshit a bullshitter, man."

"Thanks for the help," Evan said, foreclosing the topic. "I'll let you know next time I'm out your way. Tell Margie she's a brave woman."

"Always do. Laters. And make sure you get your sorry ass out here soon."

"Will do." Evan disconnected the call and rubbed his mouth. Mathematics major at MIT and a master's from U Penn? No wonder the FBI had recruited him. And he'd pegged Xav for a surfer! *What the hell are you doing in Dare's Landing, Xavier Constantine?*

JOHN WAVED Xav over to his desk as soon as Xav entered the bullpen area. The looks on his and Twyla Fay's faces were of abject relief. Xav set his valise on the desk. "Morning."

"Mornin'," they said in unison.

He looked from John to Twyla Fay and back again.

John stood and glanced around the bullpen briefly. "Twyla Fay and I need more coffee."

When John didn't move or say anything further, he looked at Twyla Fay. She stood and tried to smile and failed miserably.

"Why don't we all get coffee and a doughnut?" Xav asked with a calm that belied his deepening dread. He led them into the kitchen and reached for the mug he'd used since his arrival. He poured a cup of coffee and turned to the others, who, to no surprise given their distressed state, didn't have their mugs with them. Steeling himself for the worst, he placed the pot back on its burner. "Tell me."

Twyla Fay pulled the door from its pocket and slid it home, muting the sounds from the bustling office.

John cleared his throat and spoke sotto voce. "Well, startin' from when Charlie took over entering cases in NCMEC's system, all the kids, I mean the dispositions of the kids, are listed as found and the cases are closed."

Surprise, surprise, Xav thought bitterly. Charlie wouldn't be the first cop to go bad.

Before he could respond, Twyla Fay blurted, "I printed everything out. I even took screenshots and printed those. But I didn't want to touch the data until we talked to you."

"Thank you. You said 'starting from when Charlie took over.' What about cases that existed prior to when Charlie took over?"

John nodded rapidly. "They're still there—"

"But they're not open anymore," Twyla Fay finished nervously.

"Were the kids found?"

"No," John answered.

"Does our office have *any* open case data with NCMEC?"

"Old cases," John answered. "Cases over three years old."

"Go get your coffee mugs."

"Why?" Twyla Fay asked.

"Because I don't want to look like I'm holding you hostage in here for no apparent reason."

"Oh Lord, of course. Be right back," Twyla Fay said as she slid the door open and left the room.

"Twyla Fay's real upset. She's afraid she'll be blamed for anything wrong with the data," John said quickly.

"She won't be."

John sighed so deeply Xav thought he'd deflate. "Can I tell her that?"

Xav nodded as Twyla Fay returned, handed their mugs to John, and closed the door again.

"He says you won't be blamed," John reassured her.

"But how are you gonna know I didn't do it?" she asked as she filled her mug with coffee, then John's.

"Terminal usage, logins, comparisons to surveillance footage in the office," Xav said blandly.

"What do you want Twyla Fay to do?" John asked.

"I want you to use only the terminal at my desk to work on anything having to do with NCMEC from now on. I also want you each to create a new login and password, and then I want you to work with NCMEC to correct the data. But wait until after I speak with Sheriff Winston. Once you correct the data, my guess is that hits will start coming in."

Twyla Fay gasped and put a hand to her lips. "Oh my God, I didn't think about that."

"I can't believe Charlie was so damn concerned about his job security that he falsified data," John said in disgust.

Xav gave him a tight smile. If only it were that simple. "Where's Charlie now?"

John and Twyla Fay looked thunderstruck. "Sheriff didn't tell you?" Twyla Fay asked.

Xav shook his head once.

John shifted uncomfortably on his feet. "He's presumed dead."

CHAPTER TEN

"THEY THINK he took his boat out and got caught in a storm. It was found capsized down at Marina Point," John explained.

Things were getting worse by the minute. Xav blew a long breath. "Okay. Let me talk to Sheriff Winston. Is he with anyone now?"

Twyla Fay shook her head. "He has a conference call starting at eleven."

Xav gulped his remaining coffee. "Make sure your printouts are organized and get me a copy of the investigation file on Charlie's alleged death."

"Sheriff Winston's got it," she said quickly.

"Okay. I'll get it from him." Xav left the kitchen and headed across the bullpen to Sheriff Winston's office.

"WITH CHARLIE entering false data into NCMEC's system, the SBI had no reason to look into the missing kids, and my suspicion is that Charlie didn't drown by accident," Xav concluded. He'd didn't mention that Charlie might not have died at all, but he didn't have to. Sheriff Winston was a shrewd man.

A red flush had slowly crept up Ralph Winston's face and into his hairline as his anger rose. "I'm commencing an internal investigation. I'll reopen Charlie's case, and you'll have John and Twyla Fay correct the data with NCMEC."

"Who do you want to lead the investigation?"

"You."

Xav met the man's unflinching gaze. "Do you want to notify the SBI?"

"Not until your preliminary investigation is concluded. Then I'll have no choice but to face the music. No doubt I'll be facing early retirement."

Xav admired the man for taking it on the political chin, as it were. "Who handled Charlie's case?"

"Billy Kenner."

"Do you trust him?"

"Good and honest man." He hit the speaker button on his phone, then a speed dial button.

"Deputy Kenner," Billy answered.

"Come see me."

A knock sounded at the door within seconds, and it opened. Billy, a portly man in his late forties, entered and took a seat. Winston gave him the rundown and concluded with, "Now, I'm not saying you didn't do everything you could to find out what happened to Charlie. I'm saying new information has come to light and I need you to work with Xav, here, if only to verify your original conclusion is right."

Billy turned to Xav. "Charlie was a good man."

Xav didn't respond.

"Then your reinvestigation will bear that out, won't it?" Sheriff Winston asked sharply.

Billy seemed to rally but chose his words carefully. "Sheriff, I can't work with a homosexual. I'm a God-fearing man and it goes against my beliefs."

"You can and you will." Winston glared. "Look at it this way, Billy. I'll be retiring soon, and when that comes to pass, you're in a perfect position to run for sheriff. Equality being what it is and all, your acceptance might just be the ticket to get you there."

The man seemed to process this information, and he turned to Xav. "I didn't mean to be rude. I'm just not comfortable with your kind."

Xav kept his expression neutral. He'd known many a man like Billy Kenner and was long past justifying his sexuality. "No offense taken."

"Where do you want me to start?"

"How did Charlie's family take his death?" Xav asked.

"They didn't. His wife died of cancer ten years ago, and his son died nearly three years ago in Afghanistan. He had no family."

"Start at the beginning and work it like a new case," Xav suggested.

"What do you want me to tell Ridley, him bein' my partner and all?"

"Tell him I reopened the investigation into Charlie's disappearance," Winston interjected. "You don't need to tell him any more than that."

Billy stood. "Good enough."

"I won't need to remind you this is an *internal* investigation, right, Billy?"

"No, sir."

Sheriff Winston pulled a lower drawer out from his desk and retrieved a thick file folder. "Here's your old file. Have Twyla Fay get you your old workin' files. Thanks, Billy."

Summarily dismissed, Billy left the office.

"Pay him no mind. He's honest to a fault, and in spite of all that God-fearin', he's still got both feet on this earth. Though it might help if you saw your way to a haircut. I know you're not in uniform and I have no right to ask, but you'd do yourself some good with the men if you cut that mop off!"

Xav smiled wide. "It gives me character."

Winston snorted and smiled too. "You're one o' them, aren't ya?"

"One of whom?"

"One o' them types who always goes against the grain."

Xav ignored the tease. "Is it all right if I allow John and Twyla Fay to handle the hits as the NCMEC data is corrected?"

Winston shook his head slowly, now serious again, as if he disbelieved something like this could happen on his watch. "If you're not here, have them bring it to me."

"I've asked John to hold off on notifying the Wrigleys until we have confirmation from LA."

Winston winced. "We'll take things as they come."

Xav stood. "I'll have the evidence for the internal investigation sealed. Where do you want it stored before it goes to the SBI?"

"I guess we can't put it in our evidence room, now can we?" He sighed in frustration. "There's an empty gun safe in our weapons lockup. Have Twyla Fay clean out your office and have maintenance move it in there. Triple custody. All three of you sign for the evidence." Winston reached into a lower desk drawer, withdrew a cell phone, and tossed it to Xav.

He caught it with ease.

"Encrypted. Use it to call the SBI director when it's time."

"Suggestion?"

Sheriff gestured to him impatiently.

"The SBI has access to NCMEC. They should have been watching the data flow from each county and picked up that we had no open cases, yet we have multiple boys missing, parents clamoring for answers, and the press all over you about it."

An angry glare filled Winston's eyes. "You find out who did this and if the SBI is the slightest bit responsible, and that includes negligence, call the attorney general herself. Don't tell me until after you've made the call."

Xav admired the man even more. With a respectful nod, he thanked Sheriff Winston and left the office, closing the door on his way out. To Winston's further credit, Xav didn't hear anything shatter as he walked away.

CHAPTER ELEVEN

OVER THE next two weeks, John drove Xav around the county. They'd checked the surveillance film from the Greyhound station and found that the boys had left the building and wandered beyond the range of the cameras. Blue eyes continued to haunt Xav, and the delivery of the bad news to the Wrigleys nearly killed him. He spared the parents the lurid details of Bolivia and chose, instead, to focus on assuring them that Jeremy's remains would arrive forthwith, the FBI would see to a proper coffin for burial, and they would also continue efforts to find out who took Jeremy. The Wrigleys had no money, and John took up a collection at the office for the funeral service and burial. The contributions were woefully inadequate, and Xav paid the difference in costs without hesitation.

Xav and John reinterviewed families, reinvestigated the locations from which boys disappeared without a trace, and learned nothing new. Absolutely nothing.

"What do you think happened to them?" Xav asked one Thursday afternoon when they stopped for a greasy cheeseburger for lunch.

John ate the last of his fries and studied Xav. "I honestly don't have a clue."

"Show me the brothels and strip clubs."

John's eyes went wide. "Whorehouses? What would they want with boys?"

Xav pursed his lips. *Typical.* "Boys represent between 49 and 60 percent of the children who are sexually exploited in the US."

John's mouth gaped and his eyes went wide in utter shock and disbelief. "You mean they actually…. They would…. I can't believe that…."

"Let's go back to the office and I'll show you the data."

John sat dumbfounded after reading the links about the commercial sexual exploitation of children and listening to Xav talk. "I can't believe boys are worth more than girls are."

Xav nodded. "They don't get pregnant, and culturally, because they've been taught to man up, they're less emotional and don't cry for help. That silence makes them easier to addict to drugs and alcohol. In turn, they're easier to control and force to perform."

John scrubbed his face with both hands. "Jesus, that's so sick."

"Keep in mind that predators also have specific criteria, and statistics show that victims are more often fair-complected than not. Look at the complexions of our missing boys. They're all fair."

"So exactly what're you sayin' here, Xav?"

"We either have an incredibly active predator on our hands, or someone is collecting boys to exploit."

EVAN RUBBED the bridge of his nose and leaned back in his chair. Outside, sunset cast a pink glaze over the parking lot where only a few cars remained. Even through the hermetically sealed windows of the Carver County Courthouse Annex, the chirping and buzzing of cicadas drowned out the soft hum from the air-conditioning vent.

"Another late night?"

Evan looked up to see Carol standing in the doorway. "I'll be just a bit longer," he said. "Need me to walk you to your car?"

"I'll be fine." She smiled at him. "Tommy's downstairs with the car. You should come with us to Atlantic Beach sometime, you know. Maybe sail that boat of yours down and join us." It wasn't the first time she'd asked.

"I appreciate it." He meant it too. As always, part of him wanted to accept the invitation, but he still hadn't learned how to socialize, still didn't really know how to have relationships except for purely professional ones, and he didn't want to screw up his comfortable rapport with Carol. The voice in his mind *still* told him it was safer to keep his distance and his no-fraternization policy served him well. He silently cursed the bastards who'd fucked up his ability to relate to people—and himself for allowing the memories to hold dominion over him. "But you know I work most weekends."

She pressed her lips together and nodded.

He knew she cared about him. He liked her, and her husband was a good guy. He brushed the thoughts away. "Have a nice evening."

"We will."

She was gone a moment later, and Evan forced his eyes back to the files scattered over the desk. For the past two weeks, he'd spent his days dodging Talley's calls and prepping a case with Faison looking over his shoulder. Evenings, he'd combed through recent drug-bust cases with next to nothing to show for it. *Not nothing. More questions.*

Drug busts on the I-95 corridor were down, but Carver County had four ODs and two drug-related homicides just this month. Double the number this time last year. One of the ODs had been a kid at one of the local high schools. *The suppliers have to be bringing the stuff in another way.* He'd speak to John Carson in the morning and see what he'd be willing to share.

He glanced at the clock and ran a hand through his hair. Six thirty. He closed the file he'd been working on and gathered the rest into a pile, then locked them in a desk drawer. Faison didn't approve of his attorneys doing what he called "cop work." Not to mention, if Evan really did stumble onto something, Faison would claim credit faster than green grass through a goose. But credit wasn't the point. Evan wanted the fucking drug dealers out of his town.

LATE FRIDAY afternoon Evan entered the sheriff's department and was relieved not to see Xav as he headed over to talk to John.

"Mr. Fairchild," John said, nearly dropping the file he'd been reading as he shot up from his desk chair, back straight as an arrow.

"Relax, John," Evan said. "I'm not here on behalf of the DA. I'm trying to work through a few things, and I thought you might be able to help me."

"Of course, sir." John shifted from one foot to the other and looked a little embarrassed.

"So," Evan continued, doing his best to put John at ease, "how're things with the new boss? What's his name again...? Constantine?"

John brightened. "He's great. Knows his stuff. He's a good guy too."

"That's great."

"We're workin' a few new angles on some of the missing kid cases."

Evan liked the way John's face lit up when he spoke about Xav, although it didn't make Evan any more comfortable about learning Xav worked for the sheriff.

"Guess it's a California thing, 'cause Xav's real good about seeing things different."

I bet he is. Evan schooled his features and said, "That's great."

"Mind you," John continued, "some of the guys are still put out 'bout not promoting someone from right here on the force."

"I'm sure they'll be fine with him after a while," Evan lied. Even Faison had mentioned he couldn't believe Sheriff Winston had the gall to hire a "beach bum hippie" and put him at the head of a task force. If Evan hadn't been so irritated that Xav had turned up on his front doorstep, he might have enjoyed watching old-school law enforcement squirm.

"Anyhow, what can I do for you, sir?" John smiled and added nervously, "Off the record."

"Drug action is up. Cocaine has even made its way into schools. But busts along cocaine alley are down in spite of your increased efforts. Can you tell me what you've heard from the other men?"

John nodded. "Some. The guys are sayin' things've slowed down out in Nash and some of the other counties along the I-95 corridor too, but here, the coke on the street is way up. Don't make sense."

Evan leaned against the half wall next to John's desk. "Any ideas on how it's getting here if not down I-95?"

John frowned and shook his head. "I overheard Ridley White sayin' they don't have a clue how it's getting here."

Yet the cocaine business was alive and flourishing more than it ever had before in Carver County. Which boiled down to one thing. "They've all but taken over the town," he muttered to himself.

"Come again?"

"Sorry, just talking to myself. Thanks, John."

"Sorry I couldn't help, Mr. Fairchild."

Evan smiled. "You did help."

"Thank you, sir," John said brightly.

"Thanks again, John." Evan nodded and walked out of the office and into the muggy twilight. A few stars sparkled overhead as Evan drove with the top down from the sheriff's office to his house downtown. He sighed and breathed in the salty tang of the river. Maybe he would make the time to sail over the weekend.

CHAPTER TWELVE

ON FRIDAY night, Xav sat in an unmarked car parked in a dimly lit alley next to a brothel down at the docks. He was thankful he'd gone home to change. He couldn't imagine enduring a stakeout in a suit in this sweltering heat. An onshore breeze wafted through the car's windows and made a futile attempt at keeping him from melting in his jeans, bullet-resistant vest, and T-shirt.

He'd spent the afternoon watching trawlers head inland to drop their catch, and now he watched men and women frequent 4Play. It was ten in the evening and he was tired, and the pulsing light from the white neon sign that wrapped around the building was giving him a headache. The only new information yielded from his three nights of surveillance was that most North Carolinians were overweight, a couple of the girls at this particular house of ill repute weren't of age, and the madam wasn't a madam at all. His high-quality breast job and ample package were obvious beneath the skimpy summer dress, clearly intended to advertise the services he offered. Xav watched the she-male with particular interest after he ruthlessly slapped a girl repeatedly when she dared to sit in a front porch swing without permission. His name was Victor, and he was Hispanic, tall, thin, and meaner than a junkyard dog. Judging from the accent, he was Mexican, which only served to further pique Xav's curiosity.

The screech of an angry cat defending its territory and the clamor of plastic crates toppling over behind the car drew his attention to the rearview mirror. The neon that stretched down the side of the brothel cast an odd sheen to the cat that now perched on the lid of a dumpster. The tabby looked almost blond in the glow of the pulsing light. Xav watched as another cat growled and hissed. The two sparred for a moment, and when the back door of the brothel opened and closed, they took off. Xav went back to watching the front door.

Half an hour later, he was bored and tapped the steering wheel to the beat of Black Veil Brides' "Set the World On Fire." He'd learned nothing new and had decided to pack it in for the night when the back door of the brothel opened and closed again. He glanced in the rearview mirror and saw nothing. He stretched and reached for the keys in the ignition, and the back door of the brothel slammed open. His gaze went to the rearview mirror in time to see two blond heads pop up from behind his car.

One of them shouted, "Run!" and they shot down the alley.

It took less than a second for Xav to register the voice and pivot in his seat. It was a child's voice. A boy's voice full of fear, to be precise. God knew Xav had heard enough of them.

"Get them!" Victor shouted, and two men ran after them. The back door of the brothel slammed shut in a peal of Spanish curses.

Xav radioed the station for backup and was out of the car in an instant. He tore down the alley at high speed, deftly sidestepping and jumping over debris. Up ahead the boys scrambled onto a dumpster and climbed up and over a chain-link fence. To their advantage, the lardasses who chased them were unbelievably out of shape. Sirens sounded in the distance as Xav sped past them in the dark at the side of the alley. He jumped up and grabbed the chain-link, and was up and over it in seconds.

Gunfire sounded from behind, and Xav's hopes of escaping were dashed as a bullet whizzed past his ear. "Faster!" he shouted at the boys. They looked back at him, clearly confused. The loud wail of sirens told Xav help was near. "Keep going!" he shouted.

They turned to run again and one of the boys slipped in something oily and fell, and the other boy ran back to help him. Xavier reached them, grabbed them both by the shirt, lifted them to their feet, and half ran, half dragged them down the alley.

As they neared the street at the end of the alley, bullets strafed the concrete at their feet. Xav didn't dare look back. He took the boys to the ground, but not before bullets arced, nearly cutting them in half, and one slammed into his back. He went down, the warm blood of the boys on his hands made brilliant by the pulsing neon sign overhead. He reached for the boys, still believing he could save them, right before his world turned to black.

CHANCE PINNED Kevin against the bathroom stall door. Kevin ground himself against the knee Chance pressed to his groin. The thumping bass from the dance floor vibrated the tiles underfoot as Chance slipped his hand beneath the waist of Kevin's jeans and squeezed an asscheek.

"Fuck," Kevin hissed.

Chance squeezed harder. He could forget the whole frustrating week like this. Now if he could only get fucking Xav out of his mind, he'd be doing just fine.

The familiar ringtone of his cell brought him crashing back to reality. "Oh, fucking hell," he hissed as he released Kevin and pulled the phone from his pocket. He'd turn off the ringer and—"Shit," Chance said. "I gotta take this."

Kevin rolled his eyes. "Boyfriend?"

"No." Chance tapped the phone and left the bathroom. "Fairchild."

"Sorry to bother you, Mr. Fairchild," Donna, one of the sheriff's dispatchers, said. "Mr. Faison said you should get down to County General as soon as possible."

"Another OD?" Faison didn't need someone from the office to cover that. He'd catch Kevin and take up where they'd left off. "Look, Donna, I really don't see—"

"It's not an OD," she said breathlessly. "A deputy and two kids were shot."

EVAN THANKED his lucky stars he hadn't had much to drink at the club down in Wilmington. Although considering the piss-poor mood he was in by the time he strode into the hospital two hours later, it might have helped. As he entered the ER, John Carson waved at him from beside a woman who looked vaguely familiar.

"John." He turned to the woman and offered her his hand. "Evan Fairchild."

"Rebecca Wilhelm, Carver County Department of Social Services," she said briskly as she handed him a business card and pointed toward the double doors that led to the back of the ER. "We got a call about the boys they brought in."

"Good to meet you." Evan stepped back to avoid a nurse who ran down the hallway to the sound of alarm bells and buzzers. "Who's the deputy who was shot?"

John's expression darkened. "Deputy Constantine."

Shit! Evan struggled to maintain his composure and reminded himself he wasn't supposed to know Xav from Adam. "How is he?"

"He'll be okay. He was wearing a vest," John said, to Evan's great relief. "The kids, though…." He swallowed hard. "Last I heard one was touch and go. The other's stable."

"Twin brothers. Eleven years old. Fostered at Bright Horizons Group Home, went missing on a Saturday about three weeks ago," Rebecca added as she handed Evan a preliminary report.

Evan felt sick. "How'd they end up in a shooting?"

"We don't know," John answered. "The doctor's with Deputy Constantine now."

Rebecca guided them to one of the nurses' stations to ask about the status of the boys.

"All we know is Xav radioed for backup," John said in a low voice. "He was at the old docks. You know, near where the T.R. Martin processing plant used to be?"

Evan knew the docks all too well. Located on a contaminated estuary, the docks had once housed legitimate businesses that had since gone belly-up or moved to locations that were cleaner and safer. Nowadays, only small-time drug dealers and a few brothels—if you could call them that—plied their trades in the tumbledown buildings that once housed fish processing plants. Evan didn't handle prostitution cases. He'd heard some of the attorneys in his office complain that they should just tear down the entire couple of blocks, docks and all.

"Bad news," Rebecca said as she turned back to them. "One of the boys died in the OR. Looks like the other will be okay."

"Damn." John shook his head.

"Are you Mr. Fairchild?" one of the nurses asked.

"Yes." Evan was still thinking about the boy who'd died. *Who the hell would shoot eleven-year-old kids?*

"Sheriff Winston asked me to give you this." She handed him a sealed manila envelope. "I'll let you know when you can speak to Deputy Constantine."

"Thank you." Evan turned to John and Rebecca. "I can take it from here."

"Thank you, Mr. Fairchild," John added before guiding Rebecca away.

Evan waited until they had disappeared down the long hallway. He sat on a nearby bench and read the preliminary report Rebecca Wilhelm had given him, then opened the manila envelope from Sheriff Winston. He read the first document in it. It was a stat toxicology report showing that the two boys had cocaine in their systems. Stat tests also showed a fair quantity of powder cocaine on their clothing.

He read on. The other documents were preliminary statements the deputies had gathered about the shootings. He scanned them quickly and found nothing of interest. It had been chaos. Everyone heard gunfire and scattered. Not to mention drug addicts and prostitutes weren't known to be reliable witnesses. Then he came to the last one. An old homeless man stated that a shrimp trawler had put in during the chaos. That made no sense. The only legitimate reason a trawler put in late at night or at a dock other than its own would be if it couldn't make it to its own dock. Engine trouble? Perhaps. Trawlers carrying illegal haul or smuggling contraband put in at night.

"I'll be damned," he whispered to himself. He made a mental note to have the trawler checked out. If his hunch was right, he'd just found his first genuine clue.

CHAPTER THIRTEEN

XAV SAT on a bed in the ER and winced as the doctor prodded his back. "Tell me how the kids are."

The doctor ignored him. "You're lucky you wore a vest. I'm going to order an MRI. I'm concerned about damage to your spine."

"I've been through this before. I don't need an MRI. I'm fine."

"I see that, judging from the looks of that scar on your side."

"Tell me how the boys are," Xav demanded.

The doctor was grave. "One died on the operating table. The other is being transferred to a room now."

The news was a cerebral kick in the teeth. Blue eyes filled Xav's vision, glaring at him, accusing him of failing once again. His mind screamed at the loss and the room around him faded.

THE POWERFUL stench of smelling salts jolted Xav awake like a punch to his jaw. Startled, he struck out with his fist.

The doctor dodged it and caught his wrist. "Whoa, there!"

Xav sat up on the gurney, his heart pounding and his mind in a haze, only to come face-to-face with an angry Sheriff Winston. "What happened?"

"Sheriff...." Xav struggled to focus.

The sheriff glanced at the doctor, and the doctor nodded his okay to continue and left the room.

"Tell me what happened, Constantine."

When Xav was finished, Winston didn't look any happier. "I've taken your badge and weapon. You'll get them back if and when you're cleared."

Xav's ire rose, a furious leviathan within. "I never drew my weapon!"

"And I said you'll get them back if and when you're cleared! You're on desk duty until further notice! Now, that's the end of it!"

"I need to talk to the boy who's still alive."

"And I said you're on desk duty until you're cleared!"

Before Xav could shout back, none other than C. Evan Fairchild entered the room. That was all he needed. What in *hell* was he doing here?

"Sheriff Winston. Deputy Constantine," Chance greeted curtly.

Dressed in a T-shirt and jeans that hugged his body, his hair stylishly mussed instead of combed back the way he wore it at work, Chance looked every inch the way Xav remembered him from the bar.

"Mr. Fairchild, I'll leave you to it. Answer the man's questions, Constantine, and I want a report on my desk first thing in the morning. And cut your damn hair!" Winston ordered before he left the room.

"Mr. Fairchild, is it?" It took Xav monumental effort to keep sarcasm from his voice.

"Evan Fairchild," he confirmed.

Judging by Evan's ramrod straight posture and the unflinching way he met Xav's gaze, Xav was sure the man was daring him to argue otherwise. Xav couldn't resist. "What happened to the suit?" Maybe if Evan—Chance—*whatever in hell his name was*—lost the arrogant expression on his face, Xav would lose the sarcasm. The look Evan shot him was one of pure venom. *Serves you right, you arrogant dick.* When Evan didn't respond, he finally asked, "What can I do for you?"

"For starters, you can tell me what happened."

Un-freakin'-believable. *Well, Chance, we met in a bar, and you spent the night fucking my brains out, and the next time I saw you, you gave me the hairy eyeball. That's what happened. And you're gorgeous and I can't get you out of my head!* "Why would I do that?"

"Because I asked you to." Evan stared at him with flinty eyes and Xav decided never to engage in a staring contest with the man. Or play poker with him. Then again, strip poker might work. Though still hot as hell, Evan looked a lot sexier without the stick up his ass. Xav eyed him suspiciously. "I repeat. Why would I do that?"

Evan narrowed his eyes and a muscle twitched in his cheek. "Deputy Constantine, I prosecute drug crimes, and it would appear that our paths have crossed."

Xav's temper cooled a fraction. "I beg your pardon?"

"Just what I said."

"I'm not following. What does a shootout at a brothel have to do with drug crimes?"

"The boys ingested a substantial amount of cocaine."

It came together in Xav's mind and his heart melted. He rubbed his eyes with thumb and forefinger. "I'm not surprised."

Evan's frown deepened. "Come again?"

Xav told Evan about the stakeout, what had happened when he attempted to save the boys, and finished with, "You have eighteen boys missing in this county over the past five months. I suspect they're being abducted and trafficked."

Shock danced in Chance's eyes but vanished an instant later, replaced by *Evan's* steely gaze. "Trafficked? As in forced labor?"

"For sex." If Xav hadn't seen Evan pale before his very eyes, he would have thought the man was made of stone. "And the quickest way to make victims dependent on their handlers is to addict them to drugs. I…. *We* need to talk to the boy who survived."

Evan appeared thoughtful for a long moment. "What do you hope to accomplish by talking to him?" he asked, his voice softer now, less hostile.

"First, I'd like to ID him to see if he's one of our missing kids."

"*Your* missing kids?" Evan asked. "I'll save you the trouble. Quinn James Haverty. Eleven years old. Winter, the boy who died, was his twin. Both currently in the custody of Bright Horizons Group Home for youth and missing for three weeks. Anything else I can help you with?"

Xav felt as if someone had kicked him in the gut as he recalled the file on the boys. "He's… *they* were two of the boys who went missing. I need to interview him. He's the first and only clue we have as to what's happened to these boys."

"The first and only," Evan said flatly.

Xav thought he detected a touch of sarcasm, but Evan's face told him otherwise. "Yes. I need to interview him," he repeated.

Evan's gaze didn't waver. "No can do. You're on desk duty. Standard protocol."

As if Xav needed the reminder. *Prick.* "I'll call Winston."

Evan gave him a long, considering look, and Xav was surprised the scrutiny made him want to squirm. "Stay put. I'll be back in a few."

Xav watched Evan leave. In another universe, he might have found Evan's authoritative demeanor sexy. But it was transparent and just pissed him off. The man had some major insecurity and was very much "me against the world."

EVAN LEANED against the wall outside Xav's room and studied his cell phone without really seeing it. Xav was a fucking cowboy. At this rate he'd get himself killed. *Why the hell do I care? And why the hell am I even thinking about accommodating him?*

He needed to call Faison. *Child sex trafficking. Here in Carver County?* The thought made him physically ill. Not to mention Faison would explode. Then he'd start screaming bloody murder and get the very media attention he wanted so damn badly. Exactly the media circus Evan didn't need.

Evan knew human trafficking went hand in hand with the drug business. He just hadn't linked the missing boys in Carver County to the drugs. He shook his head in disgust. *I need to up my game.* But what did he know about sex trafficking? Particularly *child* sex trafficking. Not a damn thing. *Fuck.* He needed to learn what Xav knew, but working with the guy was out of the question. He couldn't work with a guy he'd fucked. Talk about a conflict of dickness—and a friggin' mathematician, no less. A Poindexter who saved kids. A *sexy* Poindexter who saved kids. A sexy Poindexter *he'd fucked* who saved kids. Evan pinched the bridge of his nose. The thought was too stupid to fathom.

Evan smacked the manila envelope against his leg. First things first. The surviving kid was the only witness to whatever the fuck had happened, and Evan needed to verify that he would survive. Second, the sheriff needed to investigate and solve the matter of the boy's disappearance. Third, Evan needed to find out if there *was* a link between the boys and the drugs. Then he'd make damn sure he put the fuckers who did this away.

He thought about the boy and reality began to blur.

Voices echoed above him. Cold, he pulled his knees to his chest and made himself small, trying to imagine he was sitting under the warm sun in his backyard with the dog licking his cheek. "I'll be good," he said. "I promise I won't do it again!"

CHAPTER FOURTEEN

"FAIRCHILD." XAV'S voice brought Evan back to himself. Xav steadied himself against the wall railing.

Xav looked pale, but he'd managed to pull his T-shirt back on. *Good.* He might be irritating, but Xav's body was downright fascinating. "I told you to stay put."

"I need to talk to Quinn."

Evan shook his head. "I told you—"

"Now. I need to talk to him now. Not later, after everyone else has talked to him and… and after his mind has done its best to bury the memories."

Xav's eyes had filled with something resembling sadness, but he gritted his teeth and winced. Then Evan realized he was shaking. "The doctor didn't clear you, did he?"

Without waiting for Xav's reply, Evan took Xav's arm to steady him and led him to the bench a few feet away. "Sit down before you fall down."

He waited until Xav sat, and then walked to the nurse's station and showed her his ID. "Can you tell me what room Quinn Haverty is in? And please get a cup of water for Deputy Constantine when you have a minute?"

"Of course." The nurse smiled at him briefly and typed something into the computer. "Quinn Haverty is in Room 345. Pediatric wing. I'll be right back with the water."

"Thank you."

She returned a moment later and set a Styrofoam cup on the counter. Evan took it and returned to where Xav sat and offered him the cup.

Xav looked up at him, surprise making a feeble attempt to break through the pain in his expression. "Thanks."

"You're welcome." Evan withdrew his phone from a pocket and texted Faison. *Situation under control. Will update you tomorrow.* Hopefully it would placate him. If he could show Faison things really *were* under control, maybe he'd hold off spinning the story to the press before he had all the facts. *Maybe.*

Xav stood with considerable effort and tossed the cup into a nearby wastebasket, then stared at it for a long moment. Evan wondered what he was thinking. There was no telling after a horrific night like tonight, and Evan's heart went out to him.

"I want to talk to Quinn."

"You're on desk duty," Evan repeated stubbornly, as if he could force the words through Xav's thick skull.

"Fuck desk duty."

Evan ran a hand through his hair. He'd never violated protocol. Why was he even considering this? Because he genuinely cared about what happened to the surviving kid. Evan also wasn't stupid and knew he needed Xav's help to solve this crime, and for some reason he couldn't fathom, he didn't want to see Xav beat his head against the system.

Fine. With his decision to work around protocol and let Xav speak to Quinn, he wasn't going to have any major fallout. He drew a long, slow breath. "What, specifically, do you want to learn from him?"

"I need to find out what happened to him. How he and his brother ended up in that alley. You need to ask questions about the drugs. We both need information. We have different goals, but the same mission here. And I'd lay odds I've worked with more kids than you have."

Definitely being a dick. Evan couldn't play cop. He knew that. But if he was going to try to stop drugs in this town, he needed to know if there was a link between the drugs and the missing boys, as Xav suspected. And there was no better way to begin than by learning what Xav knew. "For any number of reasons, I have to take the lead on this. Got that, *Deputy* Constantine?"

Xav grunted in response.

Breathe. Evan inhaled for four counts, held his breath for four, and exhaled for four counts. Much more of this and he'd lose it and want to strangle Xav more than he already did. He made a mental note to call Dr. Sampson and talk it through.

THEY FOUND Rebecca Wilhelm outside the door to Quinn's room.

"How's he doing?" Evan asked.

"He's in shock and not talking. I'm working on an emergency placement." She glanced at Xav. "Thank you for saving his life."

Xav clenched his jaw, clearly uncomfortable with her words, and nodded.

"Deputy Xavier Constantine," Evan said, "this is Rebecca Wilhelm, Carver County DSS."

"Nice to meet you," Xav said as he shook her hand. "Are you going to place him back in the same group home?"

"Why do you ask?" Rebecca eyed Xav warily.

"Because I suspect the people he ran from will be looking for him."

Evan tensed. He needed to delve further into Xav's suspicions.

Rebecca shot Xav an irritated look. "We'll make sure he's safe, Deputy."

"You don't under—"

"Let me know where you place him," Evan interjected, foreclosing the conversation before an argument could ensue. He was inclined to agree with Xav, if his suspicions were right, but he needed to *know* they were right. He needed *facts*.

"Of course," she said curtly. "Have a good evening, gentlemen."

They watched her walk away and Evan turned to Xav. "Fighting with her won't do a damn bit of good."

Xav let out an exasperated sigh and nodded his agreement.

Evan took another deep breath as he opened the door to Quinn's room.

UNLIKE THE stark white ER, the walls in Quinn's room were soothing pastels and covered with pictures of rabbits and ducks. But the rainbow sweetness of color didn't disguise the cloying antiseptic smell.

Quinn Haverty was small, a mere rise in the topography of bed linen that covered him. A beautiful kid with pale skin and dirty blond hair. He looked at them with blue eyes that seemed too large for his delicate face.

At Evan's side, Xav looked as if he'd seen a ghost. Evan met his eyes with concern, but Xav only motioned him forward.

"Quinn?" Evan greeted softly. "I'm Evan, and this is Xav."

Quinn's eyes grew wide. "You're… you were there."

Xav nodded once. "I was. The name's Xav," he repeated.

"Winter…." Quinn's eyes brimmed with tears.

Out of the corner of his eye, Evan saw Xav swallow hard. For reasons unknown, self-confident Xav was having a hard time. Evan breathed in calm and gathered his inner courage. The kid needed to know they were strong and steady for him in spite of the disastrous night, even if neither he nor Xav were feeling all that strong or steady at the moment. "I'm so sorry, Quinn."

Quinn said nothing more.

"Can you tell us what happened?" Evan asked, his voice ever so gentle. Evan hadn't intended to say "us," but it was too late now.

Quinn wiped tears from an eye with the back of his hand.

Evan glanced at Xav, who was obviously struggling to keep his expression inscrutable. He'd expected he'd have to rein Xav in, not *this*. Whatever *this* was.

"You and Winter have been missing from Bright Horizons for a couple of weeks," Evan began.

Quinn gathered a fistful of blanket. "We were in a hole and they… done things." Quinn's voice was a whisper on the air.

"Can you tell me about the hole?" Evan asked.

"In the floor. With bars on top of it. Wet, dark… so cold…." Quinn shivered. "We were so thirsty and hungry…." His voice trailed off. "Then they came and got Winter…." A soft mewl escaped him.

Evan rubbed his temples to stave off a wave of dizziness and will the sensation away, but the walls closed in on him fast. The room was suddenly too small, too dark, and memories of muted voices echoed large in his mind. "*…we'll teach you not to fight.*" Then his own voice, "*Please, don't put me back in there! I'll be good. I promise—*"

"Can you tell us how you got from the group home to the hole, Quinn?"

Xav's calm, resonant voice cut through the chaos in Evan's mind. He came back to himself with a start to realize Xav was standing beside him, his face etched with concern.

Quinn's blue eyes had filled with a haunted look, and he stared at some far-off vision.

A long moment passed in silence; then Evan regained his voice. "It's okay, Quinn. It's not your fault."

Quinn met Evan's eyes as if trying to ascertain the truth there, and in that instant, Evan's focus shifted. The case wasn't only about the drugs anymore. It felt as though he'd found a kindred spirit, and a memory stirred. *It's not your fault.* An echo of himself as a child remembering the first time he believed those words.

"Your mom loves you," Dr. Sampson assured him. "But she can't take care of herself, let alone you, until she chooses to help herself."

"But maybe if I'd helped, it wouldn't have been so hard for her," he said.

"If she got sick," she said, "would you have blamed yourself?" He shook his head.

"It's the same, Chance. It's a sickness. You couldn't have stopped it. It's not your fault."

As much as he wanted drugs off the streets, Evan wanted something better for Quinn and all the kids like himself and Quinn. Evan waited a moment, as much for himself as for Quinn. It took all his might to will away the tension in his body and focus on what was within his power to do. "Did you learn any of their names?" he asked at last.

Quinn shook his head. "They spoke Spanish." Quinn began to tremble, and tears spilled over his ashen cheeks.

Evan waited, but Quinn didn't say anything else. He had more questions, but now was not the time. "You did well, Quinn. Sleep now."

Quinn said nothing.

"You can ask the nurse to call me anytime if you think of anything you think I should know, okay?"

Quinn's eyes were distant.

"I'll ask the nurse to check on you." Evan said.

As he and Xav reached the door, Quinn said, "Blivian."

They turned back to him. "What?" Evan asked gently.

"Blivian," Quinn repeated.

"Bolivian?" Xav asked.

Quinn said no more as he slid down in the bed and brought the covers up to his chin.

"I'll get the nurse now," Evan said gently.

Quinn returned to kneading the blanket.

CHAPTER FIFTEEN

NO SOONER had Evan closed the door behind them than Xav turned to him and asked, "Are you okay?"

The concern on Xav's face irritated Evan to no end. "Fine," he snapped.

"No, you're not. One minute you were asking Quinn questions, and the next you spaced it. You looked like you hit the twilight zone—"

"You weren't supposed to talk!" Evan's face burned with embarrassment as he set his shoulders and met Xav's gaze.

"I only spoke because you didn't say a word for nearly five minutes," Xav shot back. "It was like you checked out—"

"I was thinking!"

"About what?"

"Nothing," Evan said, collecting himself and moderating his tone. "What's important is that we have a connection between the kids and the drugs."

"What connection?"

"Bolivia. The coke on our streets is from Bolivia."

"Half the coke in the US is from Bolivia. That's not a connection."

"Then why did Quinn mention Bolivia?"

Xav eyed Evan, but at least he'd dropped the subject of Evan's odd behavior. "I don't know, and I won't know until I can talk to Quinn again."

Evan shook his head. "Not a chance. Go do whatever it is deputies do after something like this and stay the hell away from him." He turned to leave and swore under his breath when two men in suits stepped off the elevator and headed straight toward them.

Xav followed his gaze and asked, "Who are they?"

Evan ignored Xav's question. "Gentlemen," he greeted with strained politeness. "Evan Fairchild, Carver County District Attorney's Office."

"Carter Dee from the State Bureau of Investigation," the first man said as he shook Evan's hand, and then gestured to the man beside him. "This is Special Agent Oliver Dunn. What's an ADA doing here at two o'clock in the morning on a missing persons case?" he asked pointedly.

Shit. He didn't want to say anything about his role in the case. They'd call the DEA in faster than greased lightning and Faison would have his head. "A deputy sheriff and two youth were shot, Special Agent Dee. James Faison cares about this case." *Smooth lies are me.*

"You're the deputy in question?" Dee asked Xav pointedly.

"Deputy Xavier Constantine," Evan interjected before Xav could speak. "May I ask who called you?"

"Rebecca Wilhelm," Dee answered. "We opened an investigation when the two boys went missing. She called to tell us they'd been found and one of them is dead. Is one of them dead?"

"Unfortunately, yes. Both youth were shot by assailants and one didn't survive," Evan said smoothly.

"We need a written statement from you, Deputy Constantine, as well as a copy of your incident report." Dee looked at Evan. "And a statement from the boy who survived."

"He's in shock and isn't talking," Xav said.

Evan fought like hell not to tell Xav to shut up. "Deputy Constantine is correct. The boy isn't communicative, and the nurse sedated him less than ten minutes ago. Why don't you give my office a call on Monday morning and we'll try speaking with him then?"

"Why would we need to contact your office?" Dee pressed.

Evan offered his stock at-your-service smile. "You don't. However, my office determines whether to file charges with respect to the dead boy, and I can't do that without a statement from the boy who survived. It'll be far less taxing for him to endure one interview as opposed to many, and it'll also allow our offices to avoid duplication of effort and paperwork if we're all present."

"Excuse us," Dee said as he led Dunn away to speak with him.

Evan turned to Xav and whispered, "Keep your mouth shut."

"Why?"

"Because they'll take this case from you and leave you with a job in name only." Evan's whisper was harsh.

"They can't do that."

Evan strangled a sigh. "You aren't from around here, *Deputy*. You don't know fuck-all about what they can or can't do."

Xav gave him a lazy salute. Evan didn't appreciate the sarcasm. He bit back a snarky comment about California and granola before gathering himself for round two with the SBI.

Dee and Dunn walked back to them. "We'll return Monday morning," Dee said.

Evan donned his best false smile. "Did you have a time in mind?" "Eight."

"The doctors will be doing rounds. I suggest ten, after they're gone," Xav said politely.

Evan glared at him and stifled a primal scream.

Dee tucked his chin and gave Xav a "yeah, right" look, but agreed. "We'll be back at ten on Monday morning. Good day, gentlemen." They turned and headed to the elevator.

Evan waited until the elevator door closed. "What part of shut up did you not understand?" he growled as he rounded on Xav.

Xav smiled. "I understood you."

Evan stepped closer, his face now inches from Xav's, his fury barely contained. "Then what the hell was *that* all about?"

"I want to be here too, and I don't do mornings."

Xav's suppressed grin pissed the fuck out of Evan. *For the love of Christ!* "Go home, Xavier!" Evan's heart beat so hard against his ribs it hurt. Fifteen fucking years perfecting his self-control, and a mathematician with long hair made him lose it. *What the fuck?*

"Xavier."

"What?"

Now Xav *was* grinning. "I like it when you call me Xavier."

Evan couldn't help it. He rolled his eyes. "Go home!" He turned on a heel and headed to the elevator. He would not look back at hotter-than-hell, flirty, distracting Xavier Constantine. Not a chance in hell. He would *not*.

Once safely alone behind the elevator doors, Evan took a few deep breaths before stabbing at the first-floor button with a vengeance. Then a chuckle bubbled up and he shook his head. *Unbelievable.* That had almost been fun! Too bad Xavier Constantine was a cop—Evan would have enjoyed whooping his ass in court.

But what the hell *had* happened back in Quinn's room? He'd been asking questions and everything had been fine. *Five minutes?* He'd spaced for *five* fucking minutes? The realization made his stomach churn. Quinn was the same age he had been when he'd entered foster care, but in his work for the DA, he'd sometimes dealt with kids in foster care. Those cases never brought back the memories—*nightmares*—of his past.

What does it matter? You're here to do a job, not get involved. His job was to interview Quinn as a witness to a crime. End of story.

And then there was Xav. Pushing his buttons. And that fucking grin!

You let him get to you.

Evan took another deep breath and thought about calling Faison. He pulled his phone from his pocket and tapped the screen: 2:00 a.m. Thank God, it was too late to call. He needed time to figure things out. They'd suddenly become very complicated. He needed to sleep so he could focus on the fallout tomorrow.

Once again, he shoved back the memories that threatened. It was going to be a long night.

CHAPTER SIXTEEN

XAV SIGNED the discharge paperwork, kept his copy, and left the rest on the counter. Then he realized he had no way to get to the office to get his bike. "Excuse me?" A nurse looked up from her paperwork with a small smile. "Do you have the number of a cab company?"

She looked horrified. "Good Lord. Do you mean to tell me after all *that*, no one waited for you? That's just plain rude. I'll call for you."

After the hell of the past five hours, he appreciated her sympathy. "Thank you."

"Where do you want to go?"

"Sheriff's office." He couldn't wait to get home and crash.

She picked up the phone and dialed.

He pocketed his wallet and keys, the only possessions he had left after Winston took his gun, badge, and vest, and then reached for the paper that was his touchstone.

"The cab will be here in a few minutes," she told him. "They'll pick you up right outside the doors."

"Thank you."

She looked at his paperwork, nodded her approval, and handed him a prescription for pain medication. "Every four hours as needed."

"Thank you." He reviewed the paper and shoved it in his pocket.

"You did a mighty fine thing, saving that boy," she said sincerely.

He gave her a tight smile. If only he'd saved *both* boys.

THE CAB dropped Xav in front of the station, and he didn't bother to go inside. He had no interest in answering questions from the unprofessionally curious. He headed across the parking lot to his bike. He unlocked his helmet and the saddlebag containing his jacket. He winced at the pain in his back as he slipped into his jacket, and winced again when he reached up to pull the helmet on. Maybe he was getting too old for this shit.

He rode hard down to the riverfront. Three pairs of blue eyes now looked out at him, angry, accusatory. Losing three kids in four months was more than he could process, and the unmitigated rage he felt had him nearly dumping his bike on a desolate road through the salt marshes. He pulled over, yanked his helmet off, and issued a guttural scream at the heavens. The crimes that adults committed against children were beyond monstrous—and his capacity to understand. He'd learned to channel his fury in productive ways—no matter that one man's effort in a sea of criminals was futile—and he'd kept at it, saving one boy at a time. He'd been damn good at his job, but now he questioned himself, and there was no worse feeling in the world. He looked up at the stars still twinkling in the blueberry predawn sky and wondered how much more he could take before he lost his effectiveness.

When his breathing slowed and his anger was in check, he rode on with Jason Walker's "Echo" playing through his helmet. Now Quinn was all alone. The thought of losing a brother made his chest hurt. He couldn't bear it if he lost a brother, and he couldn't imagine what it would be like to lose a twin. The needle on his anger meter threatened to shoot into the red again, and he mentally tamped it down. He'd been able to save Quinn, and he needed to focus his energy like a laser on that. He didn't have to ask why the boys had been taken. He knew why. But he hadn't expected a brothel to be a holding pen. He mentally shook his head as he concentrated on the road. Brothels were usually the last place traffickers kept kids for sale.

He came to a stop at the pier. After locking his gear, he walked down the planks and took a seat at the end to watch the sun come up. It took its time rising, effulgent as it streaked the eastern horizon with its orange, reds, and pinks.

His mind drifted to thoughts of Evan, and he wished that instead of retreating to their separate corners, they'd gone home together and woken up this morning next to each other. They could have gotten to know each other a little, maybe had an opportunity to find out if there could be something between them. Evan's lithe body pressed against him, sex as the sun streamed in through the windows, showering together, Evan kissing him while he tried to cook breakfast…. Deciding breakfast was overrated and—

He needed to stop with the alternate universe fantasy. It wasn't going to happen unless he chose to make his way past Evan's passive-aggressive behavior.

He'd worked with victims for years, and it was plain as day that Evan was battling a hidden something. Xav understood emotional damage, how it manifested, and how it rode people like an eight-hundred-pound canary and denied them an opportunity to live in happiness if they let it— the caustic, selfish, self-centered, and immature behaviors that shielded vulnerabilities in a vain attempt to maintain a bulletproof emotional shell. Sadly, those behaviors also often hid a beautiful heart.

He wondered what had so stunted Evan's emotional growth and maturity. Evan vomited his personal rage at the world in so many different ways it was like playing whack-a-mole just to talk to the guy. "I" and "me" were the only pronouns in his vocabulary except when it came to criticism. Then "you" became the pronoun du jour.

Xav had no desire to become a by-product of Evan's personal shit. He wouldn't allow himself to become collateral damage on Evan's fucked-up radar. He flicked a pebble with a finger and it skittered away as he wondered if Evan had any idea how transparent he was.

Xav shook his head. Did he really want to invest in Evan? He didn't think so. But, for now, he'd keep an open mind. He flicked another pebble away and lifted an imaginary glass to himself. *Here's to finding Evan's beautiful heart.*

He watched as trawlers set out for the day. Booms extended, they looked like giant mosquitoes engaged in an odd water dance as they paraded out to sea. There were hundreds of them. He shouldn't have been surprised, he supposed. Then again, he hadn't spent any time learning about the North Carolina fishing industry, and he made a mental note to research it that afternoon.

He looked around and found a trawler that hadn't left the docks yet. Curious, he got to his feet and walked up the pier and across the dock to get a better look at it. He watched as the crew rigged the nets and prepared to set out for the day.

"Can I help y'all with somethin'?"

Xav smiled at the fisherman. "I've never seen a trawler before."

The man chucked his dirty cap back with a smile. "Y'all ain't from around these parts?"

Xav smiled and shook his head.

"Well, step on in for a look-see."

More curious now, Xav climbed aboard the boat.

"The name's Hatch. I'm 'er captain." The man extended a gloved hand.

Xav shook it in spite of its filthy appearance. "Xav."

The captain gave him the two-bit tour, and they ended at the hopper. "This here's the hopper. It sorts catch before it goes in the hold down there."

Xav peered into the hold. "That's huge."

The man snickered. "Holds two ton on a good day."

Xav pointed to a large round vent in the shaft at the top of the hold. "What's that?"

"Water come out there so we can keep the catch wet. We can also freeze it if we want."

"Full-service trawler?"

Captain Hatch grinned with pride. "My *Jenny*'s a good boat, and it's an honest livin'."

Xav smiled at the reference to Forrest Gump's boat. "The most beautiful name in the whole wide world."

Hatch nodded with a grin before reaching down, lifting the steel grill to the hold, and throwing it over. The clank it made when it landed on deck was deafening, made only louder by the cavernous hold below. Unbidden, Quinn's words suddenly echoed in his mind. *In the floor. With bars on top of it. Wet, dark... so cold.*

"Where do you take your fish at the end of the day?" Xav asked.

"Drop it at the processors in holds like this but much bigger."

Forcing a smile, Xav asked, "Can you go down there?"

Hatch grinned. "How do ya think we clean 'er out?"

"Anyone ever get stuck in there?"

Hatch laughed. "If they was, they'd be hollerin' up ta let 'em out before they like-ta drown when we flush 'er clean."

"How do you get out of it?"

"Ladder on the wall." Hatch snickered. "Why? You plannin' on goin' down in my hold?"

Xav chuckled. "Thanks, but travelling with dead fish isn't my thing."

Hatch cracked up "'Spose not."

"I'm just trying to figure out how a hold works."

"Why, ya jus' fill 'er with catch, clean 'er, and fill 'er again!"

It was Xav's turn to laugh aloud. "I guess I should research it online before I go around bothering fishermen."

"I don't mind ya askin'. Y'all gonna open a plant?"

"Me? No. I'm a new deputy sheriff just trying to learn about the town."

Hatch's smile faltered. "Y'all ain't lookin' to cause me trouble, are ya?"

Xav's smile widened. "Absolutely not. But maybe you can help me with something."

"What's on yer mind?"

Xav thought for a moment, gauging how direct he could be. "If I wanted to smuggle something, how would I do it?"

Hatch looked away and spit, then turned back to Xav. "Depends on what yer smugglin', now, don't it?" He chucked his cap before pulling it off, stroked his hair back with a gloved hand, and put it back on. "Fer instance. If it don't need to breathe, the ballasts be a good place. But if it need to breathe, then yer only place be the holds."

"There's more than one hold?"

"Depends on the size o' boat. This here boat, I only got one hold, but I also have a bait tank that can double as a small hold."

"How big is that?"

"'Bout yay wide an' yay deep." Hatch spread his arms as wide as he could and rotated them ninety degrees upright. "What's on yer mind, there, Deputy?"

Xav toyed with the idea of telling him the truth and opted for a half-truth. "Hypothetically speaking?"

"I take yer meanin'."

"Human cargo."

CHAPTER SEVENTEEN

HATCH TSKED. "Dangerous business tryin' to bring people over."

"I don't mean in. I mean out," Xav said.

Hatch squinted and glanced around before meeting Xav's eyes again. "Yer talkin' the worst kinda pirate."

Xav nodded.

"People fit in holds. Even small holds. Hypothetically speakin', o' course."

"If I were to be the worst kind of pirate, where would I pick up my cargo? Hypothetically speaking."

Hatch met his gaze with knowing eyes. "Y'all'd make it look like yer doin' regular fish business. Drop yer catch, clean yer hold, and fill 'er again. Bein' hypothetical and all."

Xav nodded once. "Thanks for the tour, Hatch." He withdrew his wallet from his back pocket, removed a business card from it, and handed it to Hatch. "Call me if you ever need anything."

Hatch grinned, accepted it, and shook Xav's hand. "Y'all come back now."

Xav climbed out of the boat and headed back to the pier. He couldn't help the overriding suspicion that the Haverty boys had been held captive in a hold somewhere, but he had no way of knowing if it was on a boat or in a processing plant. He looked out at the trawlers on the water again. He could see how shrimp boats would be a profitable mode of smuggling drugs into the US—*or kids out of the US*—given their massive cargo holds and ballasts, the boats lost to confiscation a mere cost of doing business.

The fear in Quinn's voice as he spoke of being held captive had been an echo of Jeremy Wrigley's when Xav had asked him to run. Blue eyes filled his vision again. He swore softly and rubbed his tired eyes. Time to go home to get some sleep.

Shit. Not until he wrote his incident report and statement for Winston. He didn't think his soul had ever felt wearier than it did at that very moment.

ON SATURDAY morning Evan swung by the coroner's office after a stop at Starbucks for a latte with a double shot of espresso and a quick hello to his favorite barista, Wanda. He didn't expect the preliminary autopsy report on Winter to be ready yet, so he was surprised when Ryan Clark, the clerk on duty, returned with a folder and a grin.

"Rachelle stayed late," he told Evan as he handed him the folder. "We should have the final done Wednesday when all the blood and tissue analyses are back."

"She around?" Evan had always been on good terms with Rachelle Vickers, the county medical examiner.

"Nah. She went home an hour ago. She won't be back until Monday. Carl's on call over the weekend." Ryan leaned on the counter, his face a little too into Evan's personal space.

Evan stepped back, uncomfortable with the intrusion. "Thank you." He tucked the report in his satchel.

"Coffee sometime?" Ryan's grin came off like a leer.

When Evan first met Ryan, his gaydar had sounded louder than a preacher at a tent revival. On the rare occasion someone hit on him at work, Evan was doubly uncomfortable. His no-fraternization policy kept things right where he liked them. Nonexistent. Not to mention Ryan was definitely not his type. But Evan knew better than to outright reject an offer from someone he might need in order to do his job well. "Perhaps."

Now, back in his office, Evan sipped his third coffee. Three hours of sleep would have to do—in his five years with the DA, he was always in his office at 8:00 a.m. sharp. Even on Saturdays, he'd always spent at least the morning working. He'd chased sleep most of the night, or what had remained of it. He should only feel tired, but this felt different. *He* felt different. Emotionally drained. The loss of Winter, and the look of fear in Quinn's eyes, weighed far heavier on him than he'd expected.

He focused on the file on his desk and thanked his lucky stars yet again for Carol. Bless her, she'd come in early on a Saturday to gather what she could on the case involving the two boys and *Deputy Constantine*. She'd contacted Sheriff Winston's office and obtained copies of Xav's statement, incident report, and the crime scene and ballistics reports from forensics. He read the note she'd stuck to the front of the file: *Left message for Wilhelm at DSS asking for copy of report sent to SBI re Haverty twins missing from placement.*

He opened the folder and added the medical examiner's preliminary autopsy report, Rebecca Wilhelm's report from last night, and the stat drug tests and witness statements he'd received the night before from Sheriff Winston to it. He put the autopsy report at the bottom of the documents. He wasn't ready to read that yet. He carefully reviewed the preliminary statements again and set the unique one—the one that mentioned the shrimp trawler putting in late—aside.

He picked up the phone and dialed the forensics lab.

"Forensics, this is Ingram."

"Tom? Evan Fairchild. I'm following up on the Haverty case."

"Haverty. Oh, right. The shooting down at the old docks."

"That's the one. One of the witness statements mentions a trawler putting in late. Did you find anything out about it?"

"You're gonna have to check with the sheriff's office, Mr. Fairchild. Information can't leave Forensics without Sheriff Winston's approval."

Irritated, Evan tried a different tack. "Were you able to figure out the name of the boat?"

"You're gonna have to check with the sheriff's office on that."

"Why don't you give me the registration numbers and I'll save you the trouble of looking the registration up?"

"As I said, Mr. Fairchild. You're gonna have to check with the sheriff's office on that."

"Thanks, Tom," Evan said curtly and hung up. He finished his now cold coffee. *That was a dead end.* He glanced at the file and decided he'd start with the big picture. He began by reading the forensic report of the scene. The techs had meticulously documented the alley and everything in it. They'd noted two sets of assailants' footprints. They'd even gone so far as to show the path the assailants took to leave the scene. The assailants had escaped by running back the way they came. Evan noted that the footprints stopped where they began: at the back door of the brothel. At least the sheriff's deputies had a starting point for their official investigation.

He withdrew the computer-generated three-dimensional image estimating the source point, path, and endpoint of the ordnance. He cringed when he saw the lateral arc drawn through both boys and Xav. It was only by the grace of God that Xav and Quinn had survived. Evan withdrew the ballistics report that accompanied the image. The assailants had used identical weapons, Belgian FN Herstals. He frowned. The gun wasn't familiar to him, but a note in the report identified it as the semiautomatic pistol of choice for drug cartels. *Interesting*. The techs had tagged more than forty slugs taken from the surrounding area, thus indicating that at least one of the guns had been equipped with an extended magazine.

Evan studied the ballistics report on Xav's gun. It hadn't been drawn from its holster, let alone fired. He shuffled paper until he found the report on Xav's vest. The techs had extracted six slugs from it. It was wholly impressive that Xav could stand on his own less than four hours after the impact, and a begrudging admiration began to blossom in Evan.

Next, he looked at the pictures of Xav in the ER. Xav's torso was damn sexy even in an emergency room. The hint of definition in his abs, the narrow waist, the dusty nipples. They all complemented the slightly salty taste of Xav's skin when Evan worked his tongue over the peaks and valleys of muscle…. Disappointed in himself for allowing his mind to wander, he forced his thoughts back to his work.

He turned to the pictures of Quinn and Quinn's haunting words flooded his thoughts. *In the floor. With bars on top of it. Wet, dark… so cold.* Images from his own nightmares bounced off the walls of his mind, and he sat back in his chair and rubbed his temples. He breathed in for four counts, held it for four, breathed out for four, then held it again. Twice, three times through the exercise, and he was able to force the images from his mind. Cop work sucked.

Sitting forward again, he read the report on Quinn, gripping it as if it were a life raft in a storm. Only two bullets had reached their intended target. The first grazed Quinn's arm; the second was a through-and-through to his lower side. Both wounds merely required stitches. *Thank God*. He looked for the toxicology report on Quinn. It only confirmed what he'd seen in the stat report.

They hadn't taken pictures of Winter because he'd been whisked off to emergency surgery. Evan's heart twisted a little. He decided to brave the medical examiner's report. Four bullets to the head and neck, seven to the back, severing his spine. Evan's gut clenched. He'd prosecuted enough murders to know most people didn't survive shots to the head, but the spine shots were overkill. *Motherfuckers*. The end of the report noted clothing and personal possessions: underwear, jeans, plaid shirt, tennis shoes, a pocket Bible, and a painted seashell. Evan's heart twisted a little more as he studied the image of the pretty shell. He'd never seen anything like it and made a mental note to have it checked out.

He read the reports on Xav. The ER report reflected exactly what the doctor had said and mirrored what he'd seen with his own eyes. He hadn't realized that they'd run toxicology on him too. It was standard protocol in an officer-involved shooting, and it was no surprise that Xav was cleaner than a whistle.

The last documents were Xav's statement and incident report. Evan wondered whether Xav had slept at all last night. According to the documents, Xav had radioed for backup the moment before the pursuit commenced. He couldn't verify that the boys had exited the brothel, but since the boys hadn't passed in front of the car and there was no other way to arrive at the back of the car, it was a logical conclusion. However, he was certain that the assailants exited the brothel at someone named Victor's command. Evan read the detailed paragraph on Victor, a man Xav suspected to be operating the brothel.

The accounting of events was in keeping with the other reports. Two boys ran from behind the car, pursued by two assailants who exited the brothel, chased them down the alley, and fired weapons at them. Xav outran the assailants and attempted to protect the boys, never drawing his weapon. According to the surveillance footage taken from the docks in front of the brothel and the Handy Harry's gas station at the other end of the alley, it had all happened in less than three minutes. Not much to it.

Winston had noted that he didn't see any violation of protocol, signed off, and authorized Xav to be released for duty once Evan's office approved it. *Wonderful*. Evan wanted that responsibility like a hole in the head. If anyone found out about his tryst with Xav, it would be the end of his career. But Faison had sent him to the hospital to deal with this, so if he asked anyone else to sign off, he'd only raise suspicion. He sighed heavily as he opened his e-mail to send a note to Carol to prepare the appropriate document. Lo and behold, she'd already sent it to him. He didn't know whether to hug or choke his presumptuous, ever-efficient administrative assistant. He approved the report electronically and e-mailed it to Sheriff Winston with a copy to Carol for the file.

Evan sat back in his chair feeling somewhat vindicated. Though he hadn't proven shit yet, he was certain of the connection between the boys and drugs and the late-returning trawler.

CHAPTER EIGHTEEN

AT 10:00 a.m., Evan picked up the phone and dialed. He'd gone through several new cases and assigned them to attorneys in the office, checked to ensure documents on two cases set for preliminary hearing on next week's docket were ready to go, and reviewed and approved the stack of documents awaiting his signature. In short, he'd done everything on his desk and couldn't procrastinate any longer in calling Faison, and Faison would have heard about the SBI poking around by now.

"Fairchild? Why the hell haven't you called me? Did aliens abduct your ass? Or are you ignoring me?" Faison demanded before Evan got a word out.

"My apologies, sir. I got back from the hospital after three this morning, and I overslept," Evan lied.

"I don't pay you to sleep in when my county ends up on the front page of the *Raleigh News and Observer*."

Shit. A front-page story might cause the SBI to poke around, and Evan prayed they stayed away. He also prayed like hell the national media didn't carry the story. Faison only wanted media attention if it worked to his advantage. Namely, if he controlled the message to the public and the press painted him in the brightest limelight possible. In spite of Faison's feigned complaint, Evan knew that was exactly what Faison hoped for.

He needed Faison off his back, which would only happen if he could convince Faison they could spin the coverage in his favor. "Unfortunately, it's to be expected, sir," Evan said briskly. He needed Faison off his back. "I'll take care of it."

"Tell me what we're looking at. How bad is it?"

Evan explained the basic facts, knowing Faison would already have heard most of them. He hadn't been elected because he lacked connections. The sad thing was most of Faison's connections usually proved worthless unless they had to do with crime. Faison was a stickler about getting his facts straight. Evan dismissed the thought with a flicker of irritation. Faison was Faison. Evan had long since learned not to waste his time trying to keep ahead of the bastard's motivations.

"Thoughts?" Faison demanded.

Evan considered whether he should tell Faison about the connection he and Xav suspected between drug and child sex trafficking, then decided he'd stick to facts. "The preliminary witness statements mentioned a shrimper," he said.

"Shrimper?" Faison laughed. "If I had a dollar for every shrimper that passed by the docks, I wouldn't need a job."

"This one was spotted at night. Long after most of the boats put in for the evening." When Faison didn't immediately shut him down, he continued, "If drug suppliers are avoiding I-95 and bringing it in by water, it would explain the increase in product in Carver County—"

Faison laughed so loudly into the phone, Evan had to pull the handset away from his ear. "I know you're from up in Bertie, but you've been living here long enough to know that we've got more than our fair share of shrimpers in these parts. Ain't nothin' special about a shrimper putting in late. Probably had engine trouble. I wouldn't be surprised, given the slow season they're havin'."

"But sir, this could be what we've been looking for. Think about it. You could ship the product up from Florida and transfer—"

"I spoke to Wally about how best to manage this," Faison boomed over the receiver.

"Manage what?" Managing matters in the DA's office was *his* job as chief assistant district attorney.

"This is not your concern. This is about sending a message to criminals. Upping the ante," Faison pontificated. "We need to make a statement, and court's the best place to do it."

Evan braced for the worst. In his experience, Talley's "advice" about running the DA's office was as useless as tits on a boar.

"I want you to take that case out of Havelock," Faison continued. "What is it? Davidson?"

"Davies," Evan corrected. He knew the case well. Multiple defendants, all low-level drug dealers netted in a sting operation the sheriff's office had spearheaded.

"I want you on it," Faison repeated. "A strong presence in court will show the dealers we aren't fooling around."

"But sir," Evan protested, "Marcy Gayle is handling the Davies case. She's done a fine job—"

"Don't get all high and mighty on me, Fairchild," Faison snapped. "Just because you went to some hoity-toity law school don't mean you're too good to prosecute dealers."

Evan knew it was useless to argue, but he couldn't stop himself. He didn't mind handling low-level drug cases when the workload called for it, but this would seriously cut into the time he needed to get a handle on the bigger picture.

Five minutes later Evan hung up the phone, having gotten no further in convincing Faison that assigning him to the Davies case was a mistake. *Not just a waste of time, a fucking mistake.*

He leaned back in his chair and rubbed the bridge of his nose. He was so damn tired. Tired of the bullshit. Tired of walking on eggshells to maintain the uneasy peace. How the hell had he gotten it into his head that he should involve himself in the investigation of Winter's death?

He'd follow protocol and take the Davies case. He could ask around about the shooting, the drugs, and the tie-in to the shrimpers, but he'd let the cops do what they were supposed to do. He'd stay on the periphery of it but slowly collect the evidence he needed to cut the head off the snake. He'd figure out how to get rid of the drugs in Dare's Landing come hell or high water.

He needed to clear his mind and thought of his sailboat at the marina. A few hours on the water and he'd be able to shake the claustrophobic feeling that had plagued him all morning.

Evan arrived at his boat around 2:00 p.m., having stopped at his house to change into shorts and a T-shirt. A sleek Hunter 33 he'd purchased before he left private practice, she was compact enough for single-handing yet still comfortable enough to make the long trip through the Bahamas to the Caribbean. Not that he'd found the time to sail her much farther than the Outer Banks, with as much work as came across his desk, but the idea of a month on the water was something to aspire to.

The sun was high in the sky as he climbed aboard, but the stiff breeze off the water took the edge off the heat and humidity. He pulled off the sail covers and looked out over the Neuse River. The water rippled and sparkled with a strong southerly wind, creating white-capped waves that promised an exciting ride. A good eighteen to twenty knots.

Perfect day for a sail.

He headed toward Minnesott Beach on a close haul, riding the waves and catching spray from the bow. The boat, which he'd named *Solitary Man*, bucked against the swells. He laughed aloud as a particularly large wave splashed him, drenching his clothing. *Best kind of air conditioning.*

It felt fucking great to be at the helm, fighting the wind to keep up his speed. Here on the water, the tension that had taken up permanent residence in his gut faded. He thought about Xav, and for once, the usual need to butt heads dissolved into something mellow. With Neil Diamond's "Solitary Man" playing in the back of his mind, he imagined Xav smiling. Xav making a stupid joke. Xav looking back at him and seeing Chance as he was—accepting him, bullshit and all—instead of Evan and his hard shell. He allowed his daydream to continue. Xav up on deck holding on to the mast, smiling at him as his long hair whipped about his face. Maybe he'd put the boat on autopilot and join Xav there, watching for dolphins that chased schools of fish in the water. Xav's skin bronzed from the North Carolina summer. Smooth. Soft.

A fantasy to indulge in, and thanks to himself, nothing could ever happen. Still, Evan didn't push the reverie away. Imagining himself with someone who loved him couldn't hurt anything, could it?

CHAPTER NINETEEN

XAV WENT into the office on his way home early Saturday morning and completed his statement and incident report for Sheriff Winston, then spent the rest of the day moping and sleeping. When he woke on Sunday morning, he decided to get his shit together. He set the coffee to brew and called the office.

"Morning, Twyla Fay."

"Hello, Deputy Constantine. What can I do for you?"

She sounded too formal for Xav's comfort, and he could only imagine the rumors around the office about him fucking up and being put on desk duty. "Is John in the office?"

"No, sir. He won't be back in until tomorrow."

Silence hung over the phone line like a scratchy wet blanket. "Is Sheriff Winston in?"

"No, sir. He won't be back in until tomorrow either."

"Okay. Thanks."

He hung up without waiting for her response. *Fuck it.* He didn't need anyone's permission to go to the office or back to the crime scene.

AN HOUR later Xav had hauled the box of files on the missing boys back to the office. He turned at the front glass doors and backed through one of them with his hands full. When Twyla Fay saw him, she came to his rescue. Together, they carried everything to his desk.

"Thanks," Xav said.

"My pleasure," she said formally.

"You okay?" he asked.

She gestured nonchalantly to the kitchen. He nodded and she walked away. Hardly anyone was in the office, so he wondered why she had a need for secrecy. He organized a few things on his desk and headed to the kitchen.

He entered and she quickly slid the pocket door home. "We got trouble," she said quickly.

"Tell me," Xav said as he reached for his mug and poured a cup of coffee.

"Ryan called and said Mr. Fairchild stopped by the coroner's office yesterday morning to get the preliminary report on Winter Haverty's autopsy."

"Who's Ryan?"

"One of the clerks at the coroner's office."

"Did he give the report to Mr. Fairchild?"

"He did, and Sheriff is not goin' to be happy about it," Twyla Fay said in a huff.

"Why would he give it to him?"

She gave him a curious look.

Xav looked at her, having no idea what was on her mind. "Am I missing something?"

"Am I allowed to talk about, um, well, you know…."

Xav raised his brows in query.

"Gayness," she whispered fiercely. "'Cause, I mean…." She flushed crimson and turned away. The dirty mugs in the sink suddenly needed washing. "Y'all know I don't mean to be rude, right?"

It was all Xav could do not to burst into laughter. "It's okay to talk about gayness with me. I believe everyone in the office knows that I'm gay," he said gently.

"But is it okay to talk about it?"

She was distraught, and Xav felt bad for her. "Others may mind it, but I don't. You can talk to me about it anytime."

"Oh, thank God. I was so afraid I'd upset you."

Xav shook his head once. "Not at all. Is Ryan gay?"

She turned from the sink and reached for a paper towel to dry her hands. "He is and he's made no secret about likin' Mr. Fairchild. Why, at last year's Christmas party, it was plain as day that Mr. Fairchild was not happy about Ryan's behavior. Worse yet, one of our deputies had to drive Ryan home 'cause he was drunker than Cooter Brown and—"

"Than who?"

She pursed her lips. "He was drunk! What'd y'all think I meant?"

Xav was dying inside trying to keep a straight face. "Got it. Go ahead," he said patiently.

"That's what y'all get for not bein' from around here. Anyway, he was drunk and all he did was talk about Mr. Fairchild! Imagine that!" Her whisper was harsh.

Xav chuckled. "Ryan has a crush on Mr. Fairchild?"

"Now, I'm not sayin' Mr. Fairchild is gay, you understand, but yes, Ryan likes Mr. Fairchild."

"I understand. And Ryan gave Mr. Fairchild a copy of the medical examiner's preliminary report on Winter Haverty's autopsy. Do I have it right?"

"Yes. And Sheriff's going to be mad about it."

"Why would Ryan call here and tell you about it?"

She gave him a sardonic look. "That's just it, isn't it?"

"He's been rebuffed by Mr. Fairchild and wants to get him into trouble?"

"Yes. He is *not* a nice man, and Mr. Fairchild *is* a nice man. It's as simple as that," she said adamantly.

Xav made a mental note to stay the hell away from Ryan. "Why don't I ask Sheriff Winston if Mr. Fairchild can have information about the shooting from last night?"

"Sheriff doesn't like information to leave here without his approval, and I'm almost certain the medical examiner would not approve of a preliminary report going to Mr. Fairchild. At the very least, it'd have to be a final report."

Xav agreed. "Has Mr. Fairchild asked for anything else that you know of?"

"Carol, his assistant, called yesterday morning and asked for a copy of your statement and incident report, and the crime scene and ballistics reports from forensics, and Sheriff said it was okay to e-mail them."

"That's normal."

"It is?"

"Sure. It's an officer-involved shooting."

"You didn't shoot anybody."

"It's still an officer-involved shooting, and one person is dead. It needs to be reviewed and cleared by the district attorney."

"That doesn't seem entirely fair," she said haughtily.

He smiled. Her protectiveness was growing on him. "It isn't always, but it's the way it is."

"Well, I don't like it. Oh, my Lord, where are my manners. How are you feelin'?"

"Sore, but otherwise okay."

"I'm so sorry one of the boys died. You have to know it isn't your fault."

Xav tried to smile, but his struggle must have been obvious, because she said, "Now you listen to me, Deputy Constantine. I saw that report. Whoever shot at you wanted those boys dead for some reason. It had nothin' to do with you. Do you understand me?"

He did. All too well. "Thanks, Twyla Fay."

"I'm serious. We gotta figure out what's going on with these missin' boys. We got a job to do."

He liked her "we" rally speech. "How are you coming along on the NCMEC data?"

"Almost all caught up. I'm double-checkin' some dates and statements and things, but we should be all caught up and accurate by the end of the week."

"Thank you for working hard on it."

She gave him a caring look. "I'm sorry you had to walk into this mess. We're better than this. We really are."

Now Xav did smile. "I know you are. We'll get to the bottom of it. Any news from Billy Kenner and Ridley White on Charlie's case?"

She shook her head. "They started all the way back at the beginning like Sheriff asked 'em to. They're bein' real thorough. I know Billy Kenner has a problem with, well, gayness, but he'll do a good job. You can count on it."

"I am. What reports have come in about Friday night?"

"Forensics sent over the crime scene and ballistics reports yesterday but then called about something else today. Wouldn't say what it was. I left the message on your desk. The hospital sent over all the reports on you and the boys. All the witness reports are in, and everything is in a big file on your desk. I'm almost done with your office. Do you want to see it?"

She beamed, hopeful, and he smiled again. "Would love to."

"ALL THE printouts of the bad NCMEC data are in here." She swung the heavy door of the gun safe open.

"Very organized."

"Thank you, sir." She swung the heavy door closed, spun the combination dial, and withdrew and pocketed the key. "Your key and the combination are in your center desk drawer. John is the only other person with a key to it."

"Excellent. What did you do with all the stuff that was in here?"

"Most of it was junk that could be thrown out, and I had the maintenance man move the rest to storage. We won't be needin' any of it until next month's Shrimp Festival." She continued showing him around the office. "Then, this low file cabinet with the plants on it over here is for all the files on the missing boys."

Xav stepped back to the doorway and admired the room. "Very nice, Twyla Fay."

"These here dry-wipe boards on the wall are for makin' notes, and I got you markers in every color I could find," Twyla Fay finished, hands on hips, as she admired her work well done.

"You did a great job. You said you were almost done. Everything looks more than finished to me."

"I ordered a big wall calendar and a wall map to go with the dry-wipe boards. They'll be in this afternoon and I'll begin fillin' 'em out. I thought we might plot out exactly what days these boys went missin' and from where. See if there's any pattern to it."

Xav chuckled. "Are you sure you're not a deputy in disguise?"

She beamed again. "My first job in high school was filin' Sheriff Winston's papers after school. When I graduated, he hired me as the receptionist. I'm still here, and a girl gets to know a few things after a while."

"I couldn't have gotten luckier."

"'Bout what?"

"Having you to work with."

She blushed like a little schoolgirl and then became serious. "You think we'll find out what's happened to all these boys?"

Now it was Xav's turn to be serious. "We will, but it may not be pretty, Twyla Fay."

She sighed. "I was afraid you'd say that."

CHAPTER TWENTY

TWYLA FAY helped him bring everything from the bullpen area into his office and fill the file cabinet. He now sat at his new desk, opened the file on the Haverty boys, and went through it again.

He reread the arrest report regarding the father's attempt to sell one of the boys on a street corner for a fix. The report referred to Winter as said boy but later mentioned in the narrative that the father had identified the boy as Quinn. *Odd.* Xav decided to look the report up in the system and then realized he didn't have a computer terminal in his office. He looked at the phone, and sure enough, efficient Twyla Fay had labeled it with each intercom extension. He pressed Speaker and punched the numbers for her extension. The speaker squawked at him, and he nearly jumped from his chair and fumbled the receiver. He quickly touched the volume down button several times.

"Yes, Deputy Constantine?" she answered.

"Am I going to have a computer terminal in my office?"

"Oh, shoot. I forgot to tell you. The techs will do it tomorrow. Is there something I can help you with?"

"I'm looking at the file on the Haverty twins and I need some additional information."

"I'll be right there."

She appeared in his doorway within seconds.

"I didn't mean to take you away from your desk."

"I can watch it from here, and it's real quiet today. What can I help you with?"

"The arrest report for Mr. Haverty. It says that Winter was the boy he attempted to sell, but later in the narrative, the father stated that the boy was Quinn. I need to know if the boy in question was ever positively identified."

"He was not. John and I looked at that too when we were entering NCMEC data."

That was disappointing. "Did we get anything in from DSS or the SBI about Friday night?"

"No. And I haven't changed the NCMEC data to list Winter as deceased and Quinn as found yet because I don't have the autopsy report and a signed disposition form on Quinn."

"I'll sign the disposition sheet so you can list Quinn as found. The SBI came to the hospital early Saturday morning, and they're returning to the hospital to interview Quinn tomorrow morning. May I trouble you to follow up on the SBI and DSS reports?"

"Be happy to."

Xav stood and his back screamed at him. "I can still use the terminal at my old desk, right?"

"Sure, but I'd be more than happy to help y'all."

He smiled. "Thanks. I only need a current disposition on the Haverty parents. I can look it up."

"I can save you the trouble. John looked it up when we were entering NCMEC data. They both died of drug overdoses shortly after the boys were removed from the home."

A suspicion began in the pit of Xav's stomach, but before it came to fruition, Twyla Fay continued.

"I have a copy of the report for the file, but you had the file at home, so I couldn't put them in there."

Xav winced. "Sorry, Twyla Fay."

"Don't be. Not like you knew you were gonna be shot at."

"I'll be sure to leave the files here in the cabinet from now on."

"I'll get the report for you." She turned to leave.

"Twyla Fay?"

She turned back.

"Do you know anything about Bright Horizons Group Home?"

"Nothing other than it's a foster facility."

"Check with the state? Let me know if there are any lawsuits, citations, or incident reports?"

"Sure."

He leaned back in his chair and was reminded by his aching body that, at the ripe old age of thirty-five, he was getting too old for this shit. He read the crime scene report. It only confirmed what he already knew, including that the assailants had exited the brothel and returned to it. Deputies had all but raided the place and found nothing in the search, and of course, every employee suddenly became deaf, dumb, and blind— including that asshole Victor. Xav began a to-do list on a sticky note. *1.*

updated DSS report on Haverty; 2. updated SBI report on Haverty; 3. interview Victor—get crim history.

He withdrew the computer-generated three-dimensional image estimating the source point, path, and endpoint of the ordnance. He cringed when he saw the path drawn through the boys and himself. He thought it odd that it showed that Winter had taken the brunt of the ordnance when Winter had been between Xav and Quinn. *They were aiming for him.*

Blue eyes filled his mind, and he rubbed his eyes with the heels of his hands and willed the vision away. He reached for the ballistics report and rubbed his chest where the tattoo was.

The assailants had fired Herstals, and that piqued his curiosity. It was a drug cartel weapon of choice. He agreed with the report that at least one of the guns had been equipped with an extended magazine, given that Forensics discovered forty slugs in the immediate area.

He wrote at the top of the sticky note, *How did boys end up behind car?* and underlined it.

He glanced at the ballistics report on his own gun only long enough to verify that it confirmed his statements to Sheriff Winston. He read the report on his vest. Six slugs? No wonder his back hurt like hell. He set the report aside in favor of looking at the pictures taken in the ER. He tossed the ones of himself back in the file and looked at the pictures of Quinn. Thank God, he'd only suffered minor injuries. He and Quinn now had matching through-and-though wounds on their sides. No pictures of Winter existed because he'd been taken straight into surgery.

Blue eyes filled his mind again, and he fought them back.

He read the stat toxicology reports on Quinn and Winter. Indeed, the amount of cocaine in their systems was far more than incidental. Most handlers used drugs and alcohol to control kids and make them perform, and the drug- and sex-trafficking trades always intersected at some point. Still, Xav wasn't sure it lent to Chance's—*Evan's* suspicions about the drug angle. He added *4. Winter-autopsy report* to his to-do list. He didn't bother to read the tox report on himself.

He looked at the forensics report on surveillance footage from the alley. No clear images of the assailants. Nothing exciting. He moved on to the witness reports. Gunfire, screams, nobody knew anything. Standard. The only unique thing he read was that an old homeless drunk had mentioned seeing a trawler.

He closed the file as Twyla Fay entered with the report on the Haverty parents' drug overdoses and handed it to him. "Here you go. Nothing special in it as far as we saw."

"Thanks." He shuffled through the witness statements. "Will you please print out a history on these two witnesses?" He handed Victor's and the old man's statements to her.

She looked at them. "Oh, Grady Bishop? Most people think he's an old drunk, but he's not. I mean he's sometimes drunk, but he is not that old. He's just got a speech impediment so everybody thinks he's old and drunk all the time. He's harmless."

She pronounced "impediment" as "im-*peedy*-ment."

"No criminal history?" Xav asked.

"None to speak of. He simply prefers to be homeless since he came back from Iraq."

"Check for me anyway?"

"Yes, sir. Oh, and this one?" She humphed and held up Victor's statement. "Nothin' but trouble. Assault is his middle name, but he never gets much jail time 'cause all his victims are whor—" She put her fingers to her lips. "Sorry. I meant to say harlots."

Xav chuckled. "Get me what we have on him?"

"Will do. Did you call forensics yet?"

"I'll do that now." She left the office, and he picked up the phone and dialed the number on the message.

"Forensics. Ingram."

"Hello. This is Deputy Xavier Constantine. I received a message to call the lab."

"Glad y'all telephoned. I called to speak to Sheriff Winston, but Twyla Fay said he wasn't in, so I asked for y'all to call. She said y'all are in charge of the Haverty shooting investigation."

That was news to Xav, but he'd roll with it on proper disclosure. "I'm the deputy who was involved in the shooting. Sheriff Winston is in charge of the investigation."

"But he wasn't in yesterday and he's not in today. Thought y'all might want to know Mr. Fairchild from the DA's office called here looking for information yesterday."

"What information?"

"He asked about the identification of a trawler observed by a witness. He wanted to know if we'd been able to ID it from the dock's surveillance footage."

"Did he say why?"

"No, and I didn't ask. Sheriff has made it clear that no information leaves this lab without his okay."

"I understand. Did you ID the trawler?"

"Nope. Expenses bein' what they are and all, we don't do what isn't authorized by the sheriff's office."

Xav thought about the mystery trawler, which he didn't think was a mystery at all, because there were as many trawlers around here as there were mosquitos—woe be unto Hummer fenders—but he couldn't discount the trawler pulling in late. "May I ask you to see what you can do to identify the trawler?"

"No problem. I'll send over the form for you to sign. Just wanted to make sure you knew that Mr. Fairchild called here asking for information."

"Thanks, Mr. Ingram. I appreciate the heads-up."

The man chortled. "No one calls me that. The name's Tom."

Xav smiled to himself. "Thanks, Tom." He hung up and looked at his watch. It was almost two o'clock, and he was hungry. He'd grab something to eat on the way to the crime scene. He took the report on the Haverty parents with him to read and exited his office, nearly running smack into Twyla Fay, and came to an abrupt halt. "Pardon me."

She smiled. "Might do yourself a favor and open the blinds there." She gestured to the window between his office and the bullpen.

"Good idea."

"Here are the reports on Victor and Bish."

"Bish?"

"Grady Bishop."

"Right." He accepted them from her. Grady Bishop's sheet showed one drunk and disorderly brought about by him trying to protect a stray dog. He handed it back to her. "Will you please put that in the file on my desk?"

"Yes, sir."

Victor's sheet was ten pages long. "Busy man."

"Nasty man's more like it."

"Clearly. I'm on cell if you need me."

"Your wall map and calendar just came in, and I'll have them filled out by tomorrow morning."

"Do you ever take a day off?"

She smiled. "Yes, sir, but I come in when I have things to do. Not every weekend we have a serious crime occur, and I like to be where I'm needed."

"Thank you, Twyla Fay. I don't know what I'd do without you."

"That's what they all say. You look like you could use some Tylenol."

He smiled. "I feel like I need some Tylenol. I have some with me. Thanks again for the great job on my office."

"You're welcome. Call if you need anything else."

"See you tomorrow." He walked toward the front door as he skimmed the report on the Haverty parents. Twyla Fay had been right. Nothing unusual. Both parents had died of massive cocaine overdoses. He stopped dead in his tracks and paced backward to Twyla Fay's desk.

She smiled. "That was fancy. I'm guessin' you had another question, Deputy Constantine."

"This report says the parents died of cocaine overdoses."

"That's right."

"The arrest report says they were heroin addicts."

She frowned. "I'll check the arrest history and double-check it with the coroner's office."

"Before you finalize the NCMEC data, will you please have an officer do a welfare check on the parents of each missing boy?"

Her expression darkened. "Oh, Lord. Do you think the parents are at risk somehow?"

"No," he lied. "But I'd rather be safe than sorry."

CHAPTER TWENTY-ONE

XAV STOOD at the edge of the yellow tape emblazoned with "Crime Scene—Do Not Cross" and stared down the alley. It seemed unusually short in the bright sunlight. When he'd been running with the boys, it had seemed a mile long. He looked at the stained asphalt at his feet and was glad he hadn't eaten yet. Quinn's and Winter's blood blended with something oily, the puddles glossy in the humidity but dried black around the edges in the heat. Scraps of paper and medical tape from the EMTs littered the area. He glanced up at the now dormant neon sign that had pulsed overhead. Two cats, engaged in a battle of the ages atop half a dumpster lid, managed to bring the second half of the lid down with a bang before screeching and running like bats out of hell. *Nothing like a common foe to bring even cats together.*

Xav stared down the alley toward the brothel, now quiet on a Sunday morning. He replayed the events of Friday night in his head, and it was still hard to fathom the brothel as a holding pen for human product. Whoever was running this sick show was either bold as brass or just plain stupid. He'd run into all kinds of traffickers while working for CARD, and nothing should have surprised him anymore. And then there was Victor. The cruel handler. Xav had read his sheet filled with one petty assault after another. Otherwise, not as much as a parking ticket. He was a resident alien from Mexico, complete with a green card, and had lived locally for two years, but Xav still had an uneasy feeling about him. *Who the fuck are you, Victor?*

Xav ducked defiantly beneath the yellow tape and headed down the alley toward the brothel, careful to avoid the crime scene markers left by the techs. He gripped the chain-link fence and climbed up and over it, the sound of it clamoring against its poles louder than he'd remembered. He dropped to the dumpster lid and jumped down to the pavement, the pain in his back nagging at him as he continued down the alley. He stopped at the yellow tape strung across the alley a mere two feet from the back door of the brothel and listened. All was quiet save for the sound of running water and the clanking of pots and pans. The cleaning crew in the kitchen, no doubt.

Xav looked around the alley and saw no way Quinn and Winter could have ended up behind the car without walking in front of it first. He moved closer to the brothel and looked around the back door. No windows, no nothing. His gaze travelled down to the pavement and he saw what appeared to be a small manhole cover sitting askew. As he thought to bend down and check it out, the back door suddenly flew open. Xav started but didn't move. A Hispanic kid no older than sixteen shoved an overflowing trash can through the doorway and stopped when he saw Xav.

"Buenos días," Xav greeted.

"Use the front door," the kid said in perfect English, clearly annoyed by Xav's presence.

"I'm looking for Victor."

"Good for you." The kid pulled the plastic trash can across the alley to the now displaced trash bin. He lifted it, clearly a strain given its contents, and it slipped from his hands. It crashed to the asphalt and lost a good portion of its contents. "*Chinga*," the kid swore as he bent to pick up the slimy trash.

Xav took the opportunity and went to help clean up the filth. The kid glanced at him with an annoyed look but didn't refuse the help. When most of the trash was cleaned up, Xav hoisted the barrel with him and they dumped the contents into the bin.

"Thanks," the kid said as he headed back across the alley.

"When's a good time to talk to Victor?" Xav asked, hoping to appear benign.

The kid turned back, seeming to debate whether to respond. "Never. He's an asshole."

Xav snorted a chuckle. "Besides never, when's a good time?"

The kid all but rolled his eyes at Xav. "You're Constantine, the cop who sat out here all Friday night and is all over the news. And a very dumb cop if you think he's going to talk to you after someone put bullets in your vest."

Xav couldn't help but smile as he sized the kid up. He was smart and had guts. "What's your name?"

"For you, it's Victor."

Now Xav did chuckle and rubbed his eyebrow with his middle finger.

The kid smiled. Then it faded. "Did they make it?"

Xav debated whether to tell the truth and decided against it. It was better if everyone thought both boys died. "No."

The kid looked away, seeming to study the rippling seawater on the other side of the dock. "Sorry to hear that."

"What are you doing working in a place like this?"

The kid turned back to him now. "College isn't free, man."

"There are a lot better places to work than this," Xav ventured.

The kid shook his head. "The tips are good."

Xav wondered for a fleeting moment if the kid had fallen into the trade, but decided he hadn't. He wouldn't be emptying filthy trash cans if he had.

A beautiful woman appeared in the doorway and read the kid the Spanish riot act for wasting time in the alley, then shot Xav a look that would have slain the more faint of heart. The kid hiked the trash can and turned it. Xav debated whether to say thanks. He didn't think the kid wanted anyone to know they had spoken. He headed away.

"Hey!"

Xav turned back at the sound of the kid's voice.

"Don't come back!"

XAV LEANED against the railing at the end of the pier and looked back at the brothel. He found no solace in being right about the intended sexual exploitation of at least two of the boys who had gone missing, and his heart ached. He looked out at the water and watched the shrimp trawlers head in for the day. They'd be a perfect mode of transport for moving young merchandise to larger boats heading to other countries. He turned back to the brothel again. Hiding them in plain sight? And that nasty son of a bitch Victor was the perfect handler. If Victor found out Quinn was still alive, Quinn would be history.

Xav's cell phone rang, and he answered it with a brusque "Constantine."

"Winston. You're cleared. Your gun and badge are in your desk drawer."

"Thanks, Sheriff."

"Agent Dee called for a copy of your statement. I gave it to him."

"Thank you. Do you have a minute to speak?"

"What's on your mind?" Winston sounded stressed. No doubt, half the state was breathing down his neck. It wasn't every day Carver County made the news for a shootout involving a deputy and two kids.

"If our assailants find out Quinn is still alive, he's at risk. Can you lock down his hospital room and ask the staff to keep quiet?"

"I told 'em last night to keep their mouths shut, but it may not account for much of nothing. He's being discharged to DSS anyhow."

"When?"

"Sometime tomorrow."

"Can you put a deputy on his door tonight?"

"I don't see why not."

Winston didn't sound happy, but Xav pressed on. "What facilities do we have for protective custody?"

"We don't. We rely on the FBI for that sort of thing."

He could handle that. "Will you make the call?"

"First thing in the morning."

"Thanks, Sheriff."

"Xav, I have to ask. Do you believe all the boys who are missing have gone the route of Quinn and his brother?"

"Meaning do I believe they've been abducted for sexual exploitation?"

"That's what I'm asking."

He didn't want to give his boss false hope. "I take each case on its own merits, but I'd be dishonest if I said I didn't believe so."

"If you're right, you're going to turn this town on its ear."

Xav winced. He could feed Winston all the stats and show him how child sex trafficking had invaded even the best of neighborhoods, but it wouldn't offer any comfort. "I know."

There was a long silence before Sheriff Winston spoke again. "In the event I lose my temper and fly off the handle, I'm going to say this now. I'm happy you're here."

"Thanks, Sheriff. I'm glad to be here." Winston terminated the call, and Xav looked out over the water again. He needed to find out more about shrimping.

He spent the rest of the day researching the North Carolina fishing industry. It was all too interesting that shrimp season arrived and the boys began to disappear. Trawlers and their hauls… having nothing to do with fish. It was just too easy.

CHAPTER TWENTY-TWO

MONDAY MORNING Evan finished his review of a new assault case that had come in the night before, touched base with several of the other ADAs to see where there cases were, and spent another few hours poring over the Davies case to get up to speed. *Twenty-five fucking witnesses.* Could Faison have picked a worse case to assign to him three weeks before trial?

"What the fuck, Evan?" Marcy had said when he told her he'd be sitting first chair instead of her. "I've worked my ass off on this case."

As if that made him any happier. "Orders," he said curtly.

"Orders?" She shook her head and sat heavily in one of the chairs facing his desk. "More likely Faison's having second thoughts about a woman prosecuting the case."

He wouldn't argue with her. Knowing Faison, that was entirely possible. But he knew pushing Faison about it would mean more blowback neither of them needed. "If it helps," he said, hoping to reassure her, "you've done a great job with it. He'll insist I cross the defendants, but you can take whatever witnesses you'd like."

She sighed. "I know it's not your fault."

"Just let me know what you're thinking," he said. "I'll make it up to you with the next assignment."

"Yeah." She rose and walked to the door, then turned back, her expression serious. "You should run, you know."

"Run?"

"You know damn well what I'm talking about," she said. "You'd make a great DA."

He offered her a tight smile and ran a hand through his hair. That was the *last* thing he wanted. He liked things just the way they were. Comfortable and safe. "Not interested," he said flatly.

"You can tell His Majesty where he can stick it," she said as she walked out of the office. She knew he'd do nothing of the sort, but he understood she needed to blow off steam. She wouldn't bring the reassignment up again, and she'd do a great job in court.

Evan glanced back down at the file on his desk and paged through the pleadings. It'd take him at least three more days to get through all the discovery. His mind wandered back to Friday night and Winter Haverty, whose body still sat at the morgue, unclaimed. At least Evan hadn't needed to meet Agent Dee at the hospital. Someone from DSS had called to say Quinn had been released to their custody. Let the SBI figure out where to find him. Evan had given Rebecca Wilhelm instructions to call him the minute anyone showed up to speak to Quinn. She'd indicated that he was in no condition to speak with anyone given his injuries and emotional state, and he remained unresponsive to her attempts to interview him.

Why can't you let this one go? It wasn't even a drug case, unless you counted the coke in the kids' systems.

Evan remembered what Fred had told him about Xav. *Rabid about protecting kids.* He really wanted to hate the man. So why couldn't he get Xav out of his mind?

Because he's the best fuck you've ever had. But that wasn't the only reason. He liked Xav's tenacity. He didn't take any bullshit, and he didn't back down. *Unlike you.* There was a hint of mystery about the man—a hint of something haunted in his eyes. Something familiar, like pain. But Xav also had a sense of humor. Evan wasn't sure he liked that part yet.

Evan eyed the phone. Faison hadn't said he couldn't ask around about the trawler or Quinn. As long as he did what he was required to do at the office, a few questions wouldn't hurt. He picked up the phone and dialed.

"Rachelle Vickers" came the voice on the other end of the line.

"Rachelle, this is Evan Fairchild."

"Good to hear from you, Evan," Rachelle answered. "I heard you came by the other day. Sorry I missed you."

"I came by to pick up the autopsy report on Winter Haverty."

"It won't be ready until Wednesday when the labs are back."

Evan paused. Clearly, she didn't know Ryan had already provided a copy of the preliminary report to him. "Can you give me the highlights?"

"I suppose it wouldn't hurt. Terrible case," she replied. "Bullet to the medulla. Surgery was a waste of time. I noted in the report that he died at the moment of impact."

"Anything remarkable?"

"As you probably learned from the hospital, there was a fair amount of cocaine in his system," she replied. "And one more thing." Her voice sounded hard, almost detached.

"Yes?"

"He was raped," she said. "The final lab results will be with the autopsy report."

Evan drew a calming breath. The second coffee he'd just finished churned in his gut. He'd handled rape cases in his time with the DA, but the image of Quinn, small and frightened in the hospital bed, made the entire thing seem that much uglier. In that moment, he understood Xav's emotional reaction to the violence perpetrated on children. He wanted nothing more than to string up the bastards who'd done this to Winter and Quinn.

"Evan?" Rachelle asked after the silence lengthened.

"Right. Sorry, I'm still here." He breathed in and out a few times. "Ryan mentioned you stayed late to do the autopsy. I'm sorry."

"Comes with the job. I understand the state is going to assume responsibility for the body, but I sent Winter's personal effects to forensics. He had a small Bible and a painted seashell in his possession."

"Great. Thanks, Rachelle. I appreciate the help."

"Any time. Oh, and Evan?"

"Yes?"

"I hope they find the bastard who did this and you put him away until he rots," she said cheerfully.

The morning dragged on. The muffin Evan had snagged from Starbucks sat untouched on his desk. He couldn't get the rape of Winter Haverty out of his mind. He glanced ruefully at the muffin several times as he worked through the Davies discovery, but he still couldn't bring himself to eat. He took a swig of coffee and rubbed the bridge of his nose, where a headache threatened.

"That good?" said a familiar voice.

Evan looked up at Xav and strangled an expletive. "What are you doing here?"

Xav held up his hands in mock surrender and smirked. "I come in peace."

Deep breath. "What do you want?" Evan responded in as calm a voice as he could manage.

Xav leaned a shoulder on the doorframe. Dressed in a charcoal suit and a jade green T-shirt that hugged the muscles of his chest and made his green eyes glow, Xav made it difficult for Evan to focus. "I wanted to let you know that Quinn's been released to DSS and I'm going to talk to him again," he said.

"Not happening." Not that he had any authority to stop Xav now that he'd been cleared to work, but he wanted to be there when Xav interviewed him.

Anger flashed in Xav's eyes but was gone like a ripple in the water as he entered. He closed the door and took a seat in front of Evan's desk.

Who the fuck does he think he is?

"Why not?" Xav asked.

Evan didn't know whether to laugh or cry. The arrogant prick not only thought he could park his ass in his office but dared to question him. "You're on desk duty."

"Not any longer. You cleared me, and you're the DA's first, the guy who runs the show. Or are you going to try to convince me Faison actually knows what goes on in his office?" He leaned back into the chair, legs open, arms casually resting on the armrests.

More distraction.

"The district attorney cares—"

"Drop it, Fairchild. You and I both know it's all about the big picture. *His* picture, to be precise, and keeping the citizens happy so they'll reelect him. He doesn't get his hands dirty."

Xav was spot on, but Evan wasn't going to agree. He might not respect Faison, but he wanted to keep his job. He needed to focus on handling his damn wildcard of a boss, but he also needed to keep his fingers on the pulse of Xav's investigation.

Xav rubbed the back of his neck. "I thought we made a good team."

Evan stood, walked around to the front of the desk, and rested a lean hip on it. "Let me make something clear, Deputy Constantine. We aren't a team."

Xav's expression darkened. "I'm not here about our personal gig."

Evan shook his head and let out a soft laugh.

Xav stood, too close now for Evan's comfort. Evan gritted his teeth and stifled his body's visceral reaction. He tried to will away the tension in his neck and shoulders and his need to confront Xav head-on as he met Xav's gaze. He half wanted to punch the man, half wanted to tear his clothes off.

What the hell is wrong with me? I'm acting like a teenager with raging hormones.

The pained admission had him cursing his childhood again. He imagined Evelene telling him not to beat himself up for it. *"Accept it for what it is and let it go."*

"This is business."

"Then stop acting like an insecure dick and let's do our jobs," Xav said, his voice tinged with exasperation.

What's more important here? You or the people you want to protect? Xav's interest was in trafficking, Evan's was drugs, and they both needed to know what Quinn knew, yet Evan continued to hesitate. *You're hesitating because he gets to you. He pushes you places you're afraid to go.* But this was supposed to be about what they needed to know to do their jobs and help Quinn and boys like him, not about his own personal shit. Faison and his buddies sure as shit weren't going to do anything about the drugs or to protect kids like Quinn. *So let it go. Buck up and do what's right.*

"You're right," Evan said at last. "I am acting like an insecure dick." Evan met Xav's gaze momentarily, then walked back behind the desk. "We'll do this together."

"Good." Xav didn't gloat. He waited patiently for Evan to take the next step.

"Level with me. What do you want to learn from Quinn?"

Xav visibly relaxed and took a seat again. "It isn't a coincidence that the brothel is located on the docks. I think it's a holding pen and they're selling kids and using boats to transport kids out of the country."

The thought nauseated Evan, and he immediately thought of the trawler mentioned in the witness report, but he wouldn't tell Xav that he'd reached a different conclusion about the boat's possible cargo. He thought again about Faison blowing him off as he took a seat. His hunches were usually good. Why had he let Faison distract him? *Because you didn't want to get into a pissing match with him.*

"Now you level with me. What do you want to know from Quinn?" Xav asked.

"Ever since the fish processing plants closed, we've had problems with the abandoned buildings around those old docks. The city's been talking about tearing them down for years. There's been a lot of low-level drug dealing out of them, but there's more than just low-level activity going on in this county. I want to figure out how the drugs are getting here, and I want to go after the suppliers, not the local dealers. If there were a link between the missing boys and the drugs, those run-down buildings would make a perfect staging area for both crimes. Bottom line is that I need to know the same things you do. How and why those boys got down there, where were they held, and why did they have so much coke in their systems?"

"Let's talk to him together," Xav suggested.

"I need to think about it. I have a few fires I need to put out, and Faison isn't receptive to me looking into the drug issues outside of his specific agenda." Evan knew he was stalling, but Xav did something to his brain that muddied his thought processes, and he needed a clear head to work out how far he could chase this rabbit without ending up knee-deep in political fallout.

Xav studied him for a moment, then stood. "Don't wait too long, Cha—*Evan*," he said, the corners of his mouth edging oh-so-slightly upward. "Because whoever shot those boys wanted them dead, and if they find out Quinn's still alive, you can bet your ass they'll come after him."

Evan repressed a groan. "Noted, Deputy Constantine."

Xav nodded and left. Evan watched him leave, only allowing himself to relax when he was sure Xav was halfway out of the building. *Infuriating man.* Working with Xav was a blatant violation of his no-fraternization policy and scared the living shit out of him. Still, he didn't doubt Xav's priorities. He was sharp, dedicated, and willing to put his life on the line to save kids. Which led Evan back to the thought he'd had before Xav had showed up at his office: this wasn't his fight. Or was it?

CHAPTER TWENTY-THREE

XAV MADE it into the sheriff's station at eleven and a reporter accosted him as he parked his bike and locked his gear.

"Deputy Constantine! What do y'all have to say about Friday night's shooting?"

Xav slipped on his suit jacket and held a halting hand up. "No comment."

He entered the building to find the bullpen area bustling with activity. It stood to reason. As weather warmed, crime increased, and it had been a busy weekend. Twyla Fay was doing her best to maintain her calm while arguing with another reporter at the reception desk.

"I'm sorry, sir. Sheriff Winston is not available. Now, I'm askin' you to leave for the last time."

Xav interrupted. "Would you like me to escort the gentleman out?"

The man turned to Xav. "You can't touch—hey, you're Deputy Constantine!"

"I am. Would you like me to escort you out?"

"Only if you're willing to comment!"

"I'd be happy to comment once you're outside the building. Right this way."

Xav walked the man to the glass doors, opened one, and gestured him outside. "Please don't obstruct the sheriff's department's ability to do its work. My comment is no comment."

Xav closed the glass door and turned the lock mechanism. The reporter yelled at him and banged on the doors. Xav left him to brandish his complaints at the glass and walked back to Twyla Fay's desk. "You okay?"

Twyla Fay checked her makeup and hair in a compact mirror and snapped it shut with a crisp click. "I swear! Is there some secret code of conduct that says reporters must be rude?"

Xav chuckled. "No. They're bred that way. Put someone on the door. Let's keep it locked for now and only admit those who have sheriff's business."

"Good idea. Thank you for gettin' rid of him. He's the fourth one this mornin'. Sheriff wants to see you when you have a minute, and John and I want to talk to you about the NCMEC data and the wall calendar and map. Oh, and the computer terminal has been moved into your office."

"Thanks. Will you please let Sheriff Winston know I'll be right with him? I want to grab a cup of joe."

"Yes, sir. And how are you feeling?"

He smiled. "I'm a little stiff but good. Thanks for asking."

Cup of coffee in hand, Xav knocked on Sheriff Winston's door. "Come!"

Xav entered and took a seat. "Morning, Sheriff."

"Hell o' one, if you're askin'. What's all this I hear about Fairchild poking around the evidence on the shooting?"

"No doubt, he needed it to clear me. I don't see a problem with him having it."

The sheriff issued a deep sigh. "You'd be the first deputy to ever think that. Most don't take kindly to the DA poking around."

"I can't say I'm fond of it, but in this instance it worked in our favor. I'm cleared and it'll keep Faison from nosing around your office."

"Good points."

Xav thought for a moment and opted not to tell the sheriff he'd stopped by Evan's office on his way in. "Fairchild raised an interesting idea when I spoke with him on Friday night. He thinks there may be a connection between the increased drug trafficking in the county and the missing boys."

Sheriff Winston frowned. "What do you think?"

"It's no secret that drug and human trafficking go hand in hand, and child sex traffickers use drugs and alcohol to subdue youth and get them to perform. But whether there is a direct link between the matters, meaning whether the traffickers in question are one and the same, isn't known and should be investigated."

"You're proposing a joint task force?"

Xav shook his head. "No. In my experience, joint task forces generally lead to stepping on toes. I've found it more efficient for task forces to share and coordinate information, which, in turn, leads to working together as if you had a joint task force."

Winston narrowed his eyes before he laughed aloud. "You should be a politician."

Xav shrugged. "In spite of stereotyping, I have rarely run into an officer who hasn't earned his stripes or shouldn't have designated authority commensurate with designated responsibility."

Winston snickered. "They taught you those pretty words in the FBI, didn't they?"

Xav chuckled. "They did. Does this sound better? I have no problem calling a spade a spade when the time calls for it."

Winston was still smiling. "Now that's what I like to hear. So just what is it that you're proposing, here?"

"Who heads up your drug task force?"

"Don't have one, but Billy is the senior deputy on staff. He sees to it that cases are assigned to the right people, and I'm here when he needs oversight."

"Why don't we ask what they think about sharing information? And I'd include John in this conversation. He's my partner."

"Twyla Fay's been working on something in your office. What is it?"

"She's putting together a wall calendar and map to plot out what's happened to the missing boys as she's correcting NCMEC data. She's been an incredible help."

The sheriff punched the intercom button for Twyla Fay.

"Yes, sir?" Twyla Fay answered.

"Billy, Ridley, John, and you in my office."

"Right away, sir."

Sheriff clicked off. "I suppose it's about time I made Twyla Fay an administrative assistant. She shouldn't be saddled with answering phones."

Xav smiled. "I know she'd be elated. Did you call the FBI about protective custody?"

Winston nodded. "I did. It's ready when you're ready to move the boy. The sooner the better." He slid a piece of paper across the desk to Xav. "Your authorization from me."

"Thank you."

The office door opened and everyone filed in. Xav stood and offered Twyla Fay his seat and gestured for someone to take the other in front of the desk. No one did.

Winston looked at Twyla Fay. "I want you to find yourself a replacement."

She looked horrified.

He continued, "It's time you were promoted to administrative assistant."

She smiled wide and did a little bounce in her seat but looked a little frayed around the edges, the whiplash having spent her immediate reserves. "Thank you, sir. Can I promote Sally Ann, the weekend receptionist, and look for another part-timer?"

"Do what you think's best. You'll be working directly for Billy, Xav, and me from now on and answering our phones. We'll discuss pay separate from this meeting."

"Why, thank you, sir."

"You've earned it." He looked at Billy Kenner. "Billy, I know you and Ridley have worked your asses off trying to figure out why we have more drugs than ever in our county. Xav here has a thought." He gestured to Xav to speak.

Not having anticipated the impromptu speech, Xav took a moment to formulate his words. "I suspect the missing boys have been abducted for purposes of child sexual exploitation—"

Billy exploded. "Oh hell no! We don't have those kinds in these parts!"

"He ain't kiddin', Billy! Just listen to him for a hot minute!" John shouted back.

"That's enough!" Winston boomed over everyone. "Now, I gave Xav the floor, and y'all are gonna listen and listen good."

Billy quieted, but disgust was plain on his face.

"It's no secret that drug and human trafficking intersect. What we want to find out is whether those who are exploiting boys are also trafficking drugs into this county. I propose we share information. It will speed up our investigations not only by process of elimination but by doubling our chances of discovery and analysis of evidence."

Ridley spoke up for the first time. "What if we think some of our evidence is unrelated?"

"Such as?" Xav asked.

"Well, like, the mules we bust on I-95. I can't see how that'd be related."

Xav nodded. "I can see how you'd think that, and you might be correct. My suggestion is that you simply present a summary of that information to us. You never know what information might be important."

Twyla Fay looked up at Billy and Ridley. "I'm going to do a presentation of sorts to Xav and John as soon as we're done here on what I've plotted out about the missing boys. Why don't y'all sit in on it?"

"Excellent idea, Twyla Fay," Xav said.

Billy fidgeted with the edge of his holster before saying, "I need to know more of what you mean by child sex trafficking. I mean, I understand kiddie porn rings and whatnot, but I don't know anything about child sex trafficking."

"Can I give him and Ridley the same crash course you gave me, Xav?" John asked.

"Absolutely," Xav answered.

Winston cleared his throat. "ADA Fairchild has been poking around the evidence on Friday night's shooting. Xav and I concluded it isn't a problem because he needed it to clear Xav. Be cooperative with him, but I do not want any information whatsoever goin' to Walter Talley."

"Who is Walter Talley?" Xav asked.

"He was here with Mr. Fairchild on your first day. Remember?" John asked.

"Now I do. What does he do, exactly?"

"He's Faison's political facilitator," Sheriff Winston said with a sour face.

"Campaign manager turned press agent?" Xav asked.

Winston humphed. "The man has bordered on violatin' about every RICO statute I can think of. He'll stoop lower than a snake's belly in a wagon rut. No information goes to that man."

"Understood," Xav said.

"Now, I want y'all to share information and get to the bottom of things. Twyla Fay, you stay here. Y'all, get to it."

CHAPTER TWENTY-FOUR

"FAIRCHILD?" FAISON said, barely looking up from his computer. "What's this about?"

Evan hated Faison's office, with its dark oak paneling, heavy furniture, and signed photographs of politicians. It reminded him of everything that was wrong with the system—all show and no substance. He'd donned his best courtroom demeanor like a suit of armor. He made up his mind to do this, and he'd stick to his guns. "Sir," he said, "I'd like to discuss your assigning me the Davies case."

"We've already discussed that. We need to show the folks out there we mean business."

"With all due respect, sir, I can do far better if you let me do my job—"

"You telling me it's not your *job* to prosecute criminals?" Faison said, his puffy face reddening with anger.

"No, sir. But I think I may be onto something here with the shooting case, and I need a little leeway to follow up on it. I've reviewed the Davies case file, and Marcy's done excellent work prepping—"

"I give you *plenty* of leeway, Fairchild," Faison shot back. "You yourself signed off clearin' the deputy. Nothin' more to it. You're my chief, and I've given you the responsibility of showin' folks we mean business in court so I have time to do my job."

Evan bit back a retort. It wouldn't help to antagonize Faison any more than he already had. "I appreciate that, sir," he said, heart racing as he rose to the argument. "And that's exactly why Marcy's the right person to—"

"You've never challenged my authority before," Faison said, eyes narrowing. "Why now?"

"Sir? I've explained—"

"No." Faison scowled and eyed him with suspicion. "There's something more going on here, isn't there?"

"I don't know what you're—"

"You've been thinking about running, haven't you?" Faison all but accused.

"Running? For *your job?*" *As if!* If he ever were insane enough to consider it, he sure as hell wouldn't hide it from Faison. "Absolutely not."

"I've heard folks talkin'," Faison continued, unfazed. "They think you're some hotshot. Them *Democrats*"—he spoke the word as if it were some sort of communicable disease—"been looking at you to run, haven't they?"

"No, sir," Evan answered truthfully. He'd spoken to no one about political ambitions—he didn't have any—and other than a few colleagues who had mentioned the possibility of unseating Faison, nobody had ever approached him about it. "But since you raised the subject," he continued, knowing full well he should just keep his mouth shut but unable to contain his rising anger, "maybe you should consider paying more attention to your job than your reelection campaign."

Faison stared at him. "What did you say?" he hissed.

"Only the truth, *sir*," Evan said, his face suddenly hot. "An eleven-year-old boy is dead, and a deputy has been shot. Toxicology says both boys had cocaine in their systems, and the medical examiner says the dead boy was raped. *That's* what your constituents care about, not a handful of low-level busts that any of your ADAs could try with their eyes closed."

Faison glared at him. "Have you finished?" he demanded.

Evan took a deep breath. "Yes, sir."

"Good." Faison crossed his arms. "Then I think it's high time you get back to work. Don't you agree?"

"Yes, sir." Evan met Faison's eyes, then turned and left. Minutes later, back in his own office, he kicked the wastebasket, sending it over, its contents spilling and covering the floor. He left the mess and sat at his desk. He pulled out another stack of documents from the Davies file and began to work his way through them. *Fine. Faison'll get his fucking case.*

"AND THAT'S all we got," Ridley concluded.

Xav sat back in his chair. "Your evidence points to one or more new methods of incursion?"

Billy nodded. "We've had low-level drug activity for as long as I've been on the force, but we've never had cocaine in middle and high schools. And the drug overdoses are increasing by droves."

Xav looked to Twyla Fay. "Did you verify the Haverty parents' overdose information?"

"I did and it's exactly as you read." Xav gestured for her to share it. "They were heroin addicts, so it makes no sense that they died of cocaine overdoses."

"What're y'all thinkin'?" Billy asked.

"The file on the Haverty twins shows they were removed from the home because the father tried to sell one or both of them on a street corner for a heroin fix," Xav said.

"What do you mean, sell?" Ridley asked.

"Prostitute them," John answered.

Billy's face paled. "God Almighty."

Xav continued. "Next thing you know, both boys are abducted, then escape a brothel and are shot. I think traffickers took notice when the father attempted to prostitute them on a street corner, later took the boys, and made sure the parents weren't around to want them back. It's only a guess, but it's an educated one."

"Y'all're sayin' whoever abducted the boys murdered the parents by way of drug overdoses?" Billy asked.

Xav nodded. "With the parents out of the picture, they become throwaway kids."

"Become what?" Ridley asked.

John and Xav began to speak at the same time, and Xav stopped and gestured to John to continue.

"Nobody gets too excited when foster kids go missin'. People figure they became foster kids 'cause they did somethin' bad, had it comin' in some way, and the kids run away. Then nobody looks too hard for 'em. That makes 'em throwaway kids 'cause nobody cares about 'em."

Ridley winced.

Twyla Fay looked at Xav. "I checked the state on Bright Horizons like you asked. No complaints, but in addition to the Haverty twins, two other kids went missin' from the home six months ago."

"Boys?" Xav asked.

"Yes," Twyla Fay answered.

"You're telling me we have a total of nineteen missing boys?" Billy asked.

"Seventeen," Twyla Fay corrected.

"How'd y'all get seventeen from eighteen plus two?" Ridley asked.

"We have a disposition on the Wrigley boy and the Haverty twins. Twenty minus three is seventeen," Xav offered.

"Oh, that's right. I forgot about the Wrigley boy. Sorry."

Xav shook his head once. "Please don't apologize. We have a lot to keep track of here. Twyla Fay, did you call DSS for an updated report on the Haverty twins?"

"Got it from Rebecca Wilhelm this morning. It's in your in-box and doesn't tell us anything we don't already know. She also gave me the report on the other two boys and said she was not the supervisor of the facility when they went missin'."

Convenient, Xav thought. "Did DSS report them missing to the SBI?"

"No one seems to have an answer for that," Twyla Fay said, nervous now. She glanced at Billy. "The DSS report does say they gave Charlie a copy of it and, um, doesn't seem he ever entered the boys into NCMEC's system."

"Shit," Billy said, pronouncing *shit* as if it had two syllables.

Xav searched for the sticky note containing his to-do list and added: *5. SBI rpt re two add'l missing kids from Bright Horizons?* and crossed off item number one and part of three, Victor's rap sheet. "John, have you had a chance to perform a welfare check on all the parents of the missing boys?"

"I have. Everyone's accounted for and they all say they're okay. I made a log and kept detailed notes of each conversation."

Xav said a silent thanks to the heavens. "What do you think about checking on them weekly? If for no other reason than goodwill on the part of the sheriff's office until we find the boys?"

"Consider it done," John assured.

"Thanks. Twyla Fay, add the parents of these two additional boys to the welfare check list, please."

"I already checked. The boys were brothers and only had a mother. She died of a cocaine overdose two weeks after the boys were placed at Bright Horizons."

Xav looked at her, incredulous.

"I know, I know," she said plaintively. "But this woman had a history of usin' cocaine."

"May I use your phone?" Billy asked.

Xav stood and offered his chair to Billy, who waved him off and reached across the desk for the phone. "This is Billy. Get somebody to make a list of every drug overdose we've had in this county over the past year. I want to know what drug they overdosed from and if it was their usual drug of choice or something else…. You heard me right." Billy became irritated. "Get it from the coroner's office and do the legwork." Billy hung up.

"Twyla Fay, do we have a file on the two additional boys?" Xav asked.

"I'm compilin' it now. I just need the medical examiner's report on the mother."

"Okay." Xav considered her evenly for a long moment.

"What?" she asked.

"It would be interesting to know if Bright Horizons is the only foster facility that has kids missing."

Her eyes went wide. "I'll have Sally Ann call and get every report on every foster facility and foster home."

"Good idea. John, do we know if any other county has multiple missing children?"

"When Twyla Fay and I corrected the NCMEC data, we checked all the other counties. Every county has missing kids, but they seem to resolve within twenty-four hours or so. Mostly runaways. We're the only one with multiple missing kids and all boys."

"For information purposes, can we keep updated printouts of kids missing in other counties and clip it to our dry-wipe board?"

"I'm on it," John said.

"Great. Twyla Fay, why don't you show us what you have on your map and calendar?"

SIX HOURS later, Evan looked up from the documents he'd been reviewing and combed his fingers through his hair. Carol had long since left, and Evan guessed he was the only one remaining at the office. Outside, the sun had set and tendrils of gray clouds streaked the dimming sky, obscuring the moon. More rain. The Drought Management Advisory Council had upgraded the western part of the state from "abnormally dry" to "moderate drought," but Carver County was expecting more rain. Just as well, since the humidity had been steadily building to clothes-sticking-to-your-body thick over the past few days.

Evan returned the last stack of documents to the banker's box marked *Davies, Box 4*, and headed home for the evening.

He showered and traded his suit in favor of a pair of bermuda shorts and a polo shirt before heading downstairs to make himself some dinner. He'd just sat down at the table to eat when he heard insistent meowing from the back porch. He smiled as he filled a saucer with cat food and set it on the back steps. He looked up to see a flash of lightning on the horizon. The distant rumble of thunder followed a few moments later.

"I may just have to give you a name," he told the cat, who purred his approval as Evan stroked his gray fur. "What do you think of Thunder?"

The cat ignored this and went back to eating.

"Yeah, I thought you might say that." Evan rinsed and refilled the empty water bowl before returning to his own dinner. He gazed out the window and watched lightning dance over the clouds.

By confronting Faison, he'd accomplished nothing except pissing him off. It wasn't as though Faison ever treated him particularly well, but things would get a lot worse now. Faison would keep him more out of the loop than ever, and he'd give Talley more leeway to run things behind the scenes. But seriously, accusing him of running for DA? He wasn't the slightest bit interested in the baggage that came with elected office. He was perfectly happy doing what he was doing.

And what's that? Kowtowing to Faison? the little voice in his head nagged.

A vision of Quinn kneading his hospital blanket filled his mind. No one should have to go through what he had, let alone a kid of eleven. At least there'd been no evidence that Quinn had also been raped.

And that absolves you of guilt?

He pushed his half-empty dinner plate away. He hadn't given up private practice to sit back and do nothing. He wanted to make a difference, to make sure no kid ever had to deal with the hell of an addicted parent. He'd *asked* for drug cases. He'd gone out of his way to hire lawyers for the DA's office—*good* lawyers—who cared as much as he did. Now he was just going to back down, take it on the chin, and be a good little boy for Faison and his cronies?

He leaned back in his chair and noticed Thunder was gazing up at him. "What?"

Thunder flicked his tail and went back to eating his food.

"You think I'm being a pain in the ass too, don't you?" Evan massaged the bridge of his nose and closed his eyes. Xav was right, even if it irked him to admit it. They needed to work together on this, even if it meant fighting whatever crazy shit Xav stirred up in him.

Fuck this.

He glanced at his cell phone: 10:21 p.m. Twyla Fay had told him that Xav was in the office today, back in full swing. *After visiting me.* He picked up his cell phone and stabbed at an icon.

"Sheriff's office, Deputy Carson."

"John? It's Evan Fairchild."

"Mr. Fairchild, what can I do for you?"

"Is Deputy Constantine around, by any chance?"

"No, sir. He left about an hour ago to grab a drink with some of the guys over at Buster's. They're celebratin' because he's been cleared for duty and Twyla Fay's been promoted to administrative assistant," John explained. "Matter of fact, I'm 'bout to leave and join them."

This surprised Evan. He figured the deputies would be more standoffish with an outsider like Xav. He had to give Xav credit. "I see."

"Would you like me to give him a message for you?"

"No," Evan said. "But thanks for offering."

CHAPTER TWENTY-FIVE

FIVE MINUTES later, having slipped barefoot into a pair of well-worn boat shoes, Evan hopped in his car and made his way over to Buster's. The place wasn't much to look at, but it was popular with folks in law enforcement. Buster, a balding ex-cop who'd opened the place after retiring from Duplin County, didn't water down his drinks or the stories of his exploits when he'd been on the force. Years ago, Evan had often joined his law partners for drinks here because Buster liked to feature Carolina microbrews on tap. Since he'd come to work for the DA, Evan could count on one hand the number of times he'd paid Buster a visit, and most of them had been with defense counsel for a quick drink after a trial.

Tonight, as with most nights, the place was brimming with cops and lawyers, a few of whom recognized him and waved their hellos. Evan spotted Xav sitting with a group of deputies toward the back of the room, his face partially obscured in shadow, a beer in his hand.

"Have any Red Oak on tap?" Evan asked the bartender.

"Battlefield Bock. I've got Beer Army Angels if you want something lighter," the bartender answered.

"Battlefield."

Evan took a long drink before heading over to Xav's table, then another on the way. He needed to take the edge off his ragged nerves. He wasn't sure how Xav would respond after their conversation, and the thought of meeting him in a bar on professional time, so to speak, set him off-balance.

Evan recognized most of the men and wasn't surprised by their shocked expressions when they saw him. "Gentlemen." He raised his glass, and a few of them responded in kind.

"To what do we owe the honor, counsel?" Xav asked.

"Do you have a minute? I'd like to speak with you."

Xav raised an eyebrow.

"About that child fatality," Evan said, bristling. The last thing he wanted was to add grist to the rumor mill and have Xav's companions think this was anything but business.

Xav set his pale ale on the table, excused himself, and got to his feet.

Evan downed his beer and set the empty glass on the bar as Xav followed him outside.

"Must be pretty important, if you came looking for me," Xav said. Not hostile, merely matter-of-fact.

"It is," Evan countered, positioning himself so that Xav had his back to the brick wall of the building.

The thunder sounded closer now, and the breeze had picked up. It smelled like rain and hot asphalt and cigarette smoke. "I told you I'd think about working together, and I did. But I need you to tell me what you have in mind. How you expect this to work."

Xav eyed Evan warily, then shrugged and shoved his hands into his pockets. "In the past seven years, there's been an extraordinary increase in the number of young children taken for purposes of exploitation. Boys in particular."

Evan thought he saw something like pain flicker across Xav's features. He'd noticed it before, and now he wondered what caused it.

"Kids like Quinn and Winter—prepubescent, fair-skinned, blue-eyed—command the highest dollar for traffickers. Two to three times what girls are worth. And every boy missing from this county fits that bill."

"Shit." Evan suddenly wished he hadn't downed the beer quite so quickly. The same queasy feeling he'd had when he'd spoken to the medical examiner was back with a vengeance. "What about the drugs?"

Xav's expression turned the darkest Evan had seen it yet. "Drugs make it easier for kids to perform, and they become far easier to manage once they're addicted."

Evan clenched his jaw and forced himself to release the tension there. Breathe in for four counts, hold for four counts, exhale for four counts, hold for four counts....

"Has there been an increase in drugs on the streets since shrimp season started?" Xav asked.

It was Evan's turn to frown. When he'd calculated the numbers for Faison, he'd used annual reports. He hadn't had any reason to analyze a shorter period. "I only know the annual numbers off the top of my head, but there has been a substantial increase in cocaine usage in the county over the past year. What's the correlation?"

"I think trawlers are bringing drugs in and taking kids out."

Damn Faison and his fucked-up bullshit! No. This was *his* bullshit, not Faison's. He'd allowed Faison to make him manipulate the figures when he should have stood up to the man. Not to mention, he was certain the late trawler on the night of the shooting was key to the investigation.

Drops of rain sizzled on the sidewalk, and steam rose from the surface. A drop fell on Xav's nose. Evan resisted the urge to brush it away and returned his focus to Xav's case. "And the brothel's an old fish processing plant," Evan put in.

From the look on Xav's face, this was news to him.

"How do you want to work this?" Evan pressed.

"I need you to analyze the drug activity since shrimp season started, and I need to compare it to our activity. Then we need to find out what Quinn knows." His brow knitted in a frown. "I'm asking for your help."

Evan weighed how he wanted to manage this without having Faison all over his ass.

Before he could speak, Xav continued. "Now it's your turn."

"What?"

"I've told you what I think. Now you tell me what you think."

Evan inhaled slowly and pushed thoughts of Faison out of his mind. "I'm operating on a hunch. Cocaine traffic is up countywide, but busts are down along the usual I-95 mule route. Which means it's getting here some other way. It got me thinking about the shrimp boats. Then this thing happened with you and the boys, and a witness mentioned seeing a trawler putting in late that night."

"I saw that in the witness report, but so what? There are more trawlers around here than there are cars in LA."

"Shrimpers don't stay out late. They pull in to port much earlier in the evening. It's odd that it was out at that time of night."

Xav was thoughtful for a long moment. "Why did you space during the interview with Quinn? Something he said got to you," he asked softly.

Evan flinched. By now, the rain had begun to fall steadily. He ignored the water that dripped down Xav's forehead and cheeks. Evan's heart beat harder. Xav was too close, and every fiber of Evan's being protested, telling him he needed to get the hell out of here or something bad would happen. "It had nothing to do with—"

"I think it had *everything* to do with Quinn," Xav prodded.

"You don't know what you're talking about." Xav's intuition infuriated Evan. He read him too well. Too well and too easily. And this needed to stop. He needed to leave before he lost his temper.

"Tell me there isn't something going on with you that doesn't meet the eye and I'll drop it," Xav pressed.

"Don't try to psychoanalyze me!" He shoved Xav in the chest, and a clap of thunder overhead set Evan's heart galloping. He grabbed Xav's T-shirt and pushed him hard against the bricks, panting. He didn't know if he wanted to hit Xav for trying to tear down his walls or surrender to the gentle understanding in those deep green eyes.

Xav stared back at him, and Evan braced for a struggle, but instead of pushing back, Xav put his hands over Evan's so gently that Evan gasped in response. "I'm sorry. I didn't mean to—"

Evan wanted Xav. And for once, he didn't fight it. Adele's "Set Fire to the Rain" filled the night air when someone opened the front door of the bar, and he grabbed Xav's arm and shoved him around the corner of the building. He took Xav's face in his hands and kissed him hard, his tongue tangling with Xav's as the rain ran down their faces.

They hadn't kissed before, when they'd fucked in the seedy beach motel. But the taste of Xav's mouth, with a hint of the beer he'd been drinking, made Evan's cock fill and press against Xav's thigh. He wanted more from Xav and he wanted it *now*. He wanted Xav naked. Wanted to hear Xav moan and know *he* was the reason Xav lost it. He wanted to feel Xav's smooth skin, dig his fingers into the muscles of his ass.

Lightning lit the parking lot and a sharp crack of thunder immediately followed.

What the fuck are you doing? the voice in Evan's head yelled. He came back to himself with a start. Half the sheriff's office was inside the building, a car could pull into the lot at any moment.

Evan disengaged from Xav, backing up and nearly tripping over a concrete wheel stop at the end of the closest parking space. Xav reached out to help him, but Evan twisted to avoid the touch. He couldn't let Xav touch him again.

Xav looked as shocked as Evan felt. For a moment, neither of them spoke. Then Evan, knowing he had to do *something* to get things back on track, said, "I'll be in touch tomorrow about seeing Quinn."

Xav said nothing as Evan walked quickly to his car and slipped inside.

XAV USED his T-shirted shoulder to wipe the rain from his face as he headed back into the tavern. He stopped at the bar to order a shot of Scotch, and headed back to the group happy to see that John had joined them.

"Everything all right?" Twyla Fay asked.

Xav reclaimed his seat at the table, downed the Scotch, and chased it with the beer. "I'm hoping Mr. Fairchild will help us. He has drug stats for the county that we don't have. I'd like to have that information. I think it'll help us get to the bottom of this." Xav hoped the answer seemed a plausible enough reason for Evan to have sought him out. He raised his beer glass. "Congratulations again, Twyla Fay. Well done!"

Everyone at the table joined the toast, and the celebration resumed.

CHAPTER TWENTY-SIX

EVAN TOSSED his keys onto the kitchen counter, flipped the docked iPhone on, and slipped off his soggy shoes. His hands shook as he grabbed the kitchen towel and rubbed his dripping hair. He eyed the fridge and debated snagging a beer, then decided he needed something stronger. He walked into the living room and retrieved a bottle from the back of the sideboard cabinet. Evan Williams 23 Year Old Bourbon, a gift from one of his former partners at the law firm after he'd won a five-million-dollar verdict. He wasn't sure why he'd saved it all these years, but he *was* sure it was time to make a dent in it.

Dark. Cold.

Glass and bottle in hand, Evan settled into his ancient rocking chair on the back porch. The thunderstorm had passed, but the rain stubbornly remained. The sound of the water rushing down the old drainpipes onto the brick driveway was soothing somehow. Evan ignored his damp clothes. He figured it was penance for yet another total fuckup.

Irritated, he pushed thoughts of Xav from his mind and thought about Quinn. Xav was right, of course. He was in this up to his emotional eyeballs, and no matter what he told himself, he was at least as invested as Xav was.

He took a long swallow of the bourbon and closed his eyes as the burn bled down his throat into his chest. Quinn's face filled his mind when he closed his eyes. *"In the floor. With bars on top of it. Wet, dark... so cold...."* The words echoed in his brain, and he opened his eyes again.

The headlights of a car bounced off the house behind him, illuminating the puddles that had formed in the backyard. He swirled the alcohol around in his glass and hoped Thunder had found a dry place to spend the evening. Maybe he should get the cat a collar and let him inside at night. Somewhere it wasn't cold and wet.

"In the floor. With bars on top of it. Wet, dark... so cold...." The terror he saw in Quinn's eyes mirrored his once long-ago fear.

"Fuck." Evan finished the bourbon and poured himself another.

"Please, I can't go back there! I promise I'll be good. I promise—" Not Quinn's voice this time. His own youthful one.

Evan sucked down the second drink and the voices faded. The animals who had taken Quinn and his brother didn't care what they did to them. *Raped over and over.*

Evan tapped his foot against the wood porch, ran a hand through his damp hair, then shot to his feet. He took the bottle by its neck, gripping it so tightly his knuckles grew white. He walked to the screen door, opened it, and stepped outside.

And Faison. *Fucking bastard.* He didn't give a shit about Quinn. Didn't give a shit about Winter. Faison probably wouldn't even bother to learn their names. They were faceless victims to him. Nothing more than fodder to bolster his latest spin to show the people of Dare's Landing how much they needed him to keep them safe.

"Safe." Evan laughed, then tightened his jaw until his teeth ached. "Fuck safe. There is no safe."

"Please, I can't go back there! I promise I'll be good. I promise—"

Back inside, Evan thought it ironic that Muse's "Dead Inside" emanated from the iPhone. It mirrored how he felt as he filled his glass again. He left the bottle on the entry table and stared at himself in the front hall mirror as he drank.

He'd done nothing to help get drugs off the street, and now he was wasting all his time on a small-time case because his fucking boss wanted to make a point? This wasn't about ego. Hell, if it had been about his ego, he'd never have taken the job, let alone stayed after Faison was elected! He'd taken the job because....

Why? He'd told himself he'd taken the job because he wanted to make a difference. But it ran deeper than that. He'd seen what drugs did to people. *Good* people. People who worked their asses off and still barely made enough to make ends meet. People who actually tried to take care of their kids. He'd seen firsthand how drugs destroyed lives. The story played out the same every time like a fucking horror movie.

Sure, he'd heard there *were* missing kids, but what the fuck had he done about it? Nothing!

He still remembered watching the social worker as she'd shoved all his clothing into a black plastic bag, along with the two ratty stuffed animals he slept with. A garbage bag. Then he'd watched her carry his meager possessions out to her car. He'd been eleven.

"*I'll get you back,*" his mother had sworn to him, her cheeks streaked with tears. "*I promise.*" And he'd believed her with all his might. But six years later, she was dead from a cocaine overdose, and there was no going back.

"Fuck!" Evan threw his empty glass at the mirror. Both the mirror and the glass shattered, sending shards flying.

He heard Dr. Sampson's words. "*You have a right to be angry, Chance. But being angry isn't going to make things right.*"

He slammed a fist against the shattered mirror. He wouldn't let the bastards who took the boys do this to anyone else.

"*In the floor. With bars on top of it. Wet, dark... so cold....*"

He remembered the dark, being certain he would die of cold. Or just die. Because it was easier than going crazy piece by piece, until there was nothing left but the screams in his mind.

CHANCE STARED *up at the ceiling. He'd lost track of what day it was. At first he'd marked the days with small tracks in the dust, but some days he still seemed to lose. He guessed he'd been in this place at least forty days.*

He got to his feet and began to pace back and forth. Eight steps toward the door. Eight steps back. He dragged a finger along the seam where the cinder blocks met, briefly lifting his hand where the toilet and sink blocked the way. Back and forth. Back and forth.

He tried closing his eyes and imagining he was sitting on the banks of the creek near the trailer park with the fishing pole he'd made out of bamboo and string. He tried to smell the grass and the dirt. He tried to hear the rushing water and feel the drops that splattered upward from the rocks. But all he caught was the faint scent of bleach from when they'd mopped three nights before. At least they'd let him out for an hour, even if he couldn't go near the other kids.

"Fuck!" he shouted. "Let me the fuck out of here!" He kicked the toilet bowl and caught a whiff of urine. "Let me out! I didn't do anything. I couldn't help it. It wasn't my fault. He made me."

Nobody answered. Chance knew the guards heard him. They just didn't give a flying fuck about it.

The kid he'd fought with, Carl, had jumped him in the courtyard and grabbed him by the balls. "Little ass-fucker," Carl had said, his face so close to Chance's that Chance smelled his sour breath. "I'm gonna show you what a real man feels like." One of the other kids had stood so the guards wouldn't see them—if the guards even gave a shit—and Carl shoved a hand down Chance's pants before Chance had kneed Carl in the groin. Carl had gotten a good punch to Chance's jaw and given him a black eye before Chance nailed Carl hard enough to send him to the ground. The guards had pulled him off Carl as he'd repeatedly hit and kicked him while some of the other kids egged him on.

"Come on! Let me out. I told you he started it. Let me the fuck out of here!"

Still nothing.

Fuckers. Chance kicked the toilet again, jamming one of his toes. It hurt like a beast, but it felt better than pacing. Again and again, he kicked it. If he felt the pain, he was still alive. It had been one of the few things they'd taught him in that hellhole.

"Let me out! I didn't start it. I told you!"

This time he slapped the wall with his open hand. Still nothing. He made a fist and clenched his jaw, then punched the concrete. Holy fuck, that hurt! But maybe if he broke his fingers or hand, they'd have to take him out. He punched it again, hard this time. He punched the wall until tears streamed down his face.

"Let me out! Let me out!"

"Let me out!" Evan shouted, waking himself up. He sat up in bed, panting and covered in sweat. He hadn't had that particular dream in more than ten years. He didn't need to ask himself why. Ghosts never exorcised returned to familiar haunting grounds. Doing the right thing by Quinn and the other boys wouldn't banish the past, but it might help change the future.

XAV STOOD on his small balcony overlooking the river and shook his head in wonder. He'd never met anyone as hot as Evan, never had a need to be with someone as much as he did Evan, all while he had no intention of being part of his emotional fallout. It was clear Evan was brilliant and dedicated to his job, but as far as Xav could see, the man's demons were huge, he had no personal life—certainly no social skills—and sweated confusion like a sinner among saints.

He braced the railing with both hands and flexed his shoulders and back. The sharp pain had subsided to a dull ache, and he hoped he could begin working out again in a couple of days. Man, he hated getting shot.

His phone vibrated in his pocket, and he withdrew it and looked at the text message. *Call your mother.*

He texted back. *Your son is sleeping now. Please remind him again tomorrow.*

Within seconds, he received another text message. *Call your mother tomorrow or she'll come to North Carolina.*

Xav snorted and sent another message. *She wouldn't do that to me.*

She shot back, *She would and bring the entire family. And stay for a month.*

Xav chuckled. *Your son surrenders. He'll call tomorrow.*

She responded with a heart and *My son got his smarts from this mother.* Xav returned a heart. He was certain he had the best mother in the world.

CHAPTER TWENTY-SEVEN

EVAN WOKE up to sunlight streaming through the blinds and realized to his horror that he'd slept right through his alarm. A miserable night of bad dreams, all but one of which he blessedly couldn't remember, and now this. *Perfect*. Evan massaged away the dull pain in his hand and shrugged off the memory of the dream.

He pulled on his running shorts and a T-shirt, grabbed his phone, and padded down the creaky wooden staircase. Through the kitchen window, the sun glinted off the damp leaves of shrubs and trees in the backyard, sending sparkles of color dancing on the morning air. From his phone, he sent an e-mail to Carol to reschedule his ten thirty meeting for the next day. It could wait. He had important shit to do.

He needed a run to clear his head, even if it meant he wouldn't get to the office until after eleven. He opened the back door, hoping to find Thunder waiting beyond the screened-in porch, but he was conspicuously absent. Evan refilled the water and food anyhow, placed them on the top step, and hoped the ants wouldn't find them before the cat did. He was out the door a few minutes later, headed toward the water. He'd run along Front Street and over to the park, and maybe he'd cross the drawbridge if he felt up to it.

Already, tourists milled around the river walks and shops downtown. The season's most popular regatta would begin the weekend after next, and the population would swell as people arrived to watch the Neuse River event. As he ran by the docks where he kept his small sailboat, Evan wished he had time to compete. But as each year passed, the summers only grew busier. He'd be lucky if he could find a free weekend before Labor Day to take her out to Ocracoke Island. At least he'd gotten in a few short sails this summer. Better than nothing. He wished he had time to sail her *now*.

He thought about Xav and last night's conversation. What was it about Xav that always took him to the edge? Rather, made him lose it? He debated calling Dr. Sampson, then chuckled to himself. He'd been doing fine on his own for years now. He'd accepted that there were things he had no control over, and had been great at controlling his anger. But even now the strange push and pull of Xav Constantine dogged him. And this case with the boys…. He mulled over yet again what Freddy had told him. He and Xav were on this case to find the same answers, but for different reasons.

We all have our ghosts.

Ghosts like the ones nipping at his heels. Last night he'd wanted far more than that single kiss, but he'd run away. And even if he wanted more than a single kiss, what the hell did he have to offer Xav except a whole lot of baggage?

This isn't about you and him. It's about Quinn and boys like him. Like you once were.

He'd do something about it this time, even if it meant his job. He wouldn't sit back and let Quinn or any other kid live through that kind of hell. If he wanted to get to the bottom of this, he needed Xav's expertise. He and Xav would speak with Quinn again, together.

XAV SAT at his desk and reviewed the file on the additional two missing boys, then looked up at Twyla Fay's wall map. He stood, intending to get a closer look at the map, and his cell phone rang. He looked at it and smiled before answering. "Morning, Mom."

"You haven't called me. I'm going to hang up so you can call me."

He chuckled. "How's the most beautiful woman in the world this morning?"

"*Más o menos.* Your youngest brother needs another lecture from you."

"What did he do now?"

"Your sister has no date for prom. I told him he should take her. Can you believe he said no to me?"

"I don't believe she has no prom date. In fact, I'm willing to bet that fifty guys asked her and she's being conceited again."

"Don't get technical."

"Put her on."

"She's at school. It's Tuesday. What's the matter with you? Is your new job making your brain soft? I think it is. You didn't call me to tell me someone shot you. I have to hear it on the news. You said North Carolina was going to be safe. You said the job was less dangerous than work with the FBI. You lied. Most mothers would yell at you. I don't yell at you and still you don't call me."

Guilt flooded him. His work with CARD was almost never in the news. The only time his family knew about his injuries was when he told them. Now, he hadn't given the news a second thought. "I'm sorry, Mom. I should have called."

"Next time, if there is a next time—*Madre de Dios*, I pray there is no next time—I want to hear from you *pronto*. Call your sister and brother. I love you. Bye."

"Love you too," he said to no one. She'd already hung up. He texted his baby sister. *Pick one of the guys who asked you to prom or I'm going to be your date.*

She texted back immediately. *As if! They'll arrest you for being a dirty old man!* A few seconds later came *You're going to help me with my dress and makeup, right?*

He shook his head in exasperation and texted, *Choose.*

He received, *If he turns out to be an idiota, I'm reporting you for child endangerment.*

He snorted and sent back, *Deal. Don't text in class.*

He texted his little brother, *Got you covered. No prom.*

He got back, *#BestQueerBroEver Next time call when you get shot. Not cool, bro.*

He sighed and sent back, *#BestLittleBroEver I will.*

He rose from his chair, went to the map, and studied the little flags that impaled it. Twyla Fay had done an excellent job and even provided a legend, but there was no pattern, there were no similarities. No two locations the same. Different times of day, different days of the week. With parents, without. He backed up to the doorway to look at the map from a distance. The colorful flags looked like a psychotic connect-the-dots test.

When Twyla Fay came up behind him, his defense training kicked in without warning and he spun, sending her off-balance. He reached out to steady her as she caught herself against the wall. The look on her face was one of pure astonishment as she let out a yip.

"I'm sorry. I didn't mean to startle you," Xav said quickly.

"Like ta give a girl a heart attack with moves like that. What are y'all doing standing in the doorway?"

He breathed in calm, and breathed out his adrenaline response, his reaction having surprised him as well. "Looking at the map. I'm still looking for a pattern."

"Don't waste your time. John and me stared at it for hours. Y'all might as well throw a dart and see where it lands." He looked at her and she looked at him. "What?" she asked.

Xav turned back to look at the map. "The middle."

John walked up behind Twyla Fay. "The middle of what?"

Xav walked to the map and put the tip of his finger to the middle of the flags, and peered closely at the map. "What's at the corner of Liberty and Independence?"

"Nothin' much. A big park with a Hispanic church at the edge of it. Why?" John asked.

"What church?" Xav asked.

"Good Shepherd's. Why?" John repeated.

Xav went to his desk and shuffled paperwork until he found Victor's rap sheet. He read the profile and miscellaneous data, walked back to John and Twyla Fay, and pointed at the detail on the page. *Volunteer: LEAP Our Good Shepherd's Church.*

Twyla Fay gasped. "Oh, my Lord!"

"Go through every file and look for any link, no matter how remote, to the church and pull everything we have on it. I'll be back in a couple of hours."

XAV SAT on his bike across the street from the church. A sister carrying a large picnic basket walked a long line of children of various ages from the front doors, around the side of the church, to the park next to it. She placed the basket on a picnic table and began removing items and setting them on the table as the kids scattered to play. He reached for his cell phone and dialed Billy Kenner's direct line at the office.

Billy answered with a sharp "Kenner."

"Billy, it's Xav."

"I hear you may be onto something."

"Maybe. I'm across the street from the church. What do we know about it?"

"Padre Paolo, the monsignor, is a nice old man. Too nice if you ask me. He takes in the homeless at night, and we've had a few callouts when the drunks and drug addicts and such give him a hard time. There've been a few thefts from the church. We keep tellin' him not to take in the more questionable folks, but he sees everyone as God's children no matter how drunk or high they might be."

"Do we have anyone we can put on the inside? As a night aid or something?"

"Not who people won't know."

"Can we put a deputy in the place at night?"

"We'd have to give the padre a reason. He's big on allowing the homeless their privacy."

"Why would he allow a she-male to work with kids?"

"A what?"

"A prostitute."

"Victor's a prostitute? I mean, not that I doubt what you're sayin', but…. I don't know how to say this without offending you."

Billy was flustered and Xav felt bad for him. "You won't offend me. Please google she-dash-male." Billy sighed long and loud, and Xav listened as he typed on the computer keyboard.

"What in tarnation—is that a man or woman?"

"It's a man who has had breast augmentation coupled with hormones."

"My God. Are those breasts real?"

"Insofar as he's had breast augmentation and taken hormones, yes."

"But… why on God's green earth would a man do somethin' like that?" Billy sounded appalled.

"She-males work in the sex or pornography industries."

"Forgive me when I say there is something not right about a man doin' that to his body."

"Victor is a known sex worker, a pimp, and has a criminal record. I question why the padre would allow him to volunteer to work with kids."

"Padre Paolo believes everyone is equal in God's eyes, and truthfully, until this shooting come up, we had no reason to suspect Victor for anything other than runnin' a brothel and mistreatin' the girls. Do you want me to talk to the padre?"

Xav weighed his options. "No. Let's first pin down whether there is a link between the church and the missing boys."

EVAN STOPPED in the office just long enough to check his phone messages and e-mail, then headed out to speak to Xav at the sheriff's office.

"I'm sorry, Mr. Fairchild," Twyla Fay told him brightly, "but he's out and I don't expect him back for a few hours."

Evan knew exactly where he'd find Xav.

CHAPTER TWENTY-EIGHT

AROUND NOON, Evan arrived at the docks not far from the brothel where the shootout had taken place. The bright yellow crime scene tape fluttering in the thick breeze didn't help his mood.

"Evan?" Xav stared at him. Judging by the tone of Xav's voice, he was surprised to see him.

"Deputy Constantine." The name felt awkward on his lips, but using Xav's first name felt even stranger, and calling him Xav was entirely out of the question. Evan barely recognized Xav, dressed as he was in a well-cut suit and silk tie, the ubiquitous braid tucked under the back collar of his jacket. Sheriff Winston preferred that his plainclothes officers wore suits, and except for the first time he'd seen Xav at work, Xav had always been in jeans and a T-shirt.

Xav leaned against a pylon, a smile on his face. "You look like hell."

"And you look like you're playing dress-up in your daddy's Sunday best."

Xav grinned outright. "You wouldn't know a fashion statement if you were served with it, counsel."

"Asshole."

"Bitch."

"If you're aiming to give me a bigger headache than I already have," Evan countered, brushing the knot of his own tie with his fingers, "you'll have to do better than that."

Xav's expression grew serious. "What's your plan?"

"We both need answers from Quinn. Let's go talk to him."

"Lead the way."

Xav followed Evan to his car. "Need a lift?" Evan asked as he pulled his keys from his pocket and unlocked the driver's side door.

"I have my bike," Xav answered with a nod in the direction of the motorcycle Evan recalled from the night they'd first met. Xav admired his Jag. "Nice. '72 E-type?"

"'71," Evan said, surprised that Xav had guessed almost right. "Found her rusting in someone's garage in Elizabeth City. Rebuilt the engine myself." He didn't add that it had taken him nearly three years to do it. "A friend of mine in Greenville did the body work."

Xav nodded appreciatively. "I'm impressed."

Evan shrugged. "I like working with my hands."

"Rain check on the ride? I'd love to see how she handles."

"Sure." Evan agreed before he even considered the implications, and he wanted to kick himself in the ass. What was it about Xav that always made him forget himself?

THEY ARRIVED at the nondescript building a few blocks south of Route 70 fifteen minutes later, and Evan got out of the car holding a small bouquet of wildflowers.

Xav almost burst into laughter and raised an eyebrow.

Evan smiled a genuine smile. "Things tend to go a little smoother when I'm gentlemanly."

"Thanks for the intel."

"My pleasure. Though I highly doubt you would come remotely close to my Southern charm."

Xav responded with a snort before following Evan up the path to the front door.

To Xav, Bright Horizons looked more like a four-story prison than a group home. His suspicions were confirmed when they entered the building and met with a metal detector and two guards. Evan produced his ID and Xav produced his badge, yet they still had to go through the detector. Xav was accustomed to detectors but wasn't used to them being obvious. Every juvenile facility and nearly every school in LA had them installed in doorframes—not only to enter the buildings but to enter restrooms, classrooms, and administrative areas as well. Woe befell anyone who tried to sneak a gun or a knife into a government facility. Unfortunately, no one had invented drug detectors that worked, but schools usually had a police liaison officer who could call in a K-9 unit at will. But a foster home? Xav shook his head. The place reminded him of MacLaren Hall in LA and made his skin crawl.

Evan signed in and pushed the clipboard across the counter to Xav. He completed and signed it as Evan went to a wall phone and called upstairs. "Rebecca Wilhelm, please." A smile filled his face. "Why, yes, this is Evan Fairchild. Is this the lovely Pauline?"

Xav snorted quietly. As if lovely Pauline couldn't tell who was at the other end of the phone from the multicamera surveillance feed.

"Well, if you'd be so kind as to send an elevator down, I'd be happy to…. Thank you kindly, pretty lady." Evan hung up and Xav rolled his eyes. Evan smiled, clearly in his element.

The elevator arrived with a groan, and Xav wondered how old the building was. Xav nearly guffawed at the ancient porcelain buttons when they stepped inside. "Fourth floor, please and thank you kindly, sir," he said in his best falsetto.

Evan glared at him as he pressed the button. "Don't get cute up there."

"I'm always cute," Xav deadpanned.

"You're not funny."

"I'm always funny." Teasing Evan had become his new favorite pastime. He was so damn easy to tease!

Clearly exasperated, Evan gave up and donned a smile as the door opened, and they stepped off the elevator into a small reception area manned by the lovely Pauline. Or would that be womanned? Xav didn't know.

"Why, Mr. Fairchild! Are those for me?"

Evan leaned over the high desk and met Pauline's starry-eyed gaze. "You're looking particularly beautiful today, Pauline," he drawled as he handed the bouquet to her. "Is that a new dress?"

Xav found himself half wishing he were on the receiving end of Evan's charm.

"Why, yes, it is, Mr. Fairchild," she said as her already pink cheeks flushed crimson. "Larry bought it for my birthday in June."

"He and Larry Jr. doing well?"

"They're both just fine. Matter of fact," Pauline said, "they took second place at the Blue Marlin tournament a few months ago. Larry's still braggin' about it round town." She laughed, then added, "And so am I, it seems."

"Can't say as I blame you." Evan flashed another of his brilliant smiles and held Pauline's hand just a moment longer than necessary.

"And this is Deputy Constantine," Evan said.

Xav had had his fill of Southern charm and was relieved when Evan moved on. "It's a pleasure to meet you," Xav greeted formally.

"You've met Rufus," Pauline added as she got to her feet and motioned to a man standing near the doorway.

Evan inclined his head. "Good to see you, Rufus. Xav, this is Rufus Searles, the aide who oversees the community room."

Xav gave Rufus a curt nod in greeting.

"Nice to meet you. Right this way, please," Rufus said.

They followed Rufus through a door and into a lobby, Xav bringing up the rear as Evan and Pauline continued to chat about a recent fish fry at one of the churches and how the Walmart they'd built outside of Charlesville had put the local supermarket out of business. Xav heard several "bless his hearts." He might not speak Southern, but he knew enough to know that wasn't a compliment.

A rude buzzer sounded and a pneumatic lock turned, and Rebecca Wilhelm entered the lobby through a security door. "Mr. Fairchild," she greeted as she held a folder to her chest and shook Evan's hand. "Mr. Constantine."

Xav didn't receive a handshake. He received a nod and didn't think that was entirely fair. He decided to yank her chain a little. "Deputy," he corrected.

She cleared her throat. "Deputy Constantine."

Evan glared at him before turning to her. "Thank you for meeting us here, Mrs. Wilhelm. We appreciate your making it here on such short notice."

"You're welcome. Your assistant, Carol, called my office and asked for a copy of the report we filed with the SBI." She handed the folder to Evan.

Evan took the folder with yet another false smile. "Thank you, Mrs. Wilhelm. It's very kind of you to bring it to me."

"You're quite welcome."

Xav repressed a smirk. Wilhelm had definitely fallen under Evan's spell. "How *did* the Haverty boys leave your custody, Ms. Wilhelm?" he asked pointedly.

"That'll be in the report, Deputy Constantine," Evan said quickly. "How is Quinn doing?"

She shook her head in disappointment. "Not a word, I'm afraid. Our psychologist tried to interview him, but he ran from the room and vomited."

"Was the psychologist male?" Xav asked.

"As a matter of fact, he was, Deputy."

Xav caught Evan's eye and thought he saw a glimmer of understanding there. "You may wish to have a female psychologist work with him."

She gave Xav the hairy eyeball. "I will take your suggestion under advisement."

"I suggest a slow approach. No direct questions at first," Xav offered politely.

When she appeared unconvinced, Evan interjected. "Deputy Constantine has worked with youth throughout his career. Although he is brash and appears to be thoughtless and is most certainly being less than diplomatic, he is quite good with them," he excused blandly.

"I am," Xav agreed with a smile.

Evan glared at Xav.

"I see. Well, I hope you have better luck with him than we did. One hour, gentlemen."

"Why the time limit?" Xav asked.

She gave him a sardonic look. "It's nearly three o'clock and I'd like to go home."

"Oh. Of course. My apologies," Xav said insincerely.

Evan glowered at him and then said with exaggerated courtesy, "I greatly appreciate you meeting us here, Mrs. Wilhelm. We'll be as quick as possible."

"Room 430B. I'll be here when you return."

"Thank you kindly," Evan said and then guided Xav by the elbow to stand in front of the security door. "Is there anything I can say to persuade you to be respectful to DSS personnel?" he asked in a whisper.

"No," Xav said flatly.

Evan sighed deeply as the door buzzed, and he opened it and gestured Xav through. "Why not?" he asked as they walked down the long corridor.

"Because they're worthless."

Evan stopped dead in his tracks and turned to Xav. "I will not debate their worth with you, but I will remind you of this. They have custody of our witness and can make it damn hard for us to speak with him. Does that register in your smartass brain?"

"Yes."

"Wonderful."

CHAPTER TWENTY-NINE

WEAK FLORESCENT lights cast a pallid glow overhead as Evan continued down the corridor. Xav followed, glancing in each room they passed. The few kids he saw looked numb, merely going through the motions required by the facility. He hated places like this. Pink's "Family Portrait" filled his mind, an inconsonant strain to complement his cynicism. They were nothing more than flesh cartel game shows. *I'll take 430B for $1,000 and a chance to fuck a kid*, he thought bitterly.

They came to Quinn's room, and Evan knocked softly on the doorjamb.

Quinn was barely a bump beneath the thin institutional blanket and didn't move.

"Quinn?" Evan asked softly.

No response.

"Quinn, it's Evan. I spoke with you at the hospital, remember? May I come in?"

No response.

Xav moved past Evan into the room. He squatted approximately eighteen inches from the bed and rested an arm on his knee. "Quinn? It's Xav. I came with Evan so I could see how you're doing."

Quinn's head slowly emerged from beneath the blanket. He looked at Xav with half-dead eyes, his pallor gray, his lips parched.

"I bet you're thirsty," Xav said gently.

No response.

"Bet your head hurts too."

Quinn continued to eye him but said nothing.

Xav checked the paper cup on the small pullout table next to the bed. It was empty, and he went to the stainless toilet-sink combination and refilled the cup. He brought it back to the table and squatted again. "I'm going to get some snacks. I'll be back in a minute."

He stood and guided Evan into the hallway, out of Quinn's earshot. "He's heavily medicated and probably hasn't eaten or had much to drink since he arrived. Let's get him some food and juice and coax him out into an open space. Do they have a social room here?"

"Yes, they do. Why would they medicate him?"

"Because he lost his brother and they wanted to head any potential anger off with medication."

Evan looked pained. "I'll ask the staff to bring a meal."

"Don't. Go to the vending machines in the lobby and get some crackers, chips, and juice. He'll be cold because his blood pressure is low, so when we get to the social room, let's sit by the windows so he has some sunshine."

Evan winced.

"Here." Xav searched his pockets and came up with about two dollars in change.

"I'll take care of it," Evan said. "They'll have change out front."

Xav watched Evan walk down the hall. Even with the stick up his ass, Evan was sexy as hell. Xav sighed as he returned to Quinn's room and leaned against the wall near the doorway.

Quinn looked at him and a quiet, hoarse word emerged. "Thanks."

"You're welcome."

Quinn continued to look at him in silence.

"How are your stitches doing?" Xav asked.

"Busted."

"Hate when that happens. You'd think they'd make 'em strong enough to last through at least one fight. Did they give you new ones?"

Quinn shook his head almost imperceptibly. "Glued 'em."

"That sucks."

"You have stitches?"

"Nope. Some nice big raspberry bruises where the bullets impacted my vest."

Evan returned with his hands full of bags of chips and crackers and a couple of bottles of juice tucked beneath an arm. Xav took the bottles and set them on the table. Evan contributed the bags to the small surface.

"Anything look decent enough to eat?" Xav asked.

Quinn studied the packages and pushed the blanket back. He struggled to sit up with a hand held to his side.

Evan bent to help him, and Xav stayed him with a gentle hand. "Do you want help?" Xav asked.

Quinn shook his head as he continued to struggle until he sat upright with a small, pain-filled grunt. He reached for the cup of water with a trembling hand and knocked it over. The look of fear in his eyes had Xav's chest tightening.

Xav retrieved the towel that hung at the side of the sink and wiped up the water, then refilled the cup. He squatted next to the bed and held it out to Quinn. "Use two hands until the medication wears off."

Quinn looked at Xav, then at the cup, and back again. Xav continued to hold it out to him. After a long beat, he took the cup and gulped the water down.

"More?"

Quinn shook his head as he went to set the cup on the tray and it flipped from his fingers.

Xav caught it deftly. "Do you want to try some juice?"

Quinn reached for a bottle of apple juice.

"Two hands until the medication wears off," Xav reminded gently.

Quinn used two hands to grasp the bottle and tried to open it with trembling fingers.

"Help?"

Quinn shook his head and continued to struggle until he unscrewed the cap. He dropped the cap as he put the bottle to his lips and stopped.

"Don't worry about it," Xav said quietly.

Quinn drank half the bottle of juice greedily as he studied the bags of chips and crackers.

"Anything look good?" Xav repeated.

Quinn set the bottle of juice on the table and fingered a bag of nacho cheese Doritos before choosing the Tostitos. He pulled at the sides of the bag until it ripped open and the chips scattered over the blanket. He looked at Xav, fear in his eyes again.

Xav offered a reassuring smile. "They're still good to eat. May I have one?"

Quinn nodded and Xav selected the chip closest to the edge of the bed and popped it into his mouth. "Pretty good."

Quinn chose one also near the edge of the bed and put it into his mouth. After a few minutes, Quinn had collected each chip one by one and was eating and drinking steadily.

"More?" Xav asked.

Quinn considered the bags again. "Which ones y'all want?"

"Anything you don't want."

"You can have those." Quinn pointed to the barbecue pork rinds before he looked up at Evan, who'd been silent. "Which ones y'all want?"

Evan gave him a small smile. "Ditto Xav. Anything you don't want."

Quinn surveyed the packages again. "Those ones." He pointed to the Ritz Crackers.

"Thank you," Evan said graciously as he took the package and opened it.

During a long, slow hour, they consumed all the chips, crackers, and juice. Quinn had color in his face again, his eyes no longer looked half-dead, and the tremors in his hands had slowed.

"You up for a walk?" Xav asked.

Fear reappeared in Quinn's eyes. "Where to?"

"I'd like to sit in the sunlight in the big room. You up for it?"

"Who's out there?"

Xav turned to Evan for help.

"It's empty right now," Evan answered.

"'Kay."

Quinn pushed the covers back, slowly withdrew his socked feet, and sat on the edge of the bed. He was dressed in sweatshirt and jeans. Absent were his belt and shoes.

"Want your slippers?" Xav asked.

"I'll get 'em." Quinn tried to stand and did a slow fall back to the bed, bracing himself on his hands as he landed.

"When we get out there, I'll get you some Tylenol," Xav said. "You up to showing me your stitches?"

"Why?"

"Because I'd like to make sure they got glued back together okay."

Quinn slid his sweatshirt up to reveal a dirty, bloodstained bandage around his waist.

Xav swore silently. "Can I take a look around the back?"

Quinn nodded and tried to turn, issuing a small squelch in pain.

"Don't turn." Without touching Quinn, Xav peered around the back to find an equally stained bandage. "Tell you what, Quinn. I'm going to go get a wheelchair."

"I can walk." Quinn tried to stand again and nearly face-planted into the floor.

"Whoa, there." Evan caught him gently and guided him back to sit on the edge of the bed. "I think I'd go with Xav's idea of a chair. I'll go see what I can find."

Quinn sat on the edge of the bed, his arms wrapped around his midriff. "Who's he?"

"Do you remember speaking to him in the hospital?"

Quinn nodded. "But who is he?"

"Evan is an assistant district attorney who works for Carver County. He's working on our shooting case."

"He a DA?"

Xav smiled. "You hear that from your parents?"

"Yeah."

"He's an assistant DA. A prosecutor."

"He gonna put me away for good?"

"Nope. He's going to help me put the guys away who shot us." Quinn looked at Xav, uncertainty filling his eyes. "He's a good guy, Quinn," Xav reassured.

Evan wheeled a chair into the room and parked it next to the bed. "Your ride's here."

Quinn struggled to his feet only long enough to pivot and sit in the chair. He settled with a sigh, and Xav removed the blanket from the bed and went to place it over is legs.

"Don't want that."

"Okay." Xav draped it over his arm. "Who do you want to push you? Me or Evan?"

"You."

"You got it." Xav handed the blanket to Evan, who accepted it willingly.

A few minutes later, they settled in the social room with sun streaming through the windows. Quinn looked out at the manicured lawn of the park next door.

"Pretty day," Xav ventured.

Quinn nodded.

"Are you up to answering a few questions?" Xav asked.

Quinn continued to look out the window. "Depends."

"Okay. Let me give you my ground rules for answering questions. First, you don't have to answer any question you don't want to answer and you don't have to explain why you don't want to answer. Second, if you do want to answer, I only want you to answer if it isn't too hard on you."

Quinn looked at him now. "Any more rules?"

"Only if you want to give me some rules."

"Like what?"

"You may have certain topics that are off-limits. And if I ask about one of those topics, you can simply say it's off-limits."

"Anything?"

"Anything," Xav assured.

"'Kay."

"I read your parents' arrest report. It says that your father was trying to sell one or both of you on a street corner. Had that happened before?"

"No. But he was real high that night and wanted more."

"The first part of the report indicates it was Winter that he was trying to sell. The second part of it indicates he was trying to sell you. Was it one of you or Winter, or both of you?"

"Both. But I didn't want 'em to arrest Winter, so I told 'em it was just me."

Xav canted his head. "What made you think you would be arrested?"

Quinn snorted. "My daddy was tryin' to make us be whores, and I seen what they do to them. They take 'em away. Sometimes they come back. Sometimes they don't."

Xav gave him a small smile. "You're pretty smart. Thanks for answering my questions."

"That's it?"

"That's it for me for now."

Evan looked up from the open folder Rebecca Wilhelm had given him. "May I ask a few questions?"

Quinn turned to him. "'Bout what?"

"This report says you disappeared from the park right down there. Is that what happened?"

Quinn rubbed his side and turned back to the windows, a faraway look settling in his eyes. "Yeah."

"Did you walk away from the park?"

Quinn shook his head. "We snuck over to talk to the man with the puppies. We went to look at 'em."

"Where was he?" Xav asked.

Quinn pointed. "Over there. He's there all the time. See?"

Xav looked out the window, and Evan rose to his feet to get a better look. "Is he there every day?" Evan asked.

"Yep."

Evan retook his seat. "Then what happened?"

"Win and me were pettin' 'em, and he said he had to take a piss and asked us to watch 'em for a few minutes. Then…." Tears suddenly welled in Quinn's eyes, and he wiped at them viciously, as if the traitors had no right to appear.

Evan reached into a pocket, withdrew a handkerchief, and held it out to Quinn.

"Don't want to get it dirty," Quinn sobbed softly.

"It's okay if it gets dirty. That's what it's for. Here." He set it on Quinn's knee.

Quinn clutched it and brought it to his mouth to smother a last sob.

"Take your time," Xav said.

Quinn wrapped his arms around his midriff and rubbed his side again as he looked out the windows.

"I'm going to get you that Tylenol," Xav said as he stood. "Would you like water or juice with it?"

Quinn shrugged without turning from the windows.

Xav squatted next to the chair. "We'll try to keep these questions short and quick. I'm also going to get someone to take a look at your stitches too."

Quinn looked at him. "'Kay."

"You okay to talk to Evan for a minute?"

Quinn looked at Evan now. "'Kay."

"Okay. I'll be right back."

CHAPTER THIRTY

XAV STRODE to the supervisor's window and slid the Plexiglas aside. "I'm sorry to interrupt you."

Rufus looked up from his paperwork. "Can I help you?"

"Tylenol for Quinn, and I need the medic on staff to take a look at his stitches."

The man looked at the clock on the wall. "Medic's gone home for the day, and you gotta get Mrs. Wilhelm to authorize a change in his plan of care for the Tylenol. We got strict orders on him."

"Can you tell me where Mrs. Wilhelm is?"

"She left."

Xav turned away, livid. He withdrew his cell phone and saw it had no reception. Realizing he couldn't simply walk outside to make a call, he turned back to the man. "May I use your phone?"

"What for?"

"To call my office."

"What for?"

"Sheriff's business."

"I suppose." He touched a button beneath the counter and the door next to him buzzed and popped open. Xav entered quickly and picked up the phone.

"Dial nine first," Rufus instructed.

Xav called Winston's direct line, and Twyla Fay answered with a chipper "Sheriff Winston's office."

Xav turned his back to Rufus and spoke in low tones. "Twyla Fay, it's Xav. Please dispatch a car to Bright Horizons Park. There's a man selling puppies on the south side of the park. Have him picked up and brought in for questioning."

"For selling puppies?"

"Suspicion of soliciting minors. I'll explain more when I get there."

"Oh, Lord. What's he look like?"

"White, average height, overweight, two-fifty, gray hair, red shirt, jeans. Cardboard box at his feet alleged to contain puppies."

"I'll dispatch a car now."

"Thanks, Twyla Fay."

"Where are you and when will you be back?"

"I'm at Bright Horizons with Evan Fairchild talking to Quinn Haverty, and it'll be at least an hour before I'm back."

"See you then."

Xav hung up. "Thank you, Rufus."

"Sure thing." He pressed the button beneath the counter and the door buzzed and popped open again.

Xav strode to the water fountain, pulled two paper cups from the dispenser, and filled them with water. Luckily, he carried Tylenol with him because his back still hurt like hell at times, and he withdrew a two-pack from his pocket as he walked back to Quinn and Evan. To his surprise, they were chatting in brief sentences about a cat named Thunder.

"Thunder's the best guard cat I've ever had," Evan said softly.

Quinn almost smiled. "Naw."

"Oh, yeah. Squirrels don't come near my persimmon tree anymore."

Xav sat down, not wanting to interrupt them, and looked out the windows. Puppy Man was still there. Xav turned back to them. "There is no such thing as a guard cat," he teased.

"You haven't met Thunder," Evan said with a twinkle in his eye. "Yet."

Xav winked at Quinn. "Something tells me I don't want to. He'd probably rip my leg off."

Now Quinn did smile, and it warmed Xav's heart. "Y'all aren't from round here," Quinn said.

"Damn. You noticed? I try hard to hide the third eye in my forehead."

Quinn smiled again. "Naw, it's 'cause you talk funny."

"You're the one with the accent. Not me."

Quinn continued to smile. "Where you from?"

"Los Angeles."

"Why're y'all here?"

"I came here so I could work with boys just like you."

"Not like they don't have kids in Los Angeles."

"They have lots of them. But none with an accent."

Quinn shook his head. "Y'all're full of it, mister."

Evan stifled a laugh. "Why, he's got you pegged, Xav."

"That he does. Here's your Tylenol."

Quinn took it from Xav and quickly downed it with water.

"Are you up for some questions if we run through them real fast?" Xav asked.

Quinn's smile fell away, but he nodded.

"So the guy went to take a piss and then what happened?" Evan asked.

"A van pulled up. Two guys got out and grabbed us. They threw us in the back and put some cloth over our face and we passed out. Next thing you know, we're in some stinkin' hole."

"Stinkin'?" Xav asked.

"Wet and smelled like fish and was real cold."

"Did the place rock like a boat?" Xav asked.

"Naw, but you could hear water hitting the walls with the tide. Like we was in a giant jar in the ocean."

"Do you remember what the guys in the van looked like?" Evan asked.

Quinn's eyes took on a haunted look again. "Yeah. They're the same two who shot at us."

"What happened after that?" Xav asked.

"Days went by. They wouldn't talk to us. Wouldn't feed us. We drank salty water from the leakin' walls. Finally, one day, Win didn't wake up easy and kept goin' back to sleep when he did. So I called help for hours and no one came...."

They waited, and when he didn't continue, Xav prompted him. "What else do you remember?"

"I guess it must have been another day or so. It's hard to keep track when you have no light to go by. Then this man, Victor, came. Said for us to chew on some little Blivian leaf things with sugar on 'em and it would wake Win up good. Except it wasn't sugar. It was real bitter, but we were so hungry we didn't care. And Victor was right. Woke Win right up. We didn't sleep for a long time and kept trying to find ways to get out of the hole. There were all these vents, but we couldn't reach 'em. More time went by and we didn't get any more leafs. Got all shaky and threw up. Felt so bad...."

Xav could tell that Quinn's emotional ballast was about to give way. "When you say Blivian, did Victor pronounce it Bolivian?"

"Yeah. Just like that. Anyway, right about the time I lost my voice from callin' some more, Victor came with more leafs. That's all we ate was leafs and we'd be all up for a long time, then get sick again...." He squeezed his eyes shut. "We felt like we was gonna die." A traitorous tear made a jagged trek down Quinn's cheek, and he used Evan's handkerchief to wipe it away. "The next time Victor came, he said Win had to go with him if we wanted more leafs. It was a long time before Win came back, and when he did, he wasn't the same no more." Tears streamed Quinn's cheeks now.

"But he came back with a blanket and lotsa leafs and a pretty little painted seashell."

The mention of the seashell caught Evan's interest, but he said nothing in favor of Quinn continuing his story.

"Victor said he'd earned it. When I asked Win where he went, all he'd say was *mariposa* over and over. He kept gettin' worse and worse 'til he wouldn't talk to me no more. So I tore up the blanket and made a rope like they do in the movies. I don't know how many tries it took, but I finally got it over a pipe up high on the wall. And me and Win climbed up and out one of the vents. More like a tunnel, all slimy and tight, but we made it and ended up in the alley next to a car. Then Victor's men came after us and we ran and now Win's dead!" Quinn sobbed into the handkerchief.

"You did good, Quinn," Evan said softly.

Xav looked out the window, and Puppy Man and his box were gone. Satisfied someone had picked him up, Xav turned back to Quinn, and the windows exploded in a shower of automatic gunfire.

CHAPTER THIRTY-ONE

XAV PUSHED Quinn's chair over at the speed of light as he grabbed the front of Evan's jacket and dove for the floor. He wrapped his arms around Quinn and Evan and pulled them to him to shield them as he pressed to the floor. The gunfire abruptly ceased, and deathly quiet descended. A sultry breeze drifted through the room, and the odd tinkle of glass chimed as shards continued to fall from the window frames.

Xav withdrew his Sig Sauer from his back holster. "Stay down," he ordered. He moved over Evan, rolled onto his back, and pulled his Glock 30S from his ankle holster. Drawing a breath and steeling himself, he rose to a crouch and went to the wall beneath the now nonexistent windows. He blindly aimed the guns over the sill, prepared to fire. When no fire sounded, he raised his head to look over the ledge. The park was empty.

Sirens sounded in the distance as he crawled across the floor back to Quinn and Evan. They were stunned and wide-eyed. "Are you hurt?"

Evan shook his head. He looked pale.

"Quinn? Are you hurt?"

Quinn slowly lifted his sweatshirt to reveal his bloody bandage. "I think I busted 'em again."

Evan reached for the blanket and pressed it to Quinn's side to staunch the bleeding.

"Stay down," Xav ordered as he crouched again. Staying low, he made his way to the supervisor's window. Rufus sat still in his chair behind the counter, eyes wide open, his chest a red ruin. Xav touched the man's neck. He was dead. Xav reached over the counter and found the button to unlock the door. He pressed it and entered the office to call the station.

XAV WAS livid. The only way someone could have known that Quinn Haverty was alive and at Bright Horizons would have been to access NCMEC's system. Or if hospital or Bright Horizons personnel blabbed. He swore under his breath. Loose lips were the last thing they needed to deal with.

EMTs treated Quinn while a furious Sheriff Winston listened to Xav give a full report. When Xav finished, Winston looked at Evan. "Do you have anything to add, Mr. Fairchild?"

"Only that I agree with Deputy Constantine. Quinn needs to be moved to protective custody." Evan was shaky and his face was flushed.

"Mr. Fairchild is going to need protection as well," Xav said.

"I beg your pardon?" Evan said, indignant.

"We don't know who those bullets were meant for," Xav said calmly.

This statement gave Evan pause. "Would you excuse us for a moment, Sheriff?" Evan stepped carefully over glass as he led Xav to stand near the wall, where they had a modicum of privacy. "If you think I'm gonna let you have someone tail me day and night, you can forget it," he said in a harsh whisper. "If they were aiming for me, they wouldn't have waited until I was inside a government building. They'd have shot me on the damn street."

"Three birds with one stone."

Evan all but growled, "Conjecture."

"True. But you can't be sorry after you're dead."

"Is that some weird LA take on 'rather be safe than sorry'?" Evan asked, clearly incredulous.

"It's a practical one."

Evan shook his head vehemently. "I won't have someone following me," he shot back. "No tail."

"Then Quinn doesn't need protection either and we can leave him here."

"Over my dead body."

"That's what I'm trying to avoid."

Evan's mouth tightened, anger evident on his face. "You don't fight fair."

"Not when it comes to protecting people." Xav walked back to where Sheriff Winston stood issuing orders to his deputies.

"I made the call to the FBI for Quinn," Winston said, "and we can keep a man with Mr. Fairchild and on his home. We need to arrange transport. Not to mention we have a facility full of traumatized children we need to get statements from."

"All the kids were in their rooms, Sheriff. I'd designate one deputy to collect statements from the few who can see the park from their windows," Xav said.

Winston pursed his lips and shook his head in disgust. "Thank God for that."

"Send the ambulances away and call the medical examiner for a second truck?" Xav asked.

"Why?"

"Because you're going to tell the media that Quinn Haverty is dead."

Sheriff Winston gave him a long look before saying, "You suppose there's someone at the coroner's office we can trust."

"We can trust Rachelle Vickers. I'll call and explain," Evan offered.

"Please," Sheriff Winston said.

"Did you request female agents when you made the call to the FBI?" Xav asked.

"I did as you instructed. Two around the clock. Though I'm thinking three might be a good idea right about now."

"Your call," Xav said appreciatively. He walked over to where Quinn lay on a gurney. "How are you doing, champ?"

"They're gonna kill me like they did Win." Quinn looked pale, his eyes full of fear.

"We're going to make sure that doesn't happen. We're moving you to a safer place."

"Like in the movies?"

Xav smiled. "Yeah, like in the movies."

"I REALIZE that," Evan was saying as Xav walked up, "but I'd appreciate it if you'd contact her and ask her to call me as soon as possible. This is extremely important…. Thank you, Ryan…. I can't chat about coffee just now…. Yes, thank you again." Evan ended the call and looked at Xav. "She left the morgue several hours ago and the clerk didn't want to bother her."

"What did coffee have to do with it?"

Evan pinched the bridge of his nose in frustration. "Nothing."

"Sounded like it did."

"It didn't." Evan shoved his phone into his pocket.

"A java connoisseur, then?"

"Drop it."

"I'd like to know what coffee had to do with transporting a witness to protective custody."

"You know damn well it had nothing to do with that."

"So it had to do with you?" Evan flushed crimson, and Xav chuckled. "Someone's hot for you," he teased.

Evan was saved by his ringing phone.

"I GOTTA get in that?" Quinn asked in a small voice.

"Yep. I'll leave it unzipped near your mouth so you can breathe, and as soon as we get you into the van, we'll unzip you all the way," Xav said.

"'Kay."

Xav lifted Quinn, and Rachelle spread the body bag beneath him and unzipped it. Xav set him in it and laid him back gently. "Ready?

"Yeah."

Quinn looked frightened as hell, but there was no other way to get him out of the building. "You're going to be all right. I promise. Here we go." Xav zipped the bag up to Quinn's chin. "Right before we go outside, I'm going to zip it up a little more so they can't see your face, and I don't want you to move once we get outside."

Quinn nodded, and Rachelle pushed the gurney to the elevator.

Xav pressed the down button and was concerned when he saw that Evan had broken out in a sweat. "You okay?" he asked almost inaudibly.

Evan nodded. The elevator arrived and the gurney went in first with Rachelle and John, and Xav followed. Evan seemed to pause for the briefest of moments before stepping in.

They rode down in silence, the elevator came to a stop with a soft groan, and the doors opened. They entered the lobby, where Sheriff Winston waited for them with none other than Faison.

"Fairchild? What are you doing here?" Faison asked.

"Doing my job, sir," Evan shot back.

Faison's face grew red, but before he could say anything, Sheriff Winston said, "Wait until they're paying attention to me before you move him, and be prepared for the cameras."

Faison smoothed his thinning hair and straightened his jacket. The man had gotten here fast, a testament to his self-importance.

"Mr. Fairchild, I've impounded your car. Xav, I have your motorcycle," Sheriff Winston said.

"Why?" Evan asked with one eye on Faison.

"Because I'd like to make sure there isn't a bomb in it," Winston explained. "Ridley and Billy will transport you, Xav, and Quinn from the morgue to the house in the unmarked surveillance van and then drive you both home. If the vehicles check out, you'll have them back by morning."

Xav thought Evan looked green as he closed his eyes and breathed deeply before opening them again.

Winston continued, "Now, this goes for every one of you here! If *any* of you breathe a single word about this boy still being alive, I will personally open a can of whoop-ass on you the likes of which y'all have never seen. Do I make myself clear?"

Humble acknowledgments filled the room.

Xav nodded an okay to Sheriff Winston, and Winston and Faison exited the building to microphones and camera flashes.

"You're not okay," Xav said to Evan quietly.

"I am," Evan countered.

"Ready?" Rachelle asked.

Xav looked down at Quinn with a reassuring smile he didn't feel. "I'm going to zip you up now and we'll unzip you as soon as you're in the van."

"'Kay."

"Let's do it."

CHAPTER THIRTY-TWO

RIDLEY PULLED the surveillance van up to the wrought-iron gates and pressed the Call button.

"Wow!" Quinn exclaimed. "This is where I'm gonna stay?"

"Sure is, young man," Billy Kenner said.

Quinn turned to Xav and he nodded his confirmation.

A woman's voice came over the intercom. "Yes?"

"Cleaning service, ma'am," Ridley announced.

"Come straight up the drive. I'll open the garage door for ya."

The gates slowly opened, and Ridley drove the van up the long driveway and pulled into the three-car garage. The garage door began its descent as soon as the van cleared the threshold.

"Here we are," Xav said.

"At least I didn't have to ride in no bag this time," Quinn said.

"I know, right? Let's go check out the house."

A tall, fit woman in her midforties dressed in cotton culottes, a peasant shirt, and running shoes greeted them when Xav slid the door open.

"You must be Deputy Constantine. I'm Annie. And you must be Quinn."

"Yes, ma'am."

"Nice to meet you, Annie. This is Evan Fairchild," Xav introduced. "He is the ADA on Quinn's case."

"Well, come on in. Lynn's just inside, and we have some sweet tea waiting for y'all. It's hotter than blue blazes out there."

Her demeanor was exactly what Xav had hoped for when he'd asked Winston to call the FBI. She was warm and easygoing and had experience dealing with kids. Nothing like what you'd expect from a feeb.

Annie gave them a tour of the house, and when Lynn took Quinn into his room to show him his new clothes, she pulled Xav and Evan aside. "This is the second attempt on this boy's life. What kind of protection did they give you, gentleman?"

"Mr. Fairchild will have an officer with him at all times," Xav answered.

"What does that do for you, Deputy Constantine?" she pressed.

Evan gave Xav a pointed look, and Xav thought he saw real concern there.

"I'll be all right," Xav assured.

"Arrogant and stupid. It's a wonder you ever worked for us," she said with a smile.

Xav chuckled. She'd done her homework. "I'll be all right," he repeated.

"Suit yourself."

"He usually does." Evan met Xav's gaze with a wry smile, then pulled his phone from his jacket pocket. "I'll be back in a few." He disappeared a moment later.

"Any special instructions?" Annie asked.

Xav shook his head. "He's probably having nightmares. Be gentle."

"That's a given. Any idea on duration?"

"None."

"Very well, then. Here's my card. I'm the lead on this. The other agents' names and cell phone numbers are on the back, along with the number of the dedicated line to the house."

They each had a glass of sweet tea as Annie sorted through the bandages and medications Rachelle had provided for Quinn.

Xav went to her. "Did she send along the medication pursuant to DSS's plan of care?"

Annie frowned in obvious disgust. "She did, along with a note saying it's enough to tranquilize a horse. We have a pediatrician coming in the morning. We'll reassess."

"Thank you. I'd shoot for something that reduces anxiety. As I understand it, he also vomited when the psychologist attempted to interview him."

Annie nodded. "Thanks for letting me know. Anything else?"

"Only that I'd let him call me or Mr. Fairchild if he wants to."

"Did you want us to collect a statement from him?"

"We've done that."

She sighed. "Every time we work a case involving kids, I ask myself how you boys at CARD survive this shit. After twenty years in this business, I still can't believe people go after kids."

"Neither can I."

"Well, go on, now. We'll lay down our lives for him," she said reassuringly.

Xav offered her a small smile. "Thank you."

She pursed her lips. "I'd like to be able to say it's our pleasure, but it isn't."

Evan joined them. "All set?" Xav asked Evan, who nodded.

"Please tell me you're gonna put these bastards away for a long time," Annie said to him.

"We'll do our best, ma'am," Evan reassured.

"And if not, you shoot their asses," she said to Xav.

He chuckled. "We'll do our best, Annie. Thanks again."

"WE NEED to work this case while the details are fresh in our minds," Xav said as Ridley drove to Evan's house.

"I agree," Billy said from the front passenger seat.

Evan scrubbed his face with both hands. "Yeah."

Evan looked like Xav felt, and Xav's heart went out to him. He was certain they could both use a couple of stiff drinks. "Is there a restaurant or bar near your house?"

"A family place around the corner. Home cooking. Beer on tap," Evan said.

"You up for it, or do you want to crash?"

"I need to eat and I'm sure as hell not up to cooking. Don't suppose my *tail* would let us walk there, do you?" Evan's vitriol lacked its usual intensity.

"So long as he can chaperone us."

Evan closed his eyes and shook his head slowly. "I can't believe I let you do this to me."

Xav smiled. "You won't have it for long. We'll get these guys."

Evan opened his eyes to Xav. "The sooner, the better."

Xav leaned forward. "Ridley, drop us both at Mr. Fairchild's house."

"Like hell. My orders are to take you to your respective residences."

"He and I need to work this case. I'll call Winston and let him know where I am and get a ride home when the next guy comes on at eleven."

Ridley gave him a sour look.

Xav withdrew his cell phone from his pocket and hit the icon to dial Winston.

"Sheriff Winston's office," Twyla Fay answered, sounding more than a little stressed out.

Xav looked at his watch. After all that had happened, it was hard to believe it was only six o'clock in the evening. "You should be gone by now," Xav greeted.

"Are you tryin' to be funny? Because you're not at all. The press won't settle down."

"How's Sheriff Winston holding up?"

"The man is a rock. Other than the press, everything's pretty much wrapped up. I even got someone to board up the windows at Bright Horizons until they can replace 'em tomorrow."

"You're a miracle worker."

"I'm sure you'll remember to tell Sheriff that before my next review."

"You know it."

"I got some bad news for y'all," she said.

"Tell me."

"We got a hit on one of our NCMEC entries."

Xav rubbed his eyes. The day was wearing on him. "Verified?"

"Yes. Just breaks my heart. Little Jimmy Perkins was found down at Marina Point around the time Charlie's boat was found down there. Drowned, by the looks of it. The Collier County medical examiner is sending his remains and all the reports up to Rachelle. John said best not to notify the parents until you and he can review the reports."

Xav winced at the news but was pleased with John. He was turning out to be a great partner. "Tell him thank you for me."

"Will do. So what can I do for you?"

Xav had almost forgotten his reason for calling. "Tell Sheriff Winston that I'll be at Mr. Fairchild's home reviewing Quinn's case if he needs me. I'll catch a ride home when the deputy at his residence gets off duty."

"I can't believe you two have a mind to consider anything after almost losing your lives. How is Quinn doin'?" she asked.

"Shaken up, but happy with his new temporary residence."

"I bet he is. That Charmaigne estate is gorgeous. I'll tell Sheriff where y'all will be."

"I'm on cell if he needs me."

"I'll tell him that too," Twyla Fay said.

"See you tomorrow." Xav terminated the call. "Billy?"

Billy turned to look at him.

"Twyla Fay says we received a hit on the NCMEC data. A boy drowned down at Marina Point, where Charlie's boat was found."

"Same time?"

"Twyla Fay says near to it."

Billy winced. "I hate this case," he said in exasperation.

"We do too," Xav replied.

After a few more odd looks, Billy and Ridley dropped them both at Evan's house. They greeted the officer on duty and headed to the pub on foot.

EVAN BREATHED a sigh of relief as the heat and humidity of outdoors abated with a blast of cold air as they entered the pub. God, he loved air-conditioning. It'd take a few minutes for his shirt to unstick itself from his skin, but, as they were seated and Evan pulled off his suit jacket, he felt almost human again.

They settled into a booth at the back of Captain Patty's, having left Evan's shadow, Callum Carlisle, seated on a bench outside the restaurant door. Carlisle had protested until Xav reminded him he was a deputy too and was armed.

Xav had left his own jacket back at Bright Horizons. Evan guessed he'd gotten some blood on it, but he didn't want to ask. The afternoon had been gruesome enough, and they didn't need a reminder.

"Bourbon over ice," Evan told the waitress who took their drink order and brought them a basket of hush puppies. Xav ordered pale ale. Five minutes later Evan felt the heat of the liquor in the back of his throat. The tension in his upper body eased with each sip, and before he knew it, he'd ordered a second.

"Eat something?" Xav popped a hush puppy into his mouth and offered the basket to Evan. Evan took one of the bits of fried cornbread and dipped it into the cup of butter before biting into it. "These are good," Xav said as he reached for another.

"Best hush puppies in the area," Evan confirmed as he took a second and coated it with butter. "Even better with the added saturated fat."

"I don't do grease. Only things that are healthy without the deep-frying to clog your arteries." Xav dug in for two more hush puppies. "Don't you guys eat seafood any other way?"

"Broiled in butter?" In spite of himself, Evan smiled. The waitress took their dinner orders and disappeared again.

"I hope shrimp burgers are good." Xav appeared more than skeptical.

"Grind up shrimp, mix it with the right seasonings, and you can't go wrong," Evan answered. "Trust me."

Xav drank the last of his ale.

They finished the basket of hush puppies in silence, and the waitress brought Xav another ale. Evan's exhausted brain kept replaying the afternoon's events, and each time he thought about what he'd heard Xav tell Quinn—"*He's a good guy*"—he felt more and more like the world's biggest asshole for having been so hard on Xav from the get-go. Not to mention how Xav had protected him and Quinn at the group home.

He wanted to say something to Xav, but for the life of him, he couldn't decide what to say. No. That wasn't right. He *did* know what he wanted to say. He just couldn't say it. Because he needed to apologize. And in Evan's experience, apologizing meant you put yourself out there to get stomped on, and he was sure he couldn't handle that.

He won't do that to you.

He fucking hated the little voice in his mind. Sometimes he imagined Dr. Sampson had put it there, but he knew that was bullshit too. But part of him wasn't so sure she hadn't telepathically put Mat Kearney's "Breathe In, Breathe Out" in the pub's music system just to piss him off. It was too damn relevant for comfort.

Part of him was ready to trust someone. The part of him that was the kid he'd been before all the shit happened. Again, he wondered why Xav would be interested in him and all his baggage. But the voice at the back of his mind pointed out, *He doesn't seem to mind.* He wasn't giving Xav enough credit.

CHAPTER THIRTY-THREE

"TWO SHRIMP burgers," the waitress said as she set down their food. Curly fries spilled over the plates, and for the first time, Evan's mouth watered in appreciation.

"Need anything else?" she asked.

"I think we're fine," Evan said when Xav shook his head.

Xav bit into the burger, and Evan watched him for his reaction.

"This is really good," Xav said, surprised.

"Told you." Evan ate a bit more of his own, then popped a few fries into his mouth. The food and alcohol, sitting with Xav and not feeling at odds with him, made him feel human again. "Not the kind of haute cuisine you Californians offer up, but it sure fills you up."

Xav said something about more crunches at the gym, but it didn't take him long to finish the entire burger and make a dent in the pile of fries.

Evan stared down at his drink. *Enough putting it off.* He wasn't a kid, and he wouldn't bullshit anymore. He'd acted like a dick when Xav had been nothing but patient and kind. He *liked* Xav. More than that. He trusted Xav with the truth. "I'm sorry," he said as he picked up his glass.

"Sorry?" Xav sounded bewildered.

"For acting like an asshole." Evan took a long sip of the drink. The ice cubes rattled against the sides of the glass as he set it down. He traced a fingertip along the marred surface of the table, feeling the indentations and roughness there. Something, anything to focus on other than the twisting knot in his gut.

"Thank you." Xav seemed to know Evan needed time for this, because he said nothing else.

"You were right," Evan said. "I'm too close to this. I let it get to me. But not for the reasons you might think." He did his breathing exercise. He looked up and met Xav's patient gaze.

"Quinn…. The reason I zoned out when we first spoke to him…," Evan began. Why was it so difficult to explain? He'd spent his entire legal career being paid to explain things. Make them simple. And now, when he needed to explain, he couldn't do it.

Xav reached across the table to touch Evan's hand with the tips of his fingers. Barely a touch, but so much more. "Take your time."

Evan nodded. "Quinn…. When he said they'd locked him and Winter up, all of a sudden I was back there." He swallowed hard. He could do this. He *would* do this. He'd never told another soul except Dr. Sampson, but he'd do it now. "When I was eleven, I ended up in foster care. I never knew who my father was. My mom—" He inhaled slowly so the emotions wouldn't overwhelm him. "—she tried. But she started doing coke. Sometimes she'd be gone for a few days." He rubbed the bridge of his nose and took another long breath. "Someone called social services. I know it was the right thing, but at the time…. Anyhow, they took me into custody. Placed me in a home and gave her time to get her shit together. But she couldn't. Or maybe she wouldn't. I don't know.

"I was so angry. With her. With everything. I went from one placement to another. One school to another. I was thirteen when I got into it with my last foster father. I mouthed off…. He hit me. I hit him back." Evan gazed past Xav at a picture of a square-rigged ship sailing on the ocean. It was crooked, and he fought the urge to straighten it.

"Foster parents aren't allowed to use corporal punishment," he continued after a pause. "But he told the cops I'd hit him first, and they believed him." Evan laughed bitterly. "It shouldn't have mattered. They still can't hit. Hell, if I had been in charge of DSS, I'd have seen the asshole kicked out of the foster parenting program…." Evan pulled his hand away from Xav's and made a fist, then forced himself to relax and left his fingers barely touching Xav's.

"I ended up in juvenile court. I'd gotten in trouble a few times before. Nothing major. Shoplifting. A few fights. Stupid kid shit. But the judge decided I needed to be taught a lesson. I laughed and told the judge to fuck himself. He sent me to detention for six months."

Evan drank the rest of his drink and motioned for the waitress to bring another. "I got into it with a few guys in detention." He shrugged. "After the third or fourth time, they put me in solitary confinement."

Xav shook his head slowly. "I'm sorry."

Evan closed his eyes and breathed slowly, knowing the constricted feeling in the back of his throat wasn't real. *Breathe. In. Out. In. Out.* "I pretended I was tough. Hell, solitary meant I didn't have to deal with anyone's shit. No cellmate, nobody to hassle me, no one wanting to start something." *No assholes groping me.*

Evan opened his eyes and saw understanding in Xav's gaze. Not pity. Just understanding.

"I couldn't hack it. After about a week, I freaked. I screamed at them to let me out. Pounded on the walls." He glanced down at his hands. He could see the ghosts of the cuts and bruises, even now. Every cut, every scrape, every bruise, every ache still haunted him. "I didn't understand that every time I screamed, it gave them *another* reason to keep me in there."

The waitress brought Evan's drink. He took it with a shaking hand and drank deeply. "I was in that hellhole for months. Maybe three. I don't know." He hoped his voice didn't tremble as much as he did. "I honestly can't remember. Half the time I wasn't really there. My brain was somewhere else. I heard stuff. I *saw* stuff. Shadows. People laughing. I'm pretty sure most of it never happened." He finished the rest of the drink in one swallow.

"When were you released?" Xav asked gently.

"The prison hired a new psychologist. Her name was Evelene Sampson. The social worker recommended I talk to her." Thinking about her made Evan smile a small smile.

"Evelene convinced a judge I didn't need to be in detention. She got me a group home placement, and I worked with her. She's the reason I finished high school and went to college. She helped me get a full ride to Carolina. Then she convinced me to apply to Columbia Law School and helped me get in touch with a lawyer who had my juvenile record expunged." Evan forced his gaze back to Xav. "It was a long time ago. I should have gotten over it by now. I *thought* I'd gotten over it." He strangled a sigh. "I've never told anyone."

"What happened to your mom?" Xav asked.

"She died of an overdose the day I graduated high school. We'd been in touch. She'd been doing really well in rehab...." He shook his head. "Drugs. I hate them. It's why I quit private practice and went to work for the DA. I wanted to get that shit off the streets."

Someone at the bar laughed and shouted something at the TV. Evan couldn't believe he'd done it. He'd *told* someone. Tendrils of confidence wended their way through Evan, and for the first time in as long as he could remember, he felt a sense of triumph outside of a courtroom.

"I'm sorry, Evan," Xav said sincerely.

Evan smiled another small smile. "So, what's your story? How'd you end up here? Crazy family? Had it with LA? Bad breakup? What?"

Xav gave him a warm smile; then it faded. "None of the above. Great family. No breakups. LA is LA." He cleared his throat. "I began work for the FBI as an analyst. And after a successful bust, I had my choice of assignments. I chose CARD."

"Why?"

"As an analyst, one of the things I analyzed was child exploitation numbers. And it began to eat at me. So I went through training, went into the field, thought I knew everything, and was going to single-handedly stop child sex trafficking in its tracks."

Xav paused, and Evan thought he looked pained as he took another sip of his drink.

He shook his head in obvious self-disgust. "I thought I knew what depravity was." He ran a hand down his face. "I had no fucking idea what I was dealing with."

When he didn't continue, Evan pressed him gently. "And?"

"I rescued a lot of kids. A lot of *boys*. I had no idea that boys made up more than half of the kids who were exploited until I went into the field." He shook his head again. "And never lost one until the last operation. I was deep undercover in South America. Boys trafficked by a *cocalero*—a cocaine grower—as a lucrative sideline. The DEA didn't provide the agreed-upon representation. Both boys were gunned down before I could get them on the chopper."

Evan swallowed hard. No wonder Winter's death had shaken Xav so deeply. "So why North Carolina?"

Xav smiled again, but the smile didn't reach his eyes. "I went down there to get one boy who'd gone missing from LA. There turned out to be two. The other boy had a bus ticket in his pocket. LA to North Carolina."

"Ah, the connection."

"Just found out he's one of your missing boys." Xav raised his glass in a mock toast. "I meet you, we do our thing, I find out you're working drug cases involving cocaine, and here we are."

Xav looked pained. He obviously blamed himself for the death of the two boys, but Evan wasn't sure what to say. He was inept at relationships and thought Xav deserved something better than a quick "that sucks." So he copied Xav. "I'm sorry."

Xav nodded slowly. "I'd have gladly given my life to have those two boys alive."

Evan winced. Now they were responsible for Quinn. "We'll do our best for Quinn."

Xav smiled, and this time it was genuine. "Now, *that* I believe."

They sat for a short while in companionable silence.

"What's the *C* stand for?" Xav finally asked.

It was Evan's turn to smile a genuine smile. "Chance."

"Does not."

"Sure does. My mother said she was blessed with a good son like me purely by chance." He could still recall her face when she'd told him that. She'd been beautiful then, with her long silky hair and pale skin. The way she'd been before the drugs had destroyed her. A good memory. One Evan wanted to keep.

Xav chuckled again. "Let's get out of here."

"Let's."

EVAN UNLOCKED the door and backed inside. Xav's mouth met his the minute they were out of his bodyguard's sight. The door slammed into the wall—Evan didn't give a shit that it had probably cracked the ancient plaster there—and Xav wrapped his arms around Evan's waist. They had walked home, the five-minute trip feeling more like twenty with Evan's cock straining against the fabric of his pants.

The buzz of the alcohol added to the relief of having finally spilled his guts to Xav. Evan would deal with the aftermath later. For now, he felt good. *Damn* good, in fact. Horny—*and something else*. A feeling he almost remembered from his past but that seemed so far away he wasn't sure what to call it. The only thing that really mattered was that he knew what he needed now, and Xav seemed to be of the same mind.

"Nice place," Xav half gasped. He shoved the door shut with his foot and claimed Evan's mouth again.

Xav smelled so fucking good. No cologne Evan could detect. Xav didn't need it.

"Bedroom." Evan managed to pull away, then held out his hand.

"In a minute." Xav took the offered hand but pulled Evan back toward him. But unlike the last kiss, this one felt more introspective, almost tender. Xav carded his fingers through Evan's hair, then stroked down Evan's throat, causing Evan to shiver in response.

The thought *What the hell am I doing?* evaporated as Evan let go. He didn't want to think anymore. He only wanted Xav. He reached behind Xav's neck and released the elastic holding the tight braid there. The ubiquitous braid at the back of his head gave way to Evan's fingers, spilling soft, thick waves over Xav's shoulders, releasing a hint of citrus that mingled with the crisp masculine scent of arousal. Evan carded his fingers through Xav's long hair.

"Good thing you wear your hair back," Evan said, "or I'd never be able to concentrate."

Xav laughed. "Good to know, in case I need to use it against you."

Evan pulled Xav's shirt over his head and ghosted his hands over the muscles of Xav's shoulders. The skin felt surprisingly soft and smooth over the hard planes and divots. It moved as Xav worked his way down Evan's neck and unbuttoned his shirt. Then they were chest to chest, skin against skin, and Xav held him. Not too tightly, but close enough that Evan let out a sigh.

Xav pressed his lips to the soft skin under Evan's ear, an ephemeral touch that aroused and promised much more. Xav's feathered kisses and the hardness of Xav's body beneath Evan's fingers created a counterpoint of sensation. Evan imagined them moving in tandem, drawn by the same curiosity. They'd explored each other's bodies only briefly before; their frenzied sex had been too intense, too combative for either to slow the process down. Evan had assumed this time would be the same, but Xav had taken a different tack, and Evan was grateful for it.

Xav brought Evan's mouth back to his, guiding Evan's face so that their lips aligned, touched. This time Xav pressed inward and found Evan's tongue with his, but no tangle ensued, only a soft, exploratory caress. An invitation. Not just sex, but something more intimate. Something... frightening.

Evan pulled away. He expected disappointment on Xav's face, but instead saw understanding. Patience.

"Bedroom?" The corners of Xav's lips, pink from kisses, edged upward.

Evan answered by taking Xav's hand and leading him up the staircase. Xav paused on the landing to admire the stained-glass window that looked out over the back porch. "This place really is amazing," he said. "Did you do the work?"

Evan hadn't had many guests visit his house, and none of them had asked the question, probably because they'd all assumed he'd paid someone to restore her. "Yes," he said.

"It's beautiful." Xav's obvious appreciation of the house left Evan at a loss to answer, but before he gathered his thoughts, Xav kissed him again.

This time neither of them spoke after the kiss broke. Xav hadn't let go of Evan's hand, so Evan led him in silence up the stairs and into his room. He'd never shared this room with anyone. He'd never brought a man home. That had seemed somehow sacrilegious. Too personal. Too close to what he'd always kept safely inside where no one could use it against him. But now he wanted Xav to see the house, his room. Just as he'd wanted Xav to see what he'd hidden for nearly twenty years. He trusted Xav with this.

CHAPTER THIRTY-FOUR

XAV LOOKED around the room, then at Evan. His expression both fascinated and frightened Evan. Xav hid nothing and had nothing to hide. Evan vaguely wondered what that must feel like as he touched the Bose on the nightstand and Nickelback's "I'd Come for You" filled the air.

"You're thinking too much," Xav said.

"You're right." Evan smiled. The buzz of the alcohol had started to fade, but he wasn't running. He wasn't playing either. He stepped closer and undid Xav's belt, then unzipped his pants and pushed them down with his underwear, leaving him naked. He met Xav's gaze and held it as he shed his own clothing. "So where were we?"

Xav pulled Evan close and glided his hands over Evan's back and ass. Evan leaned into the touch, whereas in the past he might have pulled away and wrested control from Xav.

"You look better without the suit," Xav said against Evan's ear.

"Shut up," Evan shot back and backed Xav up against the bed. Xav lay back and grinned happily up at Evan, who shook his head in mock disgust. "Are you ever serious?" he joked. He leaned down to kiss Xav's chest, but Xav pulled him on top of him and wrapped his arms around him.

"Sometimes. Yeah." Xav stroked the back of Evan's neck and kissed a line over his jaw.

Evan ghosted his fingers over Xav's smooth skin and brushed a rough scar on his side. He'd noticed it when they'd first had sex. "Souvenir?" he asked.

Xav grunted but didn't explain.

We all have our ghosts. Maybe someday Xav would tell him about it. Judging by the depth and breadth of the scar, it was probably quite a story.

Xav got to his knees on the mattress and rolled Evan onto his belly. He kissed Evan's mouth, then kissed his shoulder and made his way down Evan's back, exploring with lips and tongue. At first, Evan worried Xav would pin him against the sheets, but Xav seemed to understand Evan's fear and instead kneeled at his side and leaned over him.

Evan closed his eyes and relaxed. He couldn't recall the last time he'd let someone touch him like that. His cock pressed against the bed and his body craved more, but for once he didn't feel the urgent need to fuck. He fought the voice in his mind that told him he needed to be in charge and allowed his senses to take over.

Xav squeezed the globes of Evan's ass, parting them as he nipped and licked the skin. He brushed but did not linger on the delicate skin between, but his moan of appreciation made Evan shiver.

"You good?" Xav whispered.

"I'm great." The tap-tap-tap of the fan lulled Evan into a netherworld of warmth, fueled by the alcohol and Xav's hot mouth. Without thinking, Evan raised his ass closer to Xav's mouth, causing one of Xav's thumbs to brush his hole. "Please. Touch me."

Xav rumbled his approval, and Evan felt a slippery finger tracing circles around his opening. Evan spread his legs to give Xav better access. The cool wetness of Xav's finger pressed against him but didn't breach him. With his other hand, Xav kneaded Evan's ass until it burned.

"Yes. Fuck yes!" Evan nearly laughed with the pleasure of that sting. The next thing Evan knew, Xav's tongue replaced his finger. *Oh God!* Nobody had ever done that to him, but he'd imagined it more times than he could count. Evan stilled, overcome by the sensations.

"You okay?" Xav asked.

"Shit. Don't fucking stop," Evan gasped. He imagined the grin on Xav's face, and, for once, he didn't mind.

Xav teased, pressing inward, then circling Evan's opening. Each time Evan moaned his approval, Xav pressed farther inward and used his thumbs to warm the skin of Evan's ass. Xav licked his way up Evan's back, his thumb still exerting pressure on Evan's hole, building the sweet burn of want until Evan couldn't stand it anymore. He rolled over and wrapped arms and legs around Xav's incredible body, trapping their cocks between them, then moving just enough that Xav grew as hard as he was.

"Fuck me." Evan had only spoken the words a few times in his life, mostly when he'd been drunk. He'd intended to be the one doing the fucking tonight, but now all he could think of was how amazing it would be to feel Xav filling him, watch Xav plunge into him.

Xav's eyes lit with pleasure. Evan snagged a condom and lube and handed them to Xav, rolled a pillow under his neck and caught Xav's intense gaze. Xav didn't uncap the lube right away, though. Instead, he leaned over and gave Evan a crushing kiss, then teased and mouthed Evan's nipples, took Evan's hard cock in his hand, and brushed his thumb over the tip. Using the moisture there, Xav pumped Evan a few times, and shimmied down the bed and took Evan in his mouth.

"Oh, God!" Evan shouted as Xav took him deep, held him there before clasping the base of his cock and increasing the pressure with his mouth. He moved upward, stopping at the crown, using his teeth gently against the sensitive glans and pressing his tongue into the slit. Evan, who'd been trying to keep his eyes open to watch Xav's body, finally gave up and closed them.

"Much better when you don't think," Xav murmured as he came up for air.

Evan wouldn't have argued even if he'd disagreed. Besides, he was too far gone to think clearly. He tuned out the world around him and focused on Xav's amazing mouth as the last of the day's tension fled his body. Xav laved the underside of his cock as he probed beyond with his fingers, rolling Evan's sac and lightly scraping the tender skin behind it. Xav's erection pressed against his leg, but when Evan reached to touch him, Xav pushed his hand away and said, "Later. Don't worry. This, right now? This is all about you."

The words made Evan feel amazing and incredibly uncomfortable at the same time. But his discomfort fled with the onslaught of Xav's hot mouth swallowing him again, then working his way up and down, tongue and teeth and wet. And before Evan knew it, he was on the brink and soaring over the edge of his orgasm, shooting into Xav, clinging to him and shaking with the intensity of it. Evan opened his eyes to see Xav smile at him and lick his lips. Evan figured that was the hottest thing he'd ever seen.

Xav reached for the lube and slicked his fingers, then proceeded to tease Evan again until Evan whimpered and bucked underneath his hands. "Want you in me now," Evan said, his voice rough with his release.

"Soon," Xav said as he slipped a finger between Evan's legs and pressed the tip inside.

Still thrumming from his orgasm, Evan clenched around Xav's finger, then forced himself to relax and open to the pressure.

"Much better." Xav bent down and kissed Evan's chest. His lips caused Evan to shiver and relax a bit more. Xav pulled gently at Evan's hole before slipping a second finger inside. "God, you're tight."

"Been a while," Evan said. He caught the look of pleasure on Xav's face to hear this. He ran his fingers through Xav's soft hair, pulling on it until Xav moaned in pleasure.

"Feeling good?" Xav asked as he pushed a third finger inside and fucked Evan with his fingers.

"Holy fuck, yes," Evan growled. "But if you don't fuck me for real, I'm going to lose my mind."

"You're awfully demanding in bed," Xav teased gently.

"Live with it," Evan said in a rumbled voice.

More stretching; then suddenly Evan was mourning the loss of Xav's probing fingers. The sound of the condom wrapper, Xav pushing his legs back toward his shoulders, and the press of something hard against his entrance, and—holy fucking hell, that burned!—his thoughts evaporated. The sting of Xav's thick cock as Xav pushed past that tight ring of muscle faded as Xav filled him. Once he was inside, though, the pain dissolved into a blur of sensations.

"You good?" Xav whispered against Evan's ear.

Evan shivered and nodded, wreathing his arms around Xav's neck and kissing him. He couldn't get much purchase on those pink lips, but it didn't matter. He wanted Xav to understand how incredibly good it felt and that he had no regrets.

Xav moved slowly, deliberately, his burning gaze fixed on Evan's with an intensity that made Evan feel as though he were the only person in the world. Evan saw the focus, knew Xav wanted this to last but struggled against the urge to let himself fall over the precipice.

As Evan opened his body to Xav, he also opened a piece of himself he'd held back. Tiny pieces he'd hidden floated outward from the barricades he'd created. The things that made him feel vulnerable, the things that made him give a damn about someone else and not worry that the world wasn't a perfect place and he might get his heart stomped on.

"You feel so fucking amazing," Xav said as he thrust deeper still.

Evan's cock grew hard again, trapped as it was. He stroked himself to the rhythm of Xav's movements. Sweat slicked the space between them. The overhead fan did little to quell the stifling heat, although the way it picked up Xav's hair and moved it around his face made Xav look that much more beautiful.

"Evan." The adoration in Xav's voice shot through Evan and made his entire body cry out for more of Xav. A fleeting thought that he wanted Xav to call him by his name—his *real* name—dissipated as they barreled toward climax.

"Hold me," Evan said. He wasn't sure where the words had come from, but he wanted it so badly he was willing to beg. He didn't have to, since Xav pulled him up off the bed and held him as they both came, Xav crying out against Evan's neck.

The world returned with the soft whir of the fan and the sound of leaves rustling outside the open window. Neither of them moved for the longest time, and then only so Xav could release Evan's legs and they might hold on to each other just a bit longer.

They lay on top of the duvet, sweaty and sated. Frogs chirped in the weeds outside and the slight breeze through the bedroom windows ruffled the drapes. Evan closed his eyes and settled against Xav's chest. Reality faded away, leaving only the warmth of their bodies and the beat of Xav's heart against his cheek.

Here, next to Xav, Evan felt safe. As though Xav had reached into his heart and awakened the trust Evan thought gone forever. He hesitated a fraction of a second and said, "Call me Chance."

"Chance," Xav repeated, then kissed Chance's hair.

"Much better," Chance said appreciatively.

"I could never wrap my brain around Evan," Xav said, the affection in his voice chasing away Chance's lingering doubts.

"When I was little, I liked the name Chance," he admitted. "But later...."

"I like it." Xav turned Chance's head and claimed a quick kiss. "Suits you better."

"Hmm." Chance closed his eyes again. The way Faison had ranted and raved when he'd brought up Quinn's case, Chance wasn't sure he'd have a job for much longer.

"You're thinking about Quinn, aren't you?"

"Solitary is solitary," Chance said. "Not much difference if the hole is clean. I don't want to see him locked away somewhere even if it's for his own protection."

"No solitary. That'll never happen."

"I want to get the guys that did this to him and his brother." No more bullshit. No more excuses. "Tell me what you need from me."

Xav propped himself up on an elbow and looked down at Chance. "Anything you think might help put the pieces together. Come look at what we've put together in my office. See if anything makes sense to you."

Chance didn't want to go back to a law firm, but he'd do it if he had to. This was too important for him to back down under Faison's pressure. "All right," he said. "I'll give you anything that will help us solve this mess."

Xav settled back down next to him, then leaned in and kissed him. "You and I are going to put these assholes away," he said as their lips parted. "I promise."

"PLEASE. I promise I'll be good...." Chance whimpered and pulled his knees to his chest.

Laughter. The same voice he'd heard scream. His own voice. Sometimes it talked to him. Sometimes the walls flew away and he'd be drowning in darkness. Sometimes he'd fly somewhere bright and sunny, where the walls didn't exist.

"I didn't want to hit him, but he tried to hurt me. Please. I promise the next time I'll be good."

He'd been very bad. He knew that. He'd learned that in here. He'd thought he was right to fight back, but he knew now he shouldn't have. He should have let it go. He should have hid in that place in his mind where the outside world didn't exist. Then if Carl had touched him, he wouldn't remember it anyhow.

"Please," he moaned. "I told you I didn't mean to do it. I can't stand this anymore. Please...."

He shivered. He'd never get warm. Sometimes he imagined he was walking in the sand with the sun on his face. Someplace warm. Someplace safe.

His hand ached. They'd splinted two fingers and they'd wrapped his hand up so well he couldn't move it. His other hand was wrapped too, although he couldn't remember having hurt it. Maybe they figured it'd be easier if he couldn't hurt himself again. But he wouldn't. Not anymore. He'd do whatever they told him to. He'd be good. He wouldn't fight.

"Please, no... I can't do this anymore. I promise I'll be good. I promise I won't shout. I'll be good and you won't have to worry about me anymore."

The walls laughed at him. Rumbled laughter like thunder. Closer and closer it came, closing in on him so he couldn't breathe.

"No, please. Don't let me die! No!" He gasped, tried to breathe, but the walls were about to strangle him.

"No!" CHANCE shouted. "Please. No! I promise!"

"Chance?"

Two strong arms held him. Chance began to pull away, then decided he didn't want to. The arms felt safe. *He* felt safe.

"It's okay," a voice said. A gentle voice. Familiar.

He recognized the voice. "Xav?" Chance relaxed against Xav's chest.

"Yeah."

Xav gently stroked his hair. He smelled good. Comforting. Chance focused on his breathing, which was still coming in gasps. *There's nothing to be afraid of. You can breathe. Just breathe. Breathe in, count to four. Hold it for four. Breathe out, count to four, hold it for four.* His head stopped feeling as though it would float off his body and the silver specks that dotted his vision cleared.

"Bad dream?" Xav asked after a few minutes had passed.

"Yeah." God, what kind of freak would Xav take him for? Suddenly embarrassed, Chance said, "Shit. I'm sorry. I didn't mean to—"

"Shhh. It's okay." Xav kissed the top of his head. "Nothing to be sorry for."

Something in Xav's tone told Chance that Xav had had his own experiences with nightmares.

The dream had faded to a shadow now, a familiar echo. Chance breathed normally again. Breaking Benjamin's "Ashes of Eden" found its way from the radio to his still foggy brain, and the lyrics and music comforted him. The sensation of dread lessened, and he opened his eyes. His bedroom. A safe place. *His* place, with its large windows. Lots of room to move about.

Chance slipped out of Xav's arms and out of bed. What was the matter with him? In the past day, he'd told the man his life story, invited him into his house, allowed Xav to fuck him, and now he'd freaking lost it?

"You okay?" Xav asked.

"Yeah." Chance hated the sound of concern in his voice. He wasn't that kid anymore. He didn't need anyone to hold his hand.

"I need to go for a run," Chance said as he pulled on a pair of sweatpants. He needed time to think. "I'll see you later at your office."

CHAPTER THIRTY-FIVE

XAV CAUGHT a ride home in a cab at seven in the morning and thought as he always did—*Mornings should be outlawed.* The forced cab ride was just as well. He didn't need the odd looks or questions from the deputy on duty who'd gone running after Chance. Xav chuckled to himself and pitied the guy, who'd have to run with Chance in his uniform and full gear.

He thought about Chance as he showered and got ready for work. While he couldn't profess to understand Chance yet, he now understood the combative, distant man he saw in Evan, his other persona. But he'd finally glimpsed the beautiful heart he'd hoped existed beneath all that bravado. It had been a long time since Xav had felt the rush of a crush, and he smiled to himself. There was hope for them yet.

He reached for his wallet, badge, and keys and then realized he didn't have his bike back from forensics yet. He withdrew his cell phone from his pocket and dialed the office. "Good morning, Twyla Fay."

"It is not," she said in a huff.

"How bad is it?"

"Bad. Reporters are on us like a duck on a June bug, and we had to lock the front doors again. We got all kinda reports comin' in from people who think they saw everything from Italian mobsters to Martians at Bright Horizons, and the man we picked up yesterday is threatening to call a lawyer unless we release him."

"What man?"

"The man with the puppies!" she exclaimed.

"Shit. I forgot about him," Xav said in frustration.

"It's not like you haven't had a few things on y'all's mind. Forensics has been callin' every five minutes looking for you. When are you gonna be in?"

"I was on my way in until I realized I didn't have my bike."

"Oh, for cryin' out loud. It's here. Want me to have John pick you up? He's gone out to get the Krispy Kremes because I've been so damn busy."

"Would you mind?"

"Not at all, and one more thing. The medical examiner's report on Winter came in, and you're not gonna like it at all."

Xav frowned. "Is there something you want to tell me?"

"No, but I will."

After a long beat, Xav asked, "You still there?"

"Yes. He was raped."

Xav squeezed his eyes closed. No matter how many times he'd faced it, he still had a hard time processing evidence of rape.

She continued, "You need to catch those bastards and put 'em away for good."

"I intend to do just that. I'll wait for John. Thanks for everything, Twyla Fay."

"Just doin' my job."

"MORNING," XAV said as he climbed into the front seat of the sheriff's cruiser.

"One hell of a morning, Xav," John greeted. "I took the liberty of takin' a statement from our puppy-selling man and, of course, he's innocent of all wrongdoing. As far as I can tell, unless we have evidence that he's done something wrong, we have to release him. I asked the Parks and Recreation Division to pull the surveillance footage from the park next to Bright Horizons."

"Do we have anything on him?"

"Not so much as a parkin' ticket, and he's a big one for animal rights. He's hollerin' bloody murder for havin' to stay overnight in jail."

"Release him. We can pick him up again if we find something on the surveillance footage."

"I figured you'd say that, and I got them to workin' on his release paperwork."

"Good job, John. Very thorough."

John glanced at him. "Thank you, Xav. With all that's goin' on, I'm real worried about something slippin' through the cracks. With your shooting, and the NCMEC data problem, then the new hit we got, and the two other boys missin' from Bright Horizons, things aren't looking good for us. Looks like we're fallin' down on our job."

Xav shook his head. "Don't think that. It's a sign of the times we live in, and we're doing a great job of getting everything back on track."

"Boy, I sure hope so. I'm going to pull round back of the station. The press is camped out in front."

Xav pursed his lips. "They should be satisfied with the statement Winston gave them last night."

"He wants to give another brief statement when you get in and have a chance to find out what's what with everything."

John pulled into the gated parking lot reserved for the cruisers and Sheriff Winston's personal vehicle. Xav's bike and Evan's car were parked next to Winston's car.

"Did you let Mr. Fairchild know his car has been cleared?" Xav asked.

"Twyla Fay did. He said he'd be round to pick it up shortly. Said he was comin' in to meet with you anyway."

"Us. I want you and Twyla Fay in on the meeting. I want to give him a rundown on what we know. He's going to provide us with relevant information on drug busts. We're looking at the drug angle."

John parked the car, turned off the ignition, and shook his head. "God Almighty. None of us thought of that before you came along. Do you want Billy and Ridley in on the meeting?"

"Probably wouldn't hurt."

"Then I should tell you that, ah, well, there are rumors about you and, ah, and Mr. Fairchild…. Not that it's any of my business, of course, but it don't matter to me none."

Xav smirked. "It isn't fair that people assume Mr. Fairchild is gay because I am."

"I said exactly that. Not to mention, if he was, that you two'd be seein' each other. People need to mind their own."

Xav couldn't agree more.

They got out of the car and entered the bustling office.

"Thank God you're here. Sheriff wants to see you right away," Twyla Fay announced.

"Let me grab a cup of coffee and I'll be right there. When I'm done, let's convene a meeting and see where we are on everything," Xav said.

"You got it. Sally Ann is officially on my desk now, and I've taken over the desk next to John," she said with pride.

"That's great. Congratulations again."

"Thank you, sir."

THE DOOR to Sheriff Winston's office was open, and Xav entered and took a seat. "Morning."

"Morning. You all right after yesterday?"

"Fine. Thanks for having my bike brought here. John said you wanted to give the press another statement?"

"I need to say something to get them off my back."

"Mr. Fairchild is coming to meet with us. We're going to compare notes on the missing boys and increased drug activity in the county."

An impish grin filled Winston's face. "Well, now, isn't that just finer than frog hair."

Xav stifled a laugh. Just when he thought he'd heard all the Southernisms there were to hear, someone came up with another. "Meaning?"

"Mr. Fairchild can join me in giving a statement. Give that bastard Faison a run for his money."

"Faison doesn't strike me as the kind of man who will allow anyone to get between him and his limelight, but I'll leave that up to you and Mr. Fairchild."

"How soon can you have some facts ready for me?"

"Did Twyla Fay make you aware of the two additional boys who went missing from Bright Horizons?"

"She did. She also told me that she and John checked the other counties and we're the only one with this many missing kids, by far. She's also got Sally Ann looking into kids missing from other foster facilities," Winston all but spat.

Xav nodded. "I'd keep any press release limited to facts about the Haverty boys. We know that Quinn and Winter were two of the missing boys in this county, both from a foster facility, and I'd put emphasis on the fact that you're resolving cases. We're continuing to investigate and we'll publish more information as we come to know it."

"Funeral?"

Xav blew a long breath. He'd forgotten about that, and they couldn't very well have a funeral without Quinn there. "I'll ask that Winter's body be held until the investigation is over. Given that the parents are dead, there's no rush."

Winston nodded his approval. "You know about the NCMEC hit?"

"Yes. Do you mind if I ask Billy and Ridley to consider that the boy might have been on the boat with Charlie?"

Winston shook his head in disgust. "I'd be disappointed if you didn't."

Xav's admiration for the man grew. "There are only two ways someone could have found out that Quinn had been discharged from the hospital and returned to Bright Horizons. One, the hospital personnel leaked information, two, Bright Horizons leaked information, or three, someone accessed NCMEC's data."

"Had to be hospital personnel," Winston said gruffly.

"It still bothers me that the SBI didn't question our NCMEC data." Xav let the inference hang in the air.

Winston's face darkened. "Don't tell me you think this reaches all the way to the SBI."

Xav was solemn. "You read the links I gave you about the exploitation of kids out of LA's foster system?"

Winston nodded, then issued a contradictory shake of his head. "I have a hard time believin' anything like that could ever happen here."

"I'm going to have Twyla Fay list Quinn as deceased in NCMEC's system as a precaution and issue an internal memo to you as to why I'm falsifying data."

"Good idea. Let me know when you have *something* Fairchild and I can say to the press. They're gonna break down our doors."

Xav stood. "Will do. Thank you for the latitude."

Winston looked up at him, serious. "Don't thank me yet. Something tells me it's going to get worse before it gets better."

"Agreed," Xav said before he turned to leave Winston's office, stopped, and turned back. "One more thing?"

"Shoot."

"We don't want to disclose to anyone that we had a problem with our NCMEC data. Should the subject of your reopening Charlie's case arise, I'm going to say you reopened it because a boy was found down at Marina Point around the same time Charlie's boat was found. I'll add that the Collier County medical examiner's latent match was because we only recently obtained DNA data to add to Jimmy Perkins's NCMEC file."

"Sounds reasonable. Rachelle Vickers sent the reports over. Let me know when you tell the parents."

"I'm going to ask Billy and Ridley to notify them now, but I would suggest that we hold his remains in the event further forensic testing is needed."

Winston grimaced. "That's going to be hard on the family."

"It will. On a more practical note, you may wish to disclose in your press conference that we've located another missing boy before Collier County takes the credit for it."

Winston nodded slowly in contemplation. "Let me know as soon as the family is notified."

"I'll have Billy give you a call as soon as they're done."

CHAPTER THIRTY-SIX

XAV WALKED out of Winston's office and straight to Twyla Fay's new desk. "When Mr. Fairchild gets here, I want to convene in my office and go over what we have from start to finish," he said to John and Twyla Fay.

"Do you want Billy and Ridley in the meeting?" John asked.

"Yes. But I want them to notify the Perkinses that we have a positive ID on their son first, and ask them to call Sheriff Winston as soon as they're done."

John's face soured. "I should probably do that with Billy. It's a real lousy part of the job."

Xav softened. "I agree." He weighed matters carefully and dropped his voice to a near whisper. "Make sure Billy and Ridley understand that the reason we're giving to the press for the Collier County medical examiner's latent DNA match is because we only recently obtained DNA data to add to Jimmy Perkins's NCMEC file."

"That's bendin' the truth if I ever heard it but, in a way, I s'pose it's true," John acquiesced.

"Sally Ann is done checking with the state on the other foster facilities. Only Bright Horizons has kids missing," Twyla Fay offered.

"That's good news. It narrows our investigation. I'll see you in my office when Mr. Fairchild gets here."

XAV SAT down in his chair and didn't know where to start. His in-box was overflowing, and forms plastered with red "sign here" sticky arrows covered the surface of his desk. He glanced at the clock. It felt as if half the day had passed and it was only 9:00 a.m. He carefully gathered the documents and stacked them in a neat pile, then sorted through the telephone messages. Twyla Fay hadn't been kidding. Eight messages from forensics told Xav that Tom Ingram was about to have kittens. Xav picked up his phone and dialed.

"Forensics. Ingram" came Tom's clipped greeting.

"Deputy Constantine. I'm sorry I couldn't call sooner."

"I'm sure y'all are busier than a one-armed paperhanger." Tom sounded exasperated.

"Let me give you my cell phone number," Xav offered.

"I'd sure appreciate that."

Xav rattled it off, then asked, "What's up?"

"Do y'all have time to meet with me, say, around one this afternoon? We got the personal effects of the Haverty boys in here, the surveillance footage of that trawler that Mr. Fairchild was asking about, and then we got the personal effects of Jimmy Perkins that came in. I got a lot of information to give you and need some direction as to what you'd like us to process."

Xav hadn't given Quinn's personal effects a second thought, but it made sense that they would have been sent to forensics with Winter's. "Be happy to. Would you like me to bring lunch?"

"Trust me on this when I say you'll want to have eaten before then. But I'll take a rain check."

"Done. See you at one."

"Much appreciated."

Xav hung up and read down his sticky note to-do list. He crossed off *How did boys get behind car?* Quinn had answered that question, but he still wanted to know where the boys had been held and what tunnel they'd escaped through. He added to the list, *6. Search brothel.* Then he remembered Evan's comment that the brothel had once been a fish processing plant. He added, *plans & specs for building?*

He figured he'd get the worst over with and sifted through his in-box until he found the autopsy report on Winter Haverty. Paper-clipped to it was Jimmy Perkins's autopsy report from the Collier County medical examiner. He pulled Winter's report in front of him and began to read.

Winter's organ tissue was lethally suffused with cocaine, proving he'd ingested massive amounts for at least a few days, and was in keeping with the consumption of raw coca leaves laced with powder cocaine. It was a wonder he hadn't died before the shooting. Xav flipped the report over to read the sexual assault portion. Extensive damage, multiple semen samples. In short, there were multiple assailants in a short time. That and the overkill only proved his previous suspicion. *They were aiming for him.* Xav knew it was because he could identify the traffickers.

Blue eyes filled his mind, and he fought like hell to will the vision away before he broke out in a cold sweat. *Motherfuckers.* He wanted them all to burn in hell.

The end of the report noted clothing and personal possessions: underwear, jeans, plaid shirt, tennis shoes, a painted seashell, and a pocket Bible.

His brain came to a screeching halt. A *Bible*. He reached for his cell phone and dialed Reggie in LA.

"Ohmahgawd! Is this the *real* Xavier Constantine? Calling none other than *moi*? Color me thrilled!" Reggie answered in his best falsetto.

"I miss you too. How are you doing, man?"

"Good, good. Nothing's changed, and don't expect me to admit I miss you. I don't."

"You lie."

"So what? How are you doing in Podunk.... Where are you? Arkansas?"

"North Carolina."

"You aren't happy. I know you're not. When are you coming home?"

Xav ignored the teasing. "Do you remember the Bible from my case?"

"Sure. Why?" Reggie asked, all humor gone.

"I may have another one for you to look at. What kind of time do you have?"

"For you, all the time in the world so long as you clear it with Ward. How soon?"

"I'll know more when I see it this afternoon, but probably tomorrow."

"Call Ward or he'll hurt me bad."

"Call you back when I know more. Thanks, Reggie." He looked at the image of the seashell and recognized it instantly. He'd seen thousands of them for sale for a mere ten *centavos* in the local markets in Bolivia. There was no doubt in his mind that the cocaine coming into North Carolina and the missing boys were connected. Circumstantial evidence proving the traffickers were one and the same and originated in Bolivia was mounting at the speed of light. But the only link to the *Camarón* and *cocaleros* of his fabled blown mission was the bus ticket.

All he could prove in his current cases was that Victor's goons abducted Winter and Quinn, the boys were intoxicated with cocaine, and Winter was raped. Xav had no evidence of who the perpetrators were, and needed to verify the trafficking itself. Unless he could prove the origins, destinations, and modes of transport, he had nothing to substantiate trafficking. And until he identified the traffickers, he couldn't confirm that they were the perpetrators of the missing boys, and couldn't link the cases.

He set Winter's autopsy report aside and crossed *4. Winter-autopsy report* off his to-do list. Next, he read the medical examiner's report on Jimmy Perkins. The medical examiner estimated that the body had been in the water for three days during a coastal storm. Other than severe pre- and postmortem bruising and blunt force trauma to the head causing death, nothing else appeared in the report. No lab tests, no inventory of the body or personal effects. *Lame.* He developed an immediate dislike of the Collier County medical examiner and added to his to-do list, *7. Jimmy-thorough autopsy?*

He looked at the forensics report on the DSS shootout. One hundred and three bullets pulled from nearly every facet of the common room, five extracted from Rufus during the autopsy, all fired from the same Belgian FN Herstals used in the alley shootout. Other than that the shootouts involved the same guns, there was nothing to go on. Xav tossed the report aside. Given the shooters had been aiming to kill Winter in the alley, no doubt existed in his mind that the bullets from the Bright Horizons shootout were meant for Quinn. He and Chance being there had made them no more than sitting ducks against the flappers in a pinball game of mobsters bash.

Frustrated, he sat back in his chair and rubbed his eyes. His back still ached from the alley shooting, protecting Quinn was weighing on him, and the stress that came along with unsolved cases was eating at him. Six blue eyes looked out at him from his mind, dark, angry, and accusatory. *"You promised you'd keep us safe!"* Then the eyes filled with blood. Phantom pain in his side tore through him, and he began to perspire. *Shit.* He left his chair and headed to the restroom.

He rinsed his face in cool water and silently promised the blue eyes he'd get the fuckers. He looked at himself in the mirror as he dried his hands and face with paper towels, and reminded himself to keep his shit together. He tossed the towels in the wastebasket with alacrity born of exasperation and left the restroom.

He knocked on the doorjamb of Sheriff Winston's office. Winston looked up from what he was reading and motioned him in. Xav entered and closed the door behind him.

"I think what's happening here with the boys and drugs is related to the case I worked in Bolivia."

"I know you wouldn't say that without good reason. What are we lookin' at?"

"So far, only circumstantial evidence. But Winter had a Bible on him when he died. Forensics has it and I'm going to look at it this afternoon. If it turns out to be some sort of a ledger hidden within a Bible, I'm going to ask my old office to compare it to the one found on a boy in my Bolivian case. Will you please give Ward a call and okay it?"

Winston nodded. "Anything else?"

Xav shook his head. "Not right now. I'll know more after I talk to forensics and the medical examiner. Thanks, Sheriff."

"Billy called. The Perkinses have been notified about Jimmy. It goes without saying they're unhappy about us not releasing the body."

"The Collier County medical examiner didn't perform an autopsy. I'm going to ask our medical examiner to perform one. As soon as it's done, the body can be released."

Winston shook his head in disgust. "Sometimes I wonder what we pay people for. My office being the exception, of course. Keep me posted."

"I will. Thanks, Sheriff."

Xav headed back to his office and the less-than-exciting prospect of working through his in-box and signing forms. He glanced at his watch. It was nine thirty and he found himself mildly irked that Chance hadn't shown up yet. He wanted to see him.

CHAPTER THIRTY-SEVEN

CHANCE GOT out of the taxi, balanced two Starbucks cups in one hand, and tucked his briefcase under his arm with the other. He eyed the crowd of reporters at the front entrance to the sheriff's office and promptly made a beeline for the back entrance.

"Mr. Fairchild!" someone shouted from behind him.

Too slow. Chance took a long breath and turned to face Karl Kitchen, one of the reporters from *The Carver County News*. "Good to see you, Karl."

Karl tapped the small notebook he held. "Anything new on the shooting at the group home?"

"Karl," Chance said with a smile, "you know I can't comment on an ongoing investigation."

"Word is that you might've been the target of the shooter."

"No comment." At least the rumor didn't involve Quinn.

"What about rumors that you might be lookin' at takin' Mr. Faison's job?" Karl pressed.

Chance strangled a sigh. "No comment," he said. He quickly made his way through the gated rear parking lot, opened the back door as he juggled the cups and briefcase, and slipped inside before Karl could pose another question.

He headed down the long hallway to the front of the building, and a harried-looking Twyla Fay walked toward him.

"Good to see you, Twyla Fay," he said, the cups now balanced precariously on his briefcase like a twisted game of Jenga.

"I'm so sorry, Mr. Fairchild! I saw you from the window and I went to the front door to run interference. I didn't figure you'd come in the back way."

"I appreciate it."

"The reporters have been all over this place like flies on a watermelon since early mornin'," she said with a shake of her head. "Rumors are flying."

"I heard another rumor," he said with a smile. "Something about a promotion?"

"I got promoted to administrative assistant," she said proudly.

"Congratulations and well deserved."

She blushed. He walked past her and leaned on the doorjamb to Xav's office.

"Mr. Fairchild is here," she announced as she quickly stepped between Chance and the doorjamb.

Xav looked up from a mound of paperwork and smiled, obviously pleased to see Chance. "Have the others returned?"

"They're on the way back now. We'll join you as soon as they're back." Twyla Fay flitted away before Xav could respond.

"I thought you didn't do mornings," Chance said with a glance at the clock. 9:45 a.m.

"I don't. And I'll worship you more than I already do if one of those is for me."

"It most certainly is." Chance set one of the coffees on the desk in front of Xav.

"You are a god," Xav said appreciatively. He took the cup and sipped, then motioned to the chairs in front of his desk. "Bet you're one of those people who's in the office at eight sharp every morning."

Chance took a seat. "Every day but Sunday come rain or shine, and never a minute late." The moment he said it, Chance realized it wasn't entirely true. He'd slept through his alarm since meeting Xav.

"Seriously?"

"Haven't missed getting to the office by 8:00 a.m. since I started working at the DA's office."

"I'm impressed. I was worried you'd left early this morning for other reasons."

He didn't doubt that the night before had meant something to Xav, and it pleased Chance to hear this. "Just wanted to be on time," he said offhandedly as he set his briefcase on the chair next to him and opened it. "These are for you." He pulled several files from his briefcase and set them on Xav's desk. "I copied all the recent drug cases I've tried, along with a few we declined to prosecute for lack of evidence. I can't give you the originals or any confidential documents."

"Anything in there involving trawlers?"

"Not that I saw, and believe me, I looked for a connection."

"That's unfortunate."

When Xav didn't say anything more, Chance frowned and slipped his fingers through his hair, causing a lock to fall into his eyes. He brushed it back and made a mental note to make sure he didn't look as though he'd stuck his finger in an electrical outlet after he left Xav's office.

"Chance?"

That name. Chance wasn't sure he liked Xav calling him that here. It… it felt strange. Awkward. *But I asked him to use it.*

"Would it be better if I stuck with Evan?"

Chance heard no judgment in the words, just a question. *Why am I feeling like an insecure ass?* Chance lifted his chin and stared off at a distant point. *This is why you shouldn't get involved. This is why…. You're a solitary man.* But last night had been un-fucking-believable. Better. And even though the nightmare embarrassed the hell out of him, Xav's reassuring presence had made it far more bearable. So why was he keeping Xav at a distance? He furrowed his brow and glanced back at the stack of files on the desk.

"Evan?"

Xav didn't move to touch Chance, but when Chance looked up, Xav was looking at him intently. He looked concerned. More than that. He looked almost disappointed.

"I…," Chance began. "I…. Shit." He rose and walked to the windows. Outside, a line had formed to enter the building. The media was rabid, and the one deputy at the door had a hell of a time clearing people to enter one at a—

"Evan. Talk to me."

Chance caught his own reflection in the glass. *Get your shit together.* He breathed in and out slowly and turned to face Xav. Xav, who was patient and kind. Xav, who hadn't teased him. Xav, who looked genuinely worried now.

"Chance," he said. *I am Chance.* "It *is* Chance."

Xav smiled a smile that lit his green eyes and made Chance want to kiss him. Here, in the middle of the fucking office!

"Chance," Xav repeated. "But I'll keep it Mr. Fairchild in the office."

"I'm sorry," Chance said. He'd gotten used to apologizing only when it suited his purposes and never when he was contrite. How had he apologized to Xav more times than he could count in the past two days and each time he'd genuinely meant it?

"Nothing to apologize for."

Chance walked back to the chair and took a seat. Xav looked great in a suit. Better with nothing on, but he looked damn good. "Nice suit," he teased.

Xav smirked and took another sip of coffee.

Chance had completely forgotten about the coffee. He picked up his own, and for a few minutes, they sipped their coffee in comfortable silence.

"Did you see Sheriff Winston on the way in?" Xav asked.

"No. Why?"

"He wants to give another statement to the media circus and was hoping you'd join him."

"Not happening," Chance said. "Faison is the elected DA. He gives the statements. Sheriff Winston will do it on his own." Usurping Faison's publicity was a suicide mission and would end his career in a hot minute. He'd deal with Faison on his own terms, after he figured out whether it was Talley's idea to keep him off the Haverty case or if Faison had a dog in the fight.

"The man's a waste of political space," Xav said.

"Doesn't matter. I'm not giving this up, Xav. I'll help you any way I can, but I need to keep it on the down-low. If he finds out I'm still involved in this, he'll have my head on a silver platter and make it look like Christmas dinner to all his conservative cronies." He needed Xav to let it go. He'd made his decision.

"No problem. What I thought we'd do is meet with Twyla Fay, John, Billy, and Ridley to go over what we've put together and see what you think."

Chance gestured to the wall covered with map, calendar, and charts. "That is what all this relates to?"

Before Xav could respond, Twyla Fay's voice filled the intercom. "Deputy Constantine? I'm sorry to bother you. I have an Agent Dee from the SBI on the phone demanding to speak with you. I told him you were in a meeting, but he won't take no for an answer."

Chance rolled his eyes. "'Bout time Tweedle Dee and Tweedle Dunn got around to asking about Quinn," he said with a snicker.

Xav chuckled. "I was thinking more Thing One and Thing Two."

Chance laughed aloud.

"Put him through, Twyla Fay," Xav said before he pressed the speaker button and answered with a concise "Constantine."

"Deputy Constantine, this is Supervisory Agent Dee with the SBI. Where is Quinn Haverty?"

Chance couldn't prevent his eyes from widening with surprise as Xav's eyebrows shot up. "When was the last time you checked NCMEC's system?" Xav asked.

"Monday morning. It says he's been remanded to Bright Horizons. I called there this morning and Mrs. Wilhelm indicated I had to speak with Mr. Fairchild at the DA's office before we could interview him. I called his office and he isn't in. What kind of game are you playing?"

"I'm sorry, Supervisory Agent Dee. Given the news, I thought you would have known. May I trouble you to look in NCMEC's system again?" Xav asked politely.

"What news and known what?"

"Quinn Haverty is deceased, and it's been duly reported."

"What are you talking about?"

Unbelievable. "Check NCMEC's system. It's all there," Xav said calmly.

They listened as Agent Dee pounded on his keyboard ruthlessly.

"He was in that shootout at Bright Horizons?" Agent Dee demanded.

"Yes, he was. I'll have Twyla Fay send you a copy of my incident report, if you like."

"Forthwith!" Agent Dee slammed the phone down.

Xav punched the intercom button for Twyla Fay. "Please send a copy of my incident report on the Bright Horizons matter to Agent Dee."

"I will, though I'm not sure he deserves it. Sure as God made little green apples, that man is missin' the manners gene."

"While you're at it, will you ask him to provide us with a copy of their final report on the Haverty twins?" Xav asked.

"It would be my pleasure."

"And suggest that a copy be sent to my office too," Chance added.

"Be happy to, Mr. Fairchild."

"Thanks, Twyla Fay," Xav said and clicked off.

Chance looked at Xav. "They should have known."

Xav nodded. "It's certainly strange that he claims no knowledge of the event, particularly given the media attention and the clamor over twenty missing boys."

"Twenty? You said there were eighteen boys missing."

"Twyla Fay obtained a report from Rebecca Wilhelm concerning two additional boys who went missing from Bright Horizons about six months ago. It was before Wilhelm took over the facility, so she doesn't know anything about them."

Chance couldn't hide his astonishment. "No one followed up?"

"It doesn't appear so. We're looking into that now. To answer your first question, that brought our tally up to twenty boys. As I told you last night, one of the boys was found in Bolivia by me, and we recently learned from Collier County that another washed ashore at Marina Point around the same time Charlie Cooper went missing, and we now know what happened to the Haverty twins. So we're down to sixteen missing boys."

"Who's Charlie Cooper?" Chance asked.

"The deputy I replaced. He's believed to have gone out in his boat and drowned during a storm."

The information registered as Chance recalled the headlines about Cooper's disappearance. "Have you found any evidence to link Cooper's disappearance to the boy who washed ashore?"

"Sheriff Winston reopened the investigation into Charlie's disappearance. Billy Kenner and Ridley White are on it. They're also working with us peripherally on the missing boys. They may also have additional drug information for you. We discovered that the parents of all the boys missing from Bright Horizons died of cocaine overdoses. One of the parents was a known cocaine user; the Haverty boys' parents weren't. They're looking into that too."

Chance felt as if someone had kicked him in the kidneys. "Quinn's parents are dead?"

Xav nodded.

"Has he been told?" Chance could barely ask the question as memories of his social worker informing him of his mother's death flooded his thoughts. He'd been shattered in a way he'd never recovered from.

Xav suddenly looked as pallid as Chance felt. "Truthfully, I don't know." He stood, went to a file cabinet, and withdrew a file. He looked through it as he walked back to his chair and retook his seat. "The autopsy report on the parents says the family was notified, but that doesn't mean it was the boys."

Chance quickly withdrew his cell phone from his pocket, searched for Rebecca Wilhelm's number, and tapped the icon. "Good afternoon. This is Evan Fairchild. May I please speak to Rebecca Wilhelm?"

"*Of course*, Mr. Fairchild," the operator said. "Just a moment, please."

"Thank you." Chance glanced at Xav.

"I'm hard-pressed to believe DSS wouldn't have notified the boys," Xav said.

"Mr. Fairchild?"

Chance turned his attention to the voice on the phone. "Yes, this is him. Thank you for taking my call, Mrs. Wilhelm. I'm reviewing the Haverty file and have one quick question, if you don't mind."

"Of course," she replied.

"Can you tell me if the Haverty boys were formally notified of their parents' deaths?"

"Yes, they were. I told them myself."

Relief washed over Chance. "Thank you, Mrs. Wilhelm. And thank you for taking my call."

"Is there a problem?"

"No. No problem at all. Only crossing my t's and dotting my i's in the file. Thank you again." He ended the call and sat back in his chair, the dissipating adrenaline rush leaving him shaky.

"I'm sorry. It never crossed my mind that they might not have been told," Xav said sincerely.

Chance rubbed his eyes with thumb and forefinger. "Fortunately, in this instance, the system worked correctly and they were told." He thought of his own mother and wondered if Winter and Quinn had attended their parents' funerals. He made a mental note to check back with Rebecca Wilhelm and find out if they had. When his mother had died, there'd been no burial, but the small service at the church they'd once attended had at least given him some sense of closure. Winter and Quinn more than deserved the same.

"You okay? You look a little pale."

Chance nodded. "Yeah."

"Why don't we get another cup of coffee and then start our meeting with the others?"

"Sure."

CHAPTER THIRTY-EIGHT

SALLY ANN covered Xav's desk with coffee carafes, chilled water bottles, and boxes of Krispy Kremes as Billy and John brought additional chairs into the office.

Once everyone sat facing Twyla Fay's wall of information, Xav began the meeting.

"The primary goals of this meeting are to exchange information to ensure everyone is fully informed; to consider the evidence we have, circumstantial and otherwise; to determine what more should be investigated; and to leave here with a comprehensive investigation plan.

"As you know, I believe the boys who disappeared over the past five months were abducted for purposes of commercial sexual exploitation. We know that drug and human trafficking go hand in hand. Mr. Fairchild has been kind enough to join us to share what he knows about countywide statistics and trends in drug-related matters handled by his office. Thank you for joining us."

Chance nodded briefly. "Thank you for including me."

Xav gestured to the displays on the wall and described them one by one. "Twyla Fay has done an exceptional job of displaying what we know to date. This board lists the boys by name and itemizes the circumstances under which they disappeared. This calendar shows the dates each boy disappeared. And the map plots the locations from which they disappeared.

"From the list, we see that all of the boys except the two sets of boys who disappeared from Bright Horizons came from good homes. They range in age from eight to thirteen, exhibited typical age-appropriate behavior in school and at home, were not known to use drugs, and were not sexually active, let alone promiscuous, that we know of.

"The calendar shows us that the abductions began as shrimp season began and have continued steadily at an approximate rate of one to two boys per week until I arrived and the abductions abruptly ceased."

"Oh my God. I didn't even notice that," Twyla Fay said in a breathy voice.

"I'm not so vain as to believe they stopped because *there's a new sheriff in town.*" He made air quotes with his fingers. "I believe they stopped for other reasons, and I'll get into those in a few minutes."

He gestured to the wall map. "We found no similarities among or pattern to the abductions until Twyla Fay plotted the abductions on this map. That's when one location became a location of interest." He put his fingertip on the red X. "Good Shepherd's Church became of interest when we realized that Victor is a youth volunteer there. We also know that Padre Paolo takes in the homeless irrespective of sordid background."

Chance rose and went to the map. "Do you have another colored marker?"

Xav took a blue one from the nearest dry-wipe board and handed it to him. Chance drew a small circle on the map at the opposite end of the park that abutted the church and wrote BH in the center of it.

"What's that?" Twyla Fay asked.

"I'll be damned," Billy said softly.

Xav looked at Chance in disbelief.

Chance nodded in confirmation. "Bright Horizons sits at the other end of the park from the church."

Xav shook his head in dismay. They'd marked the spots where each boy had disappeared but hadn't labeled them.

"Oh, Lord! I can't believe I didn't see that! I am so sorry, Xav!" Twyla Fay exclaimed.

"Don't apologize. None of us noticed it. Thank you, Mr. Fairchild."

"I wish I could say it was my pleasure to have pointed it out to you," he said as he retook his seat.

"I'll be sure to identify each location as soon as we're done here," Twyla Fay announced.

"I'm not sure we want to do that just yet," Xav said.

"Why not?"

"We'll only clutter the map with potentially irrelevant information. Billy, where is 4Play located?"

Billy stood, retrieved a pink marker from a dry-wipe board, and circled the old docks. "A straight shot down Liberty Avenue." He drew a line down Liberty from the old docks to the church before capping the marker and retaking his seat.

John added to the conversation. "Xav, y'all asked us to check every file to see if there was any relationship between the church and the boys who'd been abducted. We didn't find anything, but we did notice that all the boys had attended a weekly Saturday get-together at the park to build piñatas for the upcoming regatta. The Parks and Recreation Department puts on the function. Not the church."

"When did it begin?" Xav asked.

John stood, took a green marker from a dry-wipe board, and circled a date on the calendar. "The first Saturday of spring break. Not counting the two additional boys we didn't know went missin' from Bright Horizons, it was two days before the first boy in our investigations disappeared."

"I'm beginning to think it's high time we had a formal talk with Padre Paolo," Billy said as John sat down again.

Ridley nodded his agreement. "Is it worth getting a warrant to search the church?"

"We have to propose evidence for a warrant. Why don't we begin a list of potential places to search and the evidence we hope to find?" Xav suggested.

Twyla Fay jumped up from her seat and went to an empty dry-wipe board. "Start naming 'em off," she announced. "Church," she said as she wrote it on the board.

"Personal effects relating to missing boys," Xav said.

"Sunday-school attendance records," John added.

"Volunteer personnel records, including those of that... that... prostitute what's-his-name," Billy said.

Chance coughed and put a loosely cupped fist to his lips. "Excuse me?"

Xav went to his desk and searched until he found Victor's sheet. "Victor Vasquez-Molina." He handed the sheet to Chance. "He runs 4Play and volunteers for the Latino youth program at the church."

"Unbelievable," Chance said as he read the report. "How in God's name does a known sex worker become a volunteer for kids at a church?"

"Only by the grace of the Almighty and Padre Paolo," Billy spat.

"It would seem that Padre Paolo is our local Mother Teresa for the downtrodden," Xav said. "Let's move it along. We have a lot of ground to cover."

"Parks and Recreation personnel records for the piñata program?" John asked.

"Got it," Twyla Fay said as she added it to the list.

"Did we get the surveillance footage from the park?" Xav asked.

"Months of it. One of us has to sit through it all," John said.

"Start with the Saturday that Quinn and Winter were abducted. We need that surveillance footage in order to ID the two men who abducted them and obtain warrants for their arrests. Add the two unknown assailants to the warrant list, Twyla Fay," Xav instructed.

"What do you want me to call 'em?" Twyla Fay asked.

"Haverty boys' kidnappers. John, compare that footage to the footage from the alley shooting to see if you can match them to the two men who shot us."

John scribbled on a small note pad. "Got it. I'll also keep a lookout for our puppy man."

"Good. Then go through every Saturday, paying close attention to each piñata class. Does the forensics lab have any trainees?"

"Two," Billy said.

"Can we send the remaining park footage over for their review?"

"I'll give Tom a call and see what we can work out," Billy said.

"What about searching 4Play?" John asked.

Xav squinted in thought. "I've thought about that. I want to know more about the building first. Mr. Fairchild, I assume city hall has plans for the building."

"Yes. But every building down there has been modified in some way without permit, and I guarantee you they don't meet code. Some are in danger of collapse and are downright dangerous. If you intend to plan a raid, I'd include Fire and Rescue in the plan."

"Good suggestion. Twyla Fay, please add 4Play to the list, but put an asterisk next to it and denote that we need building plans and specs, and Fire and Rescue if we go in." Xav rubbed his jaw in contemplation. "All right, what do we hope to find at the brothel?"

Chance cleared his throat. "Personal effects of the Haverty boys, DNA of the Haverty boys, the blanket that Quinn tore up to escape, and cocaine residue."

"Have any of you ever been inside the building?" No one responded, and Xav smiled. "I mean for other than recreational purposes."

"Ridley and I searched the place about five years ago looking for an underage girl," Billy answered. "It's like an old warehouse that's been all gussied up and has offices turned into parlors and whatnot on the second floor."

"It's an old processing plant. It has to have lower levels where the trawlers dropped their catch and fish was processed," Chance said. "Quinn said he felt like he was in a jar in the ocean because he could hear the water hitting the walls. I'm guessing that the lower levels have deteriorated over time and might have sagged enough beneath the dock to hit the water."

Xav nodded his agreement.

Ridley shook his head. "We never found anything like stairs."

"An elevator?" Xav asked.

John, Ridley, and Billy exchanged looks before John said, "I don't think anyone ever thought to look for one, Xav."

"We need the plans for the building. Though they may no longer be accurate, we need to start somewhere."

"I'm startin' a list on this side of the board for things we need to get ahold of," Twyla Fay said.

"Let's take a ten-minute break and reconvene to look at our cases," Xav announced.

"How ARE you doing?" Xav asked as he filled one of the coffee Thermoses with a fresh pot of coffee.

Chance rinsed his coffee mug and set it in the sink. "Okay. It's a lot of information to take in. I appreciate you including me in this."

"I wouldn't have it any other way."

Chance leaned a hip against the counter and looked off into the distance. "Does it ever get to you? The missing kids?"

Xav nodded. "Yep."

"But you don't give up."

"Nope."

"How do you do it?"

Xav capped the Thermos. "I close my mind to the fury I feel and just do it and don't stop doing it and never look back."

"I can't do that," Chance said.

"You do it every day in the cases you prosecute."

Chance looked at Xav now, thoughtful. "Hadn't looked at it that way."

Xav winked at him before they left the small kitchen and returned to the meeting.

CHAPTER THIRTY-NINE

XAV RESUMED his position in front of the wall of information, now with Chance at his side. "Mr. Fairchild has information to share with us, so I'm turning the floor over to him."

Xav took a seat and Chance cleared his throat and began. "We know that cocaine busts along the I-95 corridor are down, but countywide end-user arrests are up, overdoses are up, and cocaine is showing up in our schools. This information speaks to a greater influx of drugs in our county—specifically, cocaine.

"Clearly, the decrease in arrests in the I-95 corridor speaks to new clandestine routes for drug trafficking. Given there haven't been more arrests along roadways, I had no alternative but to consider private airports and waterways. Data provided by the DEA show no marked increase in drug imports by air. That leaves us with waterways. I checked cases in my office, and we haven't seen a marked increase in marine arrests having to do with drugs. All of this information has left me stumped for months trying to determine the source of the increased influx of drugs."

He reached for a marker and went to the calendar. "I analyzed the cases presented to my office for prosecution over the past twelve months and found a sharp increase in arrests for possession about the time shrimp season began." He underlined the first week of March on the calendar.

"I was afraid you'd find that," Xav said.

Chance nodded. "There does appear to be a correlation between the disappearance of the boys and the increase in cocaine trafficking."

Billy spoke up. "I asked our personnel to gather information on the drug overdoses in the county for the past twelve months to see if users were overdosing from their usual drug of choice or not. As it turns out, the only two people who overdosed from cocaine when it was not their drug of choice were the Haverty parents. This goes to your theory that the parents were murdered after the boys were removed from the home, Xav, but I'm unsure it's enough to open a murder investigation."

Chance glanced at Xav, and Xav confirmed what Billy said. "I think traffickers took notice of the Haverty boys when the father tried to prostitute them, and made sure the parents weren't around to want the boys back."

Xav turned back to Billy. "Let's talk to the sheriff and see what his thoughts are, but my gut tells me we need to open an investigation if only to prove they were not murdered. We should also take into consideration the mother of the other two boys taken from Bright Horizons. Though cocaine was her drug of choice, we probably want to look into her habits and see if she came into contact with anyone related to any of our matters here."

Chance ran a hand through his hair and blew a long breath before he continued. "From everything that's come through my office, I'm certain that cocaine is entering this county by boat. Deputy Constantine, I mentioned a trawler putting in late the night of the alley shooting. We need to look into that. Trawlers just don't put in at nearly eleven at night unless they have engine trouble."

Xav stood and joined Chance. "Tom Ingram called about your inquiry, and I authorized him to ID it. I'm going over there this afternoon. Why don't you come with me and we'll take a look at what he found."

Chance's face lit with a smile. "Be happy to."

"I'm going to add that to our list," Twyla Fay said as she jumped up from her seat, added it to the list of things that they needed to gather on the dry erase board, and retook her seat.

Chance gestured to the files on Xav's desk. "I brought some files over. Maybe you can find things in them that relate to what you're working on."

"I'll be happy to take a look at them," John said.

"As of right now, that's all I have to give you," Chance finished and took a seat.

"Thank you, Mr. Fairchild," Xav said formally. "I'm going to share some highly confidential information with you having to do with the last case I worked with the FBI…."

Xav finished fifteen minutes later with "…and the bus ticket that was in Jeremy Wrigley's possession is the reason I moved to North Carolina."

"Jesus, Mary, and Joseph," Ridley said. "I can't imagine doin' that kinda work."

"Working for CARD is, without a doubt, the hardest thing I've ever done," Xav admitted. "You can't imagine what adults do to children."

"I don't even know why we bother prosecutin' the monsters. I'd just as soon take 'em out back and shoot 'em," Twyla Fay said.

"There's no worse case to prosecute than a child molestation case," Chance agreed.

"In any event," Xav continued, "and given that LA is the primary portal for child sex trafficking in and out of the US, we originally thought that the Wrigley boy made his way to LA and the boys were abducted from there. As it turns out, the Helm boy jumped a bus with Jeremy Wrigley, came here, and the boys disappeared from the Greyhound station. They were then taken to Bolivia. So we know there is trafficking of boys from here to South America. We also know that there is an increased influx of cocaine into this county. While we haven't proved it, it's a fair bet that it's from Bolivia. We also know that a number of boys are missing from here and, based upon the events involving the Haverty twins, boys are being abducted for purposes of sexual exploitation.

"Child sex traffickers intending to take human cargo out of the country generally do it by boat. They are ferried five miles off the coast into international waters and transferred to a larger vessel, then taken to destinations south and, from there, all over the world. During the trip south, the kids are plied with alcohol and drugs, and groomed. By the time they reach South America, they are generally compliant. Any child that doesn't comply is simply thrown overboard, often cut up before being thrown over to ensure they are consumed by predatory marine life."

"Alive?" Twyla Fay asked softly.

Xav nodded. "Examples are made of them for the other children aboard the vessel."

"Oh my God," she squeaked.

Xav continued. "We know that drug traffickers are notoriously violent, but you probably have no concept of how violent *human* traffickers can be. I can tell you from personal experience they make drug traffickers look like spoiled toddlers in a park. It is my belief that cocaine is being trafficked into North Carolina and boys are being trafficked out of North Carolina via the same boats.

"Turning our attention to our recent activity, we know the perpetrators are willing to go to great lengths to avoid being caught, including not only murder but attempted murder of witnesses, a deputy sheriff, and quite possibly Mr. Fairchild, given that he was with me and Quinn at Bright Horizons.

"Looking at our cases, we know the Wrigley and Haverty cases relate to child sexual exploitation and trafficking. Enter our missing Charlie Cooper and the Perkins boy who washed ashore near Charlie's boat. I am not convinced that Charlie is deceased."

Billy spoke up, irritation plain on his face. "Charlie was a good man."

"I know you believe that, and I hope you're right. I've merely seen too many people—not just cops but politicians, doctors, lawyers, social workers, even school teachers—go bad when it comes to child sexual exploitation."

"Aww, God, that's just disgustin'," Ridley said angrily.

Xav glanced at his watch. It was nearing the time to leave in order to get to Forensics by one. "The last piece of evidence I want to raise is the Bible found in Winter's possession. A similar Bible was found in the Wrigley boy's possession, but it wasn't a Bible at all. It was a ledger containing transactions listed in bolivianos, or Bolivian currency. The LA office of the FBI believes that Bible represents an accounting of the purchases and sales of children. We'll see what the one in Winter's possession looks like when Mr. Fairchild and I visit Forensics this afternoon, and if it is a ledger, I've asked the LA office of the FBI to compare the two.

"All said, the evidence that we have gathered to date is circumstantial, and until we prove who the traffickers are, the departure and destination points, modes of transport of drugs and children and, of course, the use of the products at both ends, we have nothing to go on.

"Starting with the traffickers, we know from Quinn that Victor is a handler. He housed and maintained the Haverty boys until they escaped. But we don't know who Victor's boss is. However, we do know from Quinn that the two men who abducted them are the same two men who shot us in the alley. John, if you can ID them from the surveillance footage, let's arrest and interrogate them. You'll also want your local immigration official available to verify passports, visas, or green cards in their possession. Mr. Fairchild, I'm going to ask you to do everything within your power to assure they are detained without bail."

Chance was thoughtful for a moment. "There won't be any problem with that."

"Don't we have enough evidence based on Quinn's statement to arrest Victor?" John asked.

"We do, but we need him free right now," Xav answered.

"Why?" John all but demanded.

"Because handlers are the go-betweens and are always in contact with two people: the abductor and the boss. I want Victor in circulation right now."

Billy humphed. "Helluva thing to leave a criminal free no matter the reason."

Xav nodded. "I know, Billy. Okay, in order to prove departure point, we need to prove method of transport, and in order to prove method of transport, we need to catch them in the act. I'm hoping Mr. Fairchild is onto something with the trawler pulling in late. Assuming trawlers are our primary mode of transport, there are hundreds if not thousands of trawlers around here. How do we isolate which trawlers would be of interest to us, and how do we catch them in the act?"

Billy shook his head slowly as he thought aloud. "Involve the Coast Guard and a lot of legwork on our part. The honest fishermen around here don't like pirates of any kind. Most of them would be willin' to name those they don't like, but we need to consider competition. Some might name others outta jealousy."

"Can you put some men on that and see if our honest fishermen name a common foe?"

Billy nodded. "I'll ask Sheriff to approve the overtime."

Xav nodded. "Time is of the essence, Billy. If any of the boys are still alive, we need to get to them as soon as possible."

"Do you think they still are?" Twyla Fay asked.

"Statistically, if we don't find children within forty-eight hours of disappearance, they're deceased. Yet, I found the two boys in Bolivia after two months of searching. It's a good sign that the Haverty twins were still alive after being missing for three weeks. It tells me whoever is at the root of this wants them alive. Let's hold on to that."

"The Perkins boy wasn't," Ridley said.

Everyone in the room shifted uncomfortably.

Xav breathed deeply. "Four out of every five kids abducted don't survive. The one kid who does makes what we do worthwhile. We're going to hold on to the fact that we saved Quinn."

Everyone nodded in agreement.

"All right. You asked why I think the abductions ceased abruptly when I arrived, and there is only one reason for that. The head honcho of the operation is local, and he put a stop to it because he's worried about something."

"The head of the snake," Chance said under his breath.

Xav nodded once.

CHAPTER FORTY

XAV CLIMBED into Chance's car and found he fit nicely in the passenger seat. "Beautiful car."

Chance smiled at him briefly before putting the key in the ignition and starting it. "And a lot of work to maintain. How do you survive with a motorcycle? Riding in the rain must be a bitch."

"I don't ride in the rain unless I'm caught in it. I have a car."

Chance glanced at him. "You probably have some kind of muscle car like a Mustang."

Xav chuckled. "Too small."

"A Camaro."

"Bigger."

"An SUV?" Chance persisted.

Xav grimaced. "Bite your tongue. Bigger."

Chance thought for a moment. "A Hummer!"

Xav chuckled again. "No comment."

Chance's jaw might as well have come unhinged. "You do, don't you!"

"Maybe."

"You're an elitist!"

"I prefer snob. Let's head over to Forensics. I promised Tom I'd be there by one."

Chance put the car in gear and pulled out of the parking lot, mumbling something about a Hummer being a combination dick truck and muscle car.

Ten minutes later, they entered the unmarked building from the back and walked down a plain hallway to the front office. The door was ajar. Chance knocked and pushed it open.

"Hey, Tom," Chance greeted.

Tom Ingram's expression wasn't welcoming. "Mr. Fairchild," he said as he stood and shook Chance's hand.

Xav extended a hand. "I'm Xav Constantine."

Tom's expression changed to be more open as he shook Xav's hand. "Nice to meet y'all. Thanks for comin'."

"I brought Mr. Fairchild with me because we're looking at possible links between cocaine trafficking and our missing boys. Whatever you have to say to me, you can say to him."

Tom nodded. "Sheriff Winston called over and said that. No offense, Mr. Fairchild. I just can't release information outta here without his okay."

"None taken," Chance said.

"Let's go into the lab and take a look at what we got." He walked across the hallway, and Chance and Xav followed. "I figured we'd start with the Haverty boys' clothes and personal effects. I got them all laid out here." He gestured to a table that ran nearly the length of the room.

Xav had seen many of these tables over the years but was still impressed each time he saw the lighting beneath the eggshell surface. Though indirect, it filled the room with bright light. He was even more impressed that the forensics department had a laboratory equipped with first-class paraphernalia.

Tom gestured to a pair of jeans. "These clothes came off of Quinn Haverty and were collected at the hospital. We did all the usual tests on 'em but didn't bother to type and identify the blood. Because they're identical twins, we'd have to spend days on it, and as I understand it from the crime scene report, you already know both were shot, so there's no point to it."

"True," Xav agreed.

"But we identified several other substances on both boys' clothes, including dog hair. Puppy hair to be precise."

Xav and Chance both nodded. "They were petting puppies right before they were abducted," Chance said.

"Okay, so you know the source of that," Tom continued. "Both boys' clothes had cocaine residue on 'em, bile and excreta containing cocaine elements. This is consistent with the autopsy report on Winter Haverty and the stat blood test results from the hospital. There was also semen in Winter's underwear, and we were able to match that to what the ME found in the autopsy, but no DNA match in the system. There were two other substances on both boys' clothes we wouldn't have thought unique but for the circumstances. If these boys had been known to play down at the docks or on a trawler, this wouldn't have been significant. But they were orphans, right? In a group home?"

"Yes. What'd you find?" Xav asked.

"Moss and mold. Specifically, the type found on a fishin' boat or in a processing plant."

"It has to be from the vent they escaped out of," Xav said.

Tom squinted. "You think they were held in a processing plant?"

"That or a fishing boat," Xav answered.

"But you don't know where, exactly?"

"No," Chance said.

Tom smoothed his mustache and seemed to give this some thought. "If you identify a potential location and we get a sample, I'll be able to compare the two and identify whether they're the same."

Xav smiled and withdrew a notepad from his pocket and scribbled on it. "We have a potential location. 4Play."

Tom frowned and shook his head. "Moving on. The only nonclothing-related item Quinn had on him was this." He reached for a sealed clear plastic bag and handed it to Xav. It contained a necklace with half a heart on it engraved with *twins forever*.

"We found the other half of the heart in Winter's pocket."

An emotional band tightened around Xav's heart. "As soon as you're done with these, I'd like to return them to Quinn."

Tom nodded as he walked a few feet down the table. "We found one additional element on Winter's clothing. It was sand. Local. Again, not unique except for the circumstances and that Quinn's clothes didn't have it."

Xav nodded. "The boys were separated at one point. The sand had to have come from wherever Winter was taken."

"Okay. Then we found these two additional items in Winter's personal effects. A Bible and a seashell."

"Can I see the seashell?" Chance asked.

Tom handed the small plastic bag containing the shell to Evan.

"They're all over Bolivia. They sell them as trinkets for a couple of cents apiece," Xav explained.

Chance looked at him now. "That's our link."

Xav shook his head. "Tentative at best."

Chance's face fell in disappointment, and Tom continued. "I flipped through the Bible, and it's the strangest-looking one I've ever seen. It looks like someone's little black book."

"It's got phone numbers in it?" Chance asked.

"Just numbers. Anyway, I thought you might be interested to see it." He went to a computer terminal and punched a few keys.

An image materialized on the screen, and déjà vu hit Xav like a ton of bricks. He quickly withdrew his cell phone and dialed Reggie. "It's the same. I'll send it over," he said without preamble when Reggie answered. He terminated the call without waiting for Reggie's response. "That Bible matches one we found on the Wrigley boy," he explained. "I want you to send it to Reggie Cook in the FBI forensics lab in LA."

Tom reached for a transfer of evidence form, slapped it down on the desk, and held a pen out to Xav. Xav signed it quickly and added Reggie's e-mail address to the form.

"What is it?" Chance asked.

"It's the ledger of financial transactions in bolivianos that I mentioned in our meeting. Winter must have stolen it from whoever raped him."

Chance looked at him in surprise. "*That's* our link."

Xav nodded. "If it proves to represent the same transactions, it is."

Tom gestured to the remnants of clothing at the end of the long table. "This is what came up from Collier County with Jeremy Perkins." They moved down the table. "There isn't much left of his clothing, and he had no underwear or shoes. But he did have this." He reached for a clear plastic bag and handed it to Xav. It was another painted seashell. "He also had the same sand in his clothing that Winter had in his, but that stands to reason after the body bein' in the water for a period of time. We found blood trace in the crotch area of his pants, but the ME didn't do an autopsy, so we have nothing to match it to."

Xav pursed his lips. "I'm going to ask our ME to perform one."

Tom nodded. "That would be a help."

Xav looked at the clothing and noticed small light blue particles. "What are the blue flecks?"

"Paint."

"You have evidence from the Charlie Cooper case, don't you?" Xav asked.

"Some. Why?"

"I want to know if Jimmy Perkins was on Charlie Cooper's boat."

Tom stroked his mustache again and Xav was coming to believe it was a habit when the man was deep in thought. "I'll pull the evidence and see what I have."

"Thank you." Xav set the plastic bag containing the seashell on the table next to the clothing.

"That's all I have for the boys' property. Oh, and this is for you." He handed a large plastic bag to Xav. "It's your suit coat from the shooting at Bright Horizons. I'm done with it. Nothing to report other than Quinn's blood is on it."

Xav accepted the bag and thought to throw it out. He wasn't sure he wanted to give it to a dry cleaner. Too many questions, and it would reek to high heaven when the bag was opened.

"Now, about that trawler you called about, Mr. Fairchild. Let's go back to my office," Tom continued.

Tom took a seat behind his desk and Xav gestured to Chance to take the only other chair in the office.

"Took a little work to blow up the image, but we were able to get a registration number off the surveillance video from the docks," Tom said as he punched keys, and an image from the surveillance footage filled the monitor. He swiveled it so both Xav and Chance could see it.

"She's got both federal and state registration. Coast Guard has her hailing port as Venture, North Carolina. State registration is under Nothing Ventured, LLC."

"What's the name of the boat?" Chance asked.

"She's registered under *M. Butterfly*," Tom said with a chuckle. "Maybe they're opera buffs."

"Mariposa," Xav said under his breath.

"What?" Chance asked.

"Quinn said all that Winter kept saying when he came back was *mariposa. Mariposa* means butterfly in Spanish."

Chance's eyes widened in surprise. "Do you think that's what he meant?"

Xav nodded slowly as he thought about the registration of the *Camarón*.

Tom continued. "I searched Nothing Ventured on the secretary of state's website. There were three entries, two of which have been administratively dissolved. The active one shows the LLC was formed in 2011, and the registered agent is a law firm located in Wilmington, North Carolina. The articles of organization show the owner of the LLC is another corporation. I checked the owner corporation, but another corporation owns it. I checked that corporation, and it's owned by yet another corporation. The fact that they've hidden the ownership beneath a pile of straw companies tells me the boat's a front for something illegal."

Xav withdrew his pad and pen and made a few more notes. "May I ask you to send that information to the Cryptology Department in LA? They'll try to match the information to what we have on the Wrigley case."

"You sign the form, I'll send it wherever you want it to go." He set another form on the desk for Xav to sign.

"You've done a great job, Tom. Thank you," Xav said as he signed the form. "Is there a way to tell where the *Butterfly* is now?"

Chance shook his head. "Ships aren't required to have AIS transponders unless they have a gross tonnage of fifty thousand or more. A good-sized trawler might have a GT of a hundred and twenty tons. Unless the owners voluntarily installed a transponder on the *Butterfly* and it's on, we can't locate her. The Coast Guard can attempt to hail her and ask where she is, but if she doesn't respond, there's no way to know where she is."

"There is no way to locate her at all?" Xav asked, incredulous.

"No, but…." Chance thought for a moment. "If she's reported missing or law enforcement has issued a BOLO, the Coast Guard will put an alert out for her. If she's spotted, you'll get a location. The problem with that is that the crew of the *Butterfly* will hear the alert too, and could try to take cover in one of the estuaries."

"Good to know," Xav said. "How do you know so much about boats?"

Chance paused. "I, ah, own a small boat."

Xav's brows shot up in query, but Chance didn't continue.

"I'll let you know when you can pick up the hearts for the boy," Tom said.

Chance stood and extended a hand. "Thanks, Tom."

Tom stood and shook both Xav's and Chance's hands. "I wish I could say it's my pleasure, but it isn't. Working on the boys' property is tough."

Chance nodded. "I can only imagine."

"Thanks, Tom," Xav said as they left the office.

CHANCE DROVE to the coroner's office and they rode in silence until Xav's phone rang. He answered it and listened. "Please add moss and mold to the warrant for 4Play. It was on the boys' clothing. And we need a warrant for the corporate documents for the ownership of a trawler by the name of *M. Butterfly*, also known as *Mariposa*. What was the color of Charlie Cooper's boat? … Thanks, Billy." Xav terminated the call. "Tell me about your boat."

Chance glanced at him. "Small sailboat."

"How big?"

"Thirty-three feet or so."

"Elitist."

"Snob."

CHAPTER FORTY-ONE

THEY ENTERED the ME's office, and none other than Ryan was at the front counter. "Hello, Ryan," Chance said formally.

"Well, hi there, Mr. Fairchild."

"This is Deputy Constantine," Chance quickly introduced. "We'd like to speak with Ms. Vickers. Please let her know we're here."

"I don't know if she's avail—"

"She is and she's waiting for us," Xav said without inflection.

Ryan turned sickly sweet. "Well, now. I see that you're not from around here. Where is it that you hail from, *Deputy*?" Ryan pronounced deputy *dep-u*-tee.

Xav wasn't interested in the reindeer games. "You have five seconds to pick up the phone and let her know we're here."

Ryan paled.

"I'd do what the man says," Chance said, stifling a smile.

Ryan picked up the phone. "We do things around here with a little more manners." He rolled his eyes, then punched the intercom with an overly deliberate fingertip.

As Ryan notified Rachelle that they had arrived, Chance turned away with an exaggerated half mortified, half humorous look at Xav. Xav winked and Chance looked as if he could hardly contain his laughter.

"She'll be right with you, gentleman," Ryan announced.

"Thank you," Xav said politely.

Rachelle opened the door to the reception area. "Mr. Fairchild, Deputy Constantine. Right this way."

They followed her down the long sterile hallway, both barely able to contain their laughter.

"I'm going to warn you ahead of time. Jimmy Perkins's body is in bad shape after being in the water."

"The report says he was in the water for three days," Xav said.

"According to the reports, he washed ashore a day after the storm. I don't know if that was when he was found or just the estimated time his body came ashore. Whoever handled this for Collier did a lousy job." She turned the handle on a door that led to a room-size refrigerator, opened it, and motioned them inside.

They entered and stood aside as she approached a gurney and drew back a sheet. The body had shriveled after bloating in seawater, and the young boy looked like an old man. The smell was horrific, and Chance put a hand over his mouth and nose and turned away.

Rachelle handed a small container to him. "Rub a little of this under your nose." She pulled several latex gloves from a nearby dispenser and handed two to Xav and two to Chance, then snapped one onto each of her hands. Xav donned his with expertise. Chance tucked them in his coat pocket and handed the small container back to Rachelle.

"Can you identify a specific cause of death?" Xav asked.

"Yes." She gripped the shoulder and hip of the body and rolled it partially over. A gaping, jagged wound covered an eight-inch area on the back of the body. "He was impaled. It went through his heart before it took a good chunk of tissue on its way out."

"Gaffed," Xav said quietly.

Rachelle nodded as she rolled the body back to rest. "That would be my guess."

"What?" Chance asked.

"He was gaffed," Xav said.

"What's that?" Chance asked.

"It's the hook they use to bring large fish up on deck," Rachelle explained.

"Oh God," Chance said softly.

"May I ask you to perform a full autopsy?" Xav asked.

Rachelle nodded. "Don't know how good the evidence will be after this much time."

"Do the best you can," Xav said.

"Was he raped?" Chance asked.

"I can't say for sure yet. Small predatory marine life attacks raw tissue, but my guess is yes," Rachelle answered.

Chance excused himself and left the refrigerator.

Xav met Rachelle's eyes. "Thanks."

"Is the news accurate?"

"What news, in particular?"

"The number of boys missing is eighteen?"

Xav went to breathe deeply and opted not to inside the refrigerator. The stench was getting to him. "There were twenty. We have a disposition on the Haverty twins, the Wrigley boy, and now the Perkins boy. Sixteen remain missing."

"This isn't the work of one psychopath, is it?"

Xav met her even gaze for a long moment. "It's a sex trafficking ring."

"Son of a bitch," she said softly as she turned and led Xav from the refrigerator.

XAV OPENED the passenger door, stepped into Chance's car, and closed the door. "You okay?"

"No," Chance said softly.

Xav reached across the divide and put a calming hand on Chance's thigh. "We'll get them."

Chance gripped Xav's hand as he looked out the windshield. "I don't know how you do it."

Xav joined Chance in looking out the windshield at the nondescript parking lot. "The only way I've been able to do what I do is to think about the boys I can save. Then I do what I have to do no matter the cost."

Chance looked at him now. "Do you think the others are still alive?"

Xav met the eyes he was falling in love with and couldn't lie. "No. But we're going to do our best to find them anyway because we want to be there for them if they are. Trust me. It'll make all the difference in the world to you if you can save even one."

Chance closed his eyes and rubbed a temple with his free hand. "This world is fucked-up."

Xav nodded. He had nothing to say to that. After a long beat he said, "Are you up for a trip to City Hall to see if we can find the building plans for 4Play?"

Chance nodded. "Thank you."

"For what?"

"Walking me through this. I thought… I thought I could figure all this out and… I don't know, prosecute these fuckers." He shook his head to himself. "It's so much more than that."

Xav smiled a gentle smile. "You're doing great."

Chance rolled his eyes. "Liar."

"You're doing good things here, Chance," Xav said sincerely.

Chance almost smiled. "Of all people, I have to meet a liar who rides a Harley and drives a Hummer. This world *is* fucked-up."

Xav laughed aloud. "Shut up about my vehicles and drive."

They arrived at City Hall twenty minutes later. "Let me do the talking," Chance said as they got out of the car.

"It's all yours," Xav said.

"I'm serious. Don't be an ass. These people have no sense of humor."

"I'm on my best behavior."

Chance gave him a crooked smile. "That isn't sayin' much."

Xav snorted softly. "Bitch."

"Asshole."

Once inside the building, Chance walked up to the counter and smiled at the old woman behind it. "Ila Jo," he said when she glared back at him, "I've missed seein' you."

"You know where to find me, Mr. Fairchild," Ila Jo answered, her expression unchanged.

"Evan," Chance corrected as he put an elbow on the counter so that he was eye to eye with her.

Ila Jo blinked and her features softened a bit. She hesitated a moment, then said in a girlish voice, "All right. Evan. What can I do for you, Evan?" she asked, her wrinkled cheeks now slightly pink.

"Ah need a copy of the buildin' plans for an establishment called 4Play located down at the old docks."

The blush on her cheeks deepened as she scribbled down the name, left the counter, and disappeared through a doorway.

XAV PACED as they waited for the clerk to retrieve the documents from the archives and copy them. "How much longer is this going to take? We've been here an hour," he griped.

"Why, Xavier Constantine," Chance drawled, "y'all look as though y'all have ants in your pants."

Xav stopped pacing. "Waiting isn't my strong suit."

"I see that."

"Does everything take this long in the South?"

Chance gave him a deadpan look. "Only when we're aimin' to irritate foreigners."

"You work at it, don't you?"

"Asshole," Chance teased.

Xav chuckled. "Bi—"

"Here we are," Ila Jo said. "That'll be $112.50."

Chance made an exaggerated gesture toward Xav. "Deputy Constantine will take care of it."

"How much?" Xav all but demanded.

"Ninety pages at $1.25 a page," she announced.

Xav forked over his credit card.

"Cash only," she said as she glared at him over her spectacles.

Xav dug in his pocket for his money clip. "Highway robbery," he muttered as he counted out $120 in twenties.

"We don't give change," she said as she snatched the money from his hand.

"Oh, please. Keep the change," he said, irritated beyond reason.

It looked as if it was all Chance could do not to burst into laughter. "Thank you kindly, Ila Jo," he said as he accepted the documents.

"It's always good to see you, Evan," she cooed. "Y'all come back now."

"You got a receipt, right?" Xav asked as they walked to the car.

"Shoot. I forgot." Chance turned to head back into the building.

"Forget it! I can't take going back in there."

Chance finally exploded in laughter. "It's stapled to the documents."

Xav glared at him. "It's because I ride a bike, isn't it?"

"Absolutely not." Chance grinned as he unlocked the door to the car. "It's because you drive a Hummer."

"Fuck you."

CHAPTER FORTY-TWO

"YOU MIND stopping at Whole Foods?" Xav asked as Chance turned off the freeway. "I'll make dinner for us. My place."

"I'll drop by the Harris Teeter. It's closer."

Xav rolled his eyes and muttered, "Shopping with Hannibal."

"What?"

"Nothing," Xav said with a chuckle.

A half an hour later, Chance pulled into the parking lot of Xav's condominium near the river. He'd never been to Xav's place, and he was more than a little curious.

Xav opened the front door into a traditional living room with vaulted ceilings and perfectly placed antique furniture. "It isn't home to me yet."

Not at all what Chance had expected, it reminded him of a spread from *Southern Living*: pretty, but didn't reflect Xav's personality.

"I rented the place furnished," Xav explained as he led the way through the living room to a large, open kitchen. He set the bags of food on a glossy marble countertop.

"I'll have them take the furniture back when I bring my stuff out from LA."

"Y'all're thinking of stayin' awhile?" Chance said in a drawl. He silently hoped Xav was planning on hanging around, although he wasn't ready to come out and say it.

Xav turned and met Chance's gaze, his green eyes sparkling playfully. "Well now, Mr. Fairchild," he answered in a passable Southern accent, "it all depends on how welcome y'all make me feel." He went to Chance and leaned in for a brief kiss.

"I'll do my best," Chance said as their lips parted. The kiss felt like a warm welcome home. A bridge to something relaxed and comfortable.

Chance pulled a bottle of merlot from one of the bags. Xav retrieved a corkscrew from one of the drawers and handed it to him, then opened a cabinet and set two wineglasses on the counter.

"Twyla Fay asked about you today," Xav said as he finished emptying the bags and setting out the ingredients for their meal.

"Did she?"

"She's a bit of a gabe."

"A what?"

"Slang for gay babe."

Chance chuckled. "As opposed to fag hag?"

It was Xav's turn to chuckle. "You got it."

"You're just figuring that out?" Chance sipped his wine and smiled.

"She has a big heart. I like that," Xav said.

"I do too."

Chance relaxed with the wine. It had felt good to have Xav at his place, but it felt even better to be at Xav's. It was as if Xav had opened a door for him and invited him into his life, and, for once, Chance had walked through it. "Need any help?" he asked as Xav began to chop shallots and brown them in a pan.

"Set the table? Dishes are in the cabinet to the right of the sink. Silverware is in the first drawer under that."

Armed with plates and silverware, Chance headed to the dining room. From the arched doorway, he noticed the bevy of photographs on the table behind the couch in the living room. He set the table and then walked over to the photos for a closer look.

The largest photograph was a formal family portrait. Chance imagined the photo's purpose might have been to send along with Christmas cards. Six children: four stair-step boys flanked their parents, the mother holding a baby girl and the father with a toddler boy on his lap. The older boys wore navy jackets and striped ties, echoes of the suit their father wore. The toddler and infant wore outfits that matched their mother's dress. Chance smiled as he recognized a smiling teenage Xav.

"My mom took us to Macy's," Xav said from behind Chance, who'd been too caught up in studying the photograph to hear Xav approach. "She wanted a proper portrait of us." He chuckled. "I had just received my acceptance letter to MIT the day before. I was so proud of myself."

Chance pointed to a photo of Xav dressed in a cap and gown, his parents on either side of him. "High school graduation?"

"Yes. And this one was MIT." Xav picked up the photograph and rubbed his thumb over the glass. "The six of us are close." He set the picture down and his hand brushed another of the photographs, this one a shot of Xav next to a large sign that read *FBI Academy, Quantico, VA.*

"Do you miss working for the FBI?" Chance asked.

"I do. But it was time for a change."

A buzzer sounded in the kitchen. Xav sighed quietly. "Time to eat."

AN HOUR later Chance stared at his empty plate. *Twenty missing boys, and no one bats an eye?*

"*Head of the snake.*" Ever since Chance had breathed those words, thoughts of Faison had bounced off the walls of his mind. All the low-level prosecutions when he'd pushed and pushed Faison to focus on the big picture, to consider the source. Faison's cavalier attitude toward the increased cocaine on the street. The way Faison had blown off evidence of something far more sinister every time he mentioned the trawler putting in late or the missing kids all over the news. Then reassigning him to a case where Faison *knew* he wasn't needed and having Talley dog his every move like a malignant shadow.

You're reading too much into this. He's an asshole, nothing more.

"Chance?" Xav studied him with obvious concern. "You all right? You barely said five words during dinner."

"Shit. Sorry. The food was terrific. Thank you."

"Good," Xav replied. "What's up?"

Chance forced a smile. "I was just thinking."

"About?"

"Winter. Quinn. The rest of the missing boys."

Xav rose from the table, walked behind Chance, and massaged his shoulders for a few minutes. Chance leaned his head against Xav's chest and closed his eyes, but his brain wouldn't shut down.

"I should go," Chance said. He saw disappointment in Xav's eyes as he got to his feet. He offered Xav another forced smile, then took his face in his hands and kissed him—a kiss he hoped would reassure Xav. "It's been a long day. I need time to think."

Xav's response was to claim Chance's lips, the blistering kiss causing Chance's determination to think things through to falter.

CHANCE DROVE home with thoughts of Faison swirling like a tempest in his mind. *Damn the man!* He couldn't just turn a blind eye to this. He needed answers. He needed to investigate the connection between the drugs and the missing boys. And he knew there was only one way to accomplish that: he'd have to confront the bastard.

CHAPTER FORTY-THREE

ON THURSDAY morning, Xav stood on the dock and looked up at the brothel's dormant neon sign in the twilight. All was quiet within, and the crime scene tape no longer fluttered in the breeze. It looked as if nothing had happened.

"How do you want to do this?" John asked softly.

It was that moment where early morning pressed the sky. The time between full night and sunrise, where the sky was still a blueberry blue and the moon still shone somewhere on the faraway horizon. It made you want to whisper. "The alley and the area beneath the docks is public property. It doesn't require that we're careful," Xav murmured.

"You don't care if they know what we're doing?" John asked.

"No." Xav walked to the alley and John followed. Xav knelt at the manhole near the back door and pulled the heavy steel cover aside with effort.

John knelt beside him and took samples of the moss and mold from the opening, capped the container, then motioned to Xav to tilt the cover up. Xav lifted the heavy steel and John swabbed samples from the bottom of it. "Done," he said softly.

Xav wrestled the cover back over the vent and stood. Small strips of black mold and moss ran along the edge of the building where it met the alley. "Take samples of that." Xav pointed.

John opened another container and swabbed samples from the crevasse where the decaying wall met the concrete, and capped the container. "Anything else?"

Xav shook his head and motioned to John to follow him back out to the edge of the dock. A diver surfaced quietly at the edge of the docks, small air bubbles bursting around him as he cleared the water.

"Anything?" Xav asked.

The diver nodded, reached up and handed the underwater digital camera to Xav, and removed his mask. "The entire lower level is sunk in the water. If I didn't know better, I'd say there are people in there. I heard voices."

"Old? Young?" Xav asked.

The diver shook his head. "Can't tell for certain. But I'd say a female crying. Are we done?"

"Yes. Thank you." Xav turned and looked back at the brothel. *I'm going to get you, Victor.*

CHANCE TOOK a deep breath and knocked on Faison's office door. He had no illusions about how the conversation would go, but he had no choice. He'd spent most of the night trying to work things out in his mind, but each time he'd thought about Faison, he couldn't find a way around that brick wall.

Chance opened the door. "Sir," he said, "I need to speak to you about the child fatality, the shooting case."

"This had better be good," Faison snapped as Chance closed the door behind himself. "We've been over this twice already. You're on the Davidson case."

"Davies," Chance corrected. "And I am, sir. We'll be ready for trial—"

"Then why the hell are you still going on about the shooting?"

"Because there's a connection between the missing kids and the increased drugs," Chance said. He approached Faison's desk but didn't take a seat.

"Cocaine in the kids' systems?" Faison countered. "Already heard about that. Probably prostituting themselves because they needed money."

Keep calm and don't take the bait. Breathe. Just breathe.

"Sir, with all due respect, neither of the Haverty boys was a prostitute. All the evidence points to kidnapping and sexual exploitation, and I believe it's related to drug trafficking."

Faison waved him away, "I've already heard that hogwash. There's no connection between the cases."

"There's more," Chance continued. "There's evidence of another boy who was killed, and that case also has a drug connection. I think they're using shrimpers to handle both types of cargo. Kids and coke."

"Then let the sheriff investigate. I didn't hire you to be a cop, Fairchild. If there's a connection, they'll find it."

"But sir," Chance protested, "if I'm right about the drugs, we might be able to put these men away—"

"Who says the sheriff won't catch them?" Faison's face grew redder as he spoke. "Bad enough that the SBI is sticking their noses into this. Why don't you pull in the DEA and the FBI while you're at it?"

Chance silently thought that might not be such a terrible thing because they could use all the help they could get. He was more certain about his suspicions now than ever. "Sir, I'm not asking for special treatment. I'm not asking for time off the Davies case. I'm only asking—"

"You're treading on thin ice, Fairchild," Faison warned.

"But sir—"

"Keep pushing this and I'll have your job." Faison looked as though he was about to burst into flames. "And if you're thinking you can go back into private practice anywhere in these parts," he continued with barely repressed rage, "think again."

Chance's gut did a few backflips. He had no intention of going back to private practice, even if it meant leaving Carver County. But that might end up being very far away if Faison had any say in it. "Sir?"

"You think you'll get anywhere around here if I have anything to say about it? Everyone will know what you are, Fairchild. A convict. A fag."

Ire suffused Chance. The only way Faison would know about the conviction that had landed him in juvenile detention was if he'd accessed Chance's juvenile case file. *Records of an expunged conviction. Records that were supposed to have been destroyed.* "What?"

"You heard what I said. You think you can come in here all highfalutin and I'll just roll over?"

The slow burn of Chance's anger erupted into fury with every word out of Faison's mouth.

"Haven't you figured it out yet?" Faison spat. "Ain't nobody gonna tell me I don't do my homework. This is *my* county. I *am* the law. You serve at *my* pleasure. And right now I've about had enough of you."

Breathe in for four counts. Hold for four counts. Breathe out for four counts. Hold for four counts.

"Cat got your tongue?" Faison said when Chance didn't answer. "I thought it might."

Let it go. Arguing with Faison would only show that he gave a fuck about what the man thought. "All I'm asking, *sir*"—he held Faison's gaze and silently cheered himself on as Faison's face grew a deeper scarlet—"is for you to think about what is best for the people of Carver County. Or is what's best for *you* more important?"

"Leave."

"That's it, isn't it?" Chance demanded. "You don't care about these kids or the drugs flowing into this town. It's all about you and your little fiefdom."

"You little piece of shit. I'll crush you so hard you won't know what hit you!" Faison hissed.

Fuck that. Fuck him. For once, Chance didn't give a shit if his anger boiled up from inside. This wasn't about losing control. This wasn't about years of making sure he always did the right thing no matter what the universe did to him. *This* was anger in the face of hypocrisy the likes of which he'd never dreamed could exist. Justified and freeing anger. And he wasn't going to back down. Not this time. "It's all about you, isn't it?" he pressed, the thrill of finally speaking his mind spurring him on. "There's a connection between these missing boys and the drugs and I'm going to get to the bottom of it if it's the last thing I do. You're so goddamn interested in holding on to your job, you don't give a shit about the drugs or kids who are exploited. You'll sacrifice anything and *anyone* to keep your power!"

"Get the hell out of my sight!" Faison shouted as he shot out of his seat.

"Happily, sir," Chance glared at Faison before he turned on his heel and headed away. As he closed the door, he heard Faison pick up the phone and dial. "Talley, it's me. We got a problem."

Fuck you, sir.

Chance pretended not to notice the look on Carol's face. He guessed his fight with Faison was all over the office. The walls in the building weren't thick enough. He headed straight back to his office and his hand shook as he pressed the button on the intercom. "Carol?"

"Yes, Mr. Fairchild?"

"I don't want to be disturbed."

"Of course, sir."

"Thank you." He rose from his desk, locked his door, and sat back down. A moment later he was back on his feet, pacing the room. *Fucking piece of shit.*

He resisted the overwhelming urge to hit something. *No. That won't help anything.* His heart pounded against his ribs. *Breathe. Just breathe!*

Fuck Faison. Chance had known he was right and his anger justified. Now he wanted to scream. *You're letting him get to you.* He'd pushed Faison to the edge, but he was allowing the asshole to do the same to him.

He would quit. Show Faison he didn't give a shit about the job. *But that's a lie, and you know it!* He loved his job and he had no intention of quitting, Faison or no Faison. More than that, in this job he made a fucking *difference*. This job gave him the power to change things.

"Shit." He stared out the window at the courthouse. He couldn't let Faison push him around. He'd done the right thing by confronting him. "Shit," he repeated. He needed to vent. To talk to someone. He gripped the telephone handset and stared at the phone for a moment, then flipped through his rolodex to the tab marked *S*.

Deep breath. You can do this. Anger burned in him, seeking a way out, and he knew he'd explode if he didn't do something to manage it. He had to dial the number twice after fucking it up the first time. He couldn't think straight. Every thought seemed to bring him back to that place. *Dark. Cold.*

"Sampson," the gravelly voice on the other end announced.

"Still smoking," he said. "I thought you'd quit."

"Chance Fairchild? I thought you'd fallen off the face of the earth," Evelene Sampson said.

"Have a minute?" he asked.

"For you? Always." He imagined her canny grin. "What's up?"

"I…." *Shit.* Where to begin?

"Take your time. Deep breath. I'm not going anywhere," she offered.

"Thanks," he said. "I need a little help with this. I've gotten rusty."

"Like riding a bike. How's that beautiful house of yours?

"Almost finished," he answered, happy to engage in idle chatter. He knew that was exactly why she'd asked. She could hear the tension in his voice and she knew he needed a minute to gather his thoughts.

"How's the DA treating you?"

"Fine."

She laughed. "Liar."

He chuckled. He liked that about her. Never any bullshit. No coddling. Face the music and face your fears.

"Anything to do with the child fatality that's all over the news?" When he didn't answer, she said, "Just say it. You'll still be there after you do."

"I feel like I'm losing it."

"Dreams?"

"They're back." The tight feeling in the back of his throat was back too.

"Talk to me, Chance. And don't forget to breathe."

He closed his eyes and gathered his thoughts.

"They raped him, killed him. Medical examiner says he was repeatedly raped. I interviewed the surviving twin."

"News says the twin died in that shooting."

"Yeah, I know. We wanted it that way until we could figure out what's going on. Anyway, I interviewed him and he's a mess."

"Like you once were?"

"Yeah."

"I thought you prosecuted drug cases."

"I do," he answered testily. "But my boss," Chance began, his shoulders drawing tight as he spoke. "I think he may be involved somehow."

"That's a serious accusation."

"When I confronted the fu—son of a bitch—he threatened me. Told me I'd never work in this area again. Fuck, he'd even pulled my juvenile records!" He inhaled a long breath, held it, and released it.

"Go on," Evelene prompted.

"I nearly lost it," Chance admitted.

"Nearly isn't losing it. Getting angry is normal. And given what you've just told me, it's reasonable. Even a good thing," she pointed out. When he didn't say anything in response, she said, "So tell me more about the case."

"We think there's a link between the trafficking of cocaine and the trafficking of boys," he explained. "And I'm having nightmares again."

"We?"

"There's a new deputy investigating missing kids. Xav Constantine." *And I'm fucking falling for him, and—*

"Hold that thought. Let's get back to the boys. What's the trigger? Last time we spoke, you hadn't had the dreams in nearly five years," she pointed out.

"One of the victims, he told me their captors kept them in a pit." *Dark. Cold.*

He heard her exhale before she said, "Go on."

"He's eleven. He and his brother were in DSS custody at a group home." Chance rubbed the bridge of his nose. "I…. It's just too close to what happened to me."

"You're blaming yourself," she pointed out. "I get the fear and the memories. You're entitled to feel that. But you take it a step further."

"How?"

"You blame yourself for feeling the old fear. Then you erect walls around yourself and deny yourself the opportunity to process it, particularly with help. It's like double the shit."

"Leave it to you to articulate it so well." He laughed a harsh laugh. She was right, of course. He hated himself for being afraid. He hated that he couldn't have a normal personal relationship with anyone. Not even a friend. He told himself it was easier to do his job if people thought he was a conceited prick, but it wasn't true.

"And this deputy. Constantine, was it?"

"Yes," he answered, regretting he'd brought Xav into the mix. "Xav."

"Tell me about Xav."

"I'm seeing him."

"Congratulations. How's it going?" she asked. No judgment, just a question.

"I…. Great."

"*But…?*" When he didn't answer, she pressed, "I'm not hearing a resounding 'hell yeah' in your voice."

"I don't know the first thing about how to be in a relationship."

"And?"

"I have a no-fraternization policy," he answered.

"And if Xav wasn't a colleague? What excuse would you use then?"

"Touché."

He briefly closed his eyes. "I can't stop thinking about those kids. And I can't help thinking that my boss is involved, if not directly, then by failing to act."

"Look, Chance," she said, her voice serious. "What you went through even *before* you spent time in detention? You don't just get over it. And it doesn't get better without work."

"I know."

"If you're being honest with yourself, what do you want?" she asked. "And don't give me the 'it sounds sappy' bullshit. I'm too old for that."

"I want to make a difference." It *did* sound sappy when he said it like that.

"And?"

"I'm tired of being alone." He twisted the phone cord around a finger and sighed. "But I'm equally afraid of being with someone."

"Trust doesn't come overnight. It's gradual," she said gently. "You've got every reason in the book not to trust anyone. This Xav. Is he a good man?"

"Better than." *And he didn't run away screaming when I lost it.*

"Have you told him about your past?"

"I gave him the bird's-eye view," he said. "And he's still around."

"Then don't stop there. Don't bullshit him. Stop running. *Talk* to him. Tell him about your boss. Trust that he'll stick around. Because the way I see it, you have two choices: go on the way you've been going, or grab the bull by the balls and move forward."

"Are you sure you're a shrink?" he said with a shake of his head.

"What do you want from me?" she shot back playfully. "Platitudes? You don't buy the bullshit, so why should I sell it?"

"Thanks."

"You got it. And remember, I'm here if you need help working through this. I've got all the time in the world for you."

"Thanks. I may take you up on that," he replied.

"Take care, Chance," she said gently.

"You too."

He hung up, leaned back in his chair, and hummed Nico and Vinz's "Am I Wrong?" as he thought about what Xav had said. *"Trust me. It'll make all the difference in the world to you if you can save even one."* Now he understood why Evelene Sampson had worked so hard to save him. And she *had* saved him. Because of her, he'd found something he never expected: happiness.

Happiness. He thought of how good it had felt to sleep curled up against Xav. He'd been mortified that he'd freaked out at the dream—that Xav had seen him like that. But there'd been something good about it too. A connection. Comfort. Comfort he'd never known before. And for just a moment, he'd trusted Xav. Bullshit or not, Xav saw through it. For once, he'd met someone other than Dr. Sampson who gave a shit about him. And that felt almost too good to be true. Almost. Now he just had to figure out how to be in a relationship.

CHAPTER FORTY-FOUR

"They're a match," Tom Ingram said to Xav as he turned from the microscope.

Xav smiled. "Thanks for the quick work, Tom."

Tom shook his head in dismay. "No need. I want you to get these criminals."

"Does that mean the Haverty boys were in the lower processing plant of 4Play?" John asked, nearly dancing in place.

Tom nodded. "The mold and moss match."

"Hallelujah," John said, excitement brimming over. "Billy's got everything ready to go. This is the last we needed for the warrants. Can we raid the place now?"

Xav nodded as he pulled his cell phone from his pocket and felt a little like a teenager when he touched the heart icon he'd preprogrammed for Chance.

"Evan Fairchild."

Xav almost smiled as Chance's familiar voice filled his ear. "We're good to go."

"How soon?" Chance asked calmly.

Xav looked at his watch. "Hour and a half."

"Meet you there."

Xav poured over the ancient plans for the old processing plant that was now 4Play as he leaned over the table. "What's this?" He pointed to a small square void in the plans.

"It used to be a drop chute," Billy explained. "We think it's now the elevator down to the lower levels."

Xav nodded. "Do we have a bulk warrant?"

Sheriff Winston nodded. "Everybody present."

"How many do you think are there?" Xav asked.

"On a Thursday and bein' as it's now past noon and the place is open for business, thirty employees, another twenty in residence not on shift," Billy said.

"Customers?" Xav asked.

"No telling," Billy said, shaking his head. "Legitimate lunch customers, twenty or so. Other patrons of a… sexual nature, could be five, could be another twenty."

"So we're looking at anywhere between seventy and ninety people?" Xav asked.

Billy nodded.

Xav turned to Winston. "Do we have enough personnel?"

Winston nodded. "Brought everyone in for this."

"Coast Guard?"

"Standing by. They'll pick up anyone who ends up in the water," Winston assured.

"The other end of the alley?" Xav asked.

"Four men," Billy answered.

"Rooftops?" Xav asked.

"Air rescue standing by," Winston further assured.

"We want them in the air for the raid. We may have runners on the rooftops," Xav said calmly.

Winston's brow knitted. "Expensive."

Xav nodded. "Sorry, Sheriff."

"Deputy Constantine?" Twyla Fay's voice sounded over the open intercom. Her voice carried the stress he knew everyone felt.

"Go, Twyla Fay," Xav said.

"Someone is calling for you and sounds frantic but won't give a name. Just demandin' to talk to you."

Xav frowned. "Male? Female? Young? Old?"

"Male, youngish, said some Spanish words but speaks perfect English, and he sounds like he's out of his gourd."

A sense of foreboding came over Xav as he strode to the phone on his desk. "Put him through." Xav punched the button for the phone line before the ring could fully sound. "Constantine."

"They killed my mother!" the voice shrieked.

The cry in Xav's ear was hysterical, but he knew who it was the minute he heard the voice. It was the kid he'd spoken to in the alley next to the brothel. "Where are you?"

"End of the docks! They killed her!"

The wail tore jagged wounds through Xav's senses. "Do they know you got away?"

"Noooooooooo! They killed her!" he sobbed.

"I'm sending a car to you now." He turned to Winston. "Undercover?"

"Dark green Impala," Winston said quickly.

"Protected witness, Hispanic male, five nine, thin, approximate age eighteen, the pay phone at the end of the docks. Now!" Xav turned back to the phone. "What color is your shirt?"

"What? Red!" the voice screamed.

"Red shirt!" he yelled at Winston.

Winston repeated what Xav said into his own phone and shouted, "You got five seconds to pick him up!"

"They killed her!" the voice screamed again.

"Listen to me! Listen to me! Dark green Impala! Don't ask questions! Just get into it!" The line went dead and Xav prayed the kid would do what he'd been told. Xav turned back to everyone in the room. "We want Victor and the two shooters. We'll sort through the rest when we get them here. I want every nook and cranny searched for kids. Closets, storage areas, under beds, behind furniture, refrigerators, everything," Xav said as evenly as he could after the hysterical phone call. "And call the ME. We have one dead female at the location."

Winston's eyes darkened with fury. "You heard what the man said! Move!" he boomed.

Xav said nothing as he followed Winston from the room, familiar adrenaline mounting as it always did when he was about to walk into a balls-out assault.

When Chance arrived, he jogged up to Xav, and Xav greeted him with a brief nod. "I've never done anything like this before," Chance said, a little out of breath.

"It actually goes pretty quick and quiet. What you hope is that no one opens fire. Then it can get messy."

Chance paled. "You're going inside?"

"I'll be okay. I'm geared up."

"I don't like this."

Xav met his eyes. "This is what I do, Chance. I'll be okay."

"I still don't like it."

Xav reached for Chance's hand and held it up. "Make a fist." Chance did. Xav bumped it once with a gloved fist. "For good luck."

A flicker of a smile crossed Chance's lips.

Xav put gloved fingertips to a concealed ear fob and listened intently as the go order came and he left Chance's side in a stealth rustle of gear.

THREE DEPUTIES gathered the few restaurant patrons who occupied 4Play and moved them to one side of the restaurant. Two more deputies cleared the kitchen and bar staff, searched them, and seated them with the patrons. They looked on with apprehension when Winston ordered no fewer than ten of his men up the banking staircase to clear the second floor, then led Xav and the remaining men to the back rooms of the brothel.

Victor yelped like a girl when Xav barged through a door marked "office" with his weapon drawn. The two goons who had shot Xav and the Haverty boys in the alley stood and drew their weapons, and Xav aimed his gun at them with a keen eye.

"Guns on the desk," Xav ordered.

They hesitated.

"Now!" Xav shouted.

Both men carefully laid their weapons on the desk.

"Hands and faces to the wall!"

The two turned and placed their hands and cheeks against the wall, and deputies went to them, kicked their feet apart, and searched them.

Victor huffed and sputtered. "You can't just—"

"Shut up," one of the deputies said as he spun Victor to face the wall, pushed him none-too-gently against it, kicked his feet apart, and searched him.

"What are you doing? You can't do this!" Victor protested as the deputy cuffed his hands with disposable double restraints and led him from the office.

Xav glared at the two bastards who'd shot him and the boys. He wanted nothing more than to take a piece out of the killers. A big piece. "Ankles too," he said as he pulled two sets of hobble restraints from his pocket and handed them to the deputies.

The deputies bound the feet of the two men and led them from the office.

Commotion sounded overhead and someone shouted, "Runner! Headed for the roof!"

Xav strode down the hallway past the two shooters and deputies and into the restaurant area. He looked up at the second-floor landing as deputies charged after the runner. Shouts sounded, a door slammed, and then something sounded like fist meeting flesh. Xav wasn't worried. They'd get the man.

"All clear!" a deputy shouted from the back area of the brothel.

"All clear!" another deputy shouted from the second-floor landing.

FOR ALL intents and purposes, the raid had gone without a hitch, and deputies now marched suspects out the front door in handcuffs. Xav trotted back to Chance, and the look of relief on his face warmed Xav's heart. He'd never had anyone who waited for him after a mission, and it felt almost like coming home. "Hey."

"Hey," Chance said lightly.

"Got Victor and the two guys," Xav said with a brief smile.

Chance held a fist up and Xav bumped it.

"You killed her!"

The shriek registered, and Xav turned. He didn't even have time to swear. He ran fifty feet straight at the kid and tackled him. A gun fired as they hit the ground, and Victor wilted to the concrete. The young man beneath Xav went limp in wracking sobs.

The EMTs wheeled the restrained young man away twenty minutes later as Winston walked up to Xav. "He didn't have a gun."

"Who fired?" Xav asked, incredulous.

Winston pointed to the rooftop. "You were right."

Xav looked up and saw several officers crowded around a figure lying flat on the roof.

"Dammit!" Xav yelled as he threw his face shield to the ground.

"What?" Winston asked.

"Someone doesn't want Victor to talk!"

Winston smiled slyly. "It was only a graze. He's fine."

Xav's jaw dropped.

"Sheriff Winston!" one of the deputies called from the front doorway of the brothel.

Winston walked to him, and Xav and Chance followed.

"You better come take a look at this," he said gravely before leading them into the brothel.

They trotted up the stairs, down the hallway, and into a back room. There, inside a large dog carrier, was a child of perhaps five curled into a ball. The body was ashen, the skin waxy, and a few wispy strands of flaxen hair graced a balding head. Nothing but a skeleton remained of the frame. The child was all but a corpse.

"I think we need the coroner up here," the deputy said.

"Wait," Xav said. He stripped his gloves off and handed them to Chance, then went to the small body. He opened the carrier door, licked a finger, making sure it was wet, and placed it laterally beneath the nostrils. A sad smile grew on Xav's face.

"You are shittin' me. He's still alive?" Billy asked.

"Barely," Xav said softly. "Anyone have candy?"

Winston patted both his pants pockets, came up with a chocolate bar, and handed it to Xav.

Xav unwrapped it, broke a small piece off, and gently pushed it between the waxy lips. Feeble hands shot out, gripped Xav's hand, and held fast as he nursed the chocolate.

"Oh God," Chance said softly.

Xav stroked the balding head ever so gently with his other hand. "It's all right. You're safe now," he said softly. He looked up at Winston. "He has minutes."

Winston tucked his chin, clearly at a loss for words.

Xav turned back to the boy, whose hands went limp as he breathed his last breath. Xav gritted his teeth, reached into the small space, and withdrew the frail body. An EMT wrapped the boy in a blanket and took him away. Xav stood and left the room. The world was a fucked-up place.

CHANCE FOUND Xav at the edge of the docks, looking out over the water. "Are you all right?"

Xav turned and gave him a smile that didn't reach his eyes. "I will be."

Chance looked out over the water too. The vision of the emaciated child dug its claws deep into his mind, leaving him distraught. He'd never imagined he'd ever see something as ghastly, and he was certain even time wouldn't cleanse the horror from his mind. How many times would he see that poor child take his last breath? "They have the area down below open for us to look at. You were right. There was an elevator. They said there's a woman's body down there."

Xav sighed as he waved an errant mosquito away. "It's the mother of the kid I tackled."

Chance made an unintelligible sound as he rubbed his eyes with thumb and forefinger.

"Let's go take a look," Xav said as he turned and headed back to the brothel.

XAV STUDIED the macabre holding tank that had served as a cell for the Haverty boys. Someone had turned the music on in the restaurant upstairs, and Enya's "May It Be" was more than he cared to hear at the moment. He toed what he thought was a small spot of mold, and when it flipped over, he bent to look at it. He turned it over with a latex-gloved fingertip. It was a decaying coca leaf dusted with white powder. Xav touched the powder with a fingertip and touched it to his tongue. "Everybody, stop moving right where you are," Xav said as he stood.

Chance, Sheriff Winston, and two crime scene techs stopped moving and looked at Xav.

"The floor is covered with decaying coca leaves coated in cocaine powder. We need to collect them." He carefully stepped over to the side of the cavernous room, where Chance stood with Sheriff Winston. "I'm going to bet the chemical composition of the coke will match the cocaine you're finding on the streets."

"That's it," Chance said quietly. "That's what we needed to link the traffickers."

Xav nodded.

CHAPTER FORTY-FIVE

CHANCE WOKE at 5:00 a.m. on Friday morning. He'd dreamed about Xav and was disappointed to wake up alone.

Chance dressed in sweats and a T-shirt and headed down to the kitchen. He found Thunder outside the back door waiting not-so-patiently to be fed. He gave him fresh water and dry cat food, then went inside to make coffee.

"Shit." He'd meant to get coffee last night, but in all the excitement, he'd forgotten. He made his way to the front door, saw the cruiser parked on the street, and was reminded he was not alone. He closed the front door behind him, descended the porch steps, and walked down the front path. Deputy Carlisle saw him coming and rolled the window down.

"Morning," Chance greeted.

"Morning, Mr. Fairchild."

"I'm headed to Starbucks. Care to join me?"

"Don't mind if I do," Deputy Carlisle said with a smile. He rolled the window up, exited the car, and locked it.

Without an infusion of caffeine, Chance was glad Deputy Carlisle seemed perfectly happy walking beside him in silence. When they reached Starbucks, Carlisle took up a position by the door, hands clasped in front of him.

"What would you like?" Chance asked.

"Large black coffee would be great," Deputy Carlisle said as he reached into his back pocket for his wallet.

"I got it," Chance said with a smile. "Be right back."

"Large latte, double shot of espresso," he told Wanda, the barista.

"As if I didn't already know," she said with a bright smile.

"Oh, and add a large coffee for the deputy over there."

She grinned. "Mighty kind of you to support our deputies." She rang up his order and got to work on the coffees a moment later. "I saw your boss on TV yesterday," she said as she filled the espresso maker.

He didn't need to be reminded of Faison, but returned her smile affably. "How's the little one? Stephen, right?" The smell of coffee made Chance's stomach rumble.

"You remembered!" Wanda blushed as she held the metal pitcher of milk beneath the frother, working it so it hissed as the milk foamed. "He's doin' great," she gushed. "Startin' kindergarten in two months." She pointed to a photograph taped to the wall behind her, then carefully poured the milk into the cup of espresso.

"Time flies. I can't believe how big he's gotten," Chance said as he studied the little boy's picture.

"He just turned five." She snapped a lid onto the cup and handed it to him. "Talkin' up a storm, that boy."

"I know you're mighty proud." In his mind's eye, Chance saw the boy they'd found during the raid of 4Play. The thought made him ever more determined not to back down from Faison.

"Couldn't be prouder. See you next time, Mr. Fairchild."

"Take care, Wanda." He handed the black coffee to Deputy Carlisle before stopping at the counter where they kept the sugar and stirrers. He carefully removed the top to his cup of latte, added a shake of nutmeg, then one of chocolate, and replaced the lid. He waved at Wanda before heading out into the morning sunshine with Deputy Carlisle sipping coffee and following in his wake.

Chance had just turned the corner onto a side street when a burly man grabbed his shoulder and turned him, causing him to drop the coffee cup. An arm snaked around his neck and someone jammed the muzzle of a gun into his back beneath his rib cage.

"What the—"

"Shut up," the man said as he shoved the gun hard into his ribs and turned Chance to face Deputy Carlisle.

Deputy Carlisle dropped his coffee and drew his gun in a flash, but not fast enough. A second man approached him from behind and clubbed him in the head with the butt of his gun. Only a muted cry of pain escaped Deputy Carlisle before he slumped to the sidewalk.

Chance stifled a grunt as a black Lincoln Town Car pulled alongside them. The driver's door opened and a man jumped out as the trunk popped open. Panic stung Chance's spine as the man who held him pulled him back toward the trunk, and he began to struggle.

The man who'd left the driver's seat came around to the back of the car and slugged him in the face. Dazed, Chance continued to struggle to no avail as the man searched Chance's pockets for his cell phone. He found it, pulled it from his pocket, and withdrew the battery. He threw the battery across the street and placed the phone in front of a back tire.

The first man released Chance's neck, grabbed the back of it with a meaty hand, and shoved him headfirst into the trunk so hard it knocked the wind out of him. He hit his forehead on the way in, and blood gushed into his eyes as someone shoved something into his mouth and slapped a piece of tape over it. They grabbed his feet and pitched his legs the rest of the way into the trunk. He blindly kicked at them as the trunk lid closed over him. Darkness screamed at him as terror clawed at his mind, and the world closed in around him.

XAV WAS rudely awakened at six by his incessantly ringing cell phone. He grabbed it from the nightstand, knocking a bottle of water and the novel he'd been reading off it in the process. He rolled onto his back and answered with a gruff "Yeah."

"Xav?" asked a small voice.

Xav opened his eyes now. "Yes. Who's this?"

"Quinn," he said in a near whisper.

"What's up? Everything okay? Where are you?"

"In bed. They come to shoot us," he whispered.

"Get under the bed!"

Xav shot out of bed as Quinn screamed, and the sound of automatic gunfire filled Xav's ear right before the line went dead. Xav punched the icon to dial the FBI.

"Priority?" a computerized voice asked.

"One! Constantine, 87539, Protection Unit 34, automatic weapons fired, agents down, one civilian." He hung up and dialed dispatch. "This is Deputy Constantine. Shots fired at the Charmaigne estate! Go now!" He hung up and pulled on a pair of sweats, slipped his feet into tennis shoes, grabbed his vest, and ran from the room. In one swipe of a hand, he collected his weapons, keys, and badge off the bar and left the condominium.

He dialed John as he raced down the stairs to his bike.

"Morning, Xav," John answered, sounding chipper. "It's kinda ear—"

"Shots fired at the Charmaigne estate! Go, go, go!" Xav shouted. He unlocked his gear at the speed of light, and shoved his weapons, badge, and vest into a saddlebag.

"On my way!" John shouted in return.

Xav pocketed the phone, pulled his helmet on without bothering to snap it, started his bike, and took off with a screech of tires that ripped through the quiet morning air like a chain saw.

Xav bore down on the throttle as the bike crested a hundred miles an hour. Breaking Benjamin's "Failure" screamed at him through his helmet, and he turned the radio off. He made it to the estate in nine minutes. Someone had crashed through the gate to the circular drive, and he had no way of knowing whether it was the good guys or the bad guys. When automatic gunfire plied the morning air, he decided it sure as hell wasn't the good guys. He kicked the bike into neutral, letting the back tire slide to the right, and turned off the ignition. He jumped off as he deliberately slow-dumped the bike in the soft, damp grass at the front hedge, then pulled his vest from the saddlebag and put it on. He clipped his badge to it, and thumbed the safeties off both guns as he took cover behind the hedge.

Sirens sounded in the distance and Xav watched a man move furtively down the walkway alongside the house. Xav crouched, took careful aim, and fired. The guy dropped with a yelp and lay still. Xav searched for others, his guns at the ready. A man exited the front door, shouted "Vámonos!" and raced down the front steps, heading left as an engine roared to life.

Xav aimed again and fired. The man yelled as he went down holding his knee.

Xav moved around the hedge onto the property, guns still at the ready. The automatic garage door suddenly began to rise, and two men fled beneath it as soon as it was three feet off the ground. They grabbed the shirt of the man who was down clutching his knee and hauled him to a plain white Chevy van that was already moving toward the gate at the other end of the circular driveway. Xav aimed again as they lifted the downed man into the van through the side door and jumped in before Xav could get a shot off. As the van roared toward the gate, he shot at the back tires, firing repeatedly. The van crashed through the gate and sped down the street, and he hoped like hell he'd hit at least one tire.

Without regard for his own safety, he ran through the garage into the house. If the motherfuckers wanted to shoot his ass, they could bring it. Nothing would stop him from getting to Quinn.

He took the stairs two at a time to the second level and kicked through the bullet-riddled door into Quinn's bedroom. "Quinn!"

"Here," Annie said, her voice laden with pain.

She was lying half under the bed in a pool of blood, and Xav went to her. Her breathing was shallow and rapid, and one shoulder was a red ruin. "Where's Quinn?" he asked as he pulled the blanket from the bed and pressed it to her shoulder.

"Here."

A small hand reached out from beneath the bed and felt around for Xav.

"Are you hurt? Are you hurt?" Xav demanded as he gripped Quinn's hand.

"I-I think I b-busted my stitches again," Quinn said through tears.

Xav lay flat on his belly on the carpeting and looked beneath the bed. "C'mere, buddy." He reached beneath it and pulled Quinn out carefully and into his arms. "Can you lift your shirt for me?"

Quinn's hands shook almost violently, and he couldn't lift it.

"Let me," Xav said as he peeled the blood-soaked pajama shirt away from Quinn's skin. "Looks like you busted 'em good."

"They was trying to kill us," he said in a tremulous voice.

"You're okay now. You're safe," Xav soothed as he stroked Quinn's hair and held him close. He glanced at Annie as he worked his cell phone from his pocket with one hand. "Lynn?"

Annie glanced at Quinn before she shook her head ever so slightly. Xav didn't need to ask more. He thumbed the icon for Sheriff Winston and only succeeded in smearing blood across the face of the phone. He swore silently as he pressed his thumb to it again.

Sheriff Winston answered with a shout. "Winston!"

"It's Xav. I'm in the safe house. It's clear, but I need an ambulance here yesterday."

"One should be pullin' in there now! The boy all right?"

"Yes."

"Hang on! I got all hell breakin' loose!" Winston's voice became muffled when he placed his palm partially over the phone receiver. "Twyla Fay! Tell John the safe house is clear and Xav's inside. They need EMTs now!" Winston's voice became clear again. "How in hell did you know to go there?"

"Quinn called me right before the shooting began. What do you mean by hell breaking loose?"

"Someone got to Victor in the hospital. He's dead. They shot right through our man on the door to get to him. Then they went after Michael."

"Who's Michael?"

"The kid whose mother died at the brothel. He's okay, and our deputy on his door will be all right."

Alarm permeated every fiber of Xav's being. "Has anyone tried to reach Evan Fairchild?"

"Why?"

"Someone's cleaning house, Sheriff," Xav said gravely.

Silence reigned supreme on the call before Winston exploded. "Twyla Fay, get whoever's at Mr. Fairchild's house on the phone right this instant! I'll call you back."

Deputies stormed the room with John in the lead, and Quinn screamed in fright.

"Clear!" Xav shouted as he held Quinn protectively to his chest with one hand and his badge held skyward with the other. "Get the EMTs up here! We have two agents down!"

"WHY CAN'T I stay with y'all?" Quinn pleaded through tears as the EMTs hiked his gurney to full height.

"I'll see you at the hospital before you know it," Xav promised.

"They're gonna kill me."

Quinn's already tight grip on Xav's fingers grew tighter, and Xav fought not to wince as he leaned down and looked into Quinn's bloodshot, teary eyes. He stroked Quinn's hair back from his forehead. "Do you trust me?"

"Yeah."

"Then you know you're safe and I'll be there soon."

"What if they get y'all?"

"They aren't going to get me." Xav looked up at the EMT and nodded nearly imperceptibly, his tacit permission to inject Quinn's IV line with a sedative. "I want you to let the doctors take a look at you when you get there, and I'll see you soon." Xav pried his fingers free and pressed Quinn's hands to the soft medical blanket. "I'll see you before you know it." Quinn blinked slowly, then closed his eyes. Xav motioned for the EMT to load him into the ambulance as he withdrew his cell phone from his pocket and headed for his bike.

CHAPTER FORTY-SIX

BEFORE XAV could dial Chance's number, Winston called.

"Fairchild's nowhere to be found, neither is Carlisle, and there's no sign of struggle in the house. No one seems to know Fairchild's usual running route, and we can't get a fix on his cell phone."

Xav swore softly. "He's in trouble. Put a BOLO out on the *Butterfly*."

"On what basis?"

"Whoever's doing this is preparing to blow town, and the *Butterfly* is all we've got to go on."

"Done. Anything else?"

"No. I'm on my way in."

THE FRONT of the station was awash with reporters and television news crews, and Xav didn't want to deal with it. He parked his bike in the gated parking lot and went into the station through the back door. He entered the bullpen area to see Winston shouting at two suited men in his office.

"Who are they?" he asked Sally Ann.

Twyla Fay came trotting over. "Agents Dee and Dunn from the SBI. They found out about the NCMEC data. Sheriff told 'em we're in the middle of an operation and they wouldn't take no for an answer," she said, out of breath.

"Come with me," he instructed. He strode to Winston's office and knocked on the doorjamb. "Excuse me," he interrupted loudly as he stepped into the office. "What seems to be the problem?"

"These gentlemen would like to discuss our NCMEC data, and I'm done tellin' 'em nicely now is not the time," Winston said angrily.

"Then I suggest you gentlemen leave," Xav said pointedly.

"We have reason to believe fraudulent data has been entered into NCMEC's system by you, Deputy Constantine, and we're here to collect your records."

"Are you referring to the data concerning Quinn Haverty?"

"As a matter of fact, we are," Agent Dee said with self-satisfaction.

"I find it fascinating that it was only publicized an hour ago over police channels that he was still alive and you already know about it. It tells me you're finally on top of the information that you should have been on top of over the past six months while twenty boys disappeared. So I'll make this simple for you. I've contacted the attorney general. She has placed your office under investigation for failing to monitor and audit this county's data. Please feel free to contact her. Now, Sheriff Winston has told you that we're in the middle of an operation. You have five seconds to vacate the premises or I'll throw you out myself."

"Just who in hell—"

"Four seconds. I will bodily remove you from the premises.... Three, two...." Agents Dee and Dunn turned and left Winston's office. "Make sure someone escorts them out, Twyla Fay."

"With pleasure."

Xav turned to Winston. "Did you get the BOLO out?"

"Yes. Did you honestly contact the attorney general?"

"Yes. She's quite pleased that you initiated your own internal investigation. It saved her the trouble. She's elated that the data is now correct and we've resolved three cases in the past two weeks. She's also of the opinion that you're the best sheriff in the state."

"You're a dangerous man, Constantine."

"Not at all. Just unafraid of confrontation and facing facts. Give Faison a call?"

"Why?"

"Because you're about to publicize that we have an all-out manhunt in progress for Chance Evan Fairchild and anyone even thinking about withholding information will be shot on sight."

"Don't think I can say that, but I'll certainly let 'em know we mean business. Carlisle's on the way to the hospital. Two Hispanic men took Fairchild right around the corner from Starbucks and knocked Carlisle out. He's lucky they didn't shoot him."

"Any more information than that?"

"Not a damn thing. What are you going to do?"

Xav shook his head in disgust. "Enlist the Coast Guard, because I'm going to bet ten to one odds that Mr. Fairchild is on the *Butterfly*."

"I'll call ahead and tell 'em we want every boat in the water and join you as soon as I've issued a statement."

Xav smiled. "Thanks, Sheriff." Xav left Winston's office and walked to Twyla Fay's desk. "Where are Billy and Ridley?"

"Just pulled into the parkin' lot."

"Tell them to stay there. They're going to the old docks with me. Find John and have him meet us down there."

THEY DRAGGED Chance from the trunk and dumped him unceremoniously on the asphalt. He landed on his shoulder and scraped his cheek. Pain lanced his arm and collarbone, and the gag muted his cry of pain. Blood had caked around his eyes and he couldn't see shit. He blindly kicked out and earned a brutal punch to the ribs in return, air leaving his lungs in a sharp whoosh.

"Get up!" one of the men shouted.

Chance could barely breathe as he rolled over and struggled to his knees. Anger tried to fight its way to the surface of his overriding fear, and he struggled to keep both in check. He couldn't take much more of a beating.

"I said get up, *cabrón*!"

The men lifted Chance by his arms and propelled him roughly to his feet. His already bruised and beaten body protested, but the pain helped him focus.

Someone shoved him forward. "Walk!"

Chance stepped tentatively as he made out where he was through the slits of his eyelids. They were at the docks, and they were pushing him toward a trawler. He looked at the rear of the boat. *Butterfly*.

Fuck. Out of all the cases he'd prosecuted and all the people who could have come after him, it was human traffickers who finally got him. *Motherfucking son of a bitch*.

Fear took hold once again. He tried to bolt and only received a kick to the kidneys in reply. He went down hard, breathing heavily through his nostrils.

One of the men put the tip of a knife to his left lower eyelid. "Next time we take your eye, *cabrón*. Now, get up!"

Chance rolled over to get to his knees again and nearly vomited.

"Pinche cabrón!" The men dragged him down the dock by his shirt and kicked him over the edge. He fell into the boat, hit his head and shoulder, and screamed through the gag when his arm dislocated.

The two men jumped into the boat, and one of them shouted orders in Spanish. Someone lifted Chance and propped him into a sitting position against the hull. He screamed in pain and vomited just as someone tore the gag from his mouth. One of the men grabbed his hair and jerked his head back.

"Where's the cop?"

Dazed, Chance couldn't respond.

"Where's the cop?" the man shouted again, his spittle showering Chance's face.

"W-what cop?" Chance coughed out.

"With the braid!"

Even if he knew where Xav was, there was no fucking way he'd tell them. "I-I don't know."

The man put the tip of the blade beneath his eye again and cut into Chance's lower lid just enough to draw blood.

"I-I don't know!"

"You will tell me, *cabrón*. It's only a matter of time."

"I don't know!" Chance shouted again right before the man kicked him in the head and he passed out.

BILLY PULLED the cruiser up to the Coast Guard station, and he, Ridley, and Xav climbed out of the car. A search and recovery Sikorski Jayhawk sat on the helipad with its rotors turning. The pilot, dressed in a gray flight suit, jumped down from it and ducked beneath the rotors as he came toward them. At the same time, the Coast Guard captain jumped to the dock from a Sentinel-class fast response cutter and came to meet them.

"I'm Captain Grimes, and your pilot is Lieutenant Nelson."

"Xav Constantine." Xav shook each man's hand and Billy and Ridley introduced themselves.

"Winston is on his way, and we're not to depart until he gets here. Does anyone know what this trawler looks like?" Captain Grimes asked.

Xav shook his head. "No idea."

"BOLO says seventy-five feet in length."

Xav nodded. "That's about all we know."

Sheriff Winston pulled into the lot with a screech of tires as he cut the siren and doused the cherries. He was out of the car in an instant and headed their way. He greeted the captain with a tip of his hat.

Captain Grimes nodded in return. "The biggest hindrance we have right now is the upcoming regatta. We got amateurs on the water practicing wild maneuvers and they're likely to get in our way, so we need to pay close attention to what we're doing."

"Which of you is going in the chopper?" Lieutenant Nelson asked.

"I will," Ridley said.

"Let's go!" Captain Grimes shouted.

SHERIFF WINSTON, Xav, and Billy settled into swivel chairs in the pilothouse. Xav looked out through the tinted windows that offered a 360-degree view as the cutter powered away from its dock.

"We've been hailing the *Butterfly* since the BOLO was issued, and she's not responded. We presume she's looking to evade the law and may have altered transom markings, so we're going to have to look at every seventy-five-foot trawler," Captain Grimes intoned evenly.

Xav pursed his lips. "Needle in a haystack."

Grimes nodded. "We've set up a checkpoint at the harbor entrance, and I had each of our substations check their ports. It helps to know that no seventy-five-footer with a working engine is in port at the moment."

"Two possibles came in on the BOLO," Sheriff Winston said.

"We're going to take a look at those first. They're located here and here." Grimes pointed to two different spots on the radar screen, then glanced at Winston. "As I understand it, they've kidnapped a DA."

"Assistant DA. Evan Fairchild," Xav clarified.

"Not that it's any of my business, but do you have any idea why?" Grimes asked.

Xav glanced at Winston, who nodded for him to answer. "He and I figured out there's a link between the increased local cocaine trafficking and the boys who have gone missing."

Grimes's eyebrows shot up. "Any idea who they are?"

"A Bolivian drug cartel that operates a child sex trafficking ring on the side."

Grimes gave him a sidelong glance before walking to the wall intercom and pressing a red button. "This is Grimes. Man the guns," he said before he released the red button and went to the most forward station in the pilothouse. "If they're out here, they're headed somewhere. Where might you think that is?"

"I think our perpetrators are looking to unload cargo first, which means they'll meet up with a larger vessel to take that cargo to South America."

"Cargo being kids?"

Xav nodded.

"Worst kind of pirate."

CHAPTER FORTY-SEVEN

CHANCE WOKE to a pounding headache and searing pain in his shoulder. He had no idea how much time had passed. The hum of an engine filled his ears, and a cold wet floor rocked beneath him. The movement felt familiar. Almost comforting. *I'm on a boat.* It took a few seconds before he remembered they'd taken him aboard the *Butterfly. Motherfucking traffickers.*

The room shifted as he tried to focus his clouded mind on his surroundings. He blinked several times, trying to clear his vision. It was dim and the place stank of rotten fish and ammonia, as though someone had tried to clean the stench but had only succeeded in adding to it. He also stank of vomit. *That* he remembered.

The realization that his hands and feet were now free hit him, but when he tried to move his shoulder, pain shot like fire down his arm and into his hand. He stifled a cry as the world wobbled and tilted, causing his stomach to lurch. He sucked in deep breaths to stem the nausea. A minute passed, then another, and the universe righted itself. He felt shaky, but at least he could see straight again. He remembered now that he'd dislocated his shoulder when they'd shoved him into the boat.

He rolled onto his back and looked around the room. He couldn't see anything in the dim light, so he rubbed the crusted blood from his eyes and tried again. The smell of fish clung to the air and the cold floor beneath him. He sat up slowly, his shoulder killing him, head spinning again.

Cold. Dark.

Panic clawed at his nerves as his eyes adjusted enough for him to make out the confines of the room. No, not a room. *Storage for the day's catch.*

He listened intently and heard muffled voices from overhead. They sounded angry, hurried, and it was clear they were in a rush to leave the dock now that they had him as cargo. He felt around his legs and found small puddles of water. He reached out and his hand met a wall. He tried to get to his feet and slipped back to the floor. Dazed and in pain, he took three more tries before he made it to his feet. He leaned against the wall, trembling and panting through the excruciating pain in his arm. He needed to pop his arm back into place or he had no chance of escaping.

He sat back down, took a deep breath, and pulled his knees to his chest. He grabbed his knees with his hands, gritted his teeth, and slowly leaned back so that the muscles of his arm and shoulder stretched. Pain shot through his shoulder and he strangled a scream. *More. Just a little more.* He leaned farther back as tears streaked his cheeks. He was just about to pass out again when his shoulder slipped back into place.

Motherfucker! he silently screamed, his breaths coming in gasps as the pain overwhelmed him. Ever so slowly, the pain abated and his vision cleared. His shoulder still hurt like a beast, but at least his arm no longer hung uselessly at his side.

Focus. Breathe. In. Out. Just breathe.

Chance continued to work to catch his breath before attempting the nearly insurmountable task of standing again. Now that the pain in his shoulder had dulled a bit, the throbbing in his head and back reasserted itself. Every inch of him ached, every joint protested. And with the pain came fear. He'd soon outlive his usefulness, and then these men would kill him.

I don't want to die here.

Fear like blackness seeped into his thoughts, and panic threatened to devour him. He forced himself through the steps of his breathing exercises, knowing it would help him focus on something other than the pain. Pain shot like shards of glass being pounded into his shoulder and chest with every movement of his body as he slowly struggled to his feet. Breathing through the pain, he braced himself against the wall until he could stand.

He reached out with one hand and felt nothing in front of him. He then ran his hand over the wall and followed it until he came to another wall. Finally, he explored upward and found a low ceiling of crisscrossed metal as he extended his hand. He pushed against the metal grate with his fingertips. It rattled but didn't move. Fear became panic as he realized he was locked inside of this place like an animal. Flashes of memory pressed at the periphery of his thoughts. He forced them back, knowing the dam that held them back was quickly crumbling.

Keep your shit together.

Terror seeped into his consciousness like a toxic cloud, clawing its way into his mind. He heard voices again, but this time, the voices were in his mind. Voices of his past.

Focus. Breathe!

He ran his fingers along the metal with trembling and desperate hands, following along it until he'd traced the confines of his cage and found the latch that held it shut. Human nature made him push at it again, though he knew the effort was futile. Panic clawed at him, cutting into his consciousness. He was falling. Voices surrounded him, shouting at him that he was helpless. Worthless.

He tried to run from the voices in his head, but he knew it was useless. He was locked in this place. They would punish him, and this time, he would drown in his fear. He slid to the floor and made himself small. Maybe if he disappeared, the voices would leave him alone.

"What did you do with the money?" his foster father demanded as he held up a coffee tin and rattled it for effect. "There was more than two hundred in here!"

At first Chance hadn't known what the man was talking about, but he figured it out quickly enough. "I… I didn't take it."

Chance had been with the Krauss family for about six weeks, and he'd experienced his foster father's temper firsthand when he'd taken the bag of chips from the cupboard without permission.

Eddie Krauss had managed to keep from killing Chance only because his wife had reminded him they couldn't spank him. "If they find out," she'd warned, "we'll lose the contract with social services."

But that night, as Chance defended himself, things escalated until Eddie backhanded him so hard, the class ring on Eddie's hand sliced a line down Chance's jaw that took several stitches to close.

"Little fucker," Eddie shouted. "Where is it?"

"I didn't take it," Chance said. He was many things, but he wasn't a thief.

Eddie hadn't believed him. "What did you take it for? Drugs? You're just like your fucking mother."

"I'm not—"

Eddie hit him again.

Chance put his hand to his face and felt blood, warm on his fingers. He struggled for control—he'd always struggled with the rage—but he kept it together until Eddie backed him against the wall and grabbed him by the throat. In that moment something inside Chance snapped. Like the gates opening to let out the horses at the track, the years of his anger—at his mother, at the social system that treated him like nothing, at the schoolkids who knew that he was homeless and no one cared about him—exploded in a haze. He hit Eddie hard enough that he staggered backward.

At first, he'd been proud of himself, showing Eddie he wouldn't be pushed around. But the genie of his anger wouldn't be easily shoved back into the bottle. And he hadn't counted on solitary. He hadn't counted on how crazy it made him.

So cold.

Somewhere outside the cell, one of the guards laughed. "*...show him how to behave.*"

The judge hadn't believed him when he'd said he hadn't hit Eddie first. No one had believed him. And when he got into one fight too many, they'd put him in solitary. It didn't matter that the other kid had tried to grab his dick.

"*Please,*" he whispered. "*No more.*" He had to get out of this cell. Another day in this place and he would lose himself. He'd drown, and there would be nothing left of him. He'd be an empty shell.

I don't want to die here!

The memories dissipated like fog and reality slowly returned. He wasn't in solitary, he was on a boat.

Breathe in. Breathe out.

He rubbed a finger over the small scar on the edge of his chin. It had faded over the years, but he still knew where to find it and he still remembered how he'd come by it. Now, for the first time, that scar reminded him that he couldn't lose it. He *wouldn't* lose it.

Dark. Cold. "Please, I promise I'll be good...."

He closed his eyes and forced the echoes away. He was so tired, he couldn't think clearly.

THE CUTTER slowed as it came alongside a trawler. It looked like all crew were on deck and none knew what in hell was going on.

"Stay put," Captain Grimes said.

"We can't take a look with you?" Xav asked.

"Sure. If you want to give away that you're on this boat. The minute that captain knows you're aboard, this'll become anything but a routine stop and you'll be all over the radio waves. It'll become a regular game of telephone on the water," Grimes griped.

Disappointed, Xav sank back into his chair and watched out the window as Grimes's crew boarded the vessel and corralled the other boat's men. Grimes stepped onto the boat and spoke with the captain, who gestured for him to look at whatever he wanted to see. It took thirty minutes, but Grimes and his men returned to the cutter and the trawler pulled away.

At thirty minutes a pop, they'd never get through the trawlers on the water, Xav thought bitterly.

The second possible from the BOLO turned out to be the same, and Xav's heart sank. This was worse than looking in cars after an AMBER Alert. His cell phone rang and he looked at it with the false hope that it would be Chance. His gut twisted when he saw it was Reggie. "Hey, Reggie, I'm kind of—"

"You lucky son of a bitch. You know that Bible you sent from wherever in hell you are?"

"Is it the same?"

"Better!"

Xav felt he should have been as eager as Reggie was, but Reggie's excitement only served to irritate him further. "Tell me."

"You know how the one from Bolivia was from the buyer?"

"I never did find out what it represented."

"It's the buyer's book! And guess what? Say please!"

He wanted to choke Reggie. He didn't have time for this. "Reggie, I'm—"

"Okay, okay, okay. I'm going to pretend you asked nicely. I always have to pretend because you never do. The book from you? Every transaction is the exact opposite of the book from Bolivia!"

"Reggie, what the fuck does that mean?"

"You found the seller! Say thank you, Reggie!"

Holy shit. That *was* good news. "Thank you, Reggie."

"Wait, wait, wait. It doesn't stop there. I got more news!"

"Tell me."

"First, tell me I'm a god."

Xav rolled his eyes. "Reggie, I'm in the middle of looking for a boat and kids' lives are at stake here!"

"Say it."

"I'm going to kill you next time I see you. You're a god."

"Your guy sent over the documents for the registration of some boat named *Butterfly*."

"And?"

"Our guys got to the bottom of it and guess what?"

"What?"

"What'd you do with your enthusiasm? Did you leave it at home today?"

"Reggie, what?" Xav yelled into the phone.

"Hey! Don't yell at me like that!"

Xav squeezed his forehead with thumb and fingers and lowered his voice. "Please tell me what you are talking about."

"She's owned by the same bastard who owns the *Camarón*! The yacht from the Bolivian operation!"

"Are you shitting me?"

"Would I do that? But there's even more! Guess where the *Camarón* is right now?"

"Where?"

"Off the coast of North Carolina! That's where you are, isn't it?"

"Reggie, you *are* a god!"

"Ha-ha! I know, I know! I am one serious motherfucking god! I sent all the stuff over to your office."

"Reggie, I could kiss you!"

"Please don't. I mean, I like you, don't get me wrong, just not *that* way, if you know what I mean."

"Good. Because you don't do a thing for me." Xav hung up and turned to Captain Grimes. "The yacht I think our bad guys are looking to drop cargo on is somewhere off our coast. How do we find it?"

"Transponder number?" Grimes asked.

Xav dialed Reggie back.

"No fuckin' way will I go out with you!"

"How'd you find out where the *Camarón* was?"

"How in hell should I know? That's where Ward said it was."

"Switch me to him, please."

"Gone. Left for the weekly at the main."

Xav swore under his breath. "Thanks. And you're still a god." He terminated the call and dialed the office. "Hi, Sally Ann. May I please speak with Twyla Fay?"

"One moment, Deputy Constantine."

"I assume you're calling about the paperwork the FBI sent to us," Twyla Fay said quickly.

"I am. Specifically the paperwork from a guy named Reggie Cook."

"That's him. Fifty-three PDF files. They're printing out now. Pages and pages. About five hundred of them."

Xav swore softly again. "I need the transponder number for a boat called the *Camarón*."

"Where do I find that?"

"Can you search each document for the word 'transponder'?"

"I'll do it as fast as I can and call you back."

"Thank you, Twyla Fay."

CHAPTER FORTY-EIGHT

CHANCE NEXT woke to the sound of the engine starting and muffled voices from up on deck. A few minutes later, the hatch opened above him and light streamed into the hold. Too bright—he shielded his eyes, then thought better of it. If there was a chance to escape, he needed to pay attention.

He squinted as his eyes adjusted to the intense light, and realized someone had a gun pointed at him from above.

"Down there! Get in!" someone shouted.

To his horror, Chance saw the outline of a small figure struggling to make his way into the cavernous hold. In spite of the gun trained at his head, Chance sat up and, to his further revulsion, saw that there were *three* boys trying to climb into the hold. One of the boys made a whimpering sound as he climbed in. Another openly sobbed. A third was silent. Stoic.

Chance got to his feet, cursing a silent blue streak when pain assailed him, and hobbled to stand beneath the opening to help the boys. They shied from him, and he let his hand fall to his side. One boy landed on an ankle the wrong way and cried out, then cowered, turning his back to Chance and the others. Throughout, the gun remained pointed at Chance's head.

Chance did his best to ignore the grate overhead as it slammed shut with a deafening boom and the cover hatch that closed over it, plunging them into darkness. He fought the dread that nearly overcame him, a tidal wave of misery against a brutalized shore, and stilled, waiting for his eyes to adjust to the pitch. He listened to the boys' whimpers, sobs, and frightened breathing, and, when his eyes slowly adjusted, he made out their faces. Beautiful. Innocent. Terrified.

With four of them in the hold, the sensation that the world was closing in on Chance was ten times worse. He squeezed his eyes shut and worked his mantra. *Breathe in for four. Hold for four. Breathe out for four. Hold for four. Focus. Get your shit together.*

The sound of renewed sobs brought him back to the present and he looked at the boys. They were so young. Ten? Twelve? Anger and hatred suddenly imbued every fiber of his being. He would not let what happened to him happen to these boys. *Motherfucking traffickers or no.*

"Hey," he said. "It's going to be all right."

One of the boys stared at him. The boy's eyes shone with fear, but his gaze was openly calculating as he assessed Chance, trying to figure out if he was a threat.

Chance glanced at the other two boys, now huddled against the wall, and back again. He guessed this boy to be about twelve and probably the oldest of the three. "My name's Chance."

The boy kept his suspicious gaze locked on Chance but didn't venture a word.

"You guys okay?"

Something flickered in the boy's eyes, but Chance couldn't make out what it was. He tried again. "What's your name?"

Tentatively, the boy who'd eyed him said, "Ray."

One of the boys on Xav's list of missing children was named Ray, and Chance would have bet the shirt on his back that this was him. Chance glanced at the other two boys. "Their names?"

"He's Lee." Ray pointed a shaky finger at the kid who was sobbing openly, his head between his knees. "And that's Jenson." He pointed to the boy who'd hurt his ankle, still whimpered, and had started coughing. "Who are you?"

"As I said, my name is Chance."

"Why'd they take ya?"

Chance frowned. "I'm not sure."

Ray edged toward the two boys against the wall and squatted next to them. Chance watched as Ray huddled with them and offered the other two soothing words, to no avail.

"Can I help?" Chance asked. "Looked like Jenson, there, hurt his ankle on the way in."

"We got it," Ray said quickly.

Chance nodded and moved across the room slowly, his body aching in too many places to count. "I'm, ah, I'm right here if you need me." He used the wall as a support and lowered himself carefully. He found a reasonably comfortable sitting position and leaned back against the wall.

Chance watched them for an indeterminable time. Of the three, Lee looked to be in the worst shape. He had inched away from the others, and every time someone spoke, he flinched. Chance sat quietly, not venturing conversation. He wanted the boys to understand he wasn't a threat to them.

"They're g-gonna k-kill us, aren't th-they?" Jenson said between quiet sobs.

"We'll be all right," Chance said, trying to sound reassuring.

Jenson sniffled and, for the first time, looked at Chance.

"How's your ankle?"

"S'okay." Jenson wiped his face on his sleeve. "D-don't think it's b-broke or nothin'."

"Mind if I take a look?"

Jenson hesitated and looked to Ray, who nodded. "'K-kay."

Chance rose and approached slowly, and waited until Jenson's breathing slowed before he squatted beside the boy.

Ray hovered over Chance's shoulder like a mother hen as Jenson tentatively exposed his foot so Chance could see it.

"Let's take a look here," he said and carefully lifted Jenson's lower leg and bare foot. His ankle had started to swell and was likely sprained, but Chance didn't think it was broken. "Tell you what. We're going to wrap this so it doesn't get any worse."

Chance began to slip his sweatshirt over his head, then paused. He had no idea what had happened to the boys, but he didn't have to be a rocket scientist to make an educated guess, and the last thing he wanted to do was to frighten them more. "I'm going to take my sweatshirt off so I can get to my T-shirt. I need to tear it up to wrap Jenson's ankle," he explained evenly.

Lee began to mewl, and Jenson looked at Ray. Clearly, Ray had become the boy in charge. Chance turned to him. "Okay?"

Ray glanced at Jenson and back again. "Yeah, okay."

Chance ignored the screaming pain in his shoulder as he quickly slipped his T-shirt and sweatshirt off in one motion, pulled the T-shirt away from the sweatshirt, and pulled the sweatshirt back on. He ripped the T-shirt into strips and was surprised at the little effort it took. *Anger does have its uses*, he thought, bittersweet. "Okay." He held the strips up to Ray. "Would you mind holding these for me?"

Ray took them from him.

"All right, Jenson. I'm going to lift your foot and rest it on my knee so I can wrap it. Is that all right with you?"

Jenson glanced at Ray again who nodded.

"G-guess so."

"Okay, here we go." Chance carefully placed the boy's foot on his knee. "Now, I have to wrap this a little tight to give it support, but you let me know if it's too tight, all right?"

Jenson looked to Ray again.

"Let him," Ray said softly.

"'K-kay."

Chance began to wrap the boy's ankle and heel, careful to keep the foot aligned with his leg. "Where are you from?" he asked idly, hoping to take Jenson's mind off what he was doing.

"H-Havelock."

"Over by the base?"

"Yeah."

"I sometimes sail my boat over there to watch the planes land and take off," Chance said. "Sometimes I imagine what it must be like to fly in one of the fast ones."

Chance felt relief as Jenson seemed to relax by inches with the familiar conversation. The boys would stand a better chance of surviving this if they stayed calm.

"There," he said as he tied the bandage off. "Can you wiggle your toes?"

Jenson did.

"Good." Chance smiled at the boy. "Do you like watching the planes too?" Chance asked as he gently manipulated Jenson's ankle to ensure the bandage wasn't too tight.

"Yeah. B-but they're real l-loud sometimes." A ghost of a smile crossed his lips.

Where Chance had seen only fear before, he now saw a faint flicker of calm. "I think you're right about the ankle. I don't think it's broken."

"Yeah."

"You're very brave."

"I-I sh-shouldn't have g-gone," Jenson said softly.

Chance frowned at the quick change of subject. "Gone where?"

"I w-wanted to s-see them, and he said m-maybe I c-could t-take one home."

"Take what home?"

Jenson began to cry again.

"Puppies," Ray said from behind Chance.

Puppies. Anger infused Chance. Just like Quinn and Winter. These motherfuckers had set up a racket to scout kids.

"…asked my m-mom… said they d-didn't want n-no puppy. So I w-went real early to s-see 'em. I d-didn't… I didn't want…." He choked on a sob. "M-my m-mom's gonna be real m-mad."

Dr. Sampson's words filled Chance's mind. The words that had gotten him through so much of his childhood hell. "*It's not your fault.*" He hadn't believed the words when Dr. Sampson had said them to him years before, but he believed them now. He glanced at Lee, whose mewling had gotten worse again. "It isn't your fault. None of this is your fault."

Jenson looked at Chance, his eyes searching, and Chance saw that the boy desperately wanted to believe his words.

"We'll be okay." He turned to Ray. "What about you. Are you hurt?"

Ray shook his head, but Chance saw him swallow hard as he tried his best to be brave.

Chance glanced at Lee. Although he no longer openly sobbed, his body shook and he'd begun to rock.

"They took him," Ray said in a low voice. He was clearly struggling not to cry.

"What do you mean?" Chance asked.

"We were somewhere on the docks. Together. Then these men took him." Ray stared at his feet. "They did something to him, 'cause he won't talk now." He blinked a few times, then wiped his eyes with the back of his hand. "I tried to stop them from takin' him, but they pushed me outta the way."

The story sounded all too familiar.

"Ray was real brave," Jenson told Chance.

"I know he was. You all are."

Ray stood a little straighter, then glanced at his feet again.

"Will you sit here with Jenson while I see if I can help Lee?"

Ray nodded solemnly and sat beside Jenson. "It's okay." He looked back at Chance, who offered him a small smile.

Chance stood and walked slowly over to Lee. He forced himself to ignore the creeping sense of doom the grate overhead created in him. *You need to be strong for* these *kids.*

He sat beside Lee—not too close—careful not to scare the boy. Lee didn't look up. Chance reached out to put a reassuring hand on Lee's shoulder, then let his hand fall away. It scared him to be touched as a boy, and he could only imagine how Lee felt now.

Lee peered at Chance over his right knee, a starling caught in the sights of a cobra, then hid his face again. His blond hair was matted and full of dirt, his face pale and tear-streaked. The tag of his T-shirt was visible at his nape—the shirt was inside out. He was missing a shoe.

"My name's Chance." Chance saw Xav in his mind's eye, back in Quinn's hospital room and interviewing Quinn. His voice, its cadence, had been soft, rhythmic, conveying only comfort. *Take your time. Go slow.*

Lee suddenly whispered, "No, please, don't...."

Christ. The coroner's report on Winter was still fresh in his mind. "I won't let them hurt you again," Chance heard himself say. He knew he had no way to guarantee it, but he'd do whatever it took to keep these boys safe. Anything and everything.

"I wanna go home." Lee began to sob again.

God, Chance wanted to do *something* to help him, to keep him safe, to keep them *all* safe. His chest ached. He needed to get them out of here. "We're all going to be okay," Chance replied with a conviction fueled by rage. He'd get them out of here even if it meant putting himself between them and the assholes with the guns. "We're getting out of here."

"How?" Ray looked expectantly at Chance.

"The police are looking for us." The words came out of nowhere, but Chance knew the instant he'd spoken them that it was true. Xav would know something was wrong by now, and he would be looking for them. *We need to be ready to escape when the opportunity presents itself.*

"They'll find us," he said aloud. He met each boy's gaze and prayed like hell that the boys believed him. "But we need to be ready."

Jenson nodded. For the first time, Lee raised his head and looked at them.

Chance would make sure they were ready when Xav came for them. They'd do this together.

"What do you want us to do?" Ray asked.

CHAPTER FORTY-NINE

XAV COULD hardly contain himself as he waited for Twyla Fay's call. Waiting drove him nuts, and when his cell phone finally rang, he actually jumped. "Hi, Twyla Fay."

"This here's Hatch"

"Who?"

"Hatch from the *Jenny*? Y'all said to call if I ever needed anything?"

"Oh, right. Hatch, I'm in the middle of something now and it isn't a good time to talk."

"I know y'all are. That's why I'm callin'. Y'all're lookin' for the *Butterfly*, right? The worst kinda pirate?"

Excitement flooded Xav. "You found the *Butterfly*?"

All eyes in the pilothouse turned to Xav.

"I'm runnin' her down as we speak."

"What do you mean, running her down?"

"Crew threw something overboard and I didn't like the way it looked, so I went to see what it was. It was a kid!"

Xav swore aloud. "Is the kid alive?"

"Barely. I got him aboard and he's bein' tended to. The *Butterfly* saw what I done and took off at a dead run. She's headin' due east at twenty-eight knots, and I don't know if I can catch her, but I am gainin' on her. I got a full load and she's obviously empty."

"Where are you?"

"Write this down and give it to yer captain."

"Hang on, hang on. I need a pen."

Sheriff Winston handed a pad and a pen to him.

"Go."

"Thirty-four point seven one eight eight three one, and seventy-six point three three five eight one seven. We're on the Outer Banks just beyond Cape Lookout. How long 'til you get out here?"

Xav showed the pad to Captain Grimes. "This is where the *Butterfly* is. How long before we get there?"

Grimes took the pad from his hand and showed it to his pilot, who said, "Seven minutes." The cutter lunged into high speed, and Billy caught Xav before he fell backward.

"Hatch, listen to me. We'll be there in seven minutes. These people are armed and dangerous. I do not want you to try to confront them."

"I'm only gonna tail her, but get out here as fast as y'all can."

"We're on our way. Be careful, Hatch!" He turned back to Grimes. "There are kids aboard."

Captain Grimes spoke into the radio handset and ordered all vessels to the coordinates Hatch provided.

Within a minute, Lieutenant Nelson's voice came over the radio. "Subject vessel in sight and appears to be headed for yacht. Nine crew visible on deck."

Xav's phone rang again and he answered it. "Twyla Fay?"

"Here's the number." She rattled it off and Xav scribbled it down. "Thanks, Twyla Fay." He terminated the call. "This is the transponder number of the *Camarón*."

Captain Grimes went to the radar terminal, slid the keyboard out from it, and punched in the number. It began to blip on the radar screen. He looked out over the horizon and pointed. The pilot nodded. Grimes turned to Winston.

"We'll head the *Butterfly* off first and make sure she continues heading toward the yacht. When we have them side by side, we'll board them both and figure out the paperwork later."

Winston nodded.

"Strap yourselves into your seats, we're in for a bumpy ride," Grimes ordered.

"We're comin' up on her port side," the pilot said a few minutes later.

Captain Grimes picked up the radio handset, flipped a switch, and ordered the *Butterfly* to cut her engines. She didn't comply.

The pilot pointed out the window. The *Jenny* was gaining on the *Butterfly*.

"The last thing we need is some cowboy on the water!" Grimes shouted "Guide the *Butterfly* off!"

The pilot poured on speed, came alongside the *Butterfly*, and bumped her port side gently. The *Butterfly* came about hard to starboard, and the *Jenny* couldn't slow down and come about fast enough. She rammed the *Butterfly* amidships with a deafening crash, and the *Butterfly* stalled in the water. Gunfire ensued from the *Butterfly*, and everyone on the *Jenny* dove below deck as the cutter veered off, bullets pinging off the pilothouse.

Once a safe distance away, the pilot slowed the cutter and brought her about. Grimes held a pair of binoculars to his face as he watched his vessels surround the *Camarón*. He threw the binoculars on the map desk, grasped the handset, and hailed his lead vessel. "Do not board the *Camarón*. I repeat. Do not board the *Camarón*."

He looked at Xav. "We have a mess on our hands."

"We need to get to the *Jenny* before she sinks, and we need to get the kids off the *Butterfly*," Xav said.

Grimes shouted to the cutter's captain. "Get Rescue to the Jenny! Now!" He turned to Xav. "Have you ever dived before?"

"I have and I'm certified."

"Then this is what we're gonna do."

THEY STOOD on the deck of the cutter, and Xav listened to Busby, the engineer, lecture on the features of the *Butterfly*.

Xav donned a wet suit and air tanks, then the diving watch he'd use to communicate from beneath the water. He typed a test message on the small keypad and received *test message acknowledged* almost instantly.

When Busby finished lecturing, Xav looked at the schematics and pointed to an opening. "This is the only entrance to the hold?"

"That's it. It's a flush and it's tight. Thirty-five-degree angle. You'll be lucky if you can get your shoulders through the shaft."

"If I can't get in there, what's plan B?"

"Surface raid only."

Sheriff Winston stepped closer. "Do you have scouts in the water for the runners?"

Busby nodded. "They'll capture 'em, and we have a chase boat to swing by and pick 'em up."

"What about the *Camarón*?" Xav asked.

"She has no choice but to stay put for now," Grimes said.

Xav gave the man a thumbs-up, sat on the edge of the cutter, and dropped backward into the water.

He swam through the murky water and debris for the quarter mile it took to reach the *Butterfly*. He stayed deep in the water until he came up beneath her. The flush opening was right where Busby had showed him on the schematics. He put his ear to the hull and listened intently. The low murmur of voices filtered through. He quickly typed out a message on his watch.

Estimate 5 canaries. Awaiting go. He sent the message and received a message back instantly.

Go.

Xav carefully unscrewed the grill covering the flush opening and sent it away. It floated up for a moment before dropping into the dark water below. He studied the opening and felt the interior walls with his fingertips. They were slick with algae, which would make the short trek easier, assuming he could find grips. He activated the silent beacon on his air tanks and slipped out of them. He quickly tied them to one of the brackets that had held the grill, took a deep breath, and closed off the air. Letting the respirator fall away from his mouth, he climbed into the shaft.

Busby hadn't been kidding when he said it would be tight. Xav stretched out, long and lean, and the algae aided his slow crawl upward. He thanked his lucky stars the interior walls were riveted. Otherwise, he'd have nothing to hold on to and less hope of traversing the inclined shaft. He used his fingers on the rivets to propel himself upward and forward. When a fish head floated in front of his mask, he nearly cursed aloud and lost his air. Damn thing had dislodged from somewhere in the tunnel. He pushed it away as he made another slow crawl upward, his lungs beginning to yearn for air. Finally, he saw where water ended and air began. He smoothed his way forward until he reached air and took a deep breath as quietly as he could. One more pull upward and he was there.

He pulled his mask off and one of the boys just happened to look up at the opening. He yelped when he saw Xav's face, and Xav quickly put his fingers to his lips. The boy silently pointed up at him.

"What?" echoed up softly.

When Xav heard Chance's familiar voice, he smiled to himself and his heart actually did a little flip-flop. He pulled himself a little more forward and peered over the lip of the shaft. The wide-eyed look on Chance's face warmed his heart in ways he couldn't have imagined. He winked and put his fingers to his lips again before typing on his watch.

In. Go.

Xav pulled himself halfway through the opening and looked to the walls immediately to his left and right. There were grips, and he used them to leverage himself into the hold.

"Thank God," Chance breathed quietly.

Xav couldn't help it. He gave Chance a quick hug. He looked at the boys in the compartment and wasn't comforted. They were in shock and bad shape.

He withdrew a small flashlight from his belt and studied the walls and ceiling of the tank. When he found the hatch, he instructed everyone to move away from it. "Let's move over into that corner," he encouraged.

Chance helped the boys move to where Xav had pointed.

"Stay as quiet as you can," Xav whispered.

"You're saving us?" one of the boys asked.

"I am trying," Xav whispered. At that moment, a gunshot rang out from above, and the cacophony that began was reminiscent of a war zone. Sirens screamed and footsteps thundered, and the explosion of gunfire was deafening. The noise slowed after a few minutes, but it seemed like an eternity to Xav. A few more pops indicated that the last had been subdued. Xav waited as minutes ticked by and more footsteps thundered overhead as Coast Guard personnel boarded the boat. The hatch above them opened within minutes and bright sunlight streamed into the hold. Everyone shielded their eyes except for Xav, who was grateful to see Sheriff Winston's face appear in the opening.

"I swear, Mr. Fairchild, I never thought I'd see the day when you needed my help!" Sheriff Winston's voice boomed down to them.

Chance didn't smile. "The sooner you get us out of here, the better."

The boat suddenly groaned, and salt water shot from the shaft that Xav had exited. Someone had opened the valve to fill the hold. "Get lines down here now!" Xav shouted over the rush of the water.

Chance and Xav gathered the boys beneath the hatch. Water was rising fast, and it would only be minutes before they'd be inundated. Five grappling lines descended, and Xav showed Chance how to wrap one around a boy and cinch it with the cleat. "Hold on here," Xav instructed as he wrapped the first boy's hands around the line. "Up!" he shouted, and the boy was hauled up and out of the hold. Xav watched Chance struggle to help one of the boys, determination etched on his face.

"Up!" Chance shouted, and the next boy went.

The water was chest high by the time the Coast Guard pulled the last boy from the tank. Xav tied the final line around Chance.

"What about you?" Chance demanded.

"I'm right behind you." Xav smiled. "Up!"

Chance rose on the line and was up and out of the hold in seconds.

Xav treaded water as the level rose, then naturally rode the water up to the hatch. A strong hand from Winston helped him out of the hold.

THE CUTTER'S medical personnel tended to them as they sat on the deck.

Busby climbed up on deck from below and motioned Winston over. Winston listened to Busby talk, and then his face flushed red with fury. Two paramedics boarded the boat with a basket stretcher, and Winston motioned Xav over.

Before Xav could ask, a furious Winston huffed, "You will not like this, and I'm going to ask you to maintain your calm."

Xav didn't have to ask. A kid was dead. Rage vibrated through every fiber of his being. "Who did it?"

"They're bringing the perpetrators up too."

Perpetrators. *Plural.*

Xav covered his mouth with a hand to prevent rage from escaping him in a primeval scream.

The paramedics descended the steps and returned a few moments later with the basket, the small contents covered by a sheet.

Everyone watched in silence as the paramedics carefully transferred the basket stretcher off the boat. One of the boys began to sob, and Chance did his best to comfort him.

"Go sit down," Winston ordered Xav.

Xav met Winston's eyes, and after a long moment, he returned to Chance and the boys.

Chance calmed the crying boy again, then stood next to Xav.

Deputies hauled a belligerent Charlie Cooper up from below. He was dressed in nothing more than a pair of boxers. Xav vowed at that moment to kill him if he ever had the legal opportunity.

"Depraved son of a fucking bitch," Chance said under his breath.

But that wasn't the worst of it.

The deputies next hauled a nude, foul-mouthed Faison up from below, the blood on his hands not a euphemism for something else.

Chance paled a white Xav didn't think possible and was reminiscent of the way Xav felt the first time he'd seen such depravity.

"No," Chance breathed.

Xav put a hand on his shoulder. "Yes," he said softly.

SOMETHING INSIDE Chance shattered.

Noooooooo! roared through his mind. But the sight of Faison grabbed him by the neck and wouldn't let go.

No. Faison had downplayed things. It was what he called good politics.

Then what about the shrimper? Faison had blown him off about that, even though the connection made total sense.

Time after time, cases against the suppliers evaporated before they even crossed Chance's desk. No SBI. No DEA. No FBI.

No one to poke around and stir things up.

Faison had reassigned him to the Davies case. A slam-dunk case, but one that would take him weeks to get up to speed on. A fucking waste of time.

Perfect way to keep me *from nosing around.*

The men who'd taken Chance wanted to know what he knew. Not about Xav. *About Faison.*

No one batted an eye about the missing kids until Xav started digging. How the hell do kids vanish without anyone realizing it?

His heart raced in his chest and he clenched his jaw. How had he not seen it? Three years, and he'd never once questioned the lack of progress on the drug cases. He'd always figured Faison was withholding information from him. He'd just never guessed it was anything more than politics. *Fucker. Goddamned motherfucker!* "You sick son of a bitch!" Chance shouted.

Faison glared at him, his eyes wild, white powder on his upper lip. He was higher than a kite. "It's just your kinda pussy, pretty boy."

Chance stilled. His thoughts, his feelings, all the rage, everything he'd ever survived, seemed to culminate into a perfect calm after a storm.

He glanced at Xav, the corners of his mouth barely quirking upward. Then, calmly, without any of the rage he'd lived all his life, Chance punched Faison in the face hard enough to send him backward down the stairs and into the boat.

CHAPTER FIFTY

CHANCE OPENED the front door of the house and stood there, staring at nothing in particular. After a stop at the hospital to check on his dislocated shoulder, he and Xav had spent the entire day debriefing. FBI, SBI, DEA. He'd lost track after a while, he'd spoken to so many people. He'd slept a few hours on the couch in the lounge at the sheriff's office. He was certain Xav had guarded the door, because no one had interrupted him and he'd woken up on his own. How Xav was still awake baffled him. The man was a machine.

"You okay?" Xav's gentle touch on his shoulder brought Chance back to himself.

"Yeah. You?"

"I'm fine." Xav looked exhausted.

Xav slipped around him into the vestibule, then turned to face Chance and offered his hand. "Bed?"

"Perfect." Chance took Xav's hand and they walked into the front hallway. He hadn't made it halfway to the stairs when he swore under his breath.

"What's the matter?"

"No one's fed Thunder."

"Got it covered," Xav said. "Carol's been feeding him since you went missing." He led Chance through the kitchen and opened the back door onto the screened-in porch. Thunder slept in a pile of blankets. There was dry food in his bowl and plenty of water.

"Carol's the best."

"Yep." Xav pulled him closer, careful not to press against the sling that held Chance's arm, and gave him a sweet kiss. "Bed now?"

Chance nodded.

They climbed the stairs in silence. Xav's hand felt warm and solid in Chance's—a reminder that the entire universe hadn't shifted sideways.

Chance went to pull off the slightly too big sweatshirt and T-shirt— Xav's clothing—but the sling got in the way.

"Let me help." Xav's warm voice made Chance shiver.

"Thanks."

"My pleasure." Xav's smile was like sunshine after a squall. Chance tried to remember the last time he'd felt so warm and safe but came up empty.

Xav removed the sling, gingerly removed the sweatshirt, and then the shirt. Chance replaced the sling as Xav worked open the buckle on his belt, then unbuttoned and unzipped the jeans. He pushed them down along with the Andrew Christians Xav had also loaned him. Chance decided he liked those enough to fight Xav for them. He'd buy a few pair when he had a minute to breathe again.

"Better?" Xav asked.

"Would be better if you were naked too." Chance's body had clearly forgotten how exhausted he was.

Xav slowly removed his T-shirt and smiled. God, Chance loved that fucking smile!

"That's not naked," Chance pointed out. "But it's not a bad start."

Xav bit his lower lip and took his sweet time shimmying out of his jeans, leaving only his underwear.

"Tease."

"Come on," Xav said. "Admit you love it."

"I'm not sure," Chance said in his best courtroom voice. "I don't have all the facts yet, Deputy."

Xav chuckled, then slipped off the briefs.

"Much better."

Xav's expression grew serious as he tenderly touched Chance's cheek. Chance closed his eyes and let himself feel that fragile human connection, skin against skin. Trust. Pleasure. Kindness. Nothing sexual in that touch, not yet.

The chaos in Chance's mind quieted with the knowledge that he could just *be*.

"That's it," Xav said, his voice a husky whisper. "Don't think for a change. Let me make you feel."

Eyes still closed, Chance sighed as Xav kissed a line over the edge of his jaw and up toward his lips. Xav drew his thumb across Chance's mouth and traced his way around it. Chance's sigh started in his toes and traveled through his chest, the warmth of relaxation spreading throughout his body.

With his fingers still lightly exploring Chance's lips, Xav found Chance's shoulder with his mouth. The smooth tip of Xav's tongue pressed gently against bone and muscle, warm and wet. Xav circled Chance's waist with his other arm and pressed against Chance's back and ass. Xav was as hard as he was, but he made no move to rush.

"What do you like?" Xav asked as he nipped at Chance's shoulder.

"Good," Chance gasped. "Just like that."

"Mmmm." Another gentle bite, then Xav's tongue again, smoothing over the sting.

"Yes."

Xav lifted Chance's arm and licked his way down until he reached the inside of Chance's elbow. Chance shivered in reply as Xav repeatedly laved the sensitive skin there.

"Want you," Chance said.

"Soon." Xav nipped Chance's neck and nipped there, then massaged Chance's shoulders until Chance wondered if he'd melt.

"Ahhhh."

"That's it. Let it go."

The tension in Chance's back and shoulders fled with the onslaught of Xav's hands and words. He leaned into Xav's chest, craving the contact where before he'd have run from it. Xav was too close, too gentle, too fucking sexy. "Xavier."

This time Xav sighed. "I love it when you call me that."

Chance opened his eyes and smiled, then turned and put his hand on Xav's cheeks to draw him in for a blistering kiss. Instead of his neat braid, Xav had fashioned a rough ponytail that now barely contained his hair. Strands of dark silk fell over his eyes and nose. Chance brushed those away and slipped the elastic from Xav's nape.

Xav shook his head and his hair tumbled free. Chance worked his fingers through the tousled mess, scraping his nails against Xav's scalp until Xav moaned his pleasure.

"I like it better this way," Chance said against Xav's ear.

"I'll try to remember that." Xav touched a spot a few inches down from Chance's shoulder, and Chance winced. "Still hurts." Not a question, an acknowledgment. Xav had a few bruises, as well.

"I'll survive."

Xav leaned down and tenderly kissed the bruise. "Better?"

"I'm not sure. Can you try that again?"

Xav kissed the bruise again.

"Definitely better." Chance touched the scar on Xav's side and looked into Xav's eyes.

"It's nothing. I survived. The two boys didn't."

Some scars ran deep. Chance understood this all too well. He pressed his lips together in an approximation of a smile, then leaned down and kissed Xav's scar. He heard Xav's stuttered inhalation in response, then kissed the scar again. "I wish they had, but I'm glad you survived."

Xav nodded. From the tight line of Xav's jaw, Chance guessed speaking about it now, after everything that had happened on the boat, was simply too overwhelming. He got that. He took Xav by the hand and led him to the bed.

Xav lay on his back and Chance straddled his hips. He ghosted a palm over Xav's slightly sweaty skin, feeling it warm to his touch. Xav's nipples hardened as Chance traced lazy circles around one, then the other, and Xav's breath came in tiny gasps that caused the skin on the back of Chance's neck to prickle with heat.

"Beautiful." The word escaped Chance's lips before he could stop it. The thought *why not say it if it's true* followed in quick succession. Xav *was* a beautiful man. Chance leaned over and Xav slipped a hand between them to press their cocks together. "So good," Xav moaned as he rubbed up and down their lengths.

"Yes. Just like that. Please," Chance begged. He was too tired to fuck, and he guessed so was Xav.

Xav licked Chance's neck as he continued to pump them both. Xav's breaths against Chance's ear made Chance that much harder. He reached beneath Xav and grabbed his ass. As Xav pressed his body upward, his muscles strained and flexed against Chance's palm.

The friction between them eased as they sweat, their bodies gliding now. Chance had long since forgotten the pain of his shoulder and sore muscles, although he guessed Xav was taking care not to press against any of the obvious injuries.

"So fucking beautiful," Chance hissed as he met Xav's gaze and held it. "I want to see you come." *I want you to forget everything but the here and now. Make me feel.*

Xav's lips parted as he came. "Chance." His voice sounded like a caress. "God, Chance."

"Xavier." Chance's climax enveloped him slowly, the sensations flooding his body: heat, fleeing tension, the way Xav smelled so damn good, the need finally filled. In that long moment, Chance's only thoughts were of Xav and the way Xav made him feel. No questions. No doubts. Nothing but a sense of rightness. Knowing he was safe. Knowing he… *loved* Xav, even though he didn't yet understand what that really meant for their future. And that was just fine.

EPILOGUE

One week later

CHANCE OPENED his eyes to find Xav asleep beside him, his body spooned against his back. Moonlight bathed the room in silver, and a cool breeze danced through the open window, a welcome relief from the oppressive North Carolina heat.

He watched Xav sleep for a few minutes, his beautiful face relaxed and untroubled. The pain he'd seen in Xav's gaze since Winter's death had faded, but Chance knew it would take time before Xav would make his peace with not being able to save both the boys. They all needed time to heal. So would the town.

Since they'd been debriefed nearly a week before, Xav had stayed with him at the house. It felt wonderful to have him there, and he hoped their future held living together.

He slipped out of bed, careful not to wake Xav, and winced as pain shot through his shoulder. He breathed deeply and the pain receded.

Outside, the moon cast shadows on the front lawn and the street beyond, making the live oaks look as though their branches might stretch all the way to the waterfront. Something furry rubbed against his bare legs. He reached down and scooped up Thunder, who purred and pressed his head against his chest, turning in his arms to expose his belly. Chance rubbed the cat absentmindedly. He was glad he'd decided to invite Thunder inside, and Thunder seemed pleased with his new digs. He'd buy a collar once he had a minute. Maybe even a bed to replace the heap of blankets he'd moved inside from the porch.

Thunder hopped down from his arms and trotted happily out of the room as the soft patter of feet—human, this time—on the wood floor preceded the strong arms that slipped around his waist. Xav pressed a soft kiss to Chance's neck. "You okay?" he asked.

Chance turned around and pulled Xav's face to his, then kissed him in reply. "Better than," he said. His life would never fall neatly into place, and he was okay with that. Xav got that too, and he didn't seem to mind. "How about you?"

"Good." Xav smiled, but Chance saw a flicker of uneasiness in his eyes.

Chance brushed his fingers over Xav's lips and met his gaze. "Nervous about the press conference?" he asked.

"No. But I'd be okay if I wasn't included," Xav answered.

"You're a hero. People need their heroes."

Xav smirked and pulled Chance tighter against him, still careful not to put too much pressure on his shoulder. "You know they'll ask whether you're going to run for DA."

Xav was changing the subject, but Chance let it go. "Yes."

"Have you decided?" Xav's breath tickled the skin beneath Chance's ear, giving him goose bumps.

"I need time. I still haven't wrapped my brain around the whole Faison thing yet." The breeze blew harder from outside, causing the drapes to flutter. "I never liked the man," Chance continued. "I always told myself I'd never wish someone dead. But I *wanted* the motherfucking bastard dead. Part of me still does."

"Reasonable, given the damage he's done to untold lives. Come back to bed?"

Xav kissed Chance's shoulder, took his hand, and led him back to the bed.

Chance turned and faced Xav, then pulled his face close and claimed his lips with a blistering kiss.

Chance swallowed hard and took a moment to gather his thoughts. If he'd learned anything from what he'd been through, it was that sometimes you needed to roll the dice and accept the risk. "Thank you."

"For what?"

"For being there for me." Chance offered Xav a gentle smile before he pressed his lips against Xav's neck.

"Thank you for being there for me too," Xav said softly.

Chance looked at him now and realized he had been there for Xav too, through thick and thin. A small new confidence filled him, and with it came the realization that he'd fallen for Xav. He loved Xav. He was *in* love with Xav. He felt it as surely as Xav's steady presence. And someday he'd have the courage to speak the words aloud.

"…HOW MUCH I appreciate your taking the time to come here today. I also want to thank Governor Branston and Mayor Smith for joining us," the attorney general said, concluding her scripted remarks.

Chance glanced at Xav and smiled. He looked hotter than hell in his gray suit with the green paisley tie, his neat braid flowing down his back where everyone could see it.

"You doing okay, Quinn?" Chance asked.

"Yeah." Quinn fidgeted, then slipped his hand into Chance's. Quinn had been holding Xav's hand since they'd made their way inside City Hall, but this was the first time he'd held Chance's hand too, and it made Chance smile.

"I'm going to ask for custody," Xav had told him that morning, as they'd gone to pick Quinn up from his new foster care placement.

Chance hadn't hesitated. "Do it." It felt right. And when Xav had asked Quinn if that was what he wanted, Quinn had run to Xav and buried his head against Xav's chest.

"It'll make all the difference in the world to you if you can save even one."

That makes two more of us, Xav.

"Thank you, Attorney General Vance," the governor said as she moved to the podium. "I'd like to take this opportunity to honor some of the brave people who went above and beyond the call of duty to keep this state's citizens safe." She glanced to her left and nodded. "Deputy Constantine? Mr. Fairchild? If you'd be so kind as to join me?"

Chance smiled at Xav, and they joined the governor at the podium with Quinn standing between them.

"I can't thank you both enough for what you did for the people of this state," the governor said. "Your heroism serves as a fine example of truly selfless service to our citizens."

"Thank you, ma'am," Chance said, briefly releasing Quinn's hand to shake the governor's, then clasping Quinn's smaller one again.

"Thank you, Governor," Xav said as he shook her hand.

"And now, Sheriff Winston?" The governor gestured to him, and he looked almost as uncomfortable as Quinn did. The dress code for his deputies might be suits, but as he tugged at the collar of his dress shirt, it was quite clear he rarely wore anything but his uniform. He stepped to the podium and his face flushed.

"For your selfless devotion to duty and service to the citizens of North Carolina." The governor handed Sheriff Winston a small plaque and shook his hand. "Thank you, Sheriff. We are grateful for your perseverance and your good work."

"Thank you, ma'am," Winston said. "It's an honor and a privilege." He glanced at Xav, who nodded and grinned. "Me and my folks would like to do a little thankin' of our own."

"By all means." The governor smiled and stepped back from the podium.

"There are a lot of folks who need thankin'," Winston said. "Not the least of which is my staff." He looked out at the audience, where John, Twyla Fay, and a half a dozen uniformed deputies stood.

"And there's one in particular who I'm mighty proud of. Without his help, we'd still be spinnin' our wheels." Winston pulled a star-shaped badge from his jacket, went to Quinn, and pinned it on his shirt. "This here's our new honorary deputy, Quinn Haverty!"

Quinn's mouth fell open and he flushed crimson when the crowd applauded and whistles and cheers filled the air.

"Thank you, Quinn," the governor said. A wide-eyed Quinn shook her hand, then quickly reclaimed Chance and Xav's hands.

"And now," the governor said, "if there are any questions? We have just a few minutes left."

"Sheriff Winston?" Rachel Crawford, a reporter with the *N & O*, asked. "What's the status of your internal investigation?"

"I've asked the attorney general to assist," Winston replied. "Billy Kenner will coordinate for my office and Marcy Gayle from the DA's will file charges if need be."

"Mr. Fairchild, are you going to run for DA now that Mr. Faison has resigned?" another reporter asked as a television camera panned the room and zoomed in on Chance at the podium.

Chance smiled and shook his head. "It's premature for me to be throwing my hat into the ring, but I'm not ruling it out. In the meantime, I'll do my job as acting DA," he said, fully aware he sounded like a million other politicians.

In his mind, he heard Evelene's words, *"What do you want? And don't give me the 'it sounds sappy' bullshit."*

Chance fucking hated politicians. Still, political bullshit might be a fair trade for making a difference. More than fair, if it meant keeping kids like Quinn safe and getting drugs off the streets.

"What about the rumor that you're involved with the deputy who headed up the rescue?" someone asked from the back of the room.

"My private life is my own," he said. He wouldn't dignify the question, but he wouldn't lie anymore. He glanced briefly at Xav and saw his green eyes sparkle.

Murmurs and conversation cascaded the room. The governor stepped forward. "We're just about out of time. Someone told me there's a regatta waiting to begin. Shall we?"

One of the governor's aides clicked the microphone off, and the governor smiled at Chance. "Off the record," she said, extending her hand, "I do hope you consider running. You'd have my support."

"Thank you, ma'am," Chance replied.

Someone opened the doors at the side of the room, and the governor and her entourage stepped out into the fresh afternoon air. The sunlight reflected off the river and sparkled, lending an almost magical feeling to the world. Chance hung back with Xav and Quinn.

Xav waited until everyone had left and the doors closed. "Honorary Deputy Haverty, you can be my partner anytime," he said as he squeezed Quinn's shoulder.

Quinn beamed.

"You did good," Chance said to Quinn.

"Thanks." Quinn's blush deepened and he looked down at the pin.

Xav squatted in front of Quinn. "I have something else for you." He withdrew a small velvet box from his pocket and handed it to Quinn.

Quinn opened it and his eyes went wide right before they filled with tears. "You found 'em?"

"Yep. They're nice and shiny and on one necklace now. Would you like me to put it on you?"

Quinn rubbed an eye with the heel of a hand in a futile attempt to hide his tears and nodded.

Xav put the necklace bearing both halves of the *twins forever* hearts on him. "Winter will always be with you." Quinn melted into Xav's arms, and Xav hugged him tightly. "You okay?"

Quinn nodded as he withdrew from Xav's arms and looked up at Chance.

Chance smiled. "No matter where you are, he'll be with you. Always."

"Thank you."

"You're welcome," Xav replied as he ruffled Quinn's hair.

Chance loosened his tie and undid the top button of his shirt. The fabric stuck to his skin beneath his suit. Maybe after this dog and pony show was over, he'd take Xav and Quinn for a sail. They could spend a day or two on Ocracoke Island and maybe Xav could teach him and Quinn to surf.

"With that comment about your private life, they'll be after you now. Watching you," Xav teased.

"I'm tired of the bullshit."

Xav grinned. "Being out just comes with a different kind of bullshit."

Chance shrugged. But as he turned toward the doors, Xav grabbed his hand, pulled him close, and kissed him soundly on the lips. Chance relaxed into the embrace as the kiss deepened.

A camera flash startled them and Chance turned to the photographer, whose face was obscured by his camera. The man quickly disappeared back down the hallway.

Quinn giggled, cheeks pinking again.

Chance just laughed. "I meant it. No more hiding."

For a split second, Chance saw tenderness in Xav's eyes that made his arms ache. Then the moment passed.

Quinn opened the door and ran out, shouting back at them to hurry or they'd miss the start of the race.

Xav brushed the back of his hand against Chance's and they followed the crowd to the edge of the waterfront park, where the boats had lined up.

"Quinn! Hey, Quinn!" Ray Jr. ran up to him, the half-dozen balloons in his hand trailing in his wake. "Y'all're comin' to my birthday party, right?" He pointed to a picnic table fifty feet away beneath a big red maple tree. Several kids chased each other around the table as Ray's mother set out paper plates and plastic cups.

Chance recognized Jenson Murcheson, one of the other boys from the boat. Ray Sr. waved at them.

"We'll meet you there in a few minutes," Xav said to Quinn.

Ray handed Quinn a balloon, and they ran off laughing, Ray chattering about how the ice cream was already melting.

"Save me a piece of cake," Chance called after them. He thought about Lee Dennison, the third boy rescued from the trawler. The last he'd heard, Lee had been released from the hospital and was back with his family. Chance hoped he'd be all right.

At the edge of the water, someone hoisted a blue flag and a horn sounded. The crowd cheered and tossed confetti into the air. At the point of land overlooking the confluence of the two rivers, a brass band played from the bandstand. Chance pulled off his jacket and slung it over his shoulder as he and Xav walked closer to the water. The breeze off the water was fresh and cool. He smiled and took Xav's hand, leaned in, and kissed him. This was what he'd wanted for as long as he could remember, and he no longer cared who saw them together. He was finally home.

I'm no longer a solitary man, Chance thought happily.

Shit! Now I have to change the name of my boat!

SHIRA ANTHONY was a professional opera singer in her last incarnation, performing roles in such operas as *Tosca*, *Pagliacci*, and *La Traviata*, among others. She's given up TV for evenings spent with her laptop, and she never goes anywhere without a pile of unread M/M romance on her Kindle.

Shira is married with two children and two insane dogs, and when she's not writing, she is usually in a courtroom trying to make the world safer for children. When she's not working, she can be found at the Carolina coast aboard *Land's Zen*, a 35' catamaran sailboat, with her favorite sexy captain at the wheel.

Shira writes what she loves, be it contemporary musicians, shifter mermen, or time-traveling vampires. Her Mermen of Ea trilogy book, *Into the Wind*, was named one of the best books of 2014 by both Scattered Thoughts and Rogue Words and Hearts on Fire Reviews, and was a finalist in the 2014 Goodreads M/M Romance Member's Choice Awards. Her Blue Notes series of classical-music-themed gay romances was named one of Scattered Thoughts and Rogue Word's "Best Series of 2012," and the most recent book in the series, *Dissonance*, was named one of the best books of 2014 by Hearts on Fire Reviews.

Shira can be found on:

Facebook: www.facebook.com/shira.anthony
Goodreads: www.goodreads.com/author/show/4641776.Shira_Anthony
Twitter: @WriterShira
Website: www.shiraanthony.com
E-mail: shiraanthony@hotmail.com

AISLING MANCY is an author of romance who lives, most of the time, on the West Coast of the United States. Aisling writes adult fantasy, adult LGBTQIA romance, and fiction for gay young adults (C. Kennedy).

Raised on the mean streets and back lots of Hollywood by a Yoda-look-alike grandfather, Aisling doesn't conform, doesn't fit in, is epic awkward, and lives to perfect a deep-seated oppositional defiance disorder. In a constant state of fascination with the trivial, Aisling contemplates such weighty questions as: If time and space are curved, then where do all the straight people come from? When not writing, Aisling can be found taming waves on western shores, pondering the nutritional value of sunsets, appreciating the much maligned dandelion, unhooking guide ropes from stanchions, and marveling at all things ordinary.

Facebook: www.facebook.com/aisling.mancy
Goodreads: www.goodreads.com/author/show/6872835.Aisling_Mancy
Twitter: @aislingmancy
Website: aislingmancy.blogspot.com

By Shira Anthony

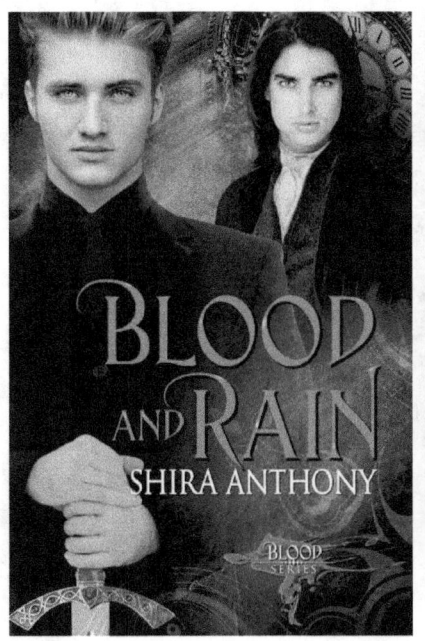

By Aisling Mancy (writing as C. Kennedy)

http://www.dreamspinnerpress.com

FOR **MORE** OF THE **BEST GAY ROMANCE**

dreamspinnerpress.com

www.ingramcontent.com/pod-product-compliance
Lightning Source LLC
Chambersburg PA
CBHW070054030726
47506CB00002B/467